REASONS

TO DECEIVE

J S Langley

The second in the 'Agaricus' series of novels. Also available is the first, ***Abuse of Privilege***, in which Mark Wilson must act as go-between in a ransom deal that is much more tricky than it first appears.

For Janet, Robert, Iain, Michael

'If you knew you were going to die tomorrow what would you do today?'

Dr G. Krai, *Nereus*, Pacific Ocean

Dr Gabriel Krai sat in his wheelchair. It had been a bad day. His pain levels were higher than usual and he knew that, over time, his symptoms would only get worse. He was gaunt, his clothes hung loose, his hair was sparse and dishevelled. Beside him on the polished surface of a mahogany writing desk lay an open laptop, its screen glowing a sea blue.

In front of him, barely six feet away, stood a man in his mid-fifties. His features were sharp, his greying hair tied back into a short ponytail, his muscled body taut beneath expensive clothing. He was becoming agitated.

'Look at you,' he said, 'you need to make way, its past your time.'

'I don't think so,' replied Dr Krai, his voice soft and toneless, 'I'm not ready.'

'You've got to listen. We don't want a vacuum at the top of the organisation ...'

'The organisation that I built.'

'That may be so, but Gabriel, nobody lives forever.'

'And if I don't want to stand aside?'

The man shrugged, his left hand moved inside his jacket, reached into a shoulder holster and emerged holding a gun, a Glock.

'We've been talking about this for months now, we can't keep just talking, the organisation is creaking, cracks are beginning to show,' he said, the gun cold in his hand, 'I don't want to do this Gabriel, don't make me do it.'

'I don't want you to do it either,' said Dr Krai, as if speaking to a small child, 'there is still time to change your mind.'

The man laughed.

'Gabriel, we've known each other a long time. I've given you unquestioning support, and loyalty, for over a decade. But time moves on, Gabriel, time moves on. Please don't make me do this, just agree to step back, let others take over the reins. I'll help, we'll do it with dignity and we'll get you the best medical care that money can buy.'

'It's because of our shared past that I give you a chance to change your mind,' said Dr Krai.

The man's face hardened and he raised the gun.

'You've become delusional,' he said.

'I'll tell you what your problem is,' said Dr Krai.

'What?'

'You've always been impetuous; you don't think ahead, you don't consider the future.'

'And you've always been quick to point out my faults,' said the man, pointing the gun at Dr Gabriel Krai's head, 'well consider this Gabriel, when ya ain't got no future there ain't much worth considering.'

The Glock kicked twice, the noise reverberating around the room.

But Dr Gabriel Krai did not die, instead two white star fractures appeared in the air between them.

'30mm laminated bulletproof glass,' said Dr Krai, 'microphones strategically placed so that we can hear each other as if it were not there.'

The fracture lines took away the screen's invisibility, its presence no longer hidden in plain sight.

The man growled and in frustration the Glock kicked again, until the trigger hammer fell on an empty chamber.

Dr Gabriel Krai wheeled himself from behind the obscuring constellation of impact sites that had pockmarked but not penetrated the intervening screen.

'Loyalty,' he said, 'is so often about knowing who holds the upper hand.'

The wheelchair moved behind the desk, Dr Krai's skeletal fingers darted across the keyboard of the open laptop. The man turned as he heard the deadlocks on the door behind him sliding home, the hiss as his area of the room was made airtight.

He rushed to the door, turned the handle, put his shoulder to it, but it was too late.

'I have wanted to test this new facility,' said Dr Krai, 'You have already experienced the quality of the sound system and the bulletproof screen which, thanks to you, I will need to replace. Now comes the interesting part.'

The man ran at the damaged screen banging on it with his fists.

'Gabriel, it was a mistake, I made a mistake. Let's forget about it, let's go back to how things were.'

'Forget that you wanted to kill me?'

The man looked at Dr Gabriel Krai imploringly.

'I'm sorry.'

'I have found that the best way to avoid having to say you're sorry is to succeed in carrying out your intentions. Planning, preparation and execution are my mantra. They have served me well.'

Dr Krai tapped again at the keyboard and then lifted his head to look at the man on the other side of the now flawed screen.

'I don't know how interested you are in the technicalities but let me tell you what is going to happen now. Sensors have confirmed that on your side of the room the space is airtight. I have initiated a sequence that will begin to introduce an extremely toxic nerve gas and although you can neither see nor smell it you may have noticed that your mouth is beginning to create more saliva, your eyes beginning to water. In a short while your vision will blur, you will find it harder and harder to breathe and you will lose control over your motor functions and be unable to move voluntarily. Then your body will begin twitching and convulsing. I'm told that at this point the pain will have become excruciating and will have spread throughout your body. Mercifully all this will not last long and you will be dead in less than 10 minutes. It will be an interesting process to watch.'

'Afterwards the room will be refreshed by high volume fans blowing clean air, the exhaust will be filtered to remove and destroy the residual nerve agent and analysers will monitor the reducing concentration.'

'Once the area is safe to enter the fans will stop and the door will be released. Your remains will then be removed and disposed of. I will see to it that suitable condolences are given to your family together with generous financial support - you do, after all, deserve that.'

The man had fallen to his knees, he was struggling for breath.

'For the love of God, Gabriel,' he wheezed.

'God has nothing to do with it. We make our choices and we have to live or die by the consequences. Anyway I hope I've proven to you that although my body may be failing my mind is not.'

Dr Gabriel Krai watched as the man slid to the floor, watched as he pulled himself into a foetal position, his muscles twitching involuntarily.

'But you have given me food for thought,' said Dr Krai to the unheeding body, 'yes, food for thought.'

Chapter 1

I don't see myself as a murderer. A murderer is someone who carries out a premeditated killing outside of the law. Sometimes the line between duty and the law gets a bit blurred, that's all.

'Just keep an eye on things that's all we're asking. Our client has a vague feeling of concern, nothing more, just enough to warrant someone being there, on the spot, watching.'

AB, my mentor, guide and boss at "The Store", was briefing me, or trying to. It all seemed pretty nebulous to me. Sitting on the business side of his polished desk, the sunlight reflecting from his bald head, AB was peering at me over his tortoiseshell rimmed glasses.

'It's purely precautionary, surveillance, get close enough to this man Dr. Krai to find out what he's up to,' he paused to glower, 'and try to be subtle; he's a dangerous man.'

I stayed silent. I'd learnt to avoid asking stupid questions.

'If you're lucky you just get an all-expenses paid 24 day cruise, but don't go soft, stay focused.'

But I'm seldom that lucky, I thought.

'For some reason Dr. Krai has decided to take a cruise across the Pacific Ocean,' said AB, 'from Sydney to Seattle. There's nothing too strange in that I suppose, if you can afford it, although, to the best of our client's knowledge, he's never done anything like this before. The fact that it's a cruise ship is particularly interesting as he normally shuns the company of Joe Public and has a phobia of water. We've put you in an outside balcony cabin a few decks below his suite, so you can be close, but not too close, to him.'

He paused and broke eye contact.

'Personally I don't believe there's anything to worry about, but you're our safety net - comprendi?'

I comprendi-ed all right; an all-expenses paid cruise in what sounded like a first class cabin. I wondered whether this was AB's way of paying me back for my efforts on the previous assignment. I must have smiled.

'And you can wipe that smirk off your face. We think we've found a way for you to get noticed by Dr. Krai despite his permanent protective entourage. But you'll only get one chance, don't fuck it up.'

Thanks for the vote of confidence, I thought.

'You'll be given a full briefing on what we know about the man; his hobbies, his likes and dislikes, that sort of thing. Make sure you do your homework.'

'Yes sir, thank you sir.' I got up to go.

'Don't take your eye off the ball on this one. You never know, they may be right,' he paused, 'and don't overdo it on the expenses,' he said to my retreating back.

I glanced at my Rolex watch, a GMT Master II with a black face and bi-coloured black/blue cerachrom bezel, and a finely polished stainless steel strap. It was a welcome leftover from a previous assignment. As if I would overdo it on expenses, well really!

From the whole tone of this one-sided conversation I was left with the distinct feeling that AB hadn't enjoyed giving me this assignment. Maybe he thought it wasn't grimy enough for me. I, on the other hand, thought it was right up my street.

Samantha, AB's secretary, PA and loyal guard dog sat at her desk and was surprised to see me exiting 'the presence' with a smile on my face. It was a unique experience for me too.

'Your detailed briefing is ready to start immediately,' she said, a quizzical look on her beautiful, high cheek-boned face, 'down in the basement, Room 11.'

'I'm right on it,' I replied cheerily.

'What are you so...?' I held up my hand.

'Can't talk, confidential, you know that.'

'You're such a tease,' she said, but without the same cheeriness in her voice.

Knowledge is power, I thought, and for this one prized moment that power was mine. I walked away whistling, just to add to her annoyance.

Chapter 2

The briefing I received on Dr Gabriel Krai was substantial, but not without its areas of uncertainty. He was an old man of failing health. He was known to have pots of money although it was largely unclear how he'd accumulated it. The briefing continued,

'War orphaned as a child Dr Krai somehow found his way to the USA where he was welcomed as an unwanted immigrant and fled to the streets. From that moment he embarked on a lifelong mission to better his circumstances. He's been remarkably successful in achieving this ambition becoming both revered and feared in equal measure and still heads the underground organisation that he built from scratch.

'Medically he is a mess and is now confined to a wheelchair. His list of allergies is long and includes penicillin, cat hair, and bee stings.'

'We estimate his age at around 80 and as he has become increasing frail he has become more unpredictable and more dangerous.'

The briefing then delved into the cities Dr Krai operated in, the schemes he was known or thought to be involved in, the history of his steady rise to 'the top'. There was even a psychological assessment full of psycho-babble, as I like to call it.

'The vague memories he has of his parents, the geographical and emotional dislocation he suffered at an early age, his experiences of living on the streets will have caused a certain degree of mental instability. He cannot identify with any particular place as 'home', is psychologically uncertain of where he belongs. Hence, even though he has achieved or exceeded his material goals and has 'arrived' he is still likely to feel unfulfilled. It is possible that now he is approaching the end of his life he does not recognise the destination he has reached as the solution he was seeking.'

See what I mean? If he were suffering from a feeling of dissatisfaction with his lot then he would have that in common with a large proportion of the world's population – including me!

One of the more useful pieces of information I was told was that Dr. Krai liked to gamble, but not to lose.

My identity for this assignment was to be Dr. David Anderson, David to his friends. I was an academic with a PhD in Ancient History and held the position of Lecturer at St Andrews University in Fife, Scotland. This was a smart move on the part of my handlers as it would explain away the Scottish lilt that I have in my voice and find almost impossible to mask.

Before moving into academia I, as Dr Anderson, had been spent some time in the army. This again was a reflection of the real me. That's the thing about subterfuge the closer the false identity is to reality, but not too close, the easier it is to pull off.

I liked the elitist feel of Dr Anderson. What I didn't like was the amount of boning up I had to do, the hours of cramming before I was passed fit to leave.

Although I did my best I could only hope that I wouldn't meet anyone who was well educated in

Ancient History and wanted to engage me in detailed conversation. I decided that if I got caught out like I would either avoid an answer (good policy), blag it (more risky) or say that my specialism lay in another era (the impact of the yak on the migration of the Mongols and hence the modern history of Europe, for example).

On a simpler, more human level, I was divorced, had no children and although an academic was going to be allowed to remain beardless.

The most painful part of the process was an enforced separation from my Rolex watch. It was like parting with a friend and I don't have too many of them. The replacement looked superficially the same but had a few extra functions. I snapped the metal strap closed. It wasn't my watch but I was willing to give it a chance.

Chapter 3

It was nice to be heading away from a blustery British Spring to the warmth of the southern hemisphere. Believing in safety statistics I boarded Qantas Airlines QF2, an Airbus A380 flight from London Heathrow Terminal 3 to Sydney Australia with an overnight stop-over in Singapore.

The A380 is properly nicknamed the 'Super-Jumbo' and is currently the world's largest passenger airliner. It has 14 First, 64 Business, 35 Premium Economy and 371 Economy seats across its two decks at an overall length of 73m and a wingspan of 80m. Its four jet engines can manage a top speed of 1,020 km/h and it has a range of over 15,000km. Understandably the airports from which it operates had to upgrade their docking facilities to accommodate it. For as little as $450m you can have one of your own. On the less comforting side it has a take-off weight of around 560 tons and contains over 300,000 litres of fuel.

I tried not to think about this as I made my way onboard.

Although "The Store" would not stretch to the purchase of First Class tickets, I had, to my personal satisfaction, talked them into Business Class by arguing that no academic worth his salt would travel in anything less.

The flight departure time was 21:15hrs and after flying for 13hrs 10mins, and with a time difference of GMT +8hrs, we should land in Singapore Changi Airport Terminal 1 at 18:25 local time.

My master plan to try and combat the inevitable jet lag was to stay awake for the whole flight, sleep like a baby in the Singapore stopover hotel, and wake refreshed for my onward flight to Sydney the next evening.

My seat number was 17B, an aisle seat on the Upper Deck. I was determined to forgo the temptation of converting it into the comfortable 2m long horizontal position. I would instead, after a light meal and a glass or two of red wine, don my headphones and make good use of the in-flight entertainment system, catching up on at least 5 or 6 different movies.

Chapter 4

I awoke sitting askew and with a stiff neck just before landing.

By the time I'd slid through the airport's slick arrivals process I was wide awake. The outside air was warm and humid, the taxi air-conditioned, the hotel room modern and full of marble.

I unpacked the little I needed, showered and shaved, and decided to walk myself back into tiredness.

It was evening on the streets but I had no idea what time my brain was on.

Singapore is the city of the clean where progress and purpose are equally matched. From the Millennium Wheel, the double-helix red lit pedestrian bridge, where human beings from across the globe stroll through a representation of their own DNA, to the harbour light show and water fountains, the laser projected holographic imagery and the live music you know you're in a place that's on the up and not afraid to show it.

The part of the city I was in was built on reclaimed land that had been allowed to settle for 10 years before the new hotels, skyscraper apartment blocks, and shopping malls had been erected.

I entered one of the shopping malls just as it was starting to rain, decided I was hungry and took the escalators down to the 24hr food hall.

It was just after 9pm local time and I was not the only one there.

The whole floor was noisy and overcrowded, vending machines lined the walls, hot food vendors competed for custom; rice, noodles, chicken, duck, seafood, breaded, flavoured, sweet, savoury were all on display in a rainbow of colours. The choice was impossibly large.

People were jostling for places to sit at the communal tables. Bathed in artificial yellow light it was like finding myself in the middle of an overpoweringly hot, humid, and claustrophobic feeding frenzy.

All around me there were families, people and children of all ages devouring the harvested produce of sea and land.

I could feel the sweat start to trickle down my back, my shirt clinging to me. Taking a few moments to try and get my bearings I came to the conclusion I was completely out of my depth and would just have to muddle through. I'd come here to eat and eat I would.

I had no change for the vending machines and the surrounding signage didn't help as it was written in what looked like Mandarin with Malay subtitles.

Observing those that appeared to better understand what they were doing, the order of the day seemed to be to choose a queue, get your food, pay for it, pick up your chopsticks and then hunt out a place at the communal tables to sit and eat it.

If a queue is long the food must be worth queuing for was my logic. I had plenty of time on my hands so I joined the longest queue. When I got to be served I took a chance and pointed to what looked like sweet and sour king prawns and fried rice and then more assuredly to a couple of bottles of chilled beer.

Pleased with this minor achievement I paid and hunted out a seat.

My chopstick ability is what could properly be called amateurish and when I finally got something into my mouth it was spicier than I had anticipated. The beer was a welcome antidote and the feel of the cool liquid in my mouth and throat was pure joy.

As I relaxed I started to look around, to take in my surroundings. This wasn't too bad after all.

It was then that I saw someone getting up to mischief.

Chapter 5

Even in thoroughly policed and regulated Singapore there are those who will take a chance and tourists are warned to beware of theft and pick-pocketing, particularly in crowded areas.

Being alert to potential mischief was one of my few areas of expertise and amongst the milling crowd I picked up some signals, like a cat sensing a mouse, and narrowed in, starting to pay more attention.

A family of very obviously unfamiliar tourists were sitting eating, talking animatedly between themselves, laughing. One of the women in the group, possibly the mother, was leaning forward showing someone else how to hold their chopsticks.

Her handbag was open at her feet. I could see her purse.

A young man, whose size and appearance indicated that he was unlikely to be a local, had done a couple of passes by their table. Dressed casually in a dark red t-shirt with a dragon motif and khaki shorts he approached once more, this time taking the opportunity of lifting the purse whilst its owner's attention was distracted, oblivious of the loss.

This wasn't a nice thing to do.

I got up from my seat and followed my target. He was a cool customer, making his way slowly towards the exit as if he'd just been talking to his granny. I caught up with him and pushed him into a quiet corner between a wall and one of the vending machines.

'What the ...!' he said.

I was both pleased and disappointed that he spoke English.

'I don't think that's yours,' I said, nodding to the purse.

'Get off me,' he hissed.

I needed him to take me seriously so I slipped my left hand between his legs and squeezed his testicles in friendly greeting. I've found this an effective way to galvanise a young man's attention, much more effective than shaking hands or saying 'Hi'.

'What the f...' he spat through clenched teeth.

'Do you want to keep these,' I asked, giving them a tweak. He winced, 'Now you listen to me, and listen carefully. Your choices are these: I turn you over to the police or you give me back that lady's purse and then run along like a good boy. Understand.'

I squeezed harder. He nodded.

'Now which is it to be?'

I backed slightly away, retaining my grip but giving him a little room.

'Now just drop it on the floor.'

He did so.

'You bastard,' he said, 'I'll rip your fucking head off for this.'

Maybe it was the pain getting to him but he should have realised that he was in no position to be issuing threats.

'Back away and leave,' I said, loosening my grip to his evident relief.

His hands went immediately to his pounding parts and then, with a snarl, he tried to head butt me.

Here I was trying to be a gentleman, giving this young man a little lesson in the hope of nudging him back onto the straight and narrow, helping him to see the error of his ways, and this was the thanks I got. I was unimpressed. When faced with two perfectly clear choices he'd chosen a third.

His lunge put him off balance and the sharp of my knee met the softness of his stomach and winded him. I pushed him backwards banging the back of his head against the wall. He slid slowly down to the floor. I laid his head against the side of the vending machine. He looked like he was sleeping.

The whole exchange had taken only a minute or two. In the crowded, noisy hall everybody was going about their business and it looked like we had not attracted any unwelcome attention. Good.

A short, wiry, wrinkled grey-haired lady of about 150 approached and started feeding coins into the vending machine. She glanced down at the recumbent youth and said something in Chinese.

'The youngsters of today,' I said, 'they just can't stand the pace.'

She shrugged then smiled and carried on with the coin feeding, hoping to win some chocolate.

I took a circuitous return route and slipped the purse back into its original place. The victim of the theft was still in deep conversation with her family.

I kicked her handbag.

'Oh sorry,' I said.

She saw me for the first time.

'No problem,' she said, her accent distinctly American, and lifted her bag onto her lap.

'Can't be too careful,' I said.

'Been to Singapore a few times, never had a problem,' she said.

I was now receiving quizzical looks from the rest of her table.

'Have a nice day,' I said and walked away.

When I returned to my original seat it was filled by someone else. My food had gone and, most disappointingly, the rest of my beer had disappeared with it.

'Thanks' I said to nobody in particular.

I was reminded of that familiar maxim "No good deed goes unpunished" and hoped it wasn't an omen.

Chapter 6

The rain had stopped by the time I left the Mall and the air felt newly washed, fresh and cool. I kept walking, took in the water, light and music show and burnt away another hour or so in the "Garden by the Bay" where the metal multifunctional "Super Trees" were interwoven with greenery whilst doubling up as water towers or housing the air conditioning exhausts from the adjacent eco-garden's giant greenhouses.

It was getting late, or early, and I was at last beginning to feel weary. I walked back to the hotel, saw one of the bars was still open and decided to make up for my lost beer.

I was ambushed by another American tourist.

'What a great place,' he said, 'You know they even have McDonald's here in Singapore?'

I said how amazing I thought that was, and that together with all the high tech up-market consumerism and Duty Free, the jewellery, the fashion, the Swiss watches and the camera-drones, having a McDonald's just put the final seal on Singapore's first world status.

He agreed enthusiastically.

I groaned internally.

'All this reclaimed land,' he said, warming to his theme, 'they're getting closer and closer to Indonesian waters you know,' I didn't, 'the Indonesians are starting to think its invasion by stealth,' he laughed, 'it can hardly amount to a lightning attack can it, but it don't stop the gunship patrols getting more and more twitchy.'

I bought him a drink in an attempt to shut him up. It didn't work.

'Other direction now, that's a different story, two big bridges linking Singapore Island to mainland Malaysia and plans for a bullet train all the way from China to Europe, a modern silk road. Paid for by the Chinese of course; god knows what they'll think of next.'

He sat on his bar stool smiling, his stomach hanging out of his cotton shirt, his bare legs protruding from pale blue shorts were covered in thick black hair. In my sleep fogged mind I couldn't decide whether he reminded me more of an American Buddha or King Kong.

It was approaching 2am. I bade him a fond farewell and went back to my room.

I showered again and got into bed.

I tried to call Teresa. I guess you could call her my girlfriend. After the death of my wife I hadn't been much on relationships but Teresa was … well something or other.

Having calculated that it was sometime mid-afternoon of the previous day in New York I thought it was worth a try. We'd agreed to meet up in Sydney and it seemed like a good idea to check there were no last minute glitches.

She didn't answer.

Chapter 7

I awoke mid-afternoon to a tapping at the door. A polite voice told me that I needed to check out and they needed to make up the room and, if I wasn't out in the next 30 minutes, they would have to charge me for an extra night. I apologised profusely and got up, washed, packed and out as quickly as I could.

The young guy at check out scowled at me and pointedly looked at his watch. I asked if I could have breakfast after I'd checked out. He said 'No' but I could have a late lunch and just pay separately for what I ate. It was more through embarrassment than anything that I declined this kind offer and made my way back to Changi Airport, the taxi dropping me off outside a mere four and a half hours before my scheduled take-off time.

My tactics for handling the time difference and associated jet lag was in tatters but I thought that if I could sleep through the overnight flight to Sydney I would be OK.

I eventually checked-in, made my way through airport security and into the departures area. I still had lots of time so to keep myself amused I tried to do the maths. I would get back onboard A380 QF2 at 19:30hrs local time and after about 8hrs flying time and a further +2hrs time difference I would be in Australia. I made that out to be an arrival time in Sydney of approximately 05:30 hrs local time. I checked the schedule, it said 05:10hrs. That was close enough. I was pleased that my brain hadn't gone completely AWOL.

Life in a departure lounge is akin to stepping into a rift in the time-space continuum or entering the waiting room of eternity. Although people came and went they were perpetually replaced and everywhere you looked you could see expectant faces and people eating, drinking and shopping to use up the time. To ensure survival and avoid Departure Lounge rage breaking out these areas operate to their own rules of peace and politeness to strangers, even though you're unlikely to meet any of them ever again.

Around me a student tour group sported bright orange team colours, giving away a lack of travel experience by taking photographs of everything, from themselves, to signs, windows, people taking photos of people taking photos. The gaggle of voices merged into white noise, the odd sound emerging temporarily from the hubbub,

'She did what?'

'I can't hear you properly; I'll call back later ...'

'What do you expect from someone like that?'

Wheeled cabin baggage rumbled across wooden floors and, under the surface fuss, cleaners, air traffic controllers and many other professionals quietly kept things going. The work of these underappreciated many being evidenced through the constantly updated electronic flight information boards, the clean toilets, with paper, and litter bins that were not overflowing.

I settled into a corner with a large black coffee and an iced bun for comfort and tried to call Teresa.

Again there was no answer.

On the way to Sydney we hit some bumpy air. It is far from comfortable when you're lying in a pressurised metal tube some 30,000 feet up in the air to find yourself bouncing up and down, feeling the metal vibrate around you and imagining the rivets groaning.

We crossed the Equator near Manado, flying over the Moluccan Sea at a speed of 555mph, approximately 2800miles from Sydney.

Chapter 8

My head felt like a moon that was in orbit around the rest of my body, tidally locked and out of place. Somehow I'd managed to land at Sydney Airport, get through customs and make my way to a four star hotel on Elizabeth Street, only walking distance from the harbour. I was in a room on the 14th Floor with panoramic views of the surrounding streets.

Although I had managed some sleep on the flight the significance of day and night was now lost on me. I tried to convince my eyes to focus. My mind was moving at the speed of treacle and my movements felt clumsy and slow.

I took a shower, gulped down one of the $8 bottles of mineral water, set the alarm for 10:00hrs and crash-landed into sleep.

The vicious shrill of the alarm woke me. I rolled over and fell out of bed.

After a shower and shave I dressed in crisp fresh clothes and descended to the 3rd floor restaurant. Here I partook of the late $30 buffet breakfast, still busy with other late rising tourists from all across the world.

Teresa was due to arrive later that day.

I asked at reception what they could recommend in the way of entertainment and was advised that the following evening there was a performance of Bizet's opera Carmen due to take place in the open air, under the stars of the southern hemisphere and against the backdrop of the iconic Opera house and brightly lit Harbour Bridge. It sounded perfect as long as it didn't rain and I walked along to the harbour area to get some tickets.

Down by the Opera House the seagulls were stealing chips. The Aussies in Sydney do not hurry and it took forever to negotiate my way through the queuing, chatting, buying process until finally I had a pair of the required tickets in my hand.

As Teresa's flight from Honolulu crossed the International Date Line she would lose a day. I'd downloaded a flight tracking app on my phone and, assuming she had actually made the flight, I was assiduously tracking her progress across the skies.

After a 10½ hour flight and a time difference of +20hrs I thought it would be better to take things easy and then enjoy the sights and sounds of Sydney the next day.

As I was to board the cruise ship Nereus the day after that and as we would both be battling different time zone differences, I knew that our meeting would be something of a whirlwind but I still hoped it would be worth it.

I liked Teresa.

Chapter 9

I'd met Teresa in the States, she'd helped me out and we'd spent some time together. I'd booked the flight for her online even though, as a successful independent business woman, I'd known that she was quite capable of doing it herself. I was just trying to show her what a chivalrous gentleman I could be and that even my Scottish thrift had limits.

We knew each other quite well by now, not to say intimately, and various underused parts of my anatomy were showing signs of awakening in anticipation of her arrival.

All went well at the start; the emotional greeting in the arrivals hall, the taxi to the hotel with smiles and banter. She even liked the double room on the 14th floor and the views over Sydney's Hyde Park. Despite her tiredness we spent an hour or so getting re-acquainted before ordering room service, showering and settling down to sleep. We left the curtains pulled back so we could lie together gazing out at the city nightscape, the coloured lighting of the street that shifted and lulled us into unconsciousness.

After a night's sleep Teresa was good to go and although she complained of being a little light-headed we had a great day walking around the harbour area, exploring the Opera House and deciding that climbing over the Sydney Harbour Bridge's iron-girdered superstructure, attached only by a thin metal cable, was a step too far for this trip.

I even bought her an "I love Sydney" T-shirt on which the word "love" was replaced by a garishly red heart shape with a white silhouette of the Opera House in the middle. Original I know. I'm just a born romantic.

She bought me an outbacker style hat that was impregnated with mozzie repellent and guaranteed to deter any possible interest from other members of the female species from at least 30 metres away.

We laughed, we joked, we seemed to be in a world built for two. It was quite special.

The evening production of Carmen under the stars was spectacular; the voices and sound projection in the outside amphitheatre was good, the production itself full of colour, vitality and, at one point, fireworks. It didn't rain and the Opera House and Harbour Bridge were both lit, forming an amazing backdrop.

With tapas and red wine available before the start and at the interval I was having a great time. Looking back it is possible that I didn't notice that Teresa, although enjoying it, was starting to flag.

It was after the Interval, with the colours swirling and the voices rising to the darkened sky, that I turned to a smiling Teresa and said, 'You are my Carmen.'

I don't know why I said it. It was a spontaneous thing. I was caught up in the moment, the emotion of the Opera, the clear, warm night, the wine, the food, the spectacle.

I'd meant it as a compliment; that Teresa was as vibrant to me as any leading lady, that I was having a good time and that I just wanted to let her know that.

It was immediately obvious that if that had been my intent then I had fallen a long way short.

She kind of smiled but I read something else in her eyes. She seemed to grow less warm and by the time we left she had become quite quiet and subdued.

I worried around her like a forlorn puppy, anxious without really understanding what was happening.

We walked back to the hotel. Teresa was not her usual talkative self.

Back at the hotel I was hopeful of a little more passion and that's when things went decidedly downhill.

Chapter 10

I had initiated what I thought would be the welcome fumblings of amorous foreplay and was surprised when Teresa, rather than returning my affections, pushed me away and stood at arm's length, her eyes flashing.

'I've got a mind you know.'

I knew that.

'I've got a voice.'

Oh, I was sure of that.

I smiled in acknowledgment. That seemed to make things worse.

'I've got intelligence!'

Indisputably Teresa was a smart woman. She'd built a successful business from almost nothing by importing goods from Costa Rica for re-sale in the United States. Her website was professionally designed and 'Teresa's Costa Rican Coffee and Crafts – Straight from the artisan to your door – Original and hassle free' was doing very well thank you very much.

'And all you want to do is squeeze my breasts and have sex.'

Erm - well actually...

The problem with me is I don't know when it's better to be a 100% honest and when it's not.

'You have nice breasts,' I said, trying to find a middle way.

It didn't work.

'I'm tired,' she said yawning to give the words added effect.

'You didn't seem tired last night,' I replied encouragingly.

'Well I am tonight, just let me have a shower and get into bed.'

This seemed like mixed messages to me with a possible undercurrent of hope.

I undressed, sat on the edge of the bed and waited patiently.

Teresa's naked body emerged from the shower room and did nothing to dull my ardour. I reached out to embrace her but she avoided my clutches and slipped naked between the crisp, cool white sheets.

'Good night,' she said.

'Yea, good night,' I replied, crestfallen.

I spent a restless night and in the morning I was feeling decidedly grumpy. Our early morning pillow talk wandered onto the unwelcome effects of jet lag and I said, 'Well at least you didn't have to buy the tickets.'

'What do you mean?' she said.

'I bought you the tickets.'

'And?'

'And I thought we would have a nice time even though I know it's rushed. You flying back today, me boarding the Ship tomorrow.'

'Because you bought the tickets?'

I know, I know, in hindsight I can see it coming too, but I was surfing on a stream of self-righteous indignation and ploughed straight into the rapids.

Teresa hauled herself into a sitting position and folded her arms across her ample breasts. It was very off-putting. Then she spoke before I had the chance to offer an apologetic climb-down.

'So you buy me the tickets, you wine and dine me and I give you sex. Is that it?'

Pow! This was escalating far too fast for me to handle.

'Effectively I am your whore am I?'

She was working herself into a tsunami of exasperation,

'I just wait for you to call do I? And when you do, out of the blue, God knows when, from God knows where, I just drop everything do I? I come running to you, ready to strip off and fling my legs over my shoulders. Is that right?'

There were parts of this that ... well best not go into that.

I got the distinct impression that there were sentiments her that had been festering beneath the surface for some time, things that had been looking for an opportunity to be vented. Too late I realised that I had unintentionally lifted the lid on a box that I would have preferred to have left shut, padlocked, chained, buried, and lowered to the bottom of the ocean. But now the lid was off and the contents were spilling out in all directions.

I thought she'd gone a bit too far and, as I've done many times before, I tried to rectify matters whilst only making them worse.

'I like having sex with you,' I said.

I'd meant it as a compliment. But it backfired.

'See! See!' she said, her voice rising, 'that's all I am to you isn't it?'

'Erm ...'

'Get out,' she was almost hysterical now.

'But it's my room,' I mentioned logically.

'Get,' she said, her eyes on fire, 'out.'

What could I do? I was completely out of my depth.

I quickly pulled on some clothes, slipped shoes onto my feet, took hold of my wallet and left with my tail between my legs both literally and metaphorically.

Chapter 11

I wandered around drinking coffee and looking idly into shop windows. I knew what time she would be leaving and left a 30 minute safety margin before going back to the room. There was no message. Every trace of her had gone. She had even made the bed.

The next morning when I was checking out I found that she'd also paid the bill.

What a woman.

I felt like an idiot although I wasn't too sure what I could have done to avoid the storm.

Before I had the chance to drive myself insane by trying to find some algebraic solution to this insoluble emotional equation I was hailed by a representative of the cruise liner company and taken off in a private car to begin the embarkation process.

Now was the time to focus on what I was here to do. To board the cruise ship, somehow make the acquaintance of Dr Gabriel Krai and find out what, if anything, he was up to.

The boarding process was both complicated and tiresome. It was like undergoing a series of regulated rights of passage ceremonies each one taking you a step further on the journey from life on dry land to a life adrift, albeit in luxury, on the sea.

It took forever. Moving from one queue to another, being subjected to repeated baggage, security, and onboard preference checks. Being asked the same questions over and over, filling out forms. There was the queue to drop off the big bags, the queue to start the check-in, the queue to check the booking, confirm your health insurance, take your photo. I even had to hand over my passport so that the crew could check visas and work with local immigration officials to speed disembarkation at the various ports of call. The fact that it was a false passport made it easier for me to cope with the loss.

Out-of-the-ordinary incidents are rare when everyone, no matter how harassed, is trying to remain polite enough to finally get themselves on board. They can complain about their treatment later in the comfort of one the bars. And they frequently do.

On this occasion however an Australian couple could not stop themselves from loudly haranguing the young uniformed steward who was in charge of the very final stage of their check-in process.

The Aussie male was large, early fifties, with a bald head and a red face. His wife was of a similar age and wearing a loose-fitting floral dress. She was in tears.

'We booked this cruise a year ago,' yelled the man, making sure we could all hear his indignation, 'for our 30th wedding anniversary. We booked a Suite. Now you tell me there's been a mistake. A mistake, and you've downgraded us to just a balcony room!'

Similar to mine, I thought, the class of cabin I had been overjoyed to have been allocated.

'It ain't good enough!'

Someone who looked like a senior steward was trying to calm the man down and shepherd him through the milling throng toward a more private side room. He handed the irate Aussie an envelope and was encouraging him to look inside. I was hoping that the side room was sound-proofed. The last I saw of him he was still shouting, the woman following behind, her head bowed in despair.

Eventually I became the proud possessor of the all-important onboard identity/pass/key card that would open my cabin door, allow me to buy things onboard, and get me through security when the time came to disembark/embark the ship for shore excursions. It was a precious object that it was important not to lose.

With my passport, visas and departure paperwork checked, copied and taken away for "safe keeping" I was feeling slightly naked and proceeded through the hand baggage X-ray and body scanner to the boarding queue where my pass was successfully swiped for the first time.

'Thank you Dr Anderson,' said a rather attractive uniformed steward, 'Welcome on board.'

Finally.

I went to find my room, number 8136 on Deck 8, but the corridor was closed off with a notice that said that I should listen out for messages over the public address system that would inform me when my cabin was ready for occupation. I went off to find a bar that was open.

None of them were.

Chapter 12

The cruise ship was named "Nereus" after a Greek sea god called by Homer "The Old Man of the Sea" who was noted for his wisdom, gift of prophecy and ability to change shape. This particular metamorphosis was capable of a cruising speed of 22 knots whilst carrying 4.000 passengers together with a crew of 1,200 to look after them. The rooms, restaurants, spa, pools, casino, theatre, helipad, shops and bars were distributed over 14 decks with, thankfully, 16 elevators as an alternative to the wide carpeted staircases.

The Nereus was the epitome of modern day cruising, a floating luxury hotel that travelled the world's oceans, touching land every now and again for a quick look and re-provisioning before continuing on its way. It was built to journey not to arrive.

Once underway, food, drink and entertainment would be available around the clock. It was a world where you were as good as your standard of room, your loyalty card rating, your fine dining and drinks package. If in America the dollar speaks then onboard the Nereus it roared.

The more you spent, the higher your tip, the better the service, the broader the smiles. It was a floating social hierarchy that you could buy into at whatever level you could afford. It was a world where ordinary people, if they were willing to blow their inheritance in a month or two, could aspire to first class treatment.

I hope this doesn't sound too cynical after all I was one of those with an outside cabin and a balcony from which I could watch the world, or mainly the sea, go by. I'd joined the club and had very little to be cynical about. Each person onboard had travelled their own way to get here and now we were all in the same boat.

I consulted my faux-Rolex watch that was a good mimic of the black faced GMT Master II with black/blue cerachrom bezel and finely polished stainless steel strap that I'd been forced to leave behind. It had the same ability to set the time in three separate time zones so I reset these to Local, London and New York. Even though it could do more than my original Rolex I still resented having to make the switch.

Then I took out my phone.

I tried to call Teresa. No answer.

I tried to call my daughter. No answer.

The public address system announced that there would be an emergency drill before we set sail. Details would be in our rooms.

I went to my room as soon as I was told it was ready. A flyer lay on the crisply made bed detailing the emergency drill procedure ending with the words **"WAIT FOR INSTRUCTIONS BEFORE PROCEEDING TO YOUR MUSTER POINT"** in large, bold type.

The drill, which was to begin at 17:00hrs, would be preceded by a PA system announcement. I obeyed the rules. I waited and then followed the PA announcement instructions.

When I got to my muster point the room was full;

most people having got themselves there 15-20mins before the exercise was officially due to start – not a very realistic beginning to an emergency drill.

With no choice of where to sit I found myself alongside the Australian couple who had had such trouble on embarkation The man was still large, early fifties, bald head and red face, and still loud. His wife chipped in occasionally to vouch for the veracity of her husband's claims.

'… 30th wedding anniversary,' he was saying to anyone who'd listen, 'booked a suite up on the 14th floor and then we got told we couldn't have it. Right as we were boarding. Just like that,' he frowned, 'somebody wanted the whole of the 14th or something. Well you can imagine I wasn't having that!'

'He wasn't having that,' echoed his partner of 30 years, 'He can get quite stroppy when he's riled.'

'Well, we were taken to talk to the Customer Cruise Director,' the man continued, 'and I let him have it. I told him what I thought and I demanded our suite. And do you know what?'

Clearly nobody did, and there wasn't a show of great interest either. The man soldiered on regardless.

'He apologized of course and then he offered us an alternative room on a lower floor, said we could have the whole cruise for free, gave us the unlimited drinks, phone and wi-fi packages and said we could enjoy speciality dining of our choice as well as access to all the VIP lounges.' He paused. 'What'd'ya think of that?'

Thankfully there was no time to find out what everybody thought of that as a young man in ship's uniform and a microphone called for our attention.

'Ladies and gentlemen thanks for turning out so promptly for this emergency drill. It is a legal requirement that all passengers attend. In a few moments we will be leading you to your specific assembly points. In the extremely unlikely event of the evacuation alarm sounding whilst we are at sea then you must take your life jacket and any medications you need and move directly to your assembly point. If you are not in your room when the alarm sounds then do not go back to your room. I repeat do not go back to your room. Instead proceed straight to your assembly point where additional life jackets will be available. Once assembled you should await further instructions. There will be members of the crew on hand to look after you.'

'Now, as I have said, it is extremely unlikely that we will ever need to use the emergency drill procedures for real but the rules of the sea and of our Company demand that we carry out this trial run and that all passengers participate. Each of your names will be carefully checked off by a member of our crew as confirmation of your attendance. As soon as the drill is complete the bars, shops, spa and other amenities will be opened.'

'Then let's get on with it,' shouted out an American voice, 'I need a drink!'

'As soon as all passenger groups are at their muster stations and have been briefed the alarm will be sounded. There will be 7 short blasts followed by one long. This is the internationally recognised Emergency Signal for a ship in distress at sea. We will then move to our assembly points out on deck.'

He stopped talking. We waited expectantly and after a few moments the alarm sounded.

As we filed out it was clear there were people who were not taking this drill very seriously. Some were slinging the proffered life jackets over one shoulder, another young man was suggesting that his name was 'Donald Duck'. This may have seemed amusing at the start but the humour soon paled and we fell like cattle into a regimented obedience to the proscribed processes.

The crew patiently demonstrated how to put on a life jacket properly, their commentary sounding like a ritualized chant.

'First put it over your head like this, then fasten the velcro straps here and here, tighten them to get a snug fit. Note the torch and the whistle; these can be used for attracting attention. Special lifejackets are available for children.'

Then, equally patiently, they used clipboards to check off each name against their corresponding room and photo key-card before passing the gathered information on for collation.

Eventually the Captain's voice echoed through the PA system. He thanked everybody for their patience, announced that the drill had been a total success and that it was now complete.

It was difficult not to be trampled underfoot in the ensuing stampede towards the bars, shops and restaurants.

Chapter 13

As the cruise ship nosed its way slowly out of Sydney harbour I stood on the balcony of my executive cabin and looked out at the iconic Harbour Bridge and Opera House as they receded into the distance. Sunglasses on and drink in hand I felt every part the tourist.

The big ship released her pilot and smoothed her way gently into the blackness of evening, past a lighthouse that was blinking out its duty, and out towards the open sea.

A few hopeful gulls flew alongside, chasing us away from Australia with their raucous cries.

There was no turning back now. Whatever it was that Dr Krai was doing onboard, if indeed he was do anything other than relaxing, I was committed to try and find out. We had 7388miles and 24 days to go to cross the Pacific and we were on our way.

I walked inside and surveyed the cases my cabin steward, a friendly chap named Jacob, had brought in for me. I unpacked carefully and then took out my phone and called in to "The Store".

'I'm on board,' I said.

'Oh good,' replied the husky tones of Samantha, 'please do try and have a good holiday.'

'It's not …'

Click.

I lay back on the bed thinking. I would go and get something to eat and find out how I might make the early acquaintance of Dr Gabriel Krai. The good thing about being marooned on a cruise ship is that he wasn't going to be going anywhere else.

My dining preference was set at "Anytime". To be honest I didn't have much of an inclination to sit down to eat at the same time, at the same table, with the same people for 24 days, no matter how interesting their lives may be or how scintillating their conversation. I was happy to forgo the waiter service and the constant temptation to order another very expensive glass of wine. I was content to just grab something to eat when I felt hungry, sit in a different place, with a different view of the world, preferably on my own. In fact it would be detrimental to my assignment to strike up more conversations than necessary or, worse, establish new relationships.

I was on a ship full of people desperate to make new friends and I was keen to keep away from them. New distractions would just present more reasons to take my eye off the ball.

The self serve buffet restaurant was on Deck 11 and I made my way there.

It was heaving.

First night gluttony had set in and I had to squeeze my way through a throng of overzealous guests to get a plate of food and then go and join the fight for an available seat.

There were a lot of Americans on board and they all wanted to talk to me. One had a large farm in the south of Texas, another lived in New Orleans. When someone asked me what I did I said I was an english academic and that this was 'my first attempt to free myself from the fetters of the merely personal, from an intellectualised existence dominated by desires, hopes, and primitive emotions, and to set out on a personal search for the elemental'.

That shut them up and I finished my meal in peace.

Chapter 14

Later that evening I went down to the casino. I knew Dr Krai was a keen poker player and if I was going to get a good first look at him I figured it would probably be there.

As I entered my eyes were assaulted by an almost overpowering blaze of red, the thick pile carpet matching the red felt of the gaming tables.

There were already people sitting with buckets of coins throwing them into the one arm bandits, happily focussed on losing their money as quickly as possible. The machines chinked and played upbeat fairground tunes and every now and then produced a metallic rush of coins that splashed into the winning trough, spilling out and onto the floor.

I glanced past the central bar, the roulette table, the black jack tables and saw that there was a second level, slightly raised and separated from the rest, partitioned off by a 3 foot high toughened glass barrier that was topped with a polished silver-chrome rail. This was where the serious poker player's tables resided; Krai's gaming territory.

One table stood apart from the rest in a corner position occupying its own private position.

I took a seat at the central bar and made myself as comfortable as possible. I ordered a drink and began to wait.

It is a sign of the times that the casino was no smoke filled room. There was a ready flow of alcohol however, even though it was ridiculously expensive.

The atmosphere was created by people anxious, against all the odds, to become winners.

About an hour later a group of four dark suited men walked in. They were quite a collection; the first was broad shouldered, tanned and bald-headed, the second was tall, black-skinned, the third was young and blonde-haired and the fourth was a wiry man of medium height.

The thick set man said something to the head croupier, a dark haired, dark skinned, slim lady in a suit, and pointed to the separated poker table where there was already a game in progress. Then the four of them walked out again. They had not been smiling.

The croupier moved to the table in question and said something that clearly upset the players. After much apologetic bowing on the one hand and grumbling on the other the game was moved to another vacant table closer to the edge of the poker playing area.

I could just hear the tail end of their conversation.

'I was happy over there, and winning.'

'So sorry, sir.'

'What's this all about?'

'That's the high stakes table, sir, I didn't think there was going to be a game tonight,' a shrug of the shoulders, 'but it appears I was wrong.'

'What's wrong is to move a game that's half way through!'

'He's right. It'll change the fall of the cards.'

'Yea, darn right, what you gonna do about that?'

The croupier sighed and pushed her long dark hair away from her face, tucking it behind her ears.

'Tonight gentlemen, and for the next hour only, your drinks are all free. Also, because I am so sorry about this inconvenience, if you give me your room numbers I'll see to it that you each get a $250 credit added to your onboard account.'

There was a pause.

'Send the barman over will you, I'm feeling thirsty.'

'Let's stop talking and let's get playing.'

'Yea, deal those cards. I'm starting to feel lucky.'

Shortly after the four dark suits returned, they were walking in a protective arc formation.

In the centre was a short, wiry individual dressed in dark slacks and a light blue open necked shirt.

It's only when you first see somebody in the flesh that you know how good your original briefing has been. This wasn't a great start. This man was walking. My briefing had been very clear that Dr Krai was wheelchair bound.

The reason for this discrepancy became immediately obvious. Krai was wearing an exoskeleton of thin black metal rods that was supporting his torso. His progress was accompanied by the soft whirring sound of several servo motors. He walked slowly, mechanically, pausing before proceeding to climb the low steps to the poker gaming area.

Four other players had been allowed to seat themselves around the separated table although the central seat was empty. Krai took this seat and nodded to the other players on either side of him.

Each player had their piles of coloured chips in front of them. The dealer, in black waistcoat, white shirt, red bow tie, and white cotton gloves waited for a nod of approval from Krai and then proceeded to announce the game rules: the opening, stakes, and limits. He then shuffled the cards, put them out to be cut twice, placed them in a card shoe and began to deal.

I moved closer.

Krai's four companions were not concentrating on the game. The one of largest build, the bald six footer, had no neck and followed my approach with his eyes. I avoided his look and, glass in hand, joined a handful of other interested observers who had gathered to watch the game unfold.

As hand followed hand it became clear that Krai was by far the better player, knowing when to fold, when to call and, most interestingly, when to bluff or call a bluff.

He began to read the other players whilst his own expression remained unfathomably blank.

Having sized things up to this point I wasn't sure how much more I was going to learn so I left the game, got myself a refill at the bar and sought out the head croupier.

'Seems like an interesting game,' I said, nodding towards Krai's table, 'how do you get involved?'

'It's invitation only,' she said politely.

'And how do you secure an invite?'

'Do you see that gentleman in the middle?'

'Yes.'

'You prove to me you've got $25,000 to spare and then you ask me nicely to suggest your name to him.' She smiled. She had a nice smile. I smiled back.

'The money's not a problem but how nice do I have to be?'

'Give me your onboard ID card,' she said.

I did so and then followed her as she went over to the bar, swung round one of the terminals, signed in, swiped my card and checked my current balance. She pursed her lips approvingly and then turned back to me.

'When would you like to play?'

'Tomorrow evening,' I said.

She turned again to the terminal and crinkled her nose.

'Well there is a game tomorrow evening. I'll see what I can do.'

Getting myself into the game was unlikely to be that easy. I was a complete unknown. The only thing I had going for me was that I could afford the entry fee.

I thought I should try to skew the odds a little more in my favour.

Chapter 15

Of the four chaperones Krai had protecting him three looked suitably unemotionally hard. The bald one looked the least likely to wish to engage in idle conversation, broad shouldered and straight backed his eyes were constantly shifting, monitoring, looking after Krai's wellbeing.

Of the remainder two stood rigidly as if made of wood, one of ebony, the other of ash. The fourth however, a razor thin man, clean shaven, was sweating and looked uncomfortable. I figured that he was my best shot. He had to go to the toilet sometime and when he did I intercepted him on his way back.

'Your boss looks like a good player,' I said casually.

'Eh?'

'Your boss,' I said, raising my glass in his direction, 'good player.'

'I don't see it's any of your business,' he said.

'Oh but it is, I've put my name down for tomorrow night's game. I'm quite looking forward to beating him.'

The thin man sneered.

'You got a big mouth.'

'And a deep pocket.'

'How deep?'

'Deep enough,' I said, pulling out a couple of $100 bills, 'cash is no use once you're on board, don't know what I should do with these.'

'You're not trying to bribe me are you mister, not for a puny couple of hundred?'

'Course not, just wondered if you were a betting man.'

He winced, 'What d'you mean?'

It was as if I'd hit a nerve.

'Heads or tails,' I took out a quarter, it shone silver in the palm of my hand, and then I flicked it spinning into the air and caught it on the back of my left hand, covering it with my right.

'Tails,' said the thin man without thinking.

I lifted my hand and looked. It was 'Heads'. I flipped it over with my thumb and then moved my right hand away to let him see.

'Tails it is.'

'Ha, knew you were a loser.'

'Name's Dr Anderson, Dr David Anderson,' I said as I handed over the money.

'Mine's, Brady. Won it fair and square didn't I. He'll eat you alive, Dr David Anderson. You won't be so cocky then.'

'We'll see,' I said.

'Yea we'll see. We'll see alright.'

He walked off smiling.

I returned to watch the rest of the game. From the height and number of piles of chips in front of him it looked like Krai was winning.

Chapter 16

The call came through early the next morning.

'Congratulations Dr Anderson. The game starts at 21:00 hrs. I've debited your account to pay for your chips. Do remember that the clocks go forward an hour today. Don't be late.'

'Thanks,' I said, 'I'm looking forward to it.'

I wasn't.

Losing on purpose doesn't come easy to me but I understood the logic. I knew how to play poker but Krai did not like to lose, therefore if I put up a reasonable fight but kept losing why wouldn't he keep me around? And being kept around Krai was my way of hoping to find out what he was, or was not, up to.

As the money I would be losing wasn't mine and I was sadly lacking in any other ideas it all seemed to make sense to me. After all, what could possibly go wrong?

I began to think through the little I thought I knew about Krai.

He was physically frail but, judging from his card play, still mentally strong. His entourage of four were not amateurs; they knew their job and followed him around like pet poodles, or maybe pet rottweiler's. They were his eyes and ears, they provided him with the protection he needed and did it with a practiced assurance.

Dr Gabriel Krai on the other hand gave the impression of constant restlessness, maybe a consequence of his condition. From what I'd seen of his demeanour he didn't seem to be greatly enjoying himself. And yet it was he who had chosen to come on this cruise, he didn't have to, there were a multitude of alternative ways he could be spending his time.

This choice was sufficiently out of Krai's character to arouse suspicion and warrant, amongst other things, my presence onboard.

He had not previously shown a penchant for luxuriating in the decadent ease of modern oceanic cruising. In fact my briefing had led me to believe that he preferred to live and eat simply. Having everything under his own control was more his way. Being in the hands of a captain and crew, a passenger not a leader, was not within his usual comfort zone.

I couldn't help thinking that I was missing something. But it was early days and if I was blissfully unaware of something critical then I still had time to search it out.

I needed to get closer to Krai and meeting Brady and getting a place at tonight's card game had given me a golden opportunity.

I just hoped that I wouldn't cock it up.

Chapter 17

I had the rest of the day to navigate my way through and after a leisurely breakfast I decided to distract myself by exploring some of the other parts of the ship. In particular I thought I'd visit the Library and borrow a book to read. That would at least help the time pass a little bit faster.

When I found what should have been the right area on Deck 7 I thought I must have made a mistake. There were comfortable black leather chairs, there were shelves lining the walls – but there were virtually no books. It took me by surprise.

'You've got to be quick if you want to get a book.'

I turned around. A grey haired man was sitting in one of the comfortable leather recliners. His small eyes were squinting at me from over the top of the book he was reading, like a nosey neighbour peeping over a fence.

'First thing people do, who know about cruising, who done it before, they come to the library soon as they can and they pick up an armful of books.' His accent was unmistakably American.

'But you can only read one book at a time.' I said.

'Yep, but if ya finish one, and ya bring it back like ya should, and them shelves are empty, just like they are now, then what d'ya do?'

'But they're only empty because so many people have taken more than they can read.'

'Exactly,' he said, 'latecomers beware, that's the motto on a cruise ship, latecomers beware!'

I was a latecomer and there were no books; Q.E.D. But I was sure there must be a flaw in his argument somewhere. It felt like accepting proof of one of the less seemly parts of the human condition; that when we find something good, we don't just take what we need we take everything we can carry and to hell with everybody else. It was other people's fault if they hadn't got there quicker, and to hell with them.

'Anyway mister, if ya can't read there's so much more time to get to know people. Some interesting people onboard this ship, y'know.'

I thought of Krai and his entourage. I guess you could call them interesting.

'You seem to have found something,' I said trying to head off a "getting to know you" type conversation.

'Not really, I'm not that interested in 'The Psychology of Sheep Shearing' fascinating though it may be to some.' He held up the book so that I could see the cover more clearly. He was telling the truth.

'Passenger from a previous cruise must have left it,' I hazarded.

'Mor'n less the last book on the shelf,' he said.

'Like the last one waiting to be picked for the team.'

I knew what that was like. I'd been asthmatic as a young kid although thankfully I'd grown out of it by the time I joined the Army. Still, bad memories die hard.

He smiled. I took the opportunity of the pause to scuttle off back to my room acquiring a chilled bottle of beer on the way.

I met Jacob in the corridor. He was standing behind his trolley of clean towels and detergents. Although neatly waist-coated the top button of his white shirt was undone. Even so there was a smile on his face and that won me over.

'Your room ready,' he said.

'Thank you,' I replied and slipped an extra 2 dollars into his hand. His smile widened and he nodded.

Once inside the room I called into "The Store" using the encrypted connection on my phone. As I gave my news Samantha yawned.

'So nothing of any consequence has happened.'

'I'm into the card game tonight.'

'Oh, well done,' she said, with an evident lack of enthusiasm, 'I look forward to your next scintillating installment.'

Click.

What can I say? I thought I'd done quite well to move so quickly. There's no pleasing some people.

I slid open the glass door and moved out onto the private balcony taking my beer with me. The Pacific Ocean rolled blue in every direction. A shearwater flew along parallel to our course. Its streamlined body cut through the air flying impossibly close to the undulating water's surface. Its eyes were focussed on catching the fish that our passing disturbed. It probably didn't even notice me.

I retrieved my phone, sat at the balcony table and this time tried to call my daughter. She didn't pick up so I left her a voicemail asking her to ring back because I needed some advice. I knew that would intrigue her, but it was also true.

As you move through your own timeline, live your own life, you collect memories. Gathered like fallen leaves, each light in itself, they accumulate, weighing on your shoulders. Not each leaf weighs the same; those of regret, mistakes, missed opportunities, lost loves, those leaves weigh most heavily.

I was carrying a lot of leaves and I thought that my daughter, being a woman, might be able to help me understand why Teresa was not speaking to me.

In the absence of this advice and rather than trying to call Teresa again, I decided to think about what I might say to her if I did call. This kind of self-examination is not my strong point so I took a swallow of beer, switched on the voice recorder on my phone, and tried a few words.

'Teresa, I've no idea why you're upset with me. Now come on, stop being silly and tell me.'

I switched off 'Record' and played it back. Even I could see that this approach would be unlikely to bear fruit. I gazed out to sea, drank some more beer, thought for a moment and then gave it another shot.

'Teresa, I know there's something wrong and I was wondering…'

My far superior effort was interrupted by a buzzing noise.

I looked around.

What looked like a european wasp was showing an unhealthy interest in me. I am not a great lover of these black and yellow striped demons and therefore instead of considering what species it might be or how it came to be here, either on the ship or more pertinently on my balcony, I instead took immediate action to try and kill the bloody thing.

As a result the buzzing grew louder and more aggressive. I managed to spill my beer, which was probably what it was after, and then moved swiftly back inside sliding the glass door closed behind me.

I wasn't fast enough.

I'd obviously annoyed it sufficiently for it to redirect its immediate priority from the partaking of sugary liquid to the repeated penetration of human skin, my skin.

I retreated in as orderly a fashion as I could, beating off its determined attacks. Backing into the toilet I snatched up a towel and hurled it in the general direction of my antagonist.

The towel fell to the floor. The buzzing took on an aggravated but muffled tone. For the next five minutes, though it seemed much longer at the time, I hunted down the wasp with deadly intent and smiled with satisfaction when I heard the exoskeleton crack and the buzzing cease.

Retrieving a white, crisp, newly laundered hand towel from the shower room I mopped the sweat from my hands, neck and face, left my vanquished foe to rest in peace and went back on to the balcony to revel in my victory.

There was still a little un-spilt beer in the bottle and I gulped it down. Looking at my phone I saw that it was still recording. I stopped it.

As I relaxed I could feel my heart rate start to slow. I'd come uncomfortably close to having pain inflicted by an angry wasp. It was a relief that, as far as I knew, I was not allergic to such stings.

When I'd recovered my composure I moved the towel containing the dead wasp into the shower room with the idea of giving it a burial at sea via the toilet flush. Before pursuing this thought however I retreated to the bedroom and used the cruise ship phone that sat on the bedside table, to ask that a replacement bottle of beer be brought to my cabin as soon as possible.

The beer arrived promptly and I was pleased to see it was nicely chilled. I took it outside and sat watching the droplets of condensation coalesce and run down the side of the bottle in rivulets. I drank it slowly.

Then a thought occurred to me.

In my briefing I had been given a summary of Krai's known medical condition including his allergies. Somewhere in the rather long list had been both bee and wasp stings. For someone with this condition the consequences of a single sting could be catastrophic, the body reacting in minutes causing the onset of anaphylactic shock. Without an injection of adrenalin to improve breathing and stimulate the heart the victim was prone to collapse with potentially fatal results. Krai would be particularly vulnerable as he was in such a poor medical condition to start with.

A Plan B therefore occurred to me. I listened to the recording I'd inadvertently made and edited out everything except the increasingly aggressive sound of the wasp. Then I transferred this recording onto my watch and made a careful note of the number of seconds it lasted.

The next step was to, very carefully, disentangle the body of the wasp from the towel and wrap it in toilet tissue. Then I went to the wardrobe and put the tissue in one of the pockets of the nearest jacket.

Chapter 18

The buffet lunch in the "Sailing By" eatery was a like a melee.

It seems that when the food is free, or at least included in the basic cost of the cruise, then people are determined to eat more. The wealth of choice only made it worse and plates were piled impossibly high in order to accommodate a portion of each of the good things on offer. People were jostling for position, eyeing other's plates to see if they'd missed anything.

There were so many people.

It was because I didn't want to have regular contact or conversation with any of my fellow passengers that I'd chosen the eat-anytime, sit-where-you-want buffet style option. I couldn't predict where this cruise was going to lead me and I didn't want to risk an attachment to anybody onboard clouding my judgment. My job was a lonely one and I was keen to keep it that way. I knew from my recent experiences with Teresa how caring about someone messes with your head.

I finally managed to salvage a vegetable curry with boiled white rice and found a seat. A forkful was on the way to my mouth when someone tapped me on the shoulder,

'Do you mind if I sit here?'

Yes, I wanted to say.

'Of course not, go ahead.'

How could I say 'No' to a guy in a wheelchair for goodness sake? Grey-haired, smartly dressed, and with medal ribbons on his left hand breast pocket, he deserved politeness.

'Escaped the wife for a bit,' he said.

A member of staff had followed him with a plate of food and now placed it down in front of him, he turned to her,

'Could you possibly bring me a glass of lemonade,' and then turning to me, 'would you like one?'

'A glass of water please.'

While we were eating I asked him about the ribbons. I couldn't help it.

'Military family,' he said, 'don't like to talk about my own service,' I knew what he meant, 'but I'm the last of three generations of soldiers.'

I nodded. He continued between mouthfuls.

'Father, Second World War, Artillery Observer, Sicily and then Italy. Grandfather, Ypres, invalided home, became a postman. The most feared man in the village.' He paused, looking out of the window, eyes seeking the blue horizon, 'I'll never forget what my father told me of my grandfather's life. He was the one who had to deliver those letters from the war office. Every day, a family's fate, their changed futures pushed through a letterbox. He would say that he could hear the screams following behind him as he walked back down the path from their front doors and closed the garden gate with a click as sharp as a rifle bullet.'

'On this one day he had to deliver so many that he couldn't stand it and just sat down on the curb and wept. An ex-soldier, an ordinary man, he just cried.'

At this point a smartly dressed, straight-backed older lady approached us. She put a hand on my companion's shoulder.

'I hope he hasn't been annoying you.' she said smiling.

'Not at all,' I rose so that she could take my seat, 'it's been nice to meet you,' I said.

It was only as I was leaving the restaurant that I realised I didn't know his name and he didn't know mine. That, at least, was one saving grace.

Chapter 19

After lunch I decided to simply wander, to get a better idea of the layout of the ship, a mental picture of which facilities were on which deck. The layout of a 14 deck cruise liner can get confusing.

As I was passing through one of the bars on a lower deck I spotted Brady seated by himself. He'd chosen an isolated corner and was speaking to someone on his mobile phone. He was sweating and seemed agitated. I thought I'd have a chat.

As I got closer I began to pick up what he was saying, the strangulated hiss of his side of the conversation.

'... listen if you just wait I'll have all the money, no problem.'

'Where from is none of your business just trust me on this, 10 days tops, that's all I'm asking.'

' .. so you want to see something down do you? $10,000 in the next 24hrs or what ...'

He snarled.

'...it ain't like I've been pissing on my own doorstep.'

'...yeh, yeh, I know Dr Krai ain't going to be happy to hear I been caught out gambling again. I just been unlucky, that's how it is with me, I never get a break.'

'...OK, OK, I'll get you something and in a coupla days you going to be begging to have me back in the game. You just wait, you'll see.'

When he saw me coming he didn't seem pleased and ended the call with 'I'll call you back later, just trust me.'

'Hello,' I said smiling, 'I'm pleased to say that I'm in the game tonight and thought I might owe you a drink for that.'

'Bourbon on the rocks,' he said, and then added, 'Don't mention it, happy to help,' in a rather insincere tone.

I got him his drink, two doubles in fact, and a lime juice for me, I wanted to stay sharp. I put the glasses in front of him and he downed the first in one, curling his lips back as the liquid seared his throat.

'So what do you want this time?'

'Just wondered if you could tell me a little about Dr Krai's approach to playing cards. I wouldn't want to make a complete fool of myself.'

He laughed in a not very encouraging way.

'You're crazy. Do you really think I would say anything to a complete stranger that would help him in a game against the boss? I'll tell you one thing though and I'll tell it you for free,' he leaned forward, I could smell his bad breath, see the sweat glistening on his skin, 'Dr Krai does not like to lose and so he never does.'

'OK then, how about a little side bet?'

'You really are crazy.'

'I'll bet you $10,000 that I beat Dr Krai tonight.'

'You'll do what?'

I repeated the proposition. I needed to find a chink in Krai's armoury and Brady was showing every sign of being it.

He looked at me searchingly.

'Get me another drink,' he said.

I brought back another two.

'Now let me get this straight, if you beat Dr Krai tonight then I owe you $10,000.'

'That's right.'

'And if you don't you give me the ten grand.'

'Spot on.'

He rubbed his chin, it was unshaven and rasped under his fingers like sandpaper.

'And what if you get knocked out early?'

'If I don't get to the head to head then all bets are off.'

'Hmm'

'What do you think?'

'I think,' he said, screwing up his eyes, 'there's going to be some weak players around that table tonight.'

'So we're on?'

He gulped down a drink.

'We got a bet Dr Anderson, we got a bet.'

He reached out a clammy hand and I took it. He had a surprisingly strong grip.

'So tell me about your colleagues,' I said.

He looked surprised.

'Why dya wanna know about them? Wadda they gotta do with the price of eggs?'

'I want to be able to concentrate on the game don't I? You've got to give me a sporting chance and if I'm always wondering what you and your three colleagues are up to I'm going to get distracted aren't I. I might even do something silly and get knocked out first up.'

He shrugged.

'Ain't gonna make much difference I s'pose, you ain't got no chance of beating Dr Krai.'

He settled back and between drinks said,

'The guy built like a bald wrestler is Marte. He's never shy to remind us of his military background, which is probably where the personal discipline he lives by was drilled into his soul, it's lodged so deep it's become his mantra; discipline, loyalty, honour.' He curled his lip showing his disdain, 'For some reason he keeps very close to Dr Krai and Dr Krai in return shows complete faith in him. No matter what I do I can't compete with that bond.'

He'd obviously tried but if he'd asked me I'd have mentioned that his gambling habit, his anxious demeanour, and his tendency to sweatiness, could also be possible reasons for his lack of success.

'You deserve better,' I said instead.

'I do the best I can. I've known Krai from his days on the streets of Chicago, when he was working his way up, didn't know nothing, learning his way, making lots of mistakes. I had to do a lot of tidying up for him. He owes me and he knows it.'

I tried to imagine a younger Brady, even more brash than today, even more full of himself. It was a frightening thought.

'The tall guy is african.'

I nodded.

'You might have guessed that from the colour of his skin. His name is Atu and he's a cold bastard, hard and very ambitious. Don't get in his way Dr Anderson, he'll walk right through you.'

Sounded like a nice guy.

'The other, the blonde man, is Gunnar Svenson. He's a Swede, a young guy learning his trade. He's quiet and easy to underestimate. But that would be a dangerous thing to do.'

His pen portraits were succinct if nothing else. I wondered how he would sum himself up but was too polite to ask.

He pushed away the last empty glass and got up to go.

'I got work to do,' he said, 'you just make sure you're good for the money, and Dr Anderson, you be careful, you go around asking too many questions you might have a long swim home.'

I ignored the threat.

'Oh, I'm good for the money,' I said, pleased that "The Store" had set me up with a sizeable slush fund.

After he'd gone I ordered a whisky and downed it in one.

That had been unexpected, I thought, but you've got to take your opportunities where you find them. I was very conscious that Brady was an unreliable ally. Time would tell if I'd done the right thing.

At least I had the names: Krai, Brady, Marte, Atu, Gunnar. These were the men I had to get in amongst. It felt like I was making progress and I was eager to take the next steps.

Chapter 20

Back in my cabin it was time to do some homework, get my mind into gear for the game tonight. Just like elite athletes if you want to do well you can't go into a poker game cold, you have to warm up. I switched on the laptop and looked for an online game.

Texas Hold'em is essentially a simple game. You aim to get a better hand than your opponent's and take their money off them.

The best and unbeatable hand is the Royal Flush a five card run of ten through to Ace of cards of the same suit. Then comes a Straight Flush, a lower run of cards all of the same suit, then Four of a Kind, the higher the better, the best being four Aces, then a Full House, a combination of three cards the same and two cards the same with the higher the three cards the better. The highest Full House is therefore three Aces accompanied by any other matching pair.

Then comes a Flush, five cards of the same suit, a Straight, five cards not of the same suit but making a run, then Three of a Kind, Two Pair, a Pair, and lastly and lowest a High Card, the higher the better.

On the Nereus the casino assigned an independent dealer, a trained member of the casino staff, and in this situation the order of play was shifted from player to player using a white disk as marker.

The player with this in front of him or her would be the last to have cards dealt to them. With the stakes set for Krai's game the player to the left of the disc would put $500 into the pot, the so-called "Small

Blind". The next player to the left would put in $1000, the "Big Blind".

Two cards would then be dealt to each player, the so-called "Pocket" cards and play would then commence from the player to the left of the "Big Blind".

The choices available to each player in turn are then pretty straightforward. If you think the two "Pocket" cards you've been dealt stand a good chance of making a winning hand you place a bet. If you think the "Pocket" cards will not stand a good chance of becoming part of the winning hand you "Fold" by throwing your cards in and taking no further part in that particular round.

For example if you have an Ace and King or a Pair, you would be a fool not to bet. If on the other hand you had a three and an eight of different suits you would probably curse your luck, fold, and wait for the next hand to bring you better fortune.

Once betting is completed the dealer places a further three cards face up on the table.

This is called "the Flop" and you try to make the best hand you can, without giving anything away to the other players, from these cards and the cards you have in your hand.

For example if you have an Ace and there are another two Aces on the table you already have a strong Three of a Kind. If you are holding an Ace and a King and on the table is dealt an eight, a six and a two in different suits then you only have an Ace High Card and what's worse is that if any of the other players are holding and eight, six, or two then they would have a Pair which is a better hand.

So all of a sudden from having a strong start you can be in a stronger or a weaker position depending on the cards the dealer lays on the table. Likewise weak looking "Pocket" cards can produce a winning hand.

Now players either continue to bet or throw in their hands.

In general the better the hand you think you have, the more you think you have the best hand, the more money you will bet.

After this round of betting is complete the dealer places another card, a fourth, face up on the table, this is called "the Turn".

The process of hand-making, betting or discarding is then repeated and a final card, "the River", is placed face up alongside the previous four.

There is then a final round of betting before the players still in the game show their hands. The best one wins and that player takes all the money bet on that hand as their winnings. The white disc is then moved to the next player, the Blinds are put in and the dealer starts to deal the next hand.

Told you it was easy.

The problem of winning consistently is made much more problematic by the chance aspect of the cards that fall on the table in the Flop, the Turn and the River together with the annoyingly dishonest and misleading behaviour of your opponents.

Putting all these things together means that it is often **not** the best hand that wins!

It would be understandable to discard a Pocket eight immediately and then if three more fall onto the table during the Flop, the Turn and the River to hold your head in your hands and wonder why you threw away a winning hand. Swallowing this misfortune without an undue show of emotion is both the sign of a true professional and the surest path to an ulcer.

In the winner-takes-all version we would be playing I bought into the game by stumping up $20,000.

As there were 5 players in the game this meant I would leave the table with $100,000 or nothing. Luckily my ambition was to achieve the latter, but to do it with aplomb. It was important that Krai noticed me sufficiently to happily to welcome me back to the table on subsequent evenings.

Having signed into an online game to warm up I played along for an hour or so, conservatively, only betting when I thought I stood a good chance of winning the hand.

Using these tactics my fortunes swung between slightly up and slightly down. I then switched to high risk betting, effectively trying to bluff my way to a win, hoping that the other players would overestimate my hand and discard their better one.

This change of tactic worked for a while but then I started losing heavily. I signed off from the game when I was $1000 down. I didn't mind the loss it was all part of the warm up.

I'd pretty much come to terms with the time difference now. If anything I was most awake in the evenings which I thought might work in my favour.

After so long hunched over a screen I decided I needed some exercise to get the blood pumping through my brain so I got changed and went for a jog around the delineated track on Deck 12, a mezzanine that overlooked the main pool on Deck 11 below.

It was warm and I jogged around in T-shirt, shorts and trainers. The sky was cloudless, the ocean an undulating mass of blue and the ship ploughed a steady path onwards in whatever direction we were supposed to be going.

I ran with a regular pace feeling the increase in adrenalin that comes with controlled exertion. It was as I began to feel the sweat begin to soak through my T-shirt that Atu passed me.

Distracted by the sound of my own breathing and thoughts of the trials to come I hadn't heard him approaching. His black chest was bare and his back muscles rippled, glistening with a sheen of sunlight as he pulled away. His stride was comfortable, effortless and long. He looked like he could run like that all day.

I laboured on feeling less capable than I had a moment ago and more like a fish out of water. Pride and my ex-military determination kept me going but when I was overtaken for the second time I decided it was time to grab a towel and go and cool off.

I made a mental note that if I was ever to get on the wrong side of Atu it would be pointless to try and run away.

Chapter 21

I took an early dinner was to ensure that the processes of digestion did not dull my senses during game.

As I made my way to the any-time restaurant at the back of Deck 11, overlooking the stern of the ship, I was conscious of the doors marked "Restricted Access", "Authorised Service Personnel", and "Crew Only". Here were the portals between the two worlds of passengers and crew with only the crew being routinely allowed to pass between the two.

The idea of a world within a world, a ship within a ship, a different life hidden behind a second skin intrigued me and I determined to find a way to familiarise myself with this secret world of service. At the moment though getting something to eat was the more pressing issue.

The problem with being confined on a cruise ship with a lot of strangers who have brought with them a holiday mindset is that most of them have decided to pretend to be interested in everybody else's business as a pretext for launching into their own stories of previous travels, either magnificent or catastrophic, their glittering careers, big houses, successful children …

It seems strange to me that people spend all this money to come away from home presumably intent on seeing new things and seeking new experiences and yet spend most of their time telling everybody about those things they've left behind or that they've already done.

People who would never normally contemplate striking up a conversation are all of a sudden transformed into curious social animals, intent on making new acquaintances, exchanging cards and addresses. But whatever the intent for expanded horizons of openness each of us brings with us our own life experiences that are cocooned within our heads together with the inescapable past that we carry in our hearts.

We're all crazy, including me.

The restaurant was again busy but I managed with plate in hand to snaffle a table by the window. It overlooked the stern, the lines of frothed white providing temporary evidence of our passing.

I'd gone for a light meal, a freshly made cheese, onion, tomato and ham omelet with a green side salad and a fresh white roll. No sooner had I sat down than one of the waiters asked if I would like a drink and I asked for a papaya juice.

With three empty seats at my table I knew I wouldn't be alone for long although I tried to avoid all eye contact and to appear as disinterested and disagreeable as possible.

'May we sit here?'

It was an Asian looking lady and her elderly parents.

'Of course,' I said, feigning a smile.

'Thank you.'

The trouble is that once you're in such close proximity to someone in a situation like this then some form of conversation is inevitable, whether you like it or not.

The lady's name was Linh. She looked to be in her late thirties or early forties and spoke very politely in polished English, her accent more refined than mine.

'May I introduce my parents,' she said, 'this is my father, Ken,' he bowed his head and I nodded back, 'and this is my mother, Thanh,' again we each nodded.

Both of Linh's parents were small and wiry, their faces deeply lined. Her father's shoulders were slightly stooped and Linh explained that he was hard of hearing.

The normal small talk about the weather and if the cruise was living up to expectations was quickly over. I was then subjected to a light interrogation.

I didn't mind this as it allowed me the opportunity to rehearse my backstory and was pleased with how easily it flowed from my tongue.

To return the compliment I asked about them. I had unwittingly opened the floodgates and their life stories flowed out of them. I listened.

Although they looked about 80 Ken and Thanh were in their 60's. Ken had fought in the Vietnam War. From a well-to-do family he had been a high school teacher before the war. Thanh had also been a teacher. A Captain on the losing side Ken had been captured by the Viet Cong after the Americans left in 1975.

As an officer he escaped the mass executions and was sent for "re-education" in one of the notorious camps dotted around what was then Saigon. Here he was ill-treated, mal-nourished and tortured for 3 years then forced to work as a peasant in the rice fields. He was unused to manual labour and it took a heavy toll on his health.

During this time his wife was scraping a living for

herself and their baby daughter as best she could and was eventually allowed to return to teaching.

When they finally got back together, a minor miracle in itself, they were treated as 2nd class citizens and became determined that their daughter would not grow up with only continuing hardship to look forward to.

They therefore borrowed, sold and saved to secretly build up the stock of small gold bars that was the black market currency.

By 1982 they had sufficient to pay for the privilege of becoming one of the many tens of thousands of Vietnamese boat people. Their particular overcrowded fishing junk made it to international waters but no further. Here their two aged outboard motors failed and they drifted, powerless, running out of food and water.

Pirates from Thailand boarded their boat and stole what few possessions they had left. It was as their boat was sinking that they were rescued by a Thai fishing boat and ended up in a refugee camp on the coast of Thailand. Here they were offered the chance to re-settle in Australia which they grabbed with both hands.

To make money to feed his family, and honour his debts back in Vietnam, Ken took a job working in the coke ovens of the Northern Australian Steel Industry. He had worked there for 32 years.

'I am now retired.' he said, rolling up his shirt sleeves to show his blackened, mottled arms, a badge of honour, 'We were very lucky. If I had not been trained in manual labour in Vietnam I could not have done this job.'

'There were hundreds of thousands of us,' said Thanh, 'so many drowned, so many killed by pirates, yes we have been lucky, so lucky, look…' she pointed towards her daughter.

'She means that I am a lawyer,' said Linh, 'my parents were determined that I should get a good education.'

'And married,' said Ken.

'Yes,' said Linh.

'And to a doctor,' said Ken.

'And with two children, a boy and a girl, our grandchildren. They're very smart too,' said Thanh.

Linh just smiled and shrugged. She knew her parents, there was no point arguing.

'Thank you for letting us sit with you, David, and letting us talk. So many people don't like to.'

'This is probably my last time at sea,' said Ken, 'I wanted a happier memory before my knees give out on me completely, and besides,' he looked at his wife, 'there are plenty of shops onboard and Thanh can never have enough of shopping for handbags and jewellery.'

I got up to leave and thanked them for their time. I envied them the closeness of their family unit. My own story, the loss of a wife to cancer, felt ordinary in comparison.

Chapter 22

Back in my cabin I took a shower and changed my clothes. I checked my watch and ensured that my jacket still had all its contents. With an hour or so still to burn I made my way to the theatre entrance on Deck 5 and took my seat for the early show.

One of the many benefits of being the occupier of an Executive Suite is that you have access to an area of preferential seating in the theatre, high to the left of the stage, a cordoned off area of the balcony.

It's not something I have ever had to worry about and I sat with the common people in a position where I could watch.

Neither Dr Krai nor any of his four closest companions attended the show but in their stead there sat a young woman who peered attentively at the stage.

The theatre was about three-quarters full and after what seemed like an age, patience not being one of my strong points, the lights went down and a be-suited compare walked out to the microphone.

The stage lighting picked out his bronzed complexion, although whether real or out of a bottle was anyone's guess. His jet black hair was slicked down tight to his skull. So much so that he appeared as if he could quite easily walk through a hurricane without getting a parting.

After the ripple of polite applause had subsided he smiled broadly, bowed and spread out his arms in welcome as if we were already acquainted and on friendly terms. Putting the microphone to his mouth he began to speak in a theatrically loud voice, dripping in self confidence.

'Welcome, ladies and gentlemen…and to you others, hello,' a titter of laughter, 'welcome to this evening's early performance. If any of you have had the pleasure of seeing Madison on stage before you will know that you are in for a treat. We feel very fortunate that she has found the time in her busy schedule to be with us here tonight and I'm sure, yes I'm sure, that you will enjoy the performance,' he paused to take a breath, 'As you can imagine she is in high demand and has travelled the world both learning and developing her hypnotic craft and has performed to audiences on every continent and on every ocean,' he paused again, giving us time to be awed, the young girl in her balcony seat was shaking her head, clearly not impressed.

'Hypnosis,' he continued, 'is both an art and a science. As I'm sure Madison will tell you the medicinal benefits of hypnosis are well proven in the relief of pain, the treatment of addiction and many other afflictions,' amazing we still need doctors, I thought.

'But also ladies and gentlemen … and you others,' less tittering than before, the joke had passed its sell-by date, 'hypnosis can also be a source of entertainment and fun and tonight that's what we are all, I'm quite sure, looking forward to. So before turning over the stage to Madison let me just remind you that the use of cameras or video equipment of any kind is not allowed and assure you that those of you who may become a part of tonight's show will not suffer any lasting effects,' a sly wink, 'other than the possible fame gained through your on-stage performance,' then, and in an undertone, 'although of course you participate at your own risk.'

He spread out his right arm towards the side of the stage, 'So now and without any further ado please welcome onto the stage,' his voice rose heightening the anticipation, 'Madison, the mind-bending, extraordinary, talented, world renowned hypnotist!!'

The spotlight swung to the left hand side of the stage whilst our compere exited right, in darkness.

To the sound of applause a tall blonde walked confidently out onto centre stage. She was wearing a glittering red sequined dress and matching high heels. Her blonde hair, swept back from her face, cascaded down her back well past shoulder length, her eyes glittered in the stage lights and her white teeth glistened between lipstick red lips.

She wore a wireless headset, the small white microphone unobtrusively positioned close to her mouth. She waited for the applause to die down.

I wondered if hypnosis could make me a more convincing card player. That's all I needed to be, a convincing loser.

The show that then followed involved linking your fingers together and putting them on the top of your head. Those in the audience who found that they couldn't separate them again were invited onto the stage and whittled down to 10 or so willing or not so willing hypno-sensitive volunteers.

After reassuring everyone that hypnosis was good for you Madison took control and entertained us by getting these poor people to humiliate themselves for our enjoyment. They cavorted around as happy dogs, played imaginary instruments, sang the Stars and

Stripes every time someone mentioned America. It was almost too easy to laugh at somebody else's discomfort whilst at the same time being mighty relieved that it wasn't you up there on stage.

I could see from her body language that the young woman seated in the balcony VIP area was not enjoying the show. About halfway through she'd had enough, got up and left.

The show ended with Madison bringing the participants out of hypnosis and back into the real world and they stood dazed, gazing around, wondering when the show would start and why there was so much applause. I was pretty sure somebody would fill them in later, perhaps even exaggerating the truth to relive the fun at their expense.

I didn't rush to leave. I waited until almost everybody else had risen from their seats and filed or pushed their way out.

This was it. My next stop was the casino.

Chapter 23

It was after 9 o'clock when I stepped onto the rich red carpet and the head croupier that I'd seen earlier welcomed me in. She gently directed me to my seat at the poker table, her dark hair swept back, her white smile contrasting attractively with her dark skin, her slim body shown to advantage by the uniformed suit she was wearing. I reminded myself that I had to focus and avoid any unnecessary distractions.

'Have a good game Dr Anderson,' she said and then pointed to her name badge clipped to the lapel of her jacket, 'my name is Rosa, and if there's anything you need just let me or one of my colleagues know. We'll be only too pleased to help.'

I noticed that she had a very pleasant American drawl to her voice.

'Thank you,' I said.

She smiled again, 'Good luck Dr Anderson.'

I wasn't sure whether it was luck or a miracle that I was in need of. You can do all the practicing you like but when you're in the real game, the heat of battle, it's all very different. I was about to find out how different.

There were five of us at the table. Krai's seat was opposite the dealer, to his right was a big man wearing a stetson and chewing gum and to his left was an already over-tanned bald man of medium build. Obliquely opposite and left of Krai sat a woman of large stature, diamonds and a happy smile and I occupied the remaining seat obliquely opposite and to Krai's right.

Krai was the last to arrive, walking slowly, the exoskeleton whirring. His seat was positioned for him by the same slim, blonde, medium height young woman of serious demeanour, but now dressed in a white knee-length Lab coat, that I had seen in the Theatre.

Brady parked himself behind Krai's shoulder with his three colleagues positioned so as to keep a surreptitious watch on both the proceedings and the rest of the room.

The casino was buzzing with people. Behind us the slot machines chinged and pinged. The noise of individual conversations blurred into the rumble of the ball on the roulette table's spinning wheel, merged with the muffled sounds of feet shuffling haphazardly across the red carpeted floor.

I switched off my phone and laid it case side up on the table in front of me. The case was a distinctive one, bright red in colour, with a large ace of spades in the centre, and in the centre of that a white Joker's face smiling back at you. It was designed to bring the owner good luck. We would see.

The dealer called us to order and then shuffled and cut, placed the white counter, watched the laying of the big and small blind bets, and then proceeded to deal the first cards. We were off.

The hands progressed slowly at first as each of us got a feel for the cards and for each other. I was looking for signals to give me a guide to the level of experience of my opponents, whether they were serious players or tourists just there to create a tale to tell and pleasantly lose their money.

I played conservatively. The man in the Stetson didn't. He played almost every hand no matter the quality of his cards and his success rate started off as erratic and quickly became disastrous. He soon left the table chewing vigorously, cursing his luck and the almost supernatural intuition of his opponents.

Standing behind Krai, Brady grinned and I wondered how carefully he had helped choose the other players. He knew he needed to help me if he was going to win our bet.

One down.

The next to fall by the wayside was the only lady in the game. From her gold bracelet to her diamond necklace and earrings it seemed that she was not short of the odd dollar or two and was playing for fun. Her husband or partner was standing behind her enjoying the joke as her pile of chips disappeared. She left the table delighted with her success, having not been the first one out.

Two down.

Brady's forehead was glistening with sweat as he chewed his upper lip. He had a lot riding on this.

So far so good.

The bald headed man played more doggedly and with intelligence born out of experience.

I saw Brady nod across to the bar and I don't think that it was a coincidence that the bald man's glass was never empty.

After an hour or so the alcohol started to take effect and he began to make a few ill considered bids, unlikely bluffs and misjudgements, getting more and more upset with himself as he did so. As the pile of chips in front of him dwindled he started to chase the game, trying too hard to win them back, becoming less and less likely to do so.

I just rode out his trauma until eventually he too had to leave the table. He was clearly unsteady on his feet as he rose, turned and proceeded to push his way out of the casino.

Three down and we'd now entered the final phase, me versus Krai, mano a mano.

Brady was clearly delighted. From his point of view the $10,000 was as good as his. Krai, as he had been throughout the game, was impassive.

I was also pleased but tried not to show it. Here I was, first game, first go and I was in the position I had been hoping for. Call it beginner's luck, albeit helped along by Brady's self-serving behind the scenes manoeuvring, call it what you like but whatever you called it here I was, exactly where I wanted to be.

I'd stuck around. Stacking and checking often I'd won a few hands on strong cards I'd been dealt and bluffed now and again with mixed success.

Now I was going head-to-head with my target, aiming to lose graciously but wanting to leave an impression that I could build on, hoping perhaps to get a direct invite to play again.

I looked across the table and met Krai's expressionless gaze. He was a cold fish so I'd have to bait my hook carefully.

Chapter 24

Now there were no distractions I could focus all my attention on Dr Krai. The first thing I noticed was the difference between the man sitting here in front of me and the photographs I had studied back in London. He was more gaunt, his face more deeply lined, and thinner. He looked much older, reduced by illness and pain to a hollowed out version of the man I'd researched. His skin was like translucent parchment, thin blue-black veins visible just below the surface. He held himself taut in the exoskeleton which gave him an angular look, like a skeleton hung out to dry.

His entourage was attentive, the young woman monitoring his condition, feeding him painkillers from time to time. There was, however, an intensity in his eyes and he exuded control proving that you don't have to look good or be the fittest to still be the boss. He had a presence and from the way he played his hands his brain was clearly sharp. What he didn't look like was someone who had come on this cruise for personal pleasure.

My plan for the rest of the game was straightforward. I was going to appear to play as well as I could and steadily lose. I've played a lot of poker over the years, enough to know that I am neither very good nor very lucky, and from what I'd already seen of Krai he was the better player so it was going to be easy for me to lose to him. I just had to shelve my competitive self.

I thought about my next steps. Over the next few days I would continue to look for Brady's help on the pretext I was keen to win my money back. I would aim to maintain my seat at the table and lose between $10-20,000 each night. After all that's why "The Store" had given me the money in the first place. Through this routine interaction I would try to slowly build a rapport with Krai, although judging from his aloofness this would be more difficult than losing the money. Either from Krai directly or from his close associates I was then going to try and find out whether there was anything going on, beyond this out-of-character choice of vacation.

For an inveterate gambler the three most important words are not 'I love you' but rather 'I won again'. I was hoping to play on this facet of Krai's character giving him pleasure by acting the reluctant but persistent loser.

I felt confident in my plan. After all what could possibly go wrong?

The rest of the game was one of attrition, neither of us getting a consistent run of better hands.

The dealer changed every hour to keep it fresh. Krai played consistently, bluffing rarely. He won some hands on weaker cards and my show of exasperation when this happened seemed to raise a glimmer of satisfaction.

I played the percentages, successfully bluffing once or twice but more often getting caught out and having more money squeezed out of me than I should have allowed. As I got more tired I increasingly hoped for a hand that would allow me to bet big but get beaten. I could see Brady, who was avidly following the game, was also starting to flag but I knew we shared the same objective: my defeat, his win.

I felt like I was beginning to run on automatic, looking for an opportunity.

And then it came.

Chapter 25

It's difficult to tell what someone else is really thinking. I learned quite early on that you can't rely on what people say as being what they actually mean. Consciously and unconsciously you take a read out from their tone of voice, their expression, their body language and then make a judgment of meaning that is filtered through your own unique set of values, experiences and knowledge. It's amazing we're able to communicate with each other at all.

Krai was making it more difficult to read him by not saying anything at all. His face was a fixed mask of inscrutability, his hands resting casually on the red baize of the table in front on him. He was looking at me with languid eyes and I wondered what he was reading from me. Did he know that I wanted to lose?

From the dealer I got dealt a pair of 2's and after cagey betting from both of us there followed a flop of the King of Clubs, 2 of diamonds, and Ace of Spades. Krai bet and raised. Assuming he wasn't bluffing this signalled a confident hand. I prayed he had two good high cards in his hand. An Ace and King would be perfect.

On a hand of three 2's I was more or less forced to bet, but if he had a combined hand of 2 Aces, 2 Kings he would also bet on the prospect of another Ace or King giving him a strong Full House and knocking my 3 2's into a cocked hat.

'Your turn, I believe,' said Krai, breaking his silence.

The temperature in the room seemed to have risen. A trickle of sweat wound its way unbidden down my cheek, like a tear. I wiped it away.

This was the moment. With only myself and Krai left in the game and the stakes high this was when I should make my move.

I bet and raised strongly. He matched and pushed further. I had to be careful because at the moment I might have the better hand. My plan could backfire and I could come out a reluctant winner.

On the other hand the chances of him beating me were high and I wouldn't look like an amateur for following my 2's and losing; perfect.

The Turn added the Ace of clubs to the mix.

I was euphoric.

I now had a Full House of 2's and Aces but if I'd guessed right Krai had a Full House of Aces and Kings, maybe he even had 4 Aces, of if he was holding 2 Kings a Full House of Kings and Aces. All of these beat me but I had to chase the betting with a Full House of my own. Not many people would throw that away.

Krai bet aggressively.

I counted the chips in front of me and pushed them forward into the centre with a theatrical show of bravado.

'All in,' I said.

There was a murmur from the small group of people who had stayed to watch the game to its bitter conclusion. I could feel the tension go up a notch or two.

The croupier counted the chips and announced the value. Krai smiled but it wasn't a smile of happiness it was the grim, set smile of the predator just before the kill, when its prey is cornered and powerless to escape.

I hoped that this investment would yield the desired return otherwise I was giving away an awful lot of somebody else's money for no good reason.

Krai pushed the required value of chips forward. I was gratified to see that this left only a handful of chips still sitting in front of him. I'd made a good fist of the game, had traded Krai blow for blow up to this point. Hopefully he was impressed.

And now this was it.

From my perspective I was confident of an honourable defeat. Brady leered at me from behind Krai's left shoulder. He seemed confident as well.

I watched as the dealer drew the last card, the River, the last card of a long game. I would lose graciously and challenge Krai to another game the following night. How could he refuse? My plan to get closer to Krai was working well.

I saw the card in the dealer's fingers even before it was flipped, before it was released to float in the still air and land on the table face up.

It was a 2.

Shit!

I had 4 2's. Please god let Krai have 2 Aces in his hand, the only way he could beat me.

There was now a strong possibility I had won by mistake. I couldn't take that risk. I had to instigate Plan B.

Trying not to draw any attention to myself I pressed one of the buttons on my watch.

At first the buzzing was low but intimidating. Krai heard it immediately and looked around, for the first time he looked unsettled.

Brady and Marte also responded and moved protectively closer to their charge.

The noise grew louder and more aggressive. The sound of an angry wasp reverberated around the table.

A pearl-necklaced lady screamed, her hands clasping her silk-wrapped cleavage, her eyes swooshing around the room trying to locate the offending insect.

I had to get the timing right. The recording would play for 5 more seconds.

4 ... as a look of alarm flashed across Krai's face, I reached into the pocket of my jacket.

3 ... I grasped the dead wasp.

2 ... I moved my eyes around as if following a flight path and shouted 'There!'.

1 ... In the confusion I took my hand out of my pocket and,

0 ... slapped it palm down onto the table with the wasp underneath it.

The buzzing came to an abrupt halt. A shard of pain shot through my hand and my first thought was that I must have slapped it down too hard.

I could feel Krai's eyes as I turned my hand over.

The wasp was not on the table where it should have been. Instead it was dangling from the palm of my hand by its sting, it's black and yellow striped abdomen pulsating rhythmically.

The bastard was dead, I thought, how the hell was it still able to sting me?

I could see Brady over Krai's shoulder trying not to laugh. He was having a great time. He wasn't even sweating.

I pulled the sting out of my hand and threw the wasp onto the red baize for all to see. It continued to twitch until the dealer placed one of the larger chips on top of it and pressed down.

I fell to sucking at my hand, attempting to extract some of the venom and relieve the pain.

It had all happened so quickly.

Krai began to raise himself from his seat, he had clearly had enough excitement for one evening. Brady, Marte, Atu, Gunnar and Krai's young nurse clustered protectively around him. As he got up he flipped over his cards; Ace of Diamonds, King of Hearts, a Full House of Aces and Kings.

I shrugged as he turned to leave.

I was more than willing to concede and if no one saw my cards then my shrug would have been enough.

Unfortunately Brady had other ideas. He clearly wanted to revel in his triumph. He wanted to look into my loser's eyes knowing he was $10,000 richer.

With my attention on the pain in my hand I wasn't quick enough to stop him.

The two 2's, the humblest cards in the pack, landed face upwards.

Brady's grin faded as he put it all together and came up with four 2's. His face changed to shock as he realised I had the winning hand. He started to sweat.

In desperation he turned to the dealer.

'Game abandoned,' he said and picked up my cards, held them in front of my face and tore them to pieces, tossing the remnants into the air. They floated down as incongruously as confetti at a funeral.

'Congratulations twice over Mr ..?' said Krai. It was the first time he'd shown any interest in me as a human being.

'Doctor,' I said, 'Doctor David Anderson.'

Krai looked at where the Dealer's chip covered the dead wasp.

'It has been an eventful evening I think,' he said before walking steadily, mechanically away flanked by Brady and Marte, followed by Atu, Gunnar and the young woman in the white Lab coat.

I watched him go. He did not look back.

At least I'd got noticed.

Chapter 26

I sat holding my hand and feeling sorry for myself. Rosa, the head croupier, appeared at my shoulder with a concerned look on her face and a bag of ice in her hand. I took the ice gratefully and closed my hand around it. The shock of cold made me wince but it soon began to numb the pain and, I hoped, reduce the swelling.

'That's quick thinking,' I said, 'Thank you.'

'Do you want to see the doctor?'

I was tempted but said that I didn't and that I would go back to my room where I had some antihistamine tablets and see how things went from there. I assured her that if the swelling or the pain got too much I would call for medical attention.

Who the hell knew that dead wasps could still sting, I thought. I got up from the table clutching the ice and leaving a trail of dripping melt water on the red baize. I had to admit to a grudging respect for the indefatigable genetic programming for the infliction of pain on their enemies that the wasp had so amply demonstrated.

I picked up my phone and slipped it into my jacket pocket and then proceeded to leave the casino, shoulders hunched, avoiding as much eye contact as possible and ignoring the varied attempts to engage me in conversation. Thankfully there were only a few punters who had witnessed the scene. I felt their eyes boring into my back as I left.

Gambling is a fool's game, I thought. I remembered my father's words from many years before 'have you ever met a poor bookmaker, son?'

As I made my painful way back to my cabin it felt like I was making my way home after a bad night in Glasgow. Bleary eyed revellers slurred past me uttering incomprehensible greetings in the universal language of the drunk.

That's the problem with these drink packages, I thought, as I tried to make my way around a large, swaying, bleary eyed lump that was blocking my way to the elevator.

'Shorry,' he said, 'so shorry,'

A well-dressed woman in an evening gown got hold of his arm.

'He thinks the cost of the drinks package is an outrage and has calculated how many drinks he has to have to break even.'

'You've got to make shure you get whatsh you pays for,' he said.

'He's good at math,' said the lady, 'made his fortune in accountancy.'

'I got me a head shtart. I'm ahead of the game,' he said.

I wasn't sure that I was. I decided to take the stairs.

'Did you have a good evening Dr Anderson?' asked Jacob as I was clumsily slotting my keycard into the door. Everything becomes more difficult with only one hand.

'I'm not sure,' I said, 'I might have done.'

Once inside I dosed myself up with painkillers and antihistamine and dowsed my hand in cold water. Then, just for my own satisfaction, I Googled "Do dead wasps sting?" and got the following result.

"Only female wasps can sting. Males do not have the egg-laying ovipositor that is modified into a stinger on female insects. Unlike bees, female wasps have the ability to sting a target multiple times. Stinging is a reflex reaction to a perceived threat and a wasp has the ability to sting for at least twelve hours after it is dead."

Now here was a bit of research that I wished I'd done earlier!

Chapter 27

I asked Jacob to bring me some more ice, wrapped it in a face cloth and put it over my throbbing palm.

Even though it was after midnight it was only early afternoon in London so I decided I'd better update "The Store" on progress.

During the evening's game I had made a number of short video and audio recordings on my watch. I transferred these, virtually one-handedly, to my phone and added a short commentary to stitch them together. Then I sent them in using my call sign "Agaricus" and pass-code as identification.

I gave it 15 minutes and then moved through the password protected firewalls on my phone to the encrypted private directory. For additional security there were no names on the contact list only descriptors.

Teresa was "Friend 3" and my finger hovered over "Delete" before scrolling down to "S" and pressing "Call".

'You have been busy,' said Samantha.

'Thanks,' I said.

'It wasn't a compliment. If I understand it right you've managed to get close to Krai - that's good - you've established a common interest in poker - that's good - you've scared the shit out of him by playing on one of his known phobias - that's not so good — you've taken the risk of putting a wasp within arm's reach of someone with a severe allergy, someone who could have gone into anaphylactic shock if he'd been stung ...'

She had a way of putting things that took the gloss off my efforts.

'... and instead of ingratiating yourself you've beaten somebody at cards who hates to be beaten at anything - that's just terrific – and, and this is the kicker, you've no idea whether he'll let you anywhere near him again - just incredible!'

'Well, when you put it like that,' I said, feeling the ice cold water trickle from my swollen hand and drip disconsolately onto the floor, 'but it is only the second day of the cruise, and I only won by mistake.'

'So being fast and incompetent makes it better does it?'

Harsh, she has always been harsh. I liked to think it was because she secretly fancied me. I stayed silent.

She sighed, 'I'll update AB but he's unlikely to be over the moon. Keep going "Agaricus" and let's hope for better news soon.'

Click.

She hadn't even asked if my hand was hurting.

I was too full of adrenalin and pain to go to sleep so I decided to cheer myself up by calling my daughter. It was early evening in New York so I hoped she'd be available. Besides I needed a woman's perspective on the "Carmen incident" with Teresa. It would be a welcome distraction.

Thankfully my daughter answered first time and after the normal pleasantries, that excluded any mention of wasps, stings or pain, I told her what had happened in Sydney as objectively as I could. I was sure she would see it from my point of view and agree that Teresa's reaction had been totally unreasonable.

'You're an idiot,' is what she actually said, 'So you effectively told her she was your whore!'

'That's not what …'

She laughed. It sounded like ridicule.

'I was trying to be …'

'Stupid, sarcastic … transactional?'

'No, romantic.'

I was finding it difficult to talk to my daughter about this but as she was one of the few people whose judgment I thought I could trust I needed to stick with it. Since my wife, her mother, had died of cancer I knew that I'd come to emotionally lean on her. It was probably a poor thing for a parent to do; a stronger man would probably have been an emotional support for her. I hoped her partner, who I hardly knew, was there for her.

Although I felt acutely awkward discussing my relationship with another woman with my daughter, the first real thing to happen to me since my wife's death over 18 months ago, I struggled on. She would have been well within her rights to be angry, furious even, that I would even look at another woman.

'Dad.'

'Er, Yes'

'This is the woman you've told me about before, right?'

Did she think I was multiple-dating? I didn't have the emotional or physical energy for that.

'Yes, of course.'

'The one that you care about?'

'Well .... er ... when you say care about ...'

'You are an idiot.'

I felt that we'd already established this fact and that repetition, although possibly warranted, was somewhat unnecessary at this stage.

'Beg,' she said.

'Beg?'

'Yes, beg.'

'But she left me. She went off without a word.'

'You didn't stop her.'

'She hasn't been in touch since.'

'You haven't spoken to her since.'

I was losing the thread.

'I've tried … she hasn't …'

'Beg.'

I got the message.

'Thanks,' I said, unconvinced and no less confused.

'And Dad,'

'Yes?'

'I love you.'

She still knew how to take my breath away, just like her mother.

'I love you too,' I said.

We ended the call and I put the phone to one side.

Life is like that isn't it, one step forward and two steps back. Even if you're an optimist it's still two forward and one back.

I knew I'd have to sort this out. Maybe I'd try and give Teresa another call.

A sharp knock at the cabin door interrupted my musings. I got up and walked across the room, reached out and turned the handle.

No sooner had the latch been disengaged than the door was thrust open, forcing me backwards, knocking me off-balance. I just had time to think what a great day I was having before I was struck forcibly on the head with something hard and darkness overtook me, tipping me into an uncomfortable dream-world of swirling streams of unconsciousness and bitter waves of nausea.

Chapter 28

My next memory was of a voice whispering into the darkness and lifting me back into a painful light.

'Dr Anderson, Dr Anderson, you okay? Dr Anderson, Dr …'

Opening my eyes a crack I groaned a response, attempting to stop the repetitious chant that sounded to me as loud as a fog horn. I was lying on my back on the bed, Jacob was stooping over me, inches from my face, and doing the anxious whispering.

As I came round I was conscious of two things; the dazzling light and a pounding pain that moved in waves from the back of my head exiting through my eyeballs.

I'd obviously been out for some time as unwelcome sunlight was streaming through the balcony windows. I found the brightness overwhelming and as I looked up at the ceiling for relief it screamed back at me in piercing unapologetic white.

I closed my eyes in self defense and raised my hand to the left side of my forehead, where there seemed to be a focus for the pain. It felt wet and sticky.

'It's okay Jacob,' I lied, 'I must have fallen over.'

As I started to raise myself into a sitting position I re-opened my eyes and felt Jacob's strong hands under my arms, helping me to sit up.

Fighting the nausea I looked around my cabin. It had been trashed.

'I guess I must have knocked into a few things,' I said. I could see from his expression that Jacob didn't believe this any more than I did.

'Give me a couple of minutes,' I said, 'maybe you could bring me some iced water.'

'Yes, of course, I go now.'

Whilst Jacob was away I tried to get my act together. I had been attacked. Knocked unconscious and my room roughly searched. I wondered what had been taken but that would have to wait.

Focusing my eyes on the face of my watch, which I was delighted was still on my wrist, I could see that it was past 7 a.m. I'd been thinking of taking a tablet to get me off to sleep. The smack on the head had clearly worked as an alternative although I couldn't say that I'd had a comfortable night.

Jacob returned and I sipped the cool water splashing some of it onto my face. He tended to me carefully and with apparent concern although whether this was genuine, or more in consideration of what his superiors might think about one of his charges getting into this kind of state, it was difficult to tell.

He helped me up and I leaned on him as I made my way to the bathroom. I left him outside as I took some time to take a shower, watching the dried blood colour the water as it swirled towards the drain.

After the shower I felt a little better. I took a couple of Paracetamol, put some antiseptic on the cuts and another layer of antihistamine cream onto my hand.

I took a look in the mirror to survey the damage. My hand was swollen, I had a gash on the head, a black eye and bruising to my right side. It could have been worse, I thought.

After a painful shave and a spearmint hit of toothpaste I felt less like an incurable invalid and exited the bathroom wearing only a large towel wrapped around my waist. Jacob was still there, waiting for me.

'Don't worry,' I said, 'if you can just find me a plaster for my head I don't think we'll need to report this any further, do you?'

His face brightened appreciably, I'd diagnosed his personal concerns correctly. At least I'd got something right. Besides it wouldn't do me any good to draw any more attention to myself than was necessary.

'That good if you okay,' he said, 'Then I make up room. You see, it be good as new. I do it. You see.'

'That's fine,' I said, 'just let me check around first.'

'No problem, you tell when ready, I go get plaster.'

After he'd gone I pulled on a clean shirt and slacks and checked out the room.

The drawers had simply been pulled out and tipped onto the floor; my suitcases had been tugged out from the wardrobe, opened, roughly examined and returned. It was a peculiar mix of care and chaos.

My laptop had been opened but was still there, my tablet lay on the bedside table. There was only one notable absence.

My phone had gone.

Either by luck or good judgment somebody had found my Achilles heel.

Shit.

Jacob came back with a box of sticking plasters and I allowed him to bandage the cut on my head as best as he could. I then tried to comb my hair to hide the damage. The black eye was red, swollen and darkening. I was beginning to think that keeping this attack quiet was going to be more difficult than I'd thought.

I clambered over the scattered clothing, pulled on a navy blue jacket and gave Jacob permission to start his clean up. I wished him luck. I'd leave him to concoct some plausible story to account for the blood on the sheets and towelling when he took them down to his friends in the laundry.

Chapter 29

After an uncomfortable, sore headed, breakfast I found a bar that was already serving and ordered a double whisky with ice, no water, trying hard to avoid the searching gaze of the bartender. Whisky for breakfast would not do my reputation any good but I thought it might at least lessen the pain of losing of my phone.

I sat at a table as far away from the bar counter as I could get, trying to avoid attention, nursing a bad head and a single malt, feeling sorry for myself.

I was in real trouble and I knew it. I had breached the most basic of professional protocols and put my daughter, Teresa and others at risk.

If my phone had been hacked, a simple task for anybody who was tech savvy, then my cover was blown.

The dark and darker things that would inevitably follow such a breach spiraled around in my head; a failed assignment, a recall, the inability to ever find out what the hell Krai was up to, if he was up to anything. But worse, much worse, was the thought of a stranger knocking on my daughter's door or ... I thought of Teresa, oh my dear god, what had I done!

I hadn't called the news into "The Store" yet. Without my phone I'd revert to using the tablet or watch but I knew the best thing to do now, the only thing to do, was to get off the ship as soon as possible and go back to face the consequences.

When we reached the first port of call, the Isle of Pines, part of the New Caledonian island group, I'd leave the ship. I didn't know if there was an airport but frankly I didn't care. Once off the ship I'd find my way home somehow or other. If it took a few extra days then that was just a temporary stay of execution. More time for my stupidity to sink in.

I finished the malt and ordered another one.

There was only one possible glimmer of hope, one thing that I kept going back to, one question, one possible saving grace; had I reactivated the firewalls before I'd answered the door?

When I'd finished the call to my daughter, when I'd heard the knock at the door, had I just let the phone drop, encrypted address book open, or had I automatically closed it down?

I couldn't remember, I just couldn't fucking remember, and now it was like sitting on a time bomb, waiting for somebody to set it off.

Looking into my half empty glass, the amber liquid glinting back the light, I knew what I had to do. I had to call this in, I had to own up to my not knowing how bad a breach this was, and take the hit. There were a lot of people who'd love to watch me fall. They'd have a field day. Fuck them!

A strong hand gripped my shoulder. A heavy presence settled in alongside me.

'Ah, just the man,' he said, 'let me introduce myself, I feel like we know each other already Dr Anderson, you can call me Marte. You may have noticed me, I was alongside Dr Krai at the game last night.'

He smiled and held out his hand, greeting me like a long lost brother.

'How lucky to bump into you like this. It looks like you have had an accident. I would very much like to talk to you. What are you drinking?'

I told him.

'Oh, it is too early even for me,' he said and signaled the barman to bring me a refill and a fresh lemon juice for himself.

He was dressed casually in cream slacks, black blazer and open-necked pale blue shirt.

'It was quite an exciting evening we had wasn't it?'

Was it only last evening? It felt like a lifetime ago.

'Yes,' I said, 'but if you don't mind I think I've had enough to drink …'

I started to get up from my seat. He placed a strong hand on my shoulder.

'No, no Dr Anderson, please sit down.'

I couldn't be bothered to argue, I may as well hear what he had to say. It would very probably form an early part of my punishment.

'Ah, that's better,' he said.

The barman brought the drinks and a plate of pistachio nuts. Marte immediately started de-shelling and popping the green nuts into his mouth. He appeared very relaxed.

My head was pounding, I was looking forward to popping some more painkillers.

He took a sip of his lemon juice, a concerned look on his face.

'I'm sorry to see that you are so under the weather,' he said, and tapped his temple indicating he had noticed my plaster.

'I fell,' I said, 'it doesn't really matter. I'll be disembarking tomorrow and then I'll get it checked out in port before I fly home.'

I hadn't really intended to say this out loud, the words just came tumbling out before I had a chance to stop them. But what did it matter, he may as well know.

'How unfortunate, and we were only just beginning to get to know you.'

He leaned forward, dropping his voice.

'Dr Krai would much rather that you stay on board.'

It was clear that this was not a request.

'And anyway I was looking to letting you know that your winnings,' he hesitated, 'your rather substantial winnings, have now been transferred into your onboard account. Congratulations Dr Anderson, you're a richer man than you were yesterday.'

I nodded. I didn't have the strength to ask him 'What winnings?' The game had been abandoned.

He shrugged.

'Dr Anderson, Dr Anderson, what can we do to convince you to stay?'

'Nothing,' was my immediate thought, 'absolutely nothing.'

He reached into an inside pocket of his jacket.

'Maybe,' he said, 'maybe this would help.'

Not more money, I thought, there isn't enough...

I stopped mid thought. In fact I stopped thinking altogether.

'You must have dropped it,' he said, pushing my phone across the table towards me, 'very careless of you Dr Anderson, you're lucky that one of our men found it and recognised your rather unique cover.'

I turned it over and stared at the ace of spades, the white joker face smiling back at me from the black centre.

'I hope you'll find that it is not broken.'

I flicked the phone on. The screen lit. I opened the functionality through fingerprint recognition and saw immediately that the firewalls to the encrypted content were active!

I tried not to show any relief, although I could hear my heart drumming in my ears. I closed it down again.

'Thank you, it seems to be in one piece.'

Marte reached over.

'May I,' he said and took the phone back again.

'Excellent, Dr Anderson. Dr Krai would very much like to see you himself,' he slipped the phone back into his inside pocket, 'I'll look after this for you in the meantime, we don't want you losing it again do we?'

He got up to go, taking a handful of pistachio nuts with him, 'Dr Krai will see you in an hour. I will come and meet you at you cabin door in 45 minutes. Enjoy your drink and, please, if possible, clean yourself up a little in the meantime.'

Chapter 30

True to his word Marte arrived at my cabin door and escorted me up to Deck 14. Krai had his own personal elevator and an area of bow section of Deck 14, containing 6 separate Suites, had been cordoned off for his use. I was lead towards what I imagined was the largest.

I waited outside in the corridor for a few moments before being invited into Dr Krai's presence. I felt like a fly being invited in by the spider.

The suite was split into two levels the lower being the living area which gave onto a large balcony with Jacuzzi hot tub, a seating or sunbathing area and panoramic views. The upper floor, that was part mezzanine, was presumably the sleeping quarters.

Krai was sitting in an electric wheelchair. Without his exoskeleton he looked exposed, like a knight without his armour or a snail without his shell.

The room with its high ceiling dwarfed him. The large glass doors leading to the balcony shone with the reflected blue light of the sea.

The young woman who I had seen in the theatre and again tending to Krai in the casino was leaning in close and unwrapping a blood pressure measuring sleeve from Krai's upper arm. She made a note on an iPad mini and then stepped away, taking a seat over by the wall so as to be within hailing distance but not intrusive. Krai's body looked fragile although his eyes were bright and piercing.

'Good morning, David,' he said as if he knew me, his voice barely audible, 'please come and sit alongside me. It is alright if I call you David I hope?'

You can call me anything you like, I thought.

'Of course,' I said.

He waved a finger towards a green leather armchair. I sat.

The young woman looked on, remaining attentive to Krai's medical condition. Hearing the timbre of his voice she got up and pressed a small white tablet into his hand. He took it obediently and swallowed it with a sip of water. She took the glass away to wash and refill in the kitchen area. He leant back with a sigh and closed his eyes. The interaction took me by surprise, it was almost affectionate.

After an uncomfortable pause he spoke, his eyes remaining closed.

'I appreciate loyalty,' he said, his voice stronger, 'and on rare occasions initiative, but I do not appreciate any of my employees being stupid.'

He coughed but waved away the offer of further help.

'I think I can, with confidence, assure you David that your privacy will, from now on, be honoured.'

I had a pretty good idea who had assaulted me. There was only one person I could think of who had what I could call "just cause". It appeared Krai was willing to take some of the responsibility, although he had not sanctioned the attack. That was a relief.

Krai leant forward and opened his eyes. The extent to which he felt he needed to approach an apology was over. That job was done. Time to move on.

'Please allow my personal physician to take a look at your injuries, David. It will be her pleasure to do so.'

At a glance from Krai the young doctor got up from her seat and motioned me to follow her. We walked out of Krai's suite, down the corridor and into one of the adjacent rooms. I followed obediently behind her petite, slim figure.

At 5' 3" tall or thereabouts and wearing a white Lab coat she walked with an authoritative step. I knew already that she was attentive and content to live in Krai's shadow.

Once inside I could see that we were in a smaller single level suite, which, although it had its own outside balcony, had been modified into a medical surgery or examination room. Krai must have been planning his trip well in advance to get this done.

All the normal accoutrements were present; a fully-adjustable hospital bed, an examination chair, surrounded by an array of machinery. The numerous shelves and cupboards that lined the walls were full of a mysterious range of tablets, ointments, bandages and the like. The floor had been tiled, presumably for hygiene reasons, and what could be seen of the walls and ceiling had beeen painted a surgical white. A faint smell of disinfectant pervaded the whole.

'Please sit here Dr Anderson,' she said, pointing to the padded examination chair. I moved in automatic obedience and she paused to snap on skintight surgical gloves.

'What's your name?' I asked.

To be honest although I'd seen her at the theatre and busying herself quietly around Krai, I hadn't really given her much thought before this moment.

She was one of those invisible people who just get on with their job but remain largely unnoticed.

She looked surprised and hesitated a moment before replying.

'My name is Dr Shavi.'

'Well hello Dr Shavi,' I said extending my hand and smiling, 'you can call me David.'

We shook hands. Although her hand was small and cold through the latex glove her grip was strong.

'I would prefer to call you Dr Anderson. Now tilt your head back.'

I did as I was told.

As she leaned over to examine my head wound I got an opportunity for my own further examination. She was certainly not unattractive. Her features where Asiatic, her hair was black and cut short, her eyes were large and brown. Under the faint smell of antiseptic I detected an even fainter smell of perfume, the distinctive sensory notes of Chanel No.5, a complex perfume for a complex character.

'Now I'm going to remove this plaster. It may hurt a little.'

She removed it in a single stoke. It hurt a lot. I winced.

'Ow,' I said.

'I'm sorry Dr Anderson, but this dressing has been most inexpertly applied and I must get a better view of your injuries if I'm going to help you. I will look at all your injuries, test you for signs of concussion and assess your general state of health.'

And I thought this was going to be quick.

She asked me several questions about my headache, shone a torch into my eyes and proceeded to push, prod, measure and medicate, her delicate fingers expertly busy, her brown eyes, focused and serious. Her hands were delicate but quick and firm and after washing my head wound she examined my bruised eye and the rest of my face.

'Now let me see your hand.'

I held out my swollen hand. I could see the sight of the wasp sting, a small black dot as if made by some malicious pinprick.

'Hmm,' she said and retreated to her cupboards and drawers returning with two sets of tablets and a glass of water.

'Take these, they will reduce the swelling and ease the pain.'

Next she applied an antiseptic spray to the cut on my head.

'I would rather not re-bandage it,' she said. 'If we keep it dry I think it will heal faster. It's not big enough to require stitches. You were quite lucky.'

I didn't feel lucky.

'Now, please take off your jacket, shirt and trousers Dr Anderson.'

Under different circumstances this could have been a welcome invitation but in the austere confines of the medical room it was anything but. Still, I did what I was told. I was thankful I'd put on fresh boxer shorts.

'I think I've seen you before,' I said.

'You mean in the casino?'

'No, I mean at the early theatre show, the hypnotist, I think you left before the end.'

Dr Shavi's lip curled in derision, 'Hypnotism is a serious thing Dr Anderson, not some circus side show where grown people cluck like chickens for other's amusement.'

I had obviously hit a bit of a nerve.

'Have you got a first name?' I asked wincing as she dug her fingers into my bruised side.

'Yana,' she said, 'but most people call me simply Doctor or Doctor Shavi.'

'May I call you Yana?'

There was a short silence.

'Please raise your arms. Thank you … you're British aren't you? I thought the British liked their formalities.' For the first time I saw a spark of playfulness through the more rigid professional façade.

'Not all of us,' I said, 'when you work in academia you're surrounded by Doctors and Professors so we revert to names. I would rather call you Yana than Shavi if that was OK with you.'

'What branch of science do you study?'

I was amused at the assumption that I studied a Science, presumably Humanities and the Arts came a poor second in her estimation.

'Well I suppose you could call it a science,' I said, 'I study Ancient History and we do use the latest techniques to analyse archaeological evidence and source manuscripts.'

She seemed less than impressed.

'You can put your clothes back on now,' she said, 'Excuse me.'

Leaving me to wrestle with my clothes she made a short call on an internal phone and then returned.

'There appears to be no serious damage Dr Anderson and there are no signs of a serious concussion. You got a hard blow to the head and what looks like a punch to the face and a number of kicks to the ribs.'

She said it matter-of-factly, as if this kind of injury, or worse, were all part of her daily grind.

The blow to the head was certainly right. I couldn't remember being punched in the face, or kicked in the ribs. I must have already been unconscious when that happened. Charming.

'Unfortunately it will take a few days for the bruising to go down, the discolouration to recede and the abrasions to heal. I could apply make-up to disguise the discolouration but the swelling would still show.'

'Thank you for your efforts, Yana,' I said.

She seemed surprised, although whether it was at my use of her first name or the simple act of thanking her, I couldn't tell. At least she didn't complain at my use of her name so I took that as permission granted.

'Time to go,' she said and I again followed behind as she led me back to Krai's suite.

Chapter 31

'I hope you are feeling better,' said Krai glancing at Dr. Yana Shavi. She nodded.

'It appears that there are no serious injuries. Let us be thankful for that.'

'Thank you for the expert attention,' I said looking across at Yana. Her head was down, she seemed to be blushing.

'I understand that you're going ashore today,' said Krai.

'Yes as soon as we're at anchor.'

'I wouldn't like anything else to happen to you Dr Anderson and I'd like you to know how much I appreciated your intervention last evening. I don't get on well with wasp stings and it seemed unfair to me that not only did you come off the worse for your act of chivalry,' he glanced down at my hand, 'but you also sacrificed a winning hand, although I'm pleased to say that I have at least been able to compensate you for that.'

He had indeed. I would find out later that my onboard account had been swollen with the injection of a generous $250,000. A much greater sum than any winnings I may have forgone.

'I'm also glad that you haven't created a fuss over this unfortunate incident. It would have been inconvenient to have people running around asking too many stupid questions,' he paused, 'As soon as I found out what had happened I let my displeasure be known. It was such a silly thing to do, such an over-reaction. I hope it is at least of some relief to you that we recovered your mobile phone, such an essential tool these days. And that now you know it's safe.'

What did he mean? Was my phone safe because he had it and I didn't? Was it safe because the invisible firewalls were in place? Was he hinting at more than he was saying? It is often the things that people don't say that disturb me the most.

'And under these circumstances it only seems proper that we look after you for a while. I understand we'll be anchoring in an hour or so off the Isle of Pines. I won't be going ashore myself and I think your leaving us at this early point in the cruise would be such a shame, don't you agree?'

'After what happened ...'

'Exactly Dr Anderson, after what has happened you don't want to be wandering around the ship attracting attention. There is so much social media traffic these days, we don't want your looks to become an internet sensation.'

'I think I'd rather leave,' I said, 'I'll find a way to get home.'

'Dr Anderson, Dr Anderson you don't understand. I don't want you to go. On the contrary I want you to stay, I want you to spend your money. I want you to enjoy the rest of the cruise.'

'I don't ...'

'A suite along this corridor has become available. Dr Shavi here can look after you better than any hospital within 1,000 kilometers and we will escort you ashore and around the ship to protect you from any unwanted attention.'

His smile was thin, somewhere between a benevolent uncle and a man-eating shark.

'I will be going ashore.' I said, wanting at least to show some semblance of backbone.

Krai shrugged, 'Of course Dr Anderson, I understand there are some fine beaches.'

He touched a button on his wheelchair. Marte entered the room.

'Whilst you were being examined we have taken the liberty of moving your belongings to your new suite. I'm sure you'll find it a significant upgrade.'

Marte moved towards me. I got up to go.

'Oh, just one more thing,' said Krai, 'It would be a shame after all this if, let me say, there were unfortunate communications made to the outside world. You know how difficult it is Dr Anderson not to inadvertently share news with your nearest and dearest. Connectivity is not so dependable out here in the ocean and I'm sure people would understand if you were incommunicado for a few days. Just until the swelling goes down, until the bruising has disappeared.'

'But...'

'It's for your own good Dr Anderson, believe me I know how pernicious media attention can be. Best keep this to ourselves. I will keep your laptop, tablet, phone safe for you in the meantime.'

He turned to Marte.

'I've asked Marte here to join you on your excursion ashore,' he said, 'he'll make sure all goes well ... and that you get back onboard safely. We can talk about your adventures over dinner tonight.'

'But...'

'Don't thank me Dr Anderson.'

'I wasn't ...'

Krai leant back and closed his eyes. I felt a familiar hand on my shoulder.

The interview was over.

I'd been effectively kidnapped. Krai obviously felt that my looks and my story could be potentially damaging to him, an unwelcome distraction.

But a distraction from what?

Chapter 32

Marte walked me to the door of my new abode. Before he let me in he stepped up close, invading my personal space,

'I've just got to get you settled in properly,' he said, 'if you could just take off your jacket.'

I did so. He searched it thoroughly before laying it down on the floor.

'Now if you could just raise your arms and stand astride.'

Again I followed his instructions and he frisked me from head to toe. When he stood back he was smiling and holding my watch in his hand unhooked and expertly unfastened, I hadn't felt it leave my wrist.

'Excellent Dr Anderson, all done.'

'And my watch?'

'It's a very nice watch.'

'I like it.'

Marte examined the Rolex before swirling it around on his finger. He was obviously thinking.

Did he know something or was it instinct that was making him suspicious?

'I have to be able to see what time it is,' I said.

He was watching me closely and I tried to play it cool but in my mind's eye I saw the watch flying into the air, the polished metal strap glinting silver in the sun before falling away towards the sea, passing from air to ocean and leaving no trace, sinking slowly into the depths, imploding as the pressure of depth exceeded the integrity limit of the housing. It was an unwelcome vision.

Marte laughed, threw the watch up into the air, caught it and handed it back to me.

Thank God. I tried not to look too relieved as I snapped it back into place.

'Thanks,' I said.

'These modern watches,' he said, 'so many functions, so many buttons.'

'It was a birthday present,' I lied.

'Very nice, you must have some wealthy friends.'

Shit, I should just have kept my mouth shut...

'Truth is it was also part payment on a gambling debt.'

'Be careful Dr Anderson,' said Marte, 'when you gamble you don't always win.'

He leaned past me and opened the door.

'Welcome to your new home. I'll see you in an hour,' he said.

The room was indeed a sizeable upgrade. It had a much larger balcony that looked out over the port side of the ship and the inside had more comfortable seating, a larger bed and all-around better facilities than my original room.

My bags had been relocated and more than that they had been unpacked and my belongings neatly stowed in the wardrobe, drawers and cupboards. It had all been done very efficiently. All that was missing was my laptop, tablet and phone, the things that really mattered.

But I still had my watch. All of a sudden it had become my closest friend, for the first time it approached superiority over its more authentic counterpart that I'd been forced to leave behind.

I took a shower, being gentle on my swellings and bruising, and then put on a change of clothes more suited to going ashore as a tourist; linen shirt, shorts and trainers.

Feeling cleaner I went out onto the balcony, leaving the glass door open, and sat staring into the blue, my back to the room. I thought of everything that had happened to me in the last few hours and gazed out at an ocean that was completely oblivious and uncaring of my fate. It was simply carrying on with its elemental dance between moon and weather.

Although I still had the watch I was concerned that it might be seen as an oversight so decided I'd better make the most of it. The communications functions operated via satellite and I pressed the right combination of bezels and pass keys to activate them.

First I sent a message to "The Store",

'Got closer to Krai. Communication might be difficult for next few days.'

I'd certainly got closer and the message had the benefit of vagueness. I'd have been interested to be a fly on the wall when Samantha was trying to interpret what I meant by that. I also omitted to mention the episode with the phone. No need to overcomplicate things.

Then to my daughter I sent, 'Entering satellite blackout area, you'll probably not be able to contact me for the next few days so best not to try. I'll let you know when we're back online.'

Not the absolute truth but I didn't want her to worry. There are times when small variations around the theme of truth seem justified.

Lastly I decided to message Teresa. I found this the most difficult and was still thinking about it when I heard a noise behind me. In haste I settled on one word 'Sorry' and pressed send.

Turning my head I saw Marte strolling through the room, unannounced and unwelcome.

I instinctively stood up and went back inside to meet him.

'You like the room?' he asked.

'Very nice,' I said.

'As you can see we moved all your stuff over and unpacked it for you as carefully as possible. I hope you don't mind.'

I could hear from his tone that 'unpacking' was another way of telling me that they'd been through everything.

'No problem,' I lied, 'I just don't seem to be able to locate my laptop.'

It was worth a try.

'Yea, sorry about that, Dr Krai is keen that you are comfortable, but like he said we don't want you to be sending out any messages you might regret later. You'll get it back safely when Dr Krai says so.'

'And when do you think that might be?'

Marte shrugged his shoulders.

'Not up to me Professor. Best you just enjoy the hospitality.'

'OK,' I said, 'has the ship anchored?'

'It has,' said Marte, 'you must have missed the announcements.'

I hadn't being paying much attention to anything.

'In that case let's go ashore.'

'No problem Dr Anderson, after you.'

Chapter 33

Before disembarking Marte wanted to pick up some cash and after seeing how I was dressed he also took a time-out to change into shorts and a T-shirt. I accompanied him to his suite, number 1402, next door to Krai.

Standing on his balcony while he got changed I could hear the sound of an incoming helicopter. Marte's balcony overlooked the helipad and the rhythmic thunder of the helicopter's rotors increased as it came into land. Once settled the rotors slowed and the noise quietened.

As I watched I could see one of the helicopter's side doors slide open. From the deck of the ship two people mis-matched in height and colouration and looking remarkably like Atu and Gunnar approached. They were carrying a stretcher.

Just then Marte came out to join me.

'Is he OK?' I asked lamely.

'Brady?' said Marte.

So my guess was confirmed.

It wasn't a very difficult thing to work out. I was supposed to be Brady's saviour by letting him win $10,000. In return he had helped by getting some weaker players around the poker table. From his point of view it was easy money. He helped me make it to the play off with Krai and expected Krai to beat me easily. With the $10,000 he could get whoever was chasing him off his back and restore the sunshine to his world.

For most of the night it must have seemed like everything was going to plan. The other players fell obediently by the wayside, even if one of them needed a little help with over-lubrication. Anyone who knew about cards could see that Krai was a better player than I was. The money was more or less in his pocket, he'd even have time to gloat.

And then that last hand, the inconvenience of the wasp, but the still overriding confidence that Krai had won. A full house of Aces and Kings was far too strong a hand to be beaten.

So desperate was he to confirm his win that he had stepped forward and flipped my cards over for all to see.

It must have been a nasty shock. I wonder how long it took him to process the information. Four 2's, four humble 2's taking down the might of the Aces and Kings. He'd done his best, he'd shouted out that the game was voided, but he knew the truth. He knew that at best he hadn't won the money and at worst he was a further $10,000 in debt, this time to an academic!

But more important was the risk that I would go shooting my mouth off about it and that if I did Dr Krai would get to know …

He must have been seething when he got to my cabin door, he must have been thinking about what to do. Did he intend to threaten me, cajole, or offer a double or nothing bet?

When he saw the door handle start to turn he must have just snapped. Fear and aggression getting the better of him. He probably didn't mean to hit me that hard or with such accuracy. He was probably both shocked and annoyed that I'd collapsed unconscious before he'd had a chance to say anything. It was all my fault and he had hit and kicked my helpless body out of frustration.

Goodness knows how long he stayed in my room or what he thought he was looking for. The search obviously started systematically as could be seen by the careful handling of the cases, but then it got more erratic as his frustration grew.

I wonder if he saw my phone and put it in his pocket without thinking? When his anger had died down he must have realised the foolishness of stealing anything. His only hope was that I wouldn't be able to identify him as my assailant.

And then what? He gets drunk? Says too much, shows somebody my phone? Who knows how it happened but here he was lying on a stretcher showing no signs of movement. Clearly, for Brady, things hadn't gone well.

Standing beside Marte I repeated my question,

'Will he be OK?'

'Do you know what happens if someone dies on a cruise ship?' said Marte.

My silence was enough.

'They get put in the freezer, that's what happens. Each of these cruise ships is legally required to have morgue facilities.'

I was so pleased.

'So Dr Anderson, does he look frozen to you?'

I looked at the horizontal figure. His head was uncovered. He didn't look well, but he didn't look rigid enough to be frozen either.

'Krai is getting soft,' said Marte, 'You can see how ill he looks, it must be effecting his judgment, there were times ... but then again he and Brady go back a long way. So you see Dr Anderson, Brady is not OK but he is lucky, very lucky.'

I thought about the half overheard phone call. I wasn't sure that Brady's luck was going to last. They were moving him from a floating frying pan into a debt-collector's fire.

'He'll be back home before we are,' said Marte, 'Let's go Dr Anderson, our tender awaits.'

Chapter 34

We'd anchored off the Isle of Pines, one of a group of French speaking islands known as New Caledonia. With a population of 3,000 it was frequently overrun by the transient visits of up to 14 major cruise ships per month. The Nereus was too large to approach the rather rudimentary harbour and passengers were ferried to and fro in the Ship's bright yellow tenders that could carry sixty or so sweating occupants at a time.

After I'd picked up a towel and a bottle of water I was about to join the queue for the next tender when Marte stopped me.

'No, no Dr Anderson, you're with me now, no need to be part of the crowd. Come this way.'

He led me to a smaller exit door that was open to the sea. I noticed that by going this way we'd somehow managed to bypass security. Bobbing in the water, waiting for us, was a much smaller bright orange craft. Marte climbed aboard and held out his hand.

'Jump in,' he said, 'this is one of the ship's Fast Rescue Boats or FRB's, we've got free use of it for the rest of the day. As it's powered by a 200 horsepower diesel marine engine I think I'll do the driving.'

Marte steered us expertly through the clear blue waters to one of the concrete landing points. I wondered how he'd managed to secure the use of the boat.

My mind had almost caught up with my recent experiences and I realized that, mainly through luck rather than judgment, I'd got closer to Krai and his entourage than I could have ever expected.

The fear of my cover being blown, my private address book falling into Krai's hands had receded. Although I didn't have my phone it seemed a small price to pay in comparison.

It was time to take advantage of the opportunity that fate had dealt me. If I could either charm or befriend Marte then maybe I could find out something useful about Krai.

Marte secured the boat and we walked on shore.

'So Dr Anderson what would you like to do?'

I tried to smile, my mind racing to try and think of something to say.

'When I was looking through the brochures for this cruise I was taken with the idea of seeing a turtle in the wild,' I said, 'I think that could be quite an experience.' I looked around at the long snaking queues, 'But I'm afraid I haven't booked anything so I don't think there's much chance.'

'Wait here,' said Marte, striding off, flip-flops flapping through the sand.

Where else was I going to go?

He returned within 10 minutes.

'This way,' he said.

We walked past the rows of waiting people. I tried to avoid eye contact.

'I've booked a boat for the two of us only, for right now.'

'Thanks,' I said, 'how did you ...'

'This way,' said Marte moving quickly, ignoring the question.

We followed a track that ran between rows of trees, the famously local species of pine, and emerged onto a white sandy beach.

A long, thin, green paint peeling boat had been expertly grounded on the shoreline. Its petrol powered engine was fastened precariously at the rear. The turquoise waters of the bay lapped gently against the sides.

I was immediately concerned about the sturdiness of this craft and hoped that this wasn't some machiavellian plot to take me somewhere remote and lose me over the side. The boat was manned by two lithe and bronze skinned islanders. One reached out his hand, his English had an American twang.

'Please sir, take my hand, step here, yes, that's right, and watch your footing.'

I felt like an old man being treated like a child but I followed his lead obediently, this rocking and unsteady boat was his territory not mine.

Marte declined assistance and climbed aboard, stumbling and nearly capsizing us. I looked away. This was not the time for me to act like a smart arse.

Our two hosts smiled, pushed the boat back from the beach and jumped in, water dripping from their shins. We headed out into the shallow clear waters. They were clearly used to handling all the different varieties of crazy tourists that came ashore from cruise ships and went about their chaperoning job with smiling confidence, chattering away to each other and seeming to enjoy life. And why not? The skies were blue, the sun was hot, the air was sweet. I decided that this was a good time to chance some small talk.

'How did you get the use of that boat?' I asked.

'The FRB you mean?'

'Absolutely.'

'Have you ever been in the military?'

I told him I had.

'Then you'll understand. I've spent a lot of my life in the navy, at one time I was more used to being at sea than I was to being on dry land. Being in the navy is like being part of a club, a brotherhood. You must know that, you learn together, live together, shit together … you help each other out,' Marte smiled, 'and even when you've left, that feeling of brotherhood doesn't goes away. So when I'm on a ship, any kind of ship, I revert to type, seek out the crew, share a few tales. Even if we speak different languages we can still understand each other. The combination of that sprinkled with Dr Krai's close relationship with the captain meant that when I suggested it as a way that we might avoid the crowds it was made available, and here we are.'

The reference to Krai's relationship to the captain was an interesting one. A thread to pick up on perhaps.

As I'd got him talking and we were still heading out to wherever we were going cutting a foaming trail through shallow waters, raising our voices above the sound of the engine, our hosts chatting together over the steering, I decided to try to learn more if I could.

'And how long have you known Dr Krai,' I asked conversationally.

'Long enough.'

Not a great start. Maybe this was a more sensitive topic for him, but I persisted.

'I know nothing about Dr Krai,' I lied, 'other than he pays his debts. Is he a good boss?'

'Good enough,' said Marte, he paused and then added, 'You ask a lot of questions Dr Anderson, take my advice … don't.'

His mouth smiled but his eyes didn't.

I decided not to press the point and turned my attention to the waters we were skimming across, the sandy bottom clearly visible, the encrusted rocks and greens of underwater vegetation. It was an idyllic spot and I began to simply enjoy the moment, soaking up a new experience, ignoring the pain from my various injuries. I thought I'd earned some respite.

We soon reached the island's big lagoon, slowed and began searching out the turtles. Hanging over the sides we peered into the water looking for signs.

Using their local knowledge our guides had taken us to a likely spot and now all of their attention was focussed on the shallow waters, scouring the corrugated sands of the seabed, punctuated with clumps of waving green. Although Marte and I joined the search we were at a slight disadvantage, they knew what they were looking for and we didn't.

We fell into a pattern of looking, moving to an adjacent area, looking again. I was beginning to think that this was going to be one of those unlucky days. Turtles after all are wild creatures, they don't have to obediently swim towards tourists, in fact if they'd learnt anything it was probably that tourists were best avoided.

There were a number of other boats out on the lagoon doing the same thing, evidence that wildlife is a business opportunity in the South Pacific, but the lagoon was so large that we were well dispersed.

After about an hour I was starting to despair but then there was excitement from one of our guides and feverish pointing,

'There! Look!'

I looked but at first I couldn't see what he was pointing at. Then one of the green clumps seemed to uproot itself and begin gliding effortlessly through the water pushing itself forward with languid strokes. A loggerhead turtle was calmly going about its business.

Our boat was being expertly maneuvered, circling to get closer, to get a better view. Then one of our guides leapt off the boat into the shallow water and, in one swift movement, caught hold of the turtle and stood holding it firmly, its head and shell partially out of the water. I hadn't expected that. I thought that at best we would watch a turtle swim past underwater, or if we were lucky maybe even more than one.

Being careful to avoid the crab-claw-breaking beak our guide was holding the turtle steady on the water's surface by its shell and his colleague touched me on the shoulder and gestured that we should jump in and join him.

Marte was already lowering himself into the waist deep water. I did the same and was pleasantly surprised at the warmth as I proceeded to stride in slow-motion over to where the turtle was being held. I could see it eyeing me as we approached.

'We are licensed to handle the turtles,' our guide explained, his voice clear and easy to understand, 'we have been trained and we keep records of what we do and what we see each day. It aids the conservation work. So you do not need to worry for the health of the turtle.'

This was obviously the answer to a question that he was regularly asked.

'We used to eat them and over the years their numbers dropped to very few but now we make more money looking after them and showing them off to people like you.'

Capitalist rules in motion, I thought. Maybe we were saviours, maybe if the cruise ships hadn't come along when they did these magnificent creatures would have been eaten out of existence. Maybe.

I looked at the turtle. I wanted it to know we were its friend.

'This one's a male. From its size I would guess it is 25 to 30 years old. As these turtles can live to be a 100 he's quite young and has, with luck, a lot of years still ahead of him. Come and take a closer look, just watch out for his mouth, it's like a beak, designed for snipping off greenery, but it's very strong, he could do you damage.'

The guide was handling him gently. We went closer and were allowed to touch the shell, slide our fingers over the slimy surface and feel the wet-leathery texture, the bumps and grooves. It was a privilege. I looked at Marte and he nodded. It seemed like he felt the same way. We were bonding over a turtle.

We repeated the slow-motion wade back to the boat, trying not to step on the numerous sea cucumbers that littered the sandy floor.

Once we'd clambered back on board the turtle was released and we watched it glide away until it was lost in the green.

Even though it had just happened it already seemed impossibly surreal. A dream that I'd had of sharing a moment with another living creature, an alien life form with whom I had little in common and no prior knowledge, supremely adapted to its environment. I had been allowed so close a contact, our worlds touching for a moment. It stirred deep thoughts. I wasn't sure the turtle had responded to the experience in the same way.

We sped away leaving him to recover from our meeting. He had probably forgotten us already.

Chapter 35

The small boat arrowed its way to a secluded beach, our white wake whispering a salty spray onto our faces before splashing back into clear water, smoothing away our passing.

Once we'd reached the beach our guides jumped out and hauled the boat onto the white sand and secured it.

'We can stay here for half an hour,' said one of them, 'the snorkelling is very good here and we have some equipment you can use.

I had just started to dry off from my last plunge but this seemed too good an opportunity to miss.

A sack was pulled from the bottom of the boat and two sets of masks, flippers and snorkels extracted.

'Please enjoy,' said out guide, 'there is just one thing, if you see a sea snake don't touch it, call me over, I know how to handle them. The problem is that they're poisonous.'

Marte and I reached out and took the masks, mouthpieces and flippers and put them on.

'This is special.' I said.

'Yes,' he said as he waddled past me towards the water and dived in.

Snorkelling among the fish, hearing only your own regular breathing as it rustles through the breathing tube is the closest I think I'll ever get to feeling like an astronaut. I'd done this many times in many different parts of the world but each time feels somehow new, like a first time.

I drifted, weightless, looking down, an observer of a another world.

Brightly coloured fish, striped or splashed with yellow, orange, and blue moved in and out of view, seemingly oblivious to my presence. Needlefish, impossibly designed, long and silvered, slid past.

It was magical and I lost track of time. Here was a non-menacing world. I started to relax. The salt water must having been doing me good because I couldn't feel any of my injuries complaining.

It was as I drifted into shallower waters that I changed my mind.

The seabed had altered from undulating sand and coppices of seaweeds to rocky crevices and sharp edges. As I watched a long body started to extract itself effortlessly from the blackness of one of the subterranean hidey-holes. Its black and white banded length identifying it unmistakably as a sea snake!

'Oh shit' I exclaimed uselessly into my snorkel sending out a chaos of bubbles.

The snake paused, part in, part out of the rock, and swayed in the lapping current. It seemed to be looking at me wondering what to do.

I am not a big fan of poisonous snakes in general and was very aware that this one could move much faster through the water than I could. I also knew that sudden movements were likely to irritate it and I didn't want to do that.

Slowly, very slowly I swept my arms forwards so that I began to move backwards in the water, my eyes not leaving the snake. It drew more of itself out from the rocks, further into the water.

I had completely forgotten my previous feelings of calmness and oneness with the sea.

It was out now and about 3 feet long with a yellow colouring to its head. Its round blue eyes were centred with black dot pupils that I was sure were looking into mine. Its long body was uniformly banded in black and silver-white.

In different circumstances, for example in an aquarium with a glass wall between us, I could have appreciated its beauty but not at this particular moment.

The snake swam towards me its body in undulating rhythm. This was very definitely its world and not mine. I felt like an overloaded super-tanker, clumsy, unwieldy and slow.

I held my breath.

The snake slid beneath me and I waited to feel the bite. As far as I could I did an impression of a large piece of driftwood, closing my eyes and concentrating on keeping still, breathing slowly and steadily.

I could no longer see the snake.

I waited. I did not feel a bite.

I waited and tried to work out from the length of the snake, the speed it was moving and the length of my body, how long it would take, how long I would have to wait, before I knew, one way or the other.

It was no good. My brain had entered suspended animation. I just had to wait.

When I felt sure I had waited long enough I started to move, very slowly, in the direction I hoped would be towards the shore. After a few moments I regained some courage, raised my head from the water and saw through my fogged facemask that I was actually not far out from the beach.

I swam slowly and then crawled, paddled and hauled myself out onto dry land. Marte and our guides were waiting for me.

'You must have been enjoying it,' said Marte, his body already dried in the sun, 'though I thought you were dead at one point, the way you were just hanging there floating face down. I was beginning to wonder how I was going to explain it to Dr Krai.'

He laughed.

I laughed.

My laugh was more hollow.

Note: *Sea Snakes (Scientific Name: **Hydrophiinae)** are found in warm coastal waters. Some are quite docile and bite only when provoked others are much more aggressive. The majority of sea snakes are highly venomous. However, even when bites to humans do occur, venom is rarely injected.*

This reassurance doesn't help when you're swimming next to one!

Chapter 36

On the way back we spotted five giant Manta Rays and paused to watch them glide through the water like delta wing airplanes. Black above they looped over to expose their white undersides as they passed beneath our boat with what looked like a smile on their faces. At a span of over 9 feet they were like something out of a sci-fi movie although it was they who were in their element and we who were the interlopers.

Once we got back to where we'd started we disembarked and Marte handed some notes to our lead guide. From the way that he steepled his hands, as if in prayer, and bowed I guessed that the payment was on the generous side. He pushed the notes into a half-torn pocket in his denim shorts, smiled and waved us farewell.

I'd just about dried off by now and suggested we find something to drink before returning to the Nereus.

Although the island was busy with tourists Marte found us a shaded table and we were soon lounging back sipping on cold beers straight from the bottle.

'That turtle,' I said, deciding I was obligated to be the one to start a conversation, 'do you think it was a good idea to disturb it? I don't know much about turtle expressions but it didn't look happy, although it didn't look massively distressed either. So what do you think? Was it a mistake for us to be responsible for disturbing a turtle that was going about its normal business in its own natural environment?'

'You've got to look at the alternatives,' said Marte, taking my question more seriously than I'd anticipated, 'They told us they were licensed and trained to handle the turtle with care. By giving them our dollars we're proving that looking after the turtles is of value, both ecologically and financially. It's sustainable. What's the alternative? They catch them and eat them as a source of protein and before long they've caught too many and they become another endangered species. No, I think we did a good thing,' he paused, 'or at least if it wasn't good it certainly wasn't bad.'

This was the first experience I'd had of Marte as something of a more caring human being, a glimpse of what might lurk inside the man that was closest to Krai. There was clearly more to him than my initial impression of the cardboard cut-out hard man.

'I'm going to hope you're right,' I said, 'the guys certainly seemed to be serious about what they were doing.'

I attracted the barman's attention and ordered another two beers.

'Do you want anything to eat?' I asked.

'What are you thinking?'

'Well I saw they were barbecuing lobster over there. It looks good.'

Marte was clearly a man of action and left me to go and investigate returning in less than 10 minutes with two grilled lobster tails lying atop some sticky rice, all wrapped in banana leaves.

'35 $ Aus each,' he said, 'tourist prices.'

'We're a captive audience,' I said, 'we overrun their island every other day, disrupt their lives, expect them to serve our needs, dance to our tune, and then we shove off and on to the next port. The least we should expect is that they screw every dollar they can out of us for the privilege.'

He nodded and we ate in silence.

The lobster was very tasty, another product of the bounteous sea. Turtles may be preserved but lobsters weren't. After we'd finished and disposed of the banana leaves we went back to the beer. In these warmer climes you have to keep up your liquid intake.

'So we have something in common,' I said.

Marte raised an eyebrow, 'Really?'

'Yes, I'm ex-army.'

Marte laughed.

'I'm not sure you could call it similar. As you know I'm ex-navy, both merchant and military, spent most of my life at sea.'

I wondered if that meant both in reality and metaphorically.

'I started at the age of 14 in the merchant navy. Travelled the world onboard cargo ships. Then I joined the military and saw the world for a second time, but a different world this time, not joined up by trade but by conflict, the only thing they had in common was that you reached them by travelling over the same waters.'

'Why did you leave?'

'Why did you leave the army?'

'I decided it was time. Wanted to try my hand at a more 'normal' life; wife, family, house, mortgage, debt all that kind of thing,' I said truthfully, 'besides I wanted to study, I've always been interested in

History,' I added less truthfully. You've always got to remember to reinforce your back-story.

'For me it was less of a choice,' said Marte, 'more of a necessity.'

I've always found it amazing how two ex-military men can fall so naturally into conversation, sharing the most private of thoughts with strangers just because they recognise in each other some kind of common understanding. The thing to watch in my game is not to drop your guard too much. If you do you could easily end up saying more than you should and that would be dangerous. As far as I knew Marte didn't have to worry about that.

'PTSD?' I asked.

Marte diverted his gaze.

'When I left I was rudderless. For the first time in my life there was no order, no one to tell me what to do. I went home and found that I didn't fit in anymore. The people I knew had moved on and I found their concerns menial, insignificant compared to what I'd seen and done and I probably didn't bother to hide it. I spiralled down pretty quickly, falling out of love with myself, falling out of love with life. Things got bleak.'

He refocused, turned his head back, his eyes steady.

'Then I met Dr Krai. It wasn't in very auspicious circumstances but he must have seen something in me and he took me under his wing. He helped me sober up. I owe him a lot Dr Anderson. Remember that, I owe him a lot.'

The fire in his eye was like a warning beacon, flashing dangerously. I got the message, 'You mess with Dr Krai and you mess with me too.'

But I still didn't want to miss this opportunity to learn more about Krai so, even though I'd been put off before, I tried again.

'As you know it looks like I'm going to be spending more time with Dr. Krai. If that's the case don't you think it's fair that I know a bit more about him?'

I could see his defenses go up.

'What do you want to know?'

'How long you've known him, what he's like as a boss, and what he's like as a person, what I should, and in particular, what I should not do. After all I don't want to upset him.'

Marte laughed, but it was dry and humourless.

'I've told you before Dr Anderson, you ask too many questions.'

'It comes with the territory, being an academic I mean.'

'Well I'll tell you this. I owe Dr Krai a lot. I've told you that when I left the navy I wasn't in great shape and the result was that I just rolled from one dirty job to another always heading downhill. Then when I met Dr Krai he said he was looking for help and it sounded like the kind of help I could offer. I knew nothing about him but I had nothing to lose. That was 10 years ago now.'

'So he's a good boss?'

'What does "good" mean? It's just a meaningless word. I would say he is clear. He's clear about what he wants and he's clear about what he'll give in return. He expects loyalty and I'm happy to give it. I can't ask for more than that.'

He wasn't enjoying the conversation any more. I had to be careful not to push it too far and ruin what little rapport we had started to build. There was just one more thing I felt I had to risk asking.

'The thing I can't quite understand,' I said, 'is why Dr Krai, in his current medical condition, would want to put himself on a cruise ship when there are so many other places, so many other things he could be doing. I mean, he's not going to be joining too many shore excursions is he and he's had to bring so many people and so much equipment along with him. What's the point?'

I'd tried to put the question as lightly as I could, using an almost jokey tone, but I'd clearly hit a nerve. Marte shuffled uncomfortably in his seat.

'I don't know,' he said, 'it's not something he's done before, in my experience.'

He lifted the bottle of cold beer to his lips and drank deeply.

I didn't want to press too hard and make him any more suspicious about me than he might already be. Almost unconsciously I looked down at my hand, the swelling was already less.

'Still hurt?'

'Not much,' I said.

Before we left I wanted him to name his colleagues. I'd learnt their names from Brady but as far as Marte was concerned I hadn't had that conversation. To avoid embarrassing blunders I needed to close the loop.

'Listen Marte, if I'm going to be around for a while at least tell me about the people I'm going to be rubbing shoulders with.'

Marte sat. He didn't say no. In fact he didn't say anything.

'What about your black skinned colleague, for example. I know he can run because he left me standing on the jogging track.'

Marte gave a dry laugh, 'His name is Atu and I wouldn't call him a colleague. He's originally from Kenya, a man with a sharp tongue and an even sharper manner. He may look gangly but he's tough. You don't want to get on the wrong side of him, you really don't.'

In my mind's eye I saw Atu's face, his cold impenetrable gaze. I thought of him as a guy I was unlikely to be able to befriend. I was better off with Marte.

'And the other?'

'His name is Gunnar, Gunnar Svenson. He is young, Scandinavian, ice cold, professional, emotionless.'

He paused.

'We really are an unsavoury bunch professor.'

I hadn't learnt anymore than I already knew but at least my acquisition of the knowledge was now above board. If Atu or Gunnar asked me where I heard their names I could now answer them truthfully that Marte had told me.

'I am wondering what I've got myself into.' I said, 'All I wanted was a restful cruise, seeing a different part of the world, and the occasional game of cards. Meeting Dr. Krai was the last thing on my mind.'

His look did not exude total belief. I pressed on.

'Well at least there's one person I might enjoy getting to know. It's quite a luxury to bring along your own medical surgery as well as a full-time doctor, even if Dr Shiva, as well as being quite cute …'

The reason I stopped mid sentence was because he had reacted so fast. His hand shot across the table and grabbed my wrist, squeezing it painfully. His face had turned a bright red, veins stood out at his temples and stretched in blue-back cords across his bald head.

'Never talk of Yana like that,' was all he said.

His reaction had taken me completely off-guard. I had had no idea that Marte had any particular feelings for her. It was just a silly quip, I back-tracked as speedily as I could.

'All I was going to say was that Dr Shiva is clearly a very good doctor. I know that by the way she examined me, and to have someone like that permanently by your side, with all the medical equipment and supplies she needs is no small thing. It takes care and planning. So Dr Krai's decision to come on this cruise cannot have been some kind of spontaneous act. He has had to plan it well ahead of time.'

I prised his fingers free from my wrist and moved my hand away.

He knew he'd overreacted.

'I do not like it when any professional woman is trivialized.'

Yea right, I thought.

'I understand and can only apologise,' I said, 'it won't happen again.'

After all I knew how sensitive talking about or to a woman could be.

We descended back into small talk, finished our beers and went to ride the FRB back to the ship.

Chapter 37

Back in my suite I tried to process the time I'd just spent on shore.

Here was a very different world to the one I normally inhabited, a world that still seemed to be in touch with itself. A world where people were a part, an integral part, of the total ecosystem, interdependent with others species of animal, reptile, insect and attuned to the environment that they all depended upon.

It was all in stark contrast to my world of concreted separation from nature, from an ingrained belief in the overwhelming superiority of *homo sapiens,* from the unquestioned premise that we are above and somehow beyond all the other components of the natural world. Industrially separated from the sources of our sustenance were bacon is something that appears by magic on a supermarket shelf, shrink-wrapped and on a three for two offer.

Being confronted with an alternative makes you wonder how this happened. How many of us happy meat-eaters would know how to cut a throat or butcher a carcass? Is it simply a consequence of our belief that enough money can buy you anything, that it is money that creates food, or clothing, or everything else, out of nothing, pre-packaged and ready to buy? That sustainability is somebody else's problem and that there is no need to nurture the "now" because somehow the future, just like the past, will look after itself.

When you experience an alternative world it makes you think.

It was about half an hour before my first dinner with Krai. Marte had given me the details,

'Dr Krai has taken over one of the speciality restaurants for his meal this evening. You will be joining him. Get yourself smartened up Dr Anderson. I'll come and collect you at 7.'

'Will there be anyone joining us?'

'Only the captain, I think. Atu, Gunnar, Yana and I will be there, but on a separate table.'

I'd showered thoroughly and washed away the remaining grains of sand that had clung persistently to various parts of my body. I'd taken Marte's advice and changed into a pale blue jacket, striped shirt and white slacks. I'd even made sure my shoes were nicely polished.

As I was completing these preliminaries there was a polite tapping at the door. It was Yana, she was still in her lab coat, and I invited her in.

'Can I ask you a mundane question,' I said after the normal pleasantries were over.

'Of course,' she said, 'ask away.'

'I need to get some laundry done and although there's a ship's phone beside my bed I don't know if I'm allowed to use it.'

She laughed.

'You're not in prison Dr Anderson, of course you can use it. You only have to pick up the phone and someone will answer. They'll do whatever you need.'

I wondered if in fact I was in a kind of prison. The phone had probably been modified to make only the one connection.

Yana looked at the pile of clothes on the bed.

'Just leave those there and I'll see that they're dealt with for you, and if you have any other questions please ask me, it's no trouble. You won't see the people who clean your room by the way because, for your convenience, they only come and do that while you're out.'

So, I thought, my contacts and communications were being tightly controlled. Other than running for the exit or misbehaving when out and about on the public parts of the ship I would just have to go along with it. It was a secret blessing that I still had my watch.

'Dr Krai has asked me to make sure that you are presentable for dinner,' Yana continued.

I turned around, showing off my choice of outfit.

'Do you want me to wear a tie?'

'That won't be necessary. I didn't mean your clothing, I meant ...' she touched the side of her face. I automatically lifted my hand to mirror hers.

'Oh I see.'

'Yes, the bruising is a little, what should I say ... noticeable.'

Becoming purple and blue I would have said.

'So if you would just follow me I'll see what I can do.'

Yana tilted back the examination chair and I found myself looking up at the ceiling.

'I just need to mix some colours to match your skin tone. It will be a little hit and miss the first time but I'll make a note of the proportions once we get it right and then it will be a lot quicker next time. Just relax, close your eyes.'

I did as I was told and could hear the unscrewing of lids and tubes, the sound of brush bristles swirling on porcelain and then the dabbing of something moist onto my skin, a 'tut' and a repeat of the process until Yana said,

'Ah, now I have it,' followed by some wider brushing and dabbing.

'The cut on your head is knitting together well,' she said, 'so, as it's mainly beneath the hairline, I think I'll just spray another protective skin of antiseptic over it and comb your hair for you.'

I felt like a manikin, a bored manikin.

'What do you do for fun?' I said, meaning to be flippant.

She thought for a moment.

'I listen to opera,' she said.

I thought that maybe she was also being flippant, a stupid answer to a stupid question.

'Do you know when Maria Callas first sang Norma?' I asked.

'November the 30th 1948 in Florence,' she said without hesitation, 'she was 24 years old.'

'I was thinking more of her first performance at the Royal Opera House, Covent Garden,' I said, wrong-footed.

'1952,' she said, 'I like her first studio recording, the one in 1949, the passion, the emotion she captures in her voice, although of course the technical quality of the recording is not up to today's standards.'

I winced as the antiseptic spray hit home.

'Painful?'

'Cold,' I said, not wishing to appear a wimp.

She went to work with the comb.

'There, you're all done. Open your eyes, tell me what you think.'

I opened my eyes, got up and strode to the wall mirror.

'Mirror, mirror on the wall…' I said.

'Very funny.'

At first glance I looked like I was back to normal. On second glance I could see evidence of swelling but could not see the join between make-up and natural skin. She'd done a good job.

'Looks good,' I said.

'Thank you. I'll give you some wipes so you can clean it off before you go to bed.'

She looked at her watch.

'10 minutes before you go to eat. I'll take you back to your suite so I can change quickly,' she said, adding, 'And I have a recording of Maria Callas on MP3 if you would like to borrow it.'

'I'd like that.'

'I'll have it left in your room for you.'

Chapter 38

There were five speciality restaurants on the Nereus and it looked like Krai had chosen the smallest. "The Boardroom's" decor was a sedate combination of wood panelling, mahogany dining tables and chairs, and thick dark green carpeting.

As I'd expected Krai had requisitioned the entire restaurant and Marte was escorting me in past a few disgruntled passengers.

'But we paid for the speciality dining package. My wife and I were very particular about that.'

'I'm very sorry sir but "The Boardroom"' is fully booked for tonight. Let me help you choose another of our restaurants and we'll refund the speciality dining fee for tonight to your onboard account.' He paused, 'and I can also offer you free wines of your choice with your meal, a small recompense for your inconvenience.'

'Ah, well...'

Upon entering the restaurant I could see that two separate tables had been prepared with about a 10 metre gap between them. At the near table sat Atu, Yana and Gunnar and at the far table sat Krai and a sturdily small man in a pristine uniform.

Marte deposited me at Krai's table and went off to sit at the other, alongside Yana.

'Good evening Dr Krai,' I said, 'I do apologise I seem to have arrived late.'

'Not at all, David, good to see you're back on board. I understand you've had an interesting time ashore. We've only just seated ourselves. Please let me introduce you to the captain of this fine vessel. Captain Sven Hayadal, Dr David Anderson.'

Captain Sven Hayadal was a short, brick built man. Smartly dressed in his uniform that displayed his 5 stripes he oozed the self-confidence that came with rank and experience.

'Pleased to meet you,' I said, holding out my non-swollen hand.

'And you,' said Captain Hayadal, half rising and exerting a vice-like grip.

I took my seat.

'There is a fixed menu for this evening,' said the Captain, 'chosen by our chef and accompanying wines chosen by our sommelier. I hope you will enjoy.'

Krai nodded.

'I'm sure I will,' I said, after the day I'd had I was feeling hungry and good wines would not go amiss either.

'So Dr Anderson,' said the Captain, 'I understand you are an academic, what is your field of study?'

I told him. I had a potted CV off pat and was pleased to have the opportunity to use it.

During my practiced monologue the starter arrived and there was a pause while the waiter explained the dish.

'Tonight the chef has prepared for your first course, hearts of palm with avocado, tomato, and champagne vinaigrette.'

Served in ovoid white dishes the food looked delicious. The waiter then produced a chilled bottle of white wine.

'And to accompany this dish our sommelier has chosen Chateau La Nerthe Blanc, a carefully blended white wine from the Chateau-neuf-du-Pape region of France.' he looked up, 'would you like to taste?'

'Only mineral water for me,' said the Captain, 'whilst on duty I stay clear of alcohol. And whilst onboard ship I'm always on duty.'

'I will join the Captain in his abstinence,' said Krai.

'I'll try some,' I said. I saw no reason not to.

The waiter seemed a little put out on the sommelier's behalf but proceeded to pour a taste sized portion into my glass, the first in a row of wine glasses that were lined up like soldiers before me. This was going to be a good night.

I whirled the wine around the glass and smelt the aroma. Then I took a little onto my tongue and savoured the taste. Dr Krai and Captain Hayadal watched my performance in polite silence.

'I hope you will notice,' said the waiter, 'that the nose is expressive and complex with pear, pastry and candied citrus tones. In contrast on the palate you will feel the wine's freshness, the subtle hints of white peach and dried candied fruits and the finish is long with floral notes, touches of pineapple and green banana sweetness.'

'Exactly,' I said and held out the glass for more.

After my tablemates had been served their mineral water and while we ate at a leisurely pace, I completed my potted history.

I noticed that Krai only picked at his food.

'And yourself, Captain,' I said, after a short and non-threatening interrogation of my studies had been completed, 'I'm fascinated to know how someone becomes a captain of a cruise ship, it's quite a responsibility.'

'There is no substitute for time in accumulating the breadth and depth of experience required to be a captain,' he said. I immediately got the impression that he was asked this question a lot and that he did not, in the slightest, mind talking about himself.

Over the main course of prime beef tenderloin served with morel mushrooms and smoked garlic-potato puree and accompanied, for me at least, with a cabernet sauvignon from the Californian Napa Valley, I learnt that Sven Hayadal, as his name suggested, was scandinavian through and through.

He was born in Narvik a town of some 20,000 people located within the Norwegian Arctic Circle. His family owned a yacht and he had inherited an almost viking-like love of exploring the sea. As he grew he joined the crews of the square rigged training ships during his summer holidays and so it was no surprise to anybody that, on leaving school, he chose to attend the Royal Norwegian Naval Academy in Bergen and went on to serve in the Royal Norwegian Navy.

What was surprising was that he had left the navy early and re-established his career in the Norwegian Merchant Fleet sailing aboard many types of cargo vessel that ploughed back and forth along the world's main trading routes.

In 1995 he joined the cruise line as a Navigation Officer and proceeded to make his way through the ranks until he became captain in 2002.

After such a long and varied career this was to be his last cruise before retirement and it was only when he said this that his stoic expression wavered for an instant. Retirement must be a worrisome prospect for someone whose whole life has been about never settling in any one port, any one ship.

Other than this one slip Captain Hayadal led us through his life's journey with a clear voice, using words efficiently and sharing information with the minimum of fuss.

'And now,' he said, 'I am responsible for over 5,000 passengers and crew and a ship worth upwards of $450m. This makes my prime responsibilities clear, it is to the ship first and foremost and it is to the safety and comfort of everyone on board. For my passengers I do my best to ensure that everyone has a wonderful time and that they make fond memories that they can look back on with pleasure.'

I rolled the dark red wine around on my tongue tasting the rich fruit, the velvety texture. Being the only one drinking alcohol and having such a lavish supply of quality wines was already starting to have an effect. I was feeling a little fuller of joie de vie.

'With so much responsibility for so many people,' I said, 'how do you sleep?'

I realized as I said it that I could have perhaps been a little more subtle, but the essence of my question was heart-felt.

The Captain smiled, 'I sleep very well, Dr Anderson. I and my first officers all have our cabins adjacent to the bridge so we are always on hand.'

'And where does the crew sleep?'

The Captain laughed.

'You seem very curious about everybody's sleeping arrangements Dr Anderson.'

'Oh, I see,' I said, 'my apologies. It's just that I'm fascinated with what goes on behind the scenes. All that happens and is largely unseen by somebody like me but is essential to the smooth running of the ship.'

'Well to answer your direct question, the majority of the crew are quartered four or six to a room on decks 1 and 2. Their cabins have bunk beds and male, female and any involved partners are separated; for obvious reasons. In general the crew sign up for 9 months. I know that's a long time for them to be away from their families but they're well paid and the jobs are highly prized. If you're really interested Dr Anderson I'd be happy to take you on a tour around the parts of the ship that are normally closed to passengers.'

'I would very much like that,' I said, wondering whether I needed to ask Krai's permission first. But why should I? I wasn't a child.

'It will be my pleasure to also introduce you to more of my team,' he paused, 'I have a very good, experienced team whose loyalty to myself and to our shared priorities is unwavering.'

Krai had been listening quietly, drinking very little and eating less. It was at the Captain's use of the word "loyalty" that he started to show interest.

'Loyalty is such an important thing,' he said.

'Yes,' replied the Captain, 'I rely upon it, without loyalty I would not sleep at night, I would not be able to ensure the smooth running of the ship.'

Krai smiled, 'Yes,' he said, 'loyalty is a concept that has occupied me greatly over the years and as I have grown in age and experience I believe I have learnt a little about human nature and in particular the true meaning of the word.'

He paused to allow our desserts to be served, a "Chocolate Sabotage" comprising a duo of chocolate mousse and ganache accompanied by chocolate lava cake and, for me alone, a glass of Malvasia madeira.

Krai then continued, his voice so low that I had to lean forward to hear,

'You will have noticed that my physical condition leaves much to be desired and, as you can imagine, as my body becomes more physically frail I have an increasing need to accept help from others. Consequently I need to be sure that those who are particularly close to me always act in my best interests, that they will always do as I ask. In other words that I can count on their loyalty.'

I swirled the madeira around my glass. The light amber colour seemed to glow with shards of orange as it clung richly to the sides before sliding back to rejoin the whole.

'The absolute worst case that could be tolerated,' said Krai, 'would be an isolated incidence of neutral behaviour, but never, in any conceivable circumstances, would I keep close to me anyone who had acted, whether in thought or in deed, against my interests. No matter who they were.'

I thought of Brady lying immobile on the stretcher. I guess he'd failed the test.

The chocolate dessert was rich, although Krai left his plate untouched, and the madeira tasted of toasted almond, spiked with tart orange. I recognised that my concentration was wavering.

'As I say I believe that over the years I have learnt something about human nature. I have learnt that there is no single path to loyalty, that to inspire loyalty is an art. For some, the simplest, their loyalty can be bought by paying more than they would get elsewhere. For as long as you continue to do this they will not let you down.'

'Others may be loyal through fear, believing that disloyalty would bring disaster upon them or those that they love. These people are constantly looking over their shoulder, seeking reassurance that they are up to the mark, believing that they are constantly watched so that nothing that they do escapes scrutiny. They are loyal because that is the path to self preservation.'

I'd eaten all that I wanted to eat. I'd drunk more than was good for me. I sat in a digestively contemplative state letting his words wash over me.

'A third possibility is loyalty voluntarily given through respect. To gain and maintain such respect is the hardest skill of all. To pay money or to engender fear are relatively simple things to do compared to this.'

'To earn these people's respect you must allow them to learn, or believe that they have learnt, something about you, your aspirations, your methods, successes, even the way that you have dealt with past failures. Allowing people to get close enough to acquire this knowledge is a risk, but should you be gain their allegiance it is freely given and it is strong. It is capable of coping with the rocky waters that come with real life. As Napoleon knew, people will die for a cause more willingly than they will give their lives for money.'

'These three aspects, purchased loyalty, loyalty grounded in fear and loyalty freely given are but three dimensional axes. Most people lie somewhere in the spaces in between, occupying their own unique spot.'

When he'd finished Krai looked across the table and met my gaze. I felt his eyes searching me out.

'And what does it take to inspire your loyalty Dr Anderson?' he asked.

Wishing I'd listened to him more closely I broke eye contact and looked away. I could feel him smiling.

'I wonder,' he said, 'I wonder.'

Chapter 39

Thankfully our conversation was interrupted by a mechanical 'buzzing' sound. The Captain reached to his waist and unclipped a small grey bleeper that was flashing blue. He read the message on the digital display and tutted.

'I am so sorry,' he said, rising to leave, 'I'm afraid there is something that needs my urgent attention.'

'Of course,' said Krai.

'A captain's work is never done,' he said after Captain Sven had left, 'It is the same in any large and complex organisation, people at the head are on call 24 hours a day, every day. The Captain is at least fortunate that he has a retirement to look forward to, some jobs you cannot retire from.'

I wasn't so sure the Captain was looking forward to retiring but kept silent on the point, Krai had said this last in such a reflective attitude that it would have been churlish to suggest that retirement was not always something to be longed for.

'Now David, shall we move on to the casino?'

I looked down at my hand.

'I think my card playing is over for the time being, Dr Krai,' I said, 'I'd rather go and watch this evening's show in the theatre.'

'That's a shame, I was looking forward to a re-match, a chance to win some of my money back,' said Krai, 'but I fully understand.'

He nodded over to the other table and Marte walked over.

'Please escort Dr Anderson to the theatre.'

Marte was far from happy.

'But...'

'It's alright,' said Krai, 'I have plenty of support for my evening at cards.'

I wanted to agree but didn't think it was appropriate. Two bodyguards and a full time doctor was more than sufficient protection for an outing to a cruise ship casino. Within the confines of the ship it was unlikely that Krai had anything to be afraid of.

Being slightly sozzled I enjoyed the theatre show. "Songs from the Musicals" was full of glitz, slick costume and scene changes and enthusiastic singing and dancing.

Marte sat alongside me and sulked the whole way through it even though the view from Krai's VIP seats made you feel that you were almost part of the performance. He made it very clear that I had badly over-stepped his babysitting tolerance threshold and Marte was in no mood for conversation. When the show had finished he whisked me back to my room as quickly as possible.

'Sleep well, Dr Anderson,' he said as he closed and locked the door of my suite, securing me for the rest of the night.

So now I was abandoned to the delights of my luxury cell and I thought vaguely that locking me in must be in stark contravention of the onboard Fire, Health and Safety Rules but realised that I was in no position to argue the point.

Lying on the bed was an MP3 player with earphones. Yana had proved herself both efficient and speedy in delivering on her promise.

After using the wipes she had given me to remove my make-up I switched my watch to one of its more special functions and did a quick sweep of the room for surveillance devices. I didn't find any. Relieved I invaded the mini-bar for four miniature bottles of Johnny Walker, picked up a glass and the MP3 player and made my way out onto the balcony to sit under the stars.

The night was warm, a bright moon lit the darkness.

The MP3 player was loaded with music of all kinds. Yana obviously had an eclectic taste and I scrolled through the listing until I found Maria Callas and pressed "Play".

As my eyes became accustomed to the dark the stars seemed to grow in brightness and to multiply. The Milky Way was washed in multitudinous pinpricks that rose up from the horizon and swept over my head.

The ship was moving steadily onwards, the shush-shush-shush of the waves remonstrating at being pushed temporarily aside. The Isle of Pines was no longer visible, lost back into the Pacific distance and retreating into memory.

With my headphones on and my eyes closed I swam on the waves of Maria Callas' uniquely impassioned voice. How can anyone not be carried away with her interpretation of the operatic music that she sang, the deep feeling in her voice.

A large whisky in my glass, the night sky riding high above me over a black undulating Pacific Ocean,

Maria Callas filling my head with sound and nobody about to hit me over the head with something hard. Things could have worked out a lot worse than this, I thought, and tomorrow I would have the opportunity to try and find out more about the enigmatic Dr Gabriel Krai.

Chapter 40

On the 4th September 1774 Captain James Cook must have been suffering from some kind of delusional fit as he stood, in full uniform, under the Pacific sun and looked out from the poop deck of his flagship the "Resolution". What he saw was a group of islands rising out of the blue waters their white sandy beaches stretching for miles. Between his ship and these beaches lay a protective reef and a rainbow of green, turquoise and blue waters. Atop the land stood a prominent species of pine tree growing to over 200ft tall. With only this scant evidence, and not bothering to land, he immediately thought 'this looks just like Scotland so I'll call it New Scotland' or, to give it a Latin twist, as was the way in those times, he called it New Caledonia.

Let me tell you, I know Scotland and these islands are nothing like it.

We had sailed through the night and reached Nouméa, the capital of New Caledonia, at 8am in the morning. Situated on Grande Terre, the biggest island in the group, Nouméa is a mix of French and Melanesian. It has a busy harbour that deals mainly in the loading and unloading of huge container ships and is deep enough for the Nereus to moor itself directly alongside one of the concreted docks.

The island itself has a central backbone of mountains rich in garnierite, a green silicate containing Nickel and it is this that drives the industrialised economy. Nouméa itself lies on a large irregular peninsula and has long, well-used, white beaches.

Yana had been kind enough to bring me a breakfast tray and I had eaten alone on the balcony. From here I could see the juxtaposition of the heavy harbour industrial machinery and the expensive private motorized yachts moored in the nearby marina and beyond these the regimented line of sea-view apartment blocks and modern hotels.

The ship's daily information sheet, delivered to every room, promised good shopping and easy transport via a hop-on/hop-off bus for a day ticket price of as little as 20$ Aus. Even so, I decided to forego these pleasures and stay on board.

There were two reasons for this. The first was that shopping amidst the graffiti, some of which I could already see from my balcony, and the prospect of a Big Mac burger meal from MacDonald's was not a big attraction for me. The second reason was that the novelty of my existence was already showing signs of wearing thin on Marte and I was getting the distinct impression that looking after me was not his most popular pastime. Therefore in an attempt to minimise annoyance I had told Yana, after thanking her for the MP3, that I was going to stay onboard today. She seemed relieved and was even smiling when she returned half an hour or so later. I guessed that she had passed on the news and that it had not been unwelcome.

'Dr Anderson, please come with me,' she said, 'I would like to examine your injuries and while you're out someone will tidy away your breakfast things and make up your room.'

Already I was feeling that my "injuries" were so superficial that they did not deserve the amount of attention they were getting.

My hand still had some swelling but the pain was minor, my face and body bruising looked worse than they were and the cut on my head was already starting to heal. Yes I was stiff and yes I was sore, but it was hardly life threatening.

'Sure,' I said and followed her out.

Back in the examination chair I glanced around the surgery and saw three layers of shelving filled with books. From their titles they were mainly about alternative therapies and included such topics as Hypnotherapy, Homeopathy, Acupuncture, Aromatherapy, Osteopathy, Meditation, Chiropractics and Herbal Medication.

'Do you believe in all these,' I said, indicating the shelves.

'I am trained and qualified in traditional medicine,' said Yana, 'but my attention is always on the patient. If there are other sources of therapy that can help to bring relief or benefit then why would I ignore them?'

It was a good question.

'But you seemed so dismissive of hypnosis,' I said, 'you clearly didn't enjoy the theatre show.'

'I was not dismissive of hypnosis per se, Dr Anderson,' Yana said, 'what I said was that it was too important a technique to be used for public amusement, as if it were a circus trick.'

'And do you use hypnotherapy on your patients?'

'Yes I do.'

'Even on Dr Krai.'

She hesitated.

'What goes on between a doctor and her patient is confidential Dr Anderson, you should know that.'

I wondered how detailed a feedback she gave on my condition. Maybe not all doctor/patient relationships were entirely confidential.

I tried again.

'I don't want to know the details, I'm only interested in the technique, whether you just leave it on the bookshelf or use it in practice.'

She seemed put out.

'I am not a theoretical doctor, I am a practical one. Of course I have tried all of these therapies,' she paused, 'and with varying degrees of success.'

'And hypnosis?'

'Is an effective therapy for many conditions. Many people are frightened by the prospect of hypnosis, they believe that they will somehow lose control of themselves and will instead be under the control of the hypnotist.'

I raised an eyebrow. I was one of those people.

'But that's simply not the case. If I were to help you into a hypnotic trance you would remain conscious of your surroundings the whole time. I would not be able to make you do anything you did not want to do.'

'Really?'

'Really. Although the precise experience of hypnosis is unique to every individual there are some general principles. It is not like sleeping, you remain aware of everything that's happening around you, you are still able to hear and sense what's going on and you are relaxed, your breathing steady and slow. One interesting thing is that your sense of time may be distorted, what seems only minutes may actually be hours.'

Yana was leaning over me, applying my make-up for the day.

'Hmm, you said "help me into a trance" not put me into one, why was that.'

'Hypnosis is an altered state of consciousness Dr Anderson, one that you voluntarily move into. No one can force you into it, that's just in the movies. But you can be helped to achieve it. It is about temporarily relaxing the connection between your conscious mind and your body and bringing the unconscious mind to the fore. Most people find it a pleasant and beneficial experience. Would you like to try it, it will help you with your pain?'

There were many questions I wanted to ask. Were there any lasting effects? What about hypnotic suggestion? But now was not the time. Now was the time to say 'No' to trying it. The risk that my unconscious mind, unshielded, might give away clues to my real purpose and identity was far too great.

'No thank you,' I said, 'I don't think my pain is severe enough to warrant the trouble. I'm feeling much better already.'

'I'm pleased to hear it,' she said, reaching down some salve and rubbing it into my hand.

I tried not to wince.

'But I can see that Dr Krai is in pain, it must be a useful technique for him,' I said

'It is, in fact as his pain increases we are doing hypno-sessions more and more frequently. Dr Krai does not believe in over-medicating with drugs. He wants to remain mentally alert more than he wishes to be free of pain. He has a strong will, in fact he is the only patient I have had that enters a hypnotic state with his eyes open, defocused, but still open.'

It seemed rather disconcerting to me, more a sign of paranoia than relaxation.

Yana took me back to my room.

'Marte will come and meet you,' she said, 'have you an idea of what you would like to do today.'

'As I'm not going ashore I thought I might make use of some of the ship's facilities,' I said vaguely, 'to be honest I would just like to get out of this room, it's a nice room but it's beginning to feel claustrophobic.'

She locked the door behind her and it was a long 30 minutes until Marte appeared, Atu at his side.

'We've decided to share your chaperoning,' Marte said, 'today its Atu's turn. You've seen him before of course. I'll leave you to get properly acquainted.'

With that he was off. I wondered who the "we" were who had done the deciding. Atu looked delighted.

'Do you like your suite, Dr Anderson?' he asked, by way of making conversation.

'It's very nice,' I said, 'although I'd have rather stayed where I was.'

'Oh, Dr Anderson you shouldn't look gift horses in the mouth. Much better your new suite than the bottom of the Pacific Ocean,' Atu smiled but he didn't seem to mean it as a joke, 'My friend Brady liked this suite, it's a shame he had to leave.'

If this was Atu's way of making friends he was desperately in need of an improvement course. I hadn't known for sure that this was Brady's suite, although his departure and its availability had seemed strangely coincidental.

Great, I thought, this is going to be fun.

'So Dr Anderson,' asked Atu, his face impassive, 'what do you want to do first.'

I didn't want to get on his wrong side, I'd been warned against that, so I thought about what I could do to calm the situation.

'Let's go for a run.'

'Good Choice,' he said.

Chapter 41

Atu left me for dead. He was showing off and smiled wider each time he lapped me.

There were a number of times in between these crossings when we were completely out of each other's sight. If I had chosen to I could easily have slipped off the jogging track and disappeared through one of the automatic sliding doors into the labyrinthine innards of the ship, getting myself quickly lost in the maze of decks and lounges. Either Atu didn't think about this or he didn't care. He certainly took his babysitting role a lot less seriously than Marte.

The next time I heard him approaching me from behind, at speed, I put my hand up. It was a kind of surrender.

'Time for a drink,' I said.

We stepped down to one of the outdoor, poolside bars on Deck 11. I ordered a whisky on ice, Atu took a tonic water. We sat contemplating life.

'Dr Krai has been good to you?' I said.

Atu raised an eyebrow.

'So, has Dr Krai has been good to you?'

'I'm not an idiot Dr Anderson. I know that Dr Krai looks for weaknesses in people and tries to exploit them,' he paused and stared straight at me, 'the thing is, if you know you're being manipulated you can work with it.'

I was surprised at his openness. His strategy of trying to manipulate a manipulator seemed fraught with difficulties to me but then again it wasn't my place to point that out to him.

'And what are your weaknesses?' I asked, trying to provoke him, just for the hell of it.

Atu laughed, his fine white teeth glistening in a black mouth.

'I would be more interested in your own situation if I were you,' he said.

This took me by surprise. I knew I had lots of weaknesses, not least of which was the incriminating information on my confiscated phone, but what could Krai possibly want from me? I thought of myself more as a inconvenient distraction.

'What do you mean?' I asked.

Atu smiled and took a drink. He looked out to sea.

'Dr Anderson,' said Atu, speaking calmly, his breathing relaxed and even, 'can you swim?'

Out of the blue this was a strange question.

'Yes, I can.'

'And are you a strong swimmer, Dr Anderson.'

'I would say that I'm quite good for an amateur,' I said.

'I am not a strong swimmer,' said Atu, 'I freely admit it. I would rather run all day than try to swim for an hour.'

'Really?'

'Yes, and that brings me to my rules.'

He at least had the quality of bluntness.

'Your rules?'

'Yes, it's better to be clear about my rules than to leave you guessing, I think.'

'And what rules are we talking about?'

'It is these. I am not a natural babysitter Dr Anderson, I have no interest in you, what you do or what happens to you.'

Not a great start but at least this had the benefit of clarity.

'So when it's my turn to look after you I may not do it with a consistent level of attention. You may feel you can take advantage of that. Please don't.'

He made an opportunity sound like a threat.

'Because if you do, Dr Anderson, you will find that it is quite easy to slip and find yourself falling overboard, falling, falling into the sea. It is not as inviting as it looks, the water is cold,' he paused for effect, 'and deep. If you were unfortunate enough to slip, Dr Anderson, then I can promise you that you will then find out how strong a swimmer you really are.'

'I see.'

I got the message and I believed he meant it.

'Good, Dr Anderson, very good, I'm pleased we understand each other,' he looked at my empty glass, 'now, would you like another drink?'

He got up and brought me another drink.

Then he sat back down opposite me and leaned forward, placing his elbows on the table, and peered into me. It was very disconcerting.

'Now at the risk of repeating myself,' he said, 'it is not that I don't like you Dr Anderson, it's that you don't matter.'

I'm sure he could have found a way to put that a bit more nicely.

'At best you are a threat that I get the pleasure of dealing with, at worst you are nothing but a nuisance, someone whose existence is to be ignored as much as possible.'

I was not sure I went along with his version of "best" and "worst". In his world I would be quite happy to be rated "worst".

'Just because Brady, the idiot, decided to take against you for some reason doesn't mean you're owed any favours.'

So Brady had kept quiet about our bet. He must have realised that admitting to it would only have made a bad situation worse. He was probably right.

'The less I see of you the better,' said Atu.

The feeling was mutual.

'I'm sorry to be a burden,' I said.

I finished my drink and said I wanted to go back to my room to read. Atu was not displeased at this suggestion. Here was immediate evidence that I had been listening to what he had said and together we left the bar.

As I re-entered my room and walked towards the bed I felt a tell-tale vibration on my wrist. The watch had detected the presence of some kind of surveillance device. Either they had just got around to placing it or perhaps they had needed the equipment to be brought onboard at Nouméa or maybe, and this was the worst alternative from my point of view, maybe my actions or intrusive questioning had raised new suspicions and I was becoming more interesting than was good for me.

I didn't want to do anything that might make my situation any worse so, having told Atu I wanted time to read, I decided I had better do just that.

The books I had brought with me had been neatly unpacked and lined on a shelf. From these I chose a modern translation of "De Vita Caesarum" more commonly known as "The Twelve Caesars".

Originally written by Gaius Suetonius Tranquillus and published in 121AD, during the reign of the Emperor Hadrian, it is part scurrilous gossip and part invaluable historical source material.

Turning to the first of the twelve, Julius Caesar, I hunted for the part where Suetonius gives a brief account of one of the most pivotal moments in Julius Caesar's life - the crossing of the Rubicon.

Being a closet geek I'd quite enjoyed, in a masochistic kind of way, some of the academic cramming that had formed part of my preparation. The real Dr David Anderson, PhD in Ancient History and Lecturer at St Andrews University, should he really exist, would have been proud of me.

Early in the 705th year since the founding of Rome, or 49BC to you and me, Julius Caesar and the 13th Legion found themselves on the banks of a small stream called the Rubicon, a stream significant only in that it marked the official border between Italy and Cisalpine Gaul.

According to the law of the Roman Republic, any provincial governor, as Julius Caesar was at this moment, who lead armed troops across the border and into Italy would be performing a traitorous act, an act of war that would have him immediately declared a public enemy of the state, the equivalent of a death penalty.

Alarmed by his growing power, the Senate had ordered Caesar to set aside his command. Caesar knew this would leave him vulnerable and there were plenty of people wishing him ill.

He was between a rock and a hard place.

He understood that Civil War, the most heinous of wars, would most likely result if he crossed the Rubicon with a fully armed and loyal Legion behind him.

If he chose to cross there would be no turning back.

According to Suetonius, whilst Caesar is still unsure whether to advance or not, a man of extraordinary height and appearance, clearly sent by the gods, turns up and begins to play music on reed pipes. Leading members of Caesar's Legion cannot do other than be attracted towards him. At their approach the apparition leaps forward, snatches up a war trumpet and rushes to bank of the river. Here he sounds a mighty blast and strides across the Rubicon and up, onto the opposite side.

Faced with this sign from the gods what else can Caesar do? He shouts out that the gods have pointed the way and that he has no choice but to follow, the die has been cast.

He crosses the Rubicon.

His troops follow him and stay loyal.

A bloody civil war ensues.

So there we are. How likely is it that this messenger from the gods actually appeared, taking the decision out of Caesar's hands?

Suetonius wrote with the benefit of 170 years of the Imperial Roman Empire behind him and the reign of 13 Emperors. He was writing the past with the sure knowledge of what happened next.

If Julius Caesar had been beaten, as was the more likely outcome, and the Republic had been restored and secured would a Roman historian of the second century AD have looked back on Julius Caser so kindly? No, Caesar would have gone down in history as a licentious brigand and traitor to the Republic. An example of what a Roman should not aspire to become.

But he won.

It's a shame that so many other innocents had to die in pursuance of his ambitions.

Maybe everyone has their Rubicon moment.

My ruminations were interrupted by a knock at the door. It was Gunnar, he'd been sent to take me to lunch. I was being passed around like a hot potato.

This was good timing as I was beginning to feel hungry and it also allowed me an opportunity to get to know Gunnar a bit better. He was someone that up until now I'd only seen hanging around in the background, mainly silent.

'Where would you like to eat,' he asked.

I told him that grabbing something from the lunch buffet would be fine for me, I didn't need anything fancy.

He seemed pleased.

Chapter 42

I went around the buffet stations and filled my plate with coconut rice topped with a chicken masala in a creamy, orange-coloured, spiced curry sauce. Gunnar followed me like a shadow but did not take anything.

Picking up a glass of chilled water I lead Gunnar to an empty table by a large window that overlooked the stern of the ship and sat down.

Gunnar simply sat and watched me eat. He didn't say a word although he appeared completely relaxed. He was a comparatively young man and although clearly not a conversationalist, at six feet tall and strongly built he wasn't someone that you would want to pick a fight with.

After I'd finished eating I asked a passing waiter to bring me a coffee and nursing the hot mug in my hands I decided to attempt a conversation.

'Hello,' I said.

He just looked past me, his eyes fixed like pale blue ice.

'Hello,' I said, trying to sound engaging.

He sighed.

'What do you want?' he said.

His voice was deep for a young man and came from inside his chest, like a dormant volcano rumbling, resonating in base notes.

'Just trying to be friendly,' I said.

'Don't.'

I took the hint and sat staring out of the window. It was raining and the wind was driving the droplets that drummed against the toughened glass and congealed into snaking rivulets that flowed down and out of sight. It looked rough out there but compared to chatting with Gunnar it was a dream.

But I'm nothing if not persistent. I had to find out what Krai was up to and Gunnar might know something. I had to try again.

I turned back from the window.

'Nice day,' I said ironically.

Gunnar glanced at the streaming windows and then back at me.

'No.'

There was no way I was going to get him warmed up by my charming small talk so I decided to jump straight in.

'How long have you worked for Dr. Krai?' I asked.

He raised an eyebrow. I'd obviously taken him by surprise. His blue eyes narrowed and darkened.

'More than a lifetime.'

I had no idea what that meant.

'I guess it takes a little while to get to know him?'

'No.'

'So he's easy to get to know?'

'No.'

This was excruciating. It would be easier to squeeze the milk out of a coconut.

'I'm looking for a bit of help here,' I said, desperation creeping into my voice, 'if I'm going to be around Dr Krai for a while I'd like to make sure I don't make any foolish mistakes.' It was the same tactic I'd used with Marte and worth another go.

'So what do you want to know?'

'How not to make foolish mistakes.'

He shrugged his shoulders, 'I'll give you one piece of good advice.'

Thanks, I thought, at least I might learn something.

'If you don't want to put your foot in it with the boss then don't ask stupid questions.'

He said it calmly, no irony in his voice, although the beginnings of a grin played around the corners of his mouth. It was the most emotional I'd seen him thus far.

I decided to shut up for a moment and drink my coffee in silence. The rain continued to pound against the window.

'I understand you're Swedish,' I said, 'my experience of Sweden is limited but it seems like a beautiful country.'

'We Swedes are built to cope with despair,' he said, 'we even have a season for it. Those dark, miserable days between the white, blue of Winter and the late rescue of the world that is the re-greening of Spring.'

This was a bit better, even bordering on the lyrical.

'But it is a beautiful country and your approach to life seems so calmly ordered. Your natural appearance, blonde and blue eyed, are the envy of us all. Why despair?'

'Without an understanding of despair you cannot properly appreciate joy,' he said, 'and, Dr Anderson, you can't hide from smoke behind a tree, but you can hide from a bear.'

He nodded in self-satisfaction.

Well, I thought, I have no idea what you're talking about. Did he mean he thought I was hiding something or that if Dr Krai was the bear then I should try and hide?

'That very much depends on whether the bear can hear your heavy breathing or smell your fear,' I said, 'it certainly isn't a foolproof strategy.'

He nodded back noncommittally. He seemed disappointed.

Our strange conversation, from which I had learnt nothing useful, was interrupted by the ringing of his mobile phone.

'Excuse me,' he said and took himself off a few yards for a short conversation.

'You're lucky your mobile phone picks up a signal onboard ship,' I said after he'd re-seated himself.

'We have a private network,' he said and then, looking at my empty plate, 'Dr Krai would like to see you, shall we go?'

It was put politely but didn't really sound like a question.

Chapter 43

Krai was sitting in his wheelchair out on the balcony looking out over the harbour. Yana was close by ready to help if necessary. Gunnar ushered me out towards Krai and then retreated into the depths of the room. He seemed relieved to have me off his hands.

'Ah, David,' said Krai, 'please take a seat, would you like a drink.'

I took a seat but declined the drink.

'Last night at dinner,' he continued, his breathing even though laboured, 'I very much enjoyed hearing about your career, your studies of ancient history but I was aware that time did not allow me to return the favour.'

He smiled, or rather his thin bloodless lips tightened across his mouth, exposing his teeth.

'I would very much like to hear your story,' I said, it would be an opportunity to compare the original briefing I'd received against his own words. After struggling with Gunnar it appeared I was going to be gifted insight from the man himself.

I'd obviously given the right answer as Krai settled back as comfortably as he could and began to speak,

'Unlike you I was a child of war, David, standing in line waiting for handouts, a refuge in my own country. I remember one particular day when a large uniformed man wearing a metal helmet sheathed in blue was walking up and down a food line, inspecting, correcting.

Although I was a small child I was determined and

I'd managed to push my way to the front of the queue by the time he came by, my rough wooden bowl held high for a spoonful of boiled rice. I was given my portion and was about to go and find a place where I could eat it quickly before one of the bigger boys stole it from me, when the man smiled, put his hand on my boney shoulder and said to the skinny brown man serving out the rice,

"Looks like we got a growing boy here, think you could fit a few more grains in that bowl?"

The skinny man said nothing but ladled an extra half portion into my bowl. I couldn't believe it.

"There you go now, you can be sure we're going be here for as long as you need us. You can trust me on that."

I heard the clicking of cameras as he moved away.

I ate well that day.'

'That's a nice story. Nice people doing nice things for others when they can. I guess that's why you remember it.'

'Not altogether,' said Krai, 'for the rest of the day I was very thankful to the stranger who had looked so big and so well-fed, and thought that if I ever saw him again I would thank him for the food he had given me, food that had filled my stomach with a little more hope.' Krai paused, I could hear his breathing, each breath emphasised, 'I never saw the man again. He'd been on a flying visit. But the skinny man serving, I saw him every day and he made me pay.'

'He must have felt humiliated, maybe the butt of later jokes. Whatever it was he used his position of power to try and get me into his line and when I held up my bowl he used to smile and give me half as much as everybody else. I nearly starved. I think he wanted me to.'

'What a bastard,' I said.

'Oh no, David,' said Krai shaking his head, 'he was just a skinny man doing a crazy job, not much better off than the rest of us, a man who did not deserve to be humiliated or laughed at. I didn't blame him. If I were him I would have given me no food at all. I thank him for his generosity.'

'No, it was the man in the blue tin hat. I came to hate his memory with a passion that burned hotter than hope. I used to imagine the ways I would kill him if we were ever to meet again. I think it was the hatred that kept me alive.'

I wondered why he was telling me this. Was it easier for him to talk to a stranger, did he need, at this stage of his life to talk about his past, to share it with anyone who would listen?

'The law of unintended consequences, David, if you don't know a culture or understand the people you are dealing with, it's easy to make a mistake. But maybe the truth in this instance is that the man in the blue tin hat didn't care. He'd got his sound bite, he'd got his photo and he'd been seen to be caring and generous for a moment in front of the cameras. It was mission accomplished from his perspective, and it was welcome to even more hell from mine.'

He paused. Yana came over and handed him two white pills and held out a glass of water. Krai swallowed them uncomfortably. Yana retreated. The whole thing lasted less than a minute, no words or looks passing between them, their movements choreographed through familiarity. Dealing so intimately with his medication, Yana was someone Krai was forced to trust.

'It's when you've got nothing to lose that you can take the greatest risks. I was 12, my father and mother dead, and I ran away from the countryside and onto the city streets.'

'There was no-one to miss me, there was no reason for any authorities to bother tracking me down. Now I started my real education and I took to it like a child prodigy who had found his calling.'

'It's amazing how easy it is to live for free, learning to steal, learning by watching others, learning how to use others to get what you want.'

'When you're on your own it's best not to stay in one place for too long. Keep moving, don't stay long enough to become attached.'

'And how did you get to America?'

'There are lots of ways, David. I learnt American from the TV, I made money and I kept it, I bought gold and I hid it. Eventually when I was 16, but probably looked like I was still 12, I found a way, on board a cargo vessel, living like a rat in the dark for 40 days, working my passage whilst being invisible. I allowed myself to be beaten without fighting back, to be punched and kicked, to be robbed of everything of value I still had. I had one objective, to get to the United States alive. Nothing else mattered. It would have been easy for me to "go missing" deep in the Pacific Ocean. No one who cared knew I was there, there was no one who cared.'

'I was carried off the ship hidden in a container, then on the back of a truck, and then finally when I reached a new city I slipped out and onto new streets and into old habits.'

'It is easy to live for nothing in American cities, there are food programs, stores leftovers and straightforward shop-lifting. I'd never eaten so well and grew stronger. I got cleaned up in rivers and streams, I collected new clothes from church give-aways and then by knocking on doors and collecting "for charity" I gained a few dollars in my pocket.'

'Nobody expected such a young-looking kid to be so worldly-wise. It was easy. Of course I got abused and learnt very quickly that the American dream was only for those with white skins, dollars and the right connections.'

'I could never have the right skin but I went to work on the other two. By joining street gangs, keeping clean, learning the ropes and not getting caught I soon had some believable identity papers.'

'The rest was just about taking opportunities, learning how people ticked and pressing the right buttons. A gang of four became eight and so on. By the time I was 25 I was someone. By the time I was 35 I was Dr Gabriel Krai. I always think a title adds gravitas, don't you David?'

I was out of my depth. I had gone from struggling to get a word out of Gunnar to this stream of consciousness from Krai himself. Why was he telling me all this? Was he playing with me or was he doing some kind of macabre rehearsal of his own obituary? And why was he teasing me about my assumed title, did he know more about me than he was letting on?

'Why are you telling me all this?' I asked.

He looked surprised.

'Because you look like a man who might be interested.'

'But you hardly know me and if what you've told me is true you're at the very least an illegal alien in the United States. What if I passed on that information?'

Krai's laugh was dry and ended in a cough.

'David, David, David,' he said as if admonishing a small child, 'if only that were the most serious charge that could be held against me. We are on a cruise ship, you have fallen into my care, and our conversation is purely circumstantial, your word against mine, what risk could you possibly be to me?'

He coughed again.

'Through life,' he said, 'we build individual memories, uniquely our own, formed from perceptions of our own successes, failures, and experiences, the more stark the event or experience, the deeper the memory. We all have our weaknesses don't we David? And sometimes we might even be able to offer a little help in exchange for something.'

His coughing got worse before he could explain what he meant. I felt threatened and off-balance.

Yana moved in and waved me away. I was sure Krai had been trying to tell me something but I'd missed the point, and now this conversation was over.

Gunnar followed me back to my cabin and deposited me there like an unwanted parcel. He locked the door and left me on my own.

I thought about Krai – what could he possibly want from me? And, in any case, I wasn't here to help him, quite the reverse.

Chapter 44

We left Nouméa at 17:00hrs.

As the cruise ship cut its way out of the harbour and into ocean waters the push of the bow wave caused silver winged flying fish to take to the air in an attempt to glide to safer waters on their stiff fins. Brown feathered gannets had cottoned on to this behaviour and their slim bodies sliced through the air, on sharp wings, hunting down the fish in mid air - missing 10, catching 1.

As I had time to burn and the surety that I was under surveillance I turned to my bookshelves once more and took down "Meditations", a book of personal and private thoughts and ideas on Stoic Philosophy by the Roman Emperor, Marcus Aurelius.

It was written sometime around 170AD and was originally meant solely for his own benefit and not that of an audience. He carried it around with him as a kind of handbook of morality against which he could check himself and his actions.

Flipping through the pages I came across "All things fade and quickly turn to myth".

On the surface this appeared a fairly bleak statement, but as a Roman Emperor such a realisation could lead you to wonder whether you could give the building of your own myth a bit of a hand whilst you were still alive. The important thing would be to leave a lasting legacy. Perhaps by constructing magnificent buildings, perhaps by conquering territories, winning wars, or recording your own achievements as history.

Making a myth that was likely to last, or at least fade away more slowly.

I thought about what we tend to remember for longest. The Titanic, for example, is remembered not because it was a great ship but because it sank under such dramatic circumstances. Her sister ships Britannic, that sank in 1916 after hitting a mine, and Olympic, nicknamed 'Old Reliable', are largely forgotten.

To capture a place in time's memory it seems that what is necessary is to do something remarkable irrespective of whether that thing can be categorised as "good" or "bad". It doesn't seem to matter as long as it's remarkable. I put the book to one side, you can have too much Philosophy.

I took my time showering and changing for dinner. Yana came to collect me early and took me into her surgery to touch up my makeup.

'You are healing quickly, Dr Anderson,' she said.

'Good,' I said, 'it's only because of your help. You're clearly very experienced at treating injuries, how long have you been a doctor?'

'Long enough.'

Oops, I'd obviously said the wrong thing. My Dad had once told me "Never piss off a woman, son. They can remember things that haven't even happened yet - and use them against you". I clearly hadn't learnt.

Yana obviously noticed my reaction.

'Sorry I snapped at you, Dr Anderson,' she said, 'it's just that ...'

She stopped and turned her head away.

'Yes?' I said.

Yana walked over to a nearby stainless steel work top, took a tissue from the dispenser and wiped her eyes. Then she returned and carried on tending to me.

'It's just that Dr Krai is getting weaker,' she said, avoiding eye contact, 'you are healing and he is dying.'

It was clear that she wished it was the other way around, but I shrugged this off.

'Have you known Dr Krai long?' I said, trying to be as conciliatory as possible, 'the care you give him is exemplary.'

Her eyes returned to mine and she paused in what she was doing.

'I never knew my parents, Dr Anderson, but I was lucky and the family who adopted me treated me like I was their own and helped me to take my education seriously.' I couldn't imagine her doing anything but take her education seriously, she seemed like she took almost everything seriously. 'And then one day, out of the blue, Dr Krai came to our school and talked to our Principal about introducing a scholarship. She readily agreed of course, no school can turn away a generous donation, and a maths, science and english competition was held to decide who would be the first beneficiary.'

'I didn't think I had a chance but I tried my best. Dr Krai himself and the Principal acted as judges and, to my amazement, I won.'

'My adopted parents were both amazed and grateful as they would not have been able to find the money for the further education I was determined to pursue.'

'Dr Krai then disappeared from my life. One short moment had changed my fortunes. To be honest, other than a name on a letterhead each time a new instalment was paid, I forgot all about him and focused only on my studies. The opportunity to train in medicine was like a dream.'

'I saw him again only after I had qualified and I was thinking through my specialisation options. He offered me a job instead, as his personal physician, promising that I could continue my training at the same time. Such financial stability was too much of a temptation and I agreed.'

'I've worked for him ever since. He's been very kind to me although he only allows me to work with him one-to-one. I was not allowed to be involved in any of his other medical treatments.'

'It is only recently, when his health has begun to fail irretrievably that I have been allowed more freedom. It is frustrating not to know everything but I have been able to concentrate on learning a range of different medical techniques, both traditional medicine and more natural treatments.'

Dr Krai being kind, the offer of sponsorship. It didn't fit with my understanding of the man, a man that never did anything without expecting more in return. What made more sense to me was that Krai had found Yana's weakness, a willing talent matched by a lack of resources, and in return had produced a professional, talented, and above all loyal medical attendant just when he needed it, at a time when he was otherwise vulnerable. I realised Yana would not see it this way so I said nothing. Maybe I was wrong, maybe he was a more complicated person than I had given him credit for.

Yana finished up, washed her hands and took off

her white lab coat that was smeared with the remnants of the makeup she had been using, and carefully hung it up. I could see that, as usual, she had thought ahead as beneath her white coat she was already dressed for dinner.

'Shall we go?' she said.

Chapter 45

Our gastronomic journey around the world continued with a visit to the Japanese speciality restaurant. Once again it had been booked for our exclusive use. Yana took my arm and escorted me past the disappointed passengers and into a relatively small space bedecked in a mixture of reds, oranges, browns, grays and blacks in geometric motifs.

I was again the last to arrive. This now seemed more by design than error and Yana went to join the separate table where Gunnar, Atu and Marte were already employed in perusing the menu, while I walked over to join Captain Hayadal and Dr Krai.

Krai did not look well but brightened up when we had placed our order and I had mentioned the subject of money.

'It is all in the decimal point,' he said, 'that's how banks make fortunes. Currency conversion is a prime example, each time you exchange money you lose a little, and that little, multiplied by millions of transactions becomes millions of profit for the exchanger. If you want to know about institutionalised stealing look no further than the cartel that fixes the exchange rates.'

I had eaten enough food to stuff a rhinoceros and without the exercise to run it off. I therefore went directly to the main course choices and settled on the "Deluxe Seafood Citrus Salad", the words deluxe, seafood and salad winning me over by the enticing juxtaposition of opulence coupled with a semblance of healthy eating.

I was surprised when both Captain Hayadal and Krai followed suit. Perhaps the cruise ship calorie excess was catching up on all of us.

Krai paused as the plates of food were served. The blanched lobster tail, octopus, and shrimp ebi, boiled, butterflied and cleaned, the pickled sweet cucumber together with kaiso seaweed, daiko sprouts and roasted sesame seeds looked and smelt like a banquet from the sea.

My companions stuck to their beloved mineral mater while I gave way to Ginjo sake, that is to regular sake what single malt scotch is to regular scotch. I knew from previous experience that only 8-9% of all sake brewed was up to the Ginjo grade.

As we ate and Krai picked ineffectually at his plate of food, he continued on his theme.

'When accounts are 99.9% accurate it's the 0.01% that matters, that's where the money is. Fractions have become my specialty, making friends with small numbers, helping them move, making them dance.'

'I discovered my talent in numbers at an early age. I have a real affinity for them. I can manipulate them like others mix and manipulate paint to make art. I have been lucky to live in an age when money and numbers have become indistinguishable. We don't pay with coins or notes any more, we pay with numbers.'

'Add, subtract, divide split, convert recombine,' he moved his hands and arms mimicking the actions, his eyes glittering and animated. It was clear that Krai loved numbers, feeling more for them than he felt for anything that had a real pulse.

'It is when you multiply that success accelerates,' he

said.

The sake was refreshing and had a delicate floral, fruit aroma. It was light and smooth, clean, and dry and suited the seafood perfectly. I poured myself another glass.

'Money, in and of itself,' continued Krai. 'is nothing. It can be a shell, a metal coin or a piece of paper. In themselves all these are useless as items of clothing, or food to eat or shelter to protect you from the rain. But the value that is placed on them has nothing to do with the physical value of the items themselves. Money derives its value from being used as a medium of exchange, a unit of measurement and a storehouse for wealth. Money allows people to exchange goods and services by providing an intermediary currency, so many dollars earned by selling potatoes, so many dollars spent to buy a tractor.'

'Money is of value only because everyone knows that everyone else will accept it as a form of payment. If that trust ever breaks down then money will have no value at all.'

The sake was going down well. Krai was making the dinner pass easily by treating us to this monologue. I couldn't remember the last time that either I or Captain Hayadal had uttered a word. We ate, we drank, we nodded our heads occasionally.

I knew from experience that sake can be deceptively strong. At about 15% alcohol it is similar to drinking wine, and much stronger than beer. The thing it has in its favour though is that, as it is simply fermented rice and water, it does not result in a serious hangover the morning after.

I wasn't as fascinated by the meaning of money as Krai and my mind was beginning to wander. We ordered coffees and Krai wound up his lecture.

'Money has been a part of human history for at least 3,000 years,' he said, 'before that it is assumed that a system of bartering was used, I'll give you this stone axe if you give me a share in your mammoth kill. Each transaction was a negotiation and negotiations can be messy, take time and have a different outcome each time. Money sets an individual value on each item in a way that can be easily understood and reproduced, increasing the speed at which business can be done.'

Krai ground to a halt.

'Very interesting,' I said, 'I'd never thought about it like that.'

The second part of my statement was true.

Yana came over with some painkillers but Krai waved them away. His animation had also acted as a distraction from his pain.

'Tomorrow we visit Mystery Island,' said Captain Hayadal, 'we should be anchored by 08:00hrs and we'll be using the tenders to shuttle people back and forth. Will you be going ashore?'

'I'd very much like to,' I said.

'Of course,' said Krai, 'it is an opportunity not to be missed, although I shall be staying on board. I'm sure Marte would love to accompany you.'

I'm sure he would, I thought.

'Now I must make my way to the casino, can I tempt you, David?'

The servo-motors on his exo-skeleton started to whirr softly as Krai prepared to rise.

'I don't think so,' I said, 'I think I'll take in the theatre show.'

'A good choice,' said the Captain, 'I believe tonight's show is particularly spectacular.'

'Do enjoy it,' said Krai, 'if you wait here I'll ask Marte to come over.'

I watched as Krai walked slowly and mechanically away, the Captain making his excuses and departing quickly.

Krai paused at the second table. I saw Marte's look of displeasure, and Atu's grin.

I was proving to be a divisive influence and wasn't sure whether that was a good or a bad thing in my quest to find out what the hell was really going on.

Chapter 46

The show was a double-header; a stand-up comedian followed by a husband and wife team of high wire acrobats.

The stand-up comedian tried to cater for his mixed audience by telling "a world of jokes". In other words he tried to insult as many of the nations of the world as he could within his allotted 40 minutes.

Obviously his jokes about the Brits were OK, there's so much to laugh about, but I didn't get a lot of the others. Marte didn't get any. He didn't want to be there and kept looking at his watch, the numerals glowing in the theatre dim.

The acrobats were outstanding. At the start of their act a rope was dropped down from the ceiling and the sequined couple climbed and swung out over our heads, the female member of the duo being in turn, thrown, caught and dangled. Although they were wearing safety ropes I did wonder what would happen if they'd just had an argument - would he still have caught her?

I mentioned this to Marte at the end of the show but he didn't respond.

His understandable grumpiness was becoming a problem. I didn't want to antagonise him, quite the opposite. I thought that if I could try and befriend him instead, or at least try and avoid annoying him more than absolutely necessary, it would be a help. I was increasingly convinced that Krai wasn't on board for the good of his health and thought that it might be possible to get something wittingly or unwittingly out of Marte.

I didn't get up to leave, instead I tried to make things better.

'I'm feeling much improved,' I said, 'the bruises are not so obvious now. Maybe I can get out of your hair and go back to my original room tomorrow.'

I glanced at his bald head thinking that perhaps I could have chosen a better idiom.

'Dr Krai will decide,' said Marte.

'Do you want me to just stay in my room until then?'

He thought about this.

'Dr Krai has offered you his hospitality, Dr Anderson, and I don't think he would be very happy to hear that you were moping around alone in your room, especially as you have already expressed a wish to go ashore tomorrow,' he paused, 'and Dr Krai hears everything.'

'Then what can I do?' I asked, 'I don't want to make your life difficult, Marte.'

At least that was the truth.

Marte softened. Trying to be nice, even if there was little I could actually do, looked like it had been a smart move.

'Dr Anderson let me tell you something,' he said, 'I do not like leaving Dr Shavi unprotected, you may have noticed that Dr Krai is becoming more erratic. It is not like him, his behaviour is changing, he is not the same man.'

This surprised me. I had assumed that his first concern would have been the danger of Atu stepping into his shoes during his enforced absences. Atu was ambitious, he would be sure to make the most of this opportunity.

'What can I do?' I asked.

'Let us see, Dr Anderson, let us see,' he smiled, 'and what would you like to do now?'

The theatre had almost emptied and I levered myself out of my seat.

'You know something, I think I'll have an early night.'

'Thank you,' said Marte as we were leaving.

If my job was to be a disruptive influence then I was certainly succeeding. Of the five people closest to Krai one had already been carried off the ship on a stretcher, one had become a very frustrated babysitter to yours truly, and one was using me as an opportunity to further his own ambitions. The other two I was trying hard to get to know better.

I had fallen into a closeness to Krai and his entourage that I could not have sensibly hoped for. If I was going to make the most out of it I had to walk a tightrope between being a non-threatening, unfortunate academic caught up in something way over his head, and a persistent inquisitor. Oh yes, and I had to survive to tell the tale.

Chapter 47

Mystery Island or more correctly Inyeug Island is a small, flat piece of land lying low atop the Pacific Ocean. It is surrounded by turquoise blue waters that lie within its protective coral Intao Reef.

Although small it actually contains a grassy airstrip, a legacy of World War 2. It is a marine sanctuary and the island itself is criss-crossed with foot-worn paths. Frequently visited by cruise ships it has market stalls, tour guides, food and drink but it is not permanently inhabited as it is believed to be the home of ghosts.

Lying adjacent to Mystery Island is the much more substantial island of Aneityum whose green clad slopes climb upwards to the rim of an extinct volcano.

Together they are the southern-most islands of Vanuatu.

We anchored on time at 8a.m and Marte and I went ashore. We spent the time snorkelling, this time without sea snakes, and afterwards Marte suggested we get a drink before going back onboard so we sat in the shade drinking Tusker, the Vanuatu brewed bottled beer. It was dry and fruity with a mild bitterness. It was just what I needed.

'It's amazing isn't it,' I said, 'you take so much of your own world for granted, the way you dress, the way you act, what success means, and then you come to a place like this and an alternative reality hits you in the face, it's a different world on the other side of the same planet.'

'That's very philosophical of you,' said Marte.

I looked across at him to see if he was taking the piss. He smiled, his face softened.

'No, really,' he said, 'you're right. It makes you challenge your thinking – what success is.'

'Yes,' I said, grabbing the opportunity to chat, to explore Marte's motives, 'I've always thought that more money, a more senior job, a bigger house and car were how to measure success. But look around you, there are no cars, houses are made out of sticks and leaves, no one is chasing a better job. And yet they seem happy with their lot.'

'Happier than we are after all our efforts,' said Marte.

'Happier than we are,' I paused, 'what do you want Marte? What kind of happiness are you chasing?'

He opened his mouth to speak but then changed his mind. He finished the rest of his beer in one and put the bottle down.

'We should be going, Dr Anderson,' he said.

Back onboard we were immediately summoned to Krai's suite. He just wanted to talk. You could see he was in pain and needed a distraction, and we would do.

Yana fussed around him whilst he talked. From all that I'd seen to date this was the normal procedure. She was tending to him like a young mother worries over a small child.

Krai asked about our time ashore.

'These are primitive people,' he said, 'they will never rise above their poverty line existence. They lack …'

Yana must have inadvertently touched a painful spot and Krai lashed out. The speed of it took me by surprise and sent Yana sprawling. From the power of the blow Krai was not as frail as I'd thought. That was worth remembering.

Marte took half a step forward. From her prone position on the floor Yana shot him a warning look and struggled quickly to her feet and made her way back to Krai.

'Sorry,' she said.

Krai nodded.

Marte stood clenching and unclenching his fists, his jaw set, his eyes narrowed. If I'd needed proof of an attachment then I'd just had it.

'Now where was I,' said Krai, completely oblivious to any harm he may have caused, 'Oh yes, they lack any form of ambition or drive ...'

I'd switched off and was only half-listening. I nodded out of politeness and did my best to appear as if I was paying attention.

As soon as I could I made my excuses and went back to my cabin.

It must have been after 17:00hrs because we were once again underway and the sun was sinking towards the sea. I stood at the rail of my balcony.

The big ahip was lumbering steadily through the pacific swell.

I showered, and wondered what dinner with Krai was going to be like. What mood he was going to be in.

Yana called at what was becoming her usual time and I sat in silence as she tended to my healing injuries and applied the makeup to my face. The bottle of nano juice that Marte had bought stood close by on one of her shelves.

I didn't want to ask directly about what I'd witnessed as I could see that she was still upset.

'Dr Krai seems to be in increasing pain,' I said.

'Yes, there is little more that I can do. He refuses stronger medication because he says he must remain mentally alert.'

'Did he hurt you?'

A tear formed in the corner of her eye but she fought it back.

'When people are in pain, Dr Anderson, they lash out. It's not their fault.'

'Sometimes at those nearest and closest to them,' I said, a flash of memory from my wife's fight with cancer colouring my cheek.

'It's not their fault, it's the pain,' said Yana.

I wasn't sure who she was trying to convince.

'Now sit still and let me get this finished.'

Chapter 48

It was Gunnar who escorted me to dinner. Capone's speciality Steakhouse was tonight's choice. It was a dimly lit and discerning affair marked out by dark woods and neutral tones.

As soon as I entered I could see that there was no question of what this restaurant was all about. It was about steak, certified Aberdeen Angus steaks to be exact. There was even a warning on the menu that there were no main course vegetarian options. Plain salads and sides were the only non-meat alternatives and even here there was no guarantee that they would not be tainted with animal protein.

It suited me. I was hungry.

After a little deliberation I went for all 3 courses; pork belly and oyster rockefeller to start followed by a 14oz New York strip steak with french fries, mushrooms and onion rings and for dessert a simple lemon coconut ice cream with toasted macadamia nuts.

I guessed my colleagues would be sticking to their mineral water but as I had an overflowing onboard account I ordered a bottle of Diamond Creek Volcanic Hill Cabernet Sauvignon 1992 from the Diamond Mountain District of the Napa Valley, California USA.

I paid no attention to what my table mates, Captain Hayadal and Dr Krai, were ordering. They could look after themselves.

What I did notice however was that Krai did not look well. It was with an effort that he returned to his favourite subject – money.

'The more money people have the meaner they grow,' he said, 'the poorest communities can be the most generous - they have nothing to lose. The rich are always watching their back, wondering who will be the next to try and steal their wealth, pull a fast one, scam them out of their money-dependent privileged positions.'

He paused to wince. Yana came over and offered him two white tablets. He took one of them.

'The difficult thing for those with money is to discriminate between flattery and friendship, true affection and emotional manipulation. Especially when they believe that the adoration might be justified.'

He paused again. Our starters were served but he didn't touch his, he carried on talking as the Captain and I ate.

'Pandering to their elevated self-image, affirming the personal veneration that he or she feels is their due. It is their Achilles' heel.' Did he mean it was his as well? 'Moneyed people tend to be capable, intelligent, sober, ruthless and perhaps even astute in all other aspects of their lives, but they can be so foolish, so lacking in common sense, when it comes to their emotional relationships with others.'

Plates were taken away, mine empty, Krai's untouched.

The main course arrived. I poured my own wine swirling it around the large-bowled glass and watching the viscous tendrils crawl satisfyingly downwards.

The steak was melt in the mouth goodness, the pepper sauce adding just the right amount of extra bite. The wine was a superb accompaniment with its aromas of blackcurrant and spices, its flavours of cocoa and berries, and its velvety smooth feeling on the tongue. I was enjoying it.

Krai was trying to manage his pain through distraction. He was talking for talking's sake. The Captain and I were a politely silent audience.

'Do you know what real weakness is?' he asked, in what was obviously a rhetorical question, 'Weakness is caring about something or someone too much. If you care then you're vulnerable. Most people could steel themselves to withstand a degree of pain, but threaten those or that thing that they care about most, threaten to hurt or destroy that, and they capitulate, they crumble before your eyes and willingly believe that if they co-operate you will keep your word and leave that thing or those others well alone. It is all so foolish. It is all so human.'

He took a sip of water. He picked at his main course. I wondered why he bothered ordering, it must simply be for appearances sake.

'I have no such weakness,' he continued, 'my choice is to have nothing in my life that anyone can threaten, nothing that if taken away would cause me a moment's anguish. My strength is in having no weaknesses; no wives, no children, nothing to care for, nothing for enemies to take advantage of.'

The physical and mental world that Krai inhabited, the world in which he thrived, was one that I did not relish. I knew I had my weaknesses and was worried that Krai could see them too. I had loved my wife, I loved my daughter and I hoped to love again. It had been difficult, my wife's illness, the pain that I could see she was suffering and that I could not take away had been horrendous and will live with me forever. But I would rather live that time over again a million times than never to have known her.

Looking at Krai, the money he had, the organization he ran, the enforced respect that he had and the choices that he had made to achieve it all. It did nothing to change my mind.

The wine tasted great but I did not want to finish the bottle. As the dessert was served I asked the waiter if he could re-cork it and have it taken to my cabin for later. He looked to Krai for permission. Krai nodded assent.

'Tomorrow is a day at sea,' said the Captain, 'I would very much like to take you on that tour of the ship that I promised you, Dr Anderson.'

'That would be great,' I said. In fact anything that got me away from the claustrophobic confines of my luxury suite was fine with me.

'Yes,' said Krai, 'I'm sure you will find it interesting, David. What time would you like him on the Bridge, Captain?'

The Captain suggested a time. I struggled to stay calm. I was being treated like a delinquent teenager that couldn't be trusted to be out on his own. I knew it was important to stick close to Krai and his entourage but the emotional price I was paying was beginning to get me down.

Another person who must have been feeling the rising tension was Yana. A number of times through the meal she had half risen from her seat in response to an obvious sign of pain from Krai only to be waved away unceremoniously.

The meal was coming to an end. Krai confirmed his intention to make his way to the casino, I said I'd make my way to the theatre. Krai called Yana across and told her to accompany me.

'But…'

He ignored her.

'See you tomorrow, Captain,' I said, trying to smooth things over, 'and good night and good luck at the table Dr Krai.'

I got up promptly and led Yana out of the restaurant. I felt Marte's eyes boring into the back of my neck. Whatever version of happiness he was seeking – this wasn't it.

Chapter 49

'I saw that Dr Krai was talking to you over dinner,' said Yana as we made our way to the elevators, 'it's therapeutic for him to talk.'

'It's sometimes easier to talk to strangers,' I said, hiding my discomfort at the mind games Krai seemed to be able to play with anyone he chose.

'Pain can be managed in a number of ways and Dr Krai has a strong mind. Keeping that mind focussed on something complex can help a lot.'

'It can hardly be a complex activity talking to strangers over dinner,' I said.

She shut up immediately. I could see that I'd lost an opportunity.

Shit!

There was something that Krai was focussed on and Yana had some knowledge of what it was. The wine had been too good and I had been too careless.

Inside the elevator I pressed 12.

'I thought we were going to the theatre,' said Yana.

'I have a surprise for you,' I said.

'But does Dr Krai ...'

'Dr Krai does not need to know everything,' I said, 'I'm a free man, a free man with lots of dollars that need spending.'

I walked her towards the entrance to the onboard Spa and Gymnasium and checked my reservation with the attractive young lady at the reception desk.

'Could I increase the treatment to include both of us?'

The young lady looked at her screen.

'I'm afraid…'

I took out a one hundred dollar bill from my inside jacket pocket and laid it on the desk. I find it is always a good idea to carry plenty of cash.

'I'm really sorry …'

I took out another two bills, one a hundred the other a fifty, and put them with the first. With so much money in my onboard account I didn't need to penny pinch. The young lady looked at the money, hesitated, and then reached out and took it.

'Ah,' she said, 'now I see there's been a cancellation. I don't know how I missed it before.'

Yana was tugging at my sleeve and pulled me a little distance away. She looked up at me with fire in her deep brown eyes.

'What is all this?'

'It's a spa,' I said.

She stamped her foot in frustration. I have that effect on women.

'I made a booking for a hot stone massage,' I said, 'I didn't know who would be accompanying me after dinner so I thought that it would be easier to pay a "no show" than turn up with no reservation at all.'

'And you think that because it's me …'

'I think that we could both do with some relaxation.'

'But I mustn't let you out of my sight,' she said. I really was being treated like a potentially naughty school kid.

I walked back to the desk and had a word with the young lady. She was very accommodating.

'They have a room with two tables side by side,' I said.

'But we'll be partially undressed?'

'I promise not to look if you don't.'

She smiled for the first time.

'Oh, come on,' I said, 'It's only for an hour.'

Smoothed black volcanic stones of varying sizes, chosen for their heat retaining properties, were warmed in a bath of 60^{0}C water. We got undressed in separate cubicles, wrapped ourselves in soft white towels and then proceeded to the massage tables.

We lay face down and as my towelling was peeled away the purple-blue bruising to my side was revealed. The masseuse, an athletic-looking young man with a crew-cut, sucked in his breath.

'I slipped in the shower,' I said, 'don't worry it hardly hurts.'

'I see,' he said, 'yes, the bathroom floors can get slippery. I'll go very gently around those areas, you must tell me if it hurts.'

Oh, I will, I thought, I most certainly will.

The treatment started with a traditional Swedish massage and I could feel my muscles relaxing, knots being unknotted under the therapist's expert hands. I hoped Yana was feeling the same benefits.

The masseuse picked up one of the hot stones and held it in his hands before continuing to smooth away my tension. He laid the hard smooth stone on just the right spot to deliver deep tactile relief beneath my skin. As it cooled he replaced the stone and expertly laid down others as the rhythmic extent of the massage moved slowly from my neck towards the base of my spine.

Finally he lined stones of decreasing size along my back. I could feel the flow of energy they released.

This was 100% worth the money.

Yana and I hadn't spoken a word throughout the treatment but after we had changed back into our clothes and were preparing to leave the spa I could see she felt better.

'Very interesting,' she said, 'the combination of heat and the minerals in the stone, the movement of the hands and the ambience of the room. They all played a part in the therapy. It has given me some ideas to think about.'

I smiled, you can take a young woman to a spa but you can't take the enquiring doctor out of the woman.

Back in my cabin I took the remaining half bottle of Diamond Creek cabernet sauvignon that had been dutifully delivered to my room and moved out onto the balcony. I filled a glass, turned off all the lights and sat just gazing over the black sea that rolled relentlessly under a star-filled sky.

Krai said that he had no weaknesses. I had many. But I would not swap my life with his. Now that he was approaching the end you could sense that those old choices were finally coming home to roost.

I'd been shocked by some of Krai's behaviour, his switch from relative calm to raw aggression and back again, his penchant for taunting. Wasn't this the behaviour of a psychopath?.

His bouts of antisocial behaviour, his impaired empathy and his apparent lack of any remorse, his uninhibited egotistical traits it all seemed to fit the bill.

I sometimes feel as if I inhabit my own body like an astronaut inhabits a spaceship. With all that had happened today and under the influence of the strong wine I started to drift into a kind of shallow sleep …

Krai was sitting in front of me, he was younger, full of his own energy.

'Pain, David, is such a strange thing, sometimes it is your friend but more often it is your enemy.'

'If you put your hand into a flame, David, it is pain that warns you to withdraw it. The pain is working in your best interests. If you fall and break your leg, the pain tells you that the damage is significant; it prevents you putting your weight on it and making it worse. It forces you to look for ways to heal the damage.'

'But if your pain is chronic like mine, it becomes debilitating, it saps your strength, it does not help you towards a recovery but rather it prevents you from doing anything other than managing it - it is only when you take the pain away that you get a part of your life back.'

'That's what I do, David, I manage the pain using anything that works - drugs, hypnotherapy, massage, whatever gives me some respite.'

In my dream Krai's watery eyes then focused on me,

'So you see I know a lot about pain and its effects. I like to put my personal knowledge to use, David, when I think it will be of benefit to me.'

I could see my own face. I could feel the sweat rise unbidden on my forehead and see it begin to trickle down my cheek. I wanted to wipe it away but when I looked down I saw that my hands were tied. I couldn't move.

'I can see,' said Krai, 'that you understand your rather unfortunate predicament.'

He was speaking slowly, calmly. His voice was much clearer and filled with purpose than the Krai I had just had dinner with.

'I will ask you a few simple questions, David, and the quality and clarity of your answers will determine the level of pain you will endure. Do you understand?'

I saw myself say,

'I understand.'

The anticipation of pain produced a feeling of nausea. In some perverse way I wanted the real pain to start, to bring the waiting to an end. I just wanted him to get on with it.

'So now let us see how far into the flame you are willing to reach and for how long you can stay there. Let the battle between pain and will begin – knowing, David, that in the end it is always the pain that wins.'

I have been trained to cope with situations like this. For me one of the most successful techniques is to take myself mentally out of the situation, to separate my body from my mind.

When I have to do this I have a place I go to.

I am sitting on the bank of a river, my fingers are running through the cool green grass. In the distance, through the full-leaved trees, I can see a house on the top of a nearby hill, standing whitewashed against the clear blue of the sky.

I peer at the house looking for any signs of movement, signs of the lives being lived there.

The sound of the river drowns out all other sounds, and fills my head with its noise.

It is an English Spring day and I can smell the musty chemistry of growth and reincarnation. I pluck a stem of Wheatgrass and chew on it. Chlorophyll-laden and dew *moistened it tastes fresh and green.*

Slowly I edge my way to the very brink of the river. It is running in a torrent, violent eddies have scooped out a section of the riverbank paradoxically creating a relatively calm area of pooling, a safe harbour amongst the turmoil.

I look into this pool. Its sunlit surface gives back a clear reflection.

But I do not see my face looking back. I see a man tied to a chair, his shoulders hunched, and another man, small, wizened and grey, his face close. He is saying something, his lips are moving.

The grass in my mouth begins to feel bitter, the river begins to roar too loudly and I am sucked into the reflection. I do not want to go. I do not want to leave this safer place.

I fight against the pull but it is no good. Inexorably I am drawn into the river, slipping back, rejoining my body, feeling its pain.

I woke in a sweat, still seated on the balcony. I felt cold. The glass of wine had spilled its red contents forming a silver–black pool on the table. I got up, searched out a drink of water, took a shower and got into bed.

Tucking myself in beneath the duvet I tried to think of sweeter things, of my daughter, of Teresa, even of Samantha at "The Store".

Chapter 50

I awoke feeling dejected. I was in the middle of something I didn't understand and although I felt I was sinking deeper into it I had no idea what it was I was sinking into. I knew Dr Krai and his entourage better now but none of them had said anything at all that was of any help to me.

I breakfasted in my room on fried eggs and bacon and lots of strong black coffee.

I thought about the ship.

The occupation of most of the people I'd encountered was "retired" and although there were a few families with young children on board, a smattering of teens, a passion of singletons and honeymooners, the majority of the demographic were golden-agers, 65+ and flush with saved, hoarded, earned or pension-pot $'s.

These golden-agers must be the perfect cruise line clientele. They're unlikely to break things, too weak to fight and too tired to get too badly drunk too often. They could be expected to be appreciative of good food and fine wines, fond of shopping, being entertained and not averse to paying for the privilege.

The ship was being kept afloat by the grey dollar. It provided a sanctuary that was cheaper per day than the cost of a care home. I recalled a passing conversation with one of these grey-haired nonstop cruisers,

'I've sold the house and I'm spending the inheritance,' she'd said proudly, 'I know every ship in the line and I'm on first name terms with most of the officers and some of the crew. As long as I don't live past 97 then I'm fine. I'm 84 now.'

Or maybe I was just getting cynical, a landlubber lost at sea.

I was beginning to lose track of what was real life and what was only a distraction. Was this life on the cruise ship the real "real life" and my daughter, Teresa, and "The Store" some shades of the past or figments of my imagination, or were they the "real life" and this surreal world some form of temporal aberration.

I was out in the Pacific Ocean where you can see the weather coming from miles away. The dark clouds, the drifting mist of rain as it falls like a veil. From a distance this can look enchanting but when you reach its outer limits and begin to disappear into its dark depths it loses it's magic.

I realised I was losing the plot and had to refocus if I wanted to find out what Krai was up to. I was becoming certain he was up to something.

Gunnar called for me around 09:30hrs and we made our way to the Bridge to meet Captain Hayadal and commence our behind-the-scenes tour of the ship.

'Excellent,' he said ebulliently as soon as we arrived, 'let's get started, there's lots of interesting things I want to show you.'

We took the service elevators to Deck 4 in order to visit the largest of the seated dining rooms. The Head Waiter was there to greet us. Most of the crew seemed to originate from Thailand or the Philippines and he was no exception.

'In this main seated restaurant we have two sittings

each night, 192 waiters serving 1900 guests. The waiters work every day, there are no days off. They enjoy a 7 month contract and then a 2 month break.'

It was as if he was reading from a prepared script, heading off the "frequently asked questions" by answering them before they could be asked.

'We use a "Point of Sale" ordering system to avoid food wastage. Each individual order goes straight to the kitchen where they have control over which choices are proving most popular and manage themselves accordingly.'

His English was better than mine. I was interested but Gunnar appeared bored. We thanked him and moved on to the main galley, a huge area of stainless steel surfaces, noise and humidity.

'Altogether we serve 12 to 13,000 meals per day. Just think of the complexity of managing the ingredients,' said the Captain, 'to ensure we can cope we have 146 chefs on board who fall into a colour-coded hierarchy and each wear a coloured scarf to identify rank. Red is the highest, then blue, then yellow. Then there is a culinary team of approximately 190. We have a total of 13 galleys spread across the ship to cater for all the various eating places including the speciality restaurants, some of which we have already enjoyed together,' he smiled, he was in his element, 'there are three main galleys of which this is one. Let me introduce you to the Executive Chef.'

We walked past a huge dishwashing and cutlery cleaning operation, the rattling plates and steam precluded any further conversation until we got to a quieter area. The Executive Chef was a big Samoan-looking man wearing a red scarf. As we approached he wiped his hands on a stained cloth that hung from the belt of his white uniform. He reached out a hand. It was like shaking hands with a vice. I withdrew as quickly as possible. With one hand still slightly swollen I couldn't afford to damage the other one.

'Health and hygienic paramount,' said the Chef, 'we got 30 different work stations for meat, chicken, fish, vegetarian, desserts,' he waved at a bank of screens, 'computer breakdown what we need, how much of each food.'

He walked us around his kingdom, it was shiningly clean and we were mainly ignored as everybody got on with their allotted task.

'We spend about $37,000 a day on food,' said the Captain, 'about 15 pallets worth of provisions.'

'We're a greedy bunch,' I said.

'You question, you ask,' said the Chef as we were walking past the fruit station.

Gunnar continued his silence, seeming to just want to move on. I was more interested.

'I see you take hygiene very seriously,' I said, raising my voice to be heard above the general clatter and gesturing at the mirror clean stainless steel surfaces.

'Yes,' he said, in a voice deep enough to belong to Davy Jones and his Locker, 'we not stop. So many mouths to feed. We prepare, cook, serve, clean, we even bake own bread.'

It really was a slick operation. I pointed to someone with a very sharp knife who was preparing fresh pineapples at olympic speed.

'Wouldn't it be easier to use canned fruit?' I asked.

The Executive Chef's face changed from sunshine to thunderstorm, his eyes shot out bolts of lightning, 'In my kitchen we use fresh. Fresh, fresh, fresh.'

He fired the words at me like machine gun bullets. I was aware of the possibility that I had said the wrong thing. The Captain backed away from me. I was on my own.

'Only as last resort, very last, we lower standards so low!' said the Chef.

'Of course,' I said, deciding not to share with him my love of tinned pineapple chunks that brought back so many fond family teatime memories.

'And as one of your customers I would like to say that I appreciate your consistent attention to detail and quality.' I said instead.

His expression softened to a glower. The Captain touched my arm, 'Shall we move on?'

Gunnar smiled, at last there was something that he had enjoyed.

I thanked the Chef and retreated with the little dignity I had left. I could feel his eyes piercing me between the shoulder blades, burning me to the exit.

As we made our way down to Deck 1 the Captain said, 'It takes decades to amass the qualifications and experience to captain a $1 billion cruise ship. You've heard about the kind of contracts the crew are on, well I get home for two weeks every 3 month or so. It's not ideal but it's better than it has been,' he paused, '40 years at sea is just about enough for me, after this cruise is over I move into retirement or at best a land-based job. I want to see if I can make up for some lost time. There was so much of the kid's lives that I just wasn't there to see.'

I wanted to tell him that lost time was one of the things that couldn't be made up, but I didn't.

'Why the land-based job?' I asked, 'Do you think you'll get bored?'

The Captain laughed.

'No, Dr Anderson, I will have plenty to keep me busy. But pensions are not so large and I have been unlucky in my attempts to invest savings over the years,' he glanced at Gunnar, 'but I am trying to improve that situation.'

I wished him luck with that.

Chapter 51

Deck 1 was deep in the bowels of the ship.

'And here are the medical facilities,' announced the Captain, 'we have one full-time doctor on board, a nurse and most of the crew are trained in basic First Aid.'

He opened the door to a small airless room with a bed and cabinets full of bandages and medications. The first thing that struck me was the lavishness of Krai's facilities compared to this. One man was being looked after much better than the other 5,000.

'With the demographic of your passengers,' I said, meaning "old and infirm", 'is this really enough?'

The Captain smiled rather sheepishly.

'Probably not. We have more medical supplies in storage if the doctor needs them and, of course, we also have the morgue.'

I gave the surprised reaction he'd been hoping for. He obviously enjoyed talking about the more macabre aspects off his ship.

'People die every day, even on vacation, even on a cruise,' he said, 'sadly this happens more often than you might think. Worldwide the latest estimate I have read is about three deaths at sea per week, particularly on cruises with a preponderance of older passengers.'

'Like this one,' I said.

'Potentially. Let's keep our fingers crossed, Dr Anderson. Most of the recorded deaths are due to a sudden heart attack, something for which we don't have the depth of facilities that you would hope to find in a large hospital on land.'

He bowed his head as if in reverence to the unlucky dead.

'We can do minor operations,' he continued, 'but clearly there are limits although we pride ourselves that we have better facilities on board than a lot of the Pacific islands have available to them.'

'But you have had deaths onboard on previous cruises?'

'Oh yes, of course,' he said, moving us further along and pointing at a steel door.

'And if the worst does come to the worst then the bodies can be stored in here. This is the door to the morgue.'

It looked cold and uninviting.

'Though we don't want to store bodies for much longer than a week. For hygiene reasons we do provide body bags and as you can see the morgue is well separated from any food storage or handling areas.'

That's re-assuring, I thought.

'We've got room for up to six bodies.'

Marvellous. It was good to know the ship was so well prepared for death.

'The main problem is repatriating the bodies. A lot of the smaller ports of call can refuse to take responsibility for them and then we have no choice but to keep the bodies onboard until we reach a more accommodating off-loading point. You can imagine the effect this can have on whoever might be travelling with the newly deceased. It can ruin their holiday,' he smiled, enjoying his own dark humour 'so we have members of the crew who are properly trained in grief counselling. They try and help the friends and relatives that are on board come to terms with what's happened,' he paused, 'and they also help them through all the necessary paperwork.'

Very thoughtful.

'We tend to keep incidents like this as quiet as we possible. We don't want to alarm or spoil the enjoyment of any of our other passengers.'

"Incident" meaning death, I thought. But fair enough, after all the ship was the equivalent of a small town at sea and all life, or in this case death, was bound to be a part of it.

I thought about Krai. If his condition continued to deteriorate there was a real possibility that he would die while we were at sea. He must know that, he wasn't stupid. So what was the attraction of spending what could potentially be the last of your days taking a holiday on a cruise ship? Although with modern communications technology I was very aware that you could do almost anything from almost anywhere these days. Maybe it wasn't about where he was but rather where he didn't want to be?

The Captain moved us on again and pointed to another heavy steel door this time looking like the door to a bank vault. It was double mortice locked and only relieved from complete solidity by the presence of a window hatch which was currently closed.

'And this is the jail,' he said, 'we don't get much serious crime as a rule so it's more of a cooling-off space really.'

I opened the small hatch and peered in through the grill. There were two sets of bunk beds crammed against the side walls and on the far wall facing me was a small sink with a mirror above it and a bucket on the floor underneath. It was stuffy and sweaty and didn't look at all inviting. It was not a place where anyone would choose to spend their time.

Our next stop was the Engine Room and we had to go through a further security scan before we were allowed entry. The smell of oil and grease seemed to bring Gunnar back to life.

'To become a Chief Engineer takes between 10 and 15 yrs,' said the Captain, 'it's a combination of qualifications, experience and working your way through the ranks from 1st Engineer to 2nd to 3rd and so on.' he paused and looked at me sternly, 'By the way while you're in here, don't touch anything.'

The room was full of meters, screens, mechanical drawings and serious looking people. The Chief Engineer, a stern looking Latvian, gave us the facts,

'We monitor everything on these consoles,' he said, 'and maybe have to deal with up to 3,000 alarms a day.'

Personally, I didn't find this reassuring. Gunnar was nodding and smiling.

'We have 80 trained people including electrical, refrigeration, mechanical and all that and we work a 24 hour shift system.'

I should hope so, I thought. I didn't like the idea of the engines being left to look after themselves.

'The Nereus has 6 engines driven by 14 Megawatt generators. We only ever use a maximum of 5 engines so we always have a spare, this gives us the capability to do on-going maintenance, lubrication and repairs. Using only 2 engines we can reach a speed of 13.3 knots and consume 4 ton per hour of heavy fuel oil and diesel to do it. Our top speed is 24 knots. We have 4 stabilisers to reduce roll and bow thrusters to increase the ship's agility. Any questions?'

It was all too much for me. I didn't have any. Gunnar had one.

'How do you produce drinking water?'

The Chief Engineer smiled. Gunnar was obviously a man after his own heart.

'A good question,' he said, 'the ship uses about 900 tons of potable water every day. In order to satisfy this need we have 3 onboard water desalination systems that remove the salt and impurities from sea water by evaporation so it is completely safe for human consumption. It is one of our most important systems, we might be on an ocean but we must make sure we do not run out of water to drink.'

The Chief Engineer stepped forward and slapped Gunnar on the back and asked if he wanted a beer later. Assuming this wasn't a rather weird spontaneous gesture I took it to mean that they knew each other already.

I didn't listen to his answer.

Our next stop was the Provisions Area or store rooms. They were cavernous and for the moment were looking rather empty.

'We'll be taking on a lot of new stock when we reach Fiji,' said the Captain in explanation, 'our orders are normally placed at least 3 months in advance and we buy local produce wherever possible so we can do a little to support the countries that we visit. We have room temperature, chilled and refrigerated storage spaces and most of our inventory is delivered on stretch-wrapped pallets. Just to give you an example of our needs, we consume about 20,000 eggs per day.'

You can't make an omelet without breaking eggs, I thought, for no apparent reason. The tour was pushing me into fact overload and I was beginning to feel hungry.

Our penultimate stop was to see the windowless shared cabins that existed below the ship's waterline and slept up to six crew members at a time. They were fairly basic and I could see why working around the higher decks to avoid spending a lot of time down here had its attractions. The Captain however was keen to let us know that the crew had their own mess, their own chef and underwent training whilst onboard. They also had their own gym facilities and internet room - a real home from home if you still had enough energy after working the long hours.

And finally we moved through to the Laundry which was oppressively hot and full of heavy duty machines including 9 industrial sized washing machines taking 125kg of clothing per load that churned and steamed the dirt away. There were also 7 dryers and 2 machines to iron sheets that took 4 people to operate them. Each individual item of laundry was tagged, tracked and traced. 1,000's of pieces of clothing and bedding were handled by a smiling team of 15 people working 24/7 who were constantly on the move.

I determined never to take a clean shirt for granted again.

We returned to the Bridge and Captain Hayadal introduced us to two more of his senior officers; Staff Captain Morgan, a straight-backed American from Georgia, and Chief Officer Douglas, a dour Glaswegian, and explained that the three of them together were responsible for the more tricky ship manoeuvres including harbour docking and undocking.

The Bridge itself consisted of a large main navigation console positioned in the centre and two wing consoles located in windowed extensions that stuck out beyond the main superstructure of the ship on both the port and starboard sides and allowed an uninterrupted view towards the stern. The Captain explained that when undertaking tight manoeuvres in and out of dock steering control could be routed to either of the wing consoles and the ship driven with precision, and eye-line view, from there.

He then tried to explain in simple terms the roles of the multitude of screens on the main console that seemed to me to be displaying some kind of indecipherable constantly scrolling techno-Chinese.

The Bridge was operated by a minimum of 2 or more normally 3 people. It didn't seem enough somehow for such a big ship.

'If the Bridge is compromised for any reason,' explained the Captain, 'the ship can also be navigated from the Engine Control Room and two other locations that are confidential.'

They seemed to be prepared for anything.

He then pointed to a secondary layer of monitors.

'We have 3 Radar and VHF, HF and MF satellite Radio for communications. Here we can see anything within our vicinity to a distance of about 70 nautical miles both on the sea and in the air.'

'And underwater as well?' I asked.

Gunnar looked at me as if I was stupid.

'High frequency radio waves like those used for cell phones are disrupted through salty water. Everybody knows that. That's why we use sonar.'

It's a good job I'm not sensitive. I'm not a big fan of being talked to like a 5 year old.

Captain Hayadal must have picked up on my high frequency irritation signals because he took over the explanation.

'In the case of submarines for example,' he said in the calming tones of a peacemaker, 'they can avoid detection from the air by staying submerged at a minimum depth of about 300 feet. Conversely to communicate most effectively they need to surface. They can also communicate using special equipment at extremely low frequencies, known as ELF, because signals in these ranges can travel long distances and penetrate seawater, like the songs of the humpback whale.'

'On land Wi-Fi is transmitted using radio waves but, like your phone for example, they too drop out under water. Sound waves, on the other hand, travel well in water which is why submarines use sonar for navigation.'

It was all too much for me. My brain was now too overloaded with information to take anything else in. Gunnar however appeared to be hanging on every word with rapt attention. I smiled and nodded as the Captain concluded,

'With our quarters close to the Bridge and pagers with us at all times myself and the other senior officers can be easily contacted at any time, day or night. Finally, if you look sternwards out of these windows you can see our array of lifeboats. We carry 8 tenders, 18 lifeboats, 80 inflatable life rafts and 2 FRB's; enough to safely disembark all passengers and crew. I, of course, would be the last to leave.'

He asked if we had any more questions. I decided I should at least ask one more as a kind of 'sod you' gesture to Gunnar.

'Is there anyone occupying the jail right now?' I asked lamely.

'No,' answered the Captain, 'and there's no-one in the morgue either.'

Gunnar asked some more sensible questions. Captain Hayadal seemed pleased and answered them at length.

My stomach was beginning to ask if my throat had been cut. Our clocks had clicked forward +1 hr at midday and it had clicked onto empty.

Chapter 52

After we'd given our thanks and left the Captain on his Bridge, Gunnar escorted me to lunch. I couldn't help noticing that as a good-looking young man in his mid-thirties, with blonde hair, a lean physique and a sharp dress sense Gunnar was turning more heads than I was.

I'd suggested the simplicity of another buffet meal, or smorgasbord as Gunnar's scandinavian sensibilities would have it, and chose a piece of pan seared ocean trout with orange. Gunnar chose ricotta and spinach gnocchi with mushrooms and we each helped ourselves from the variety of side salads on offer. To drink we both picked up a glass of iced water, its value highly prized now that I understood the amount of effort that had gone into producing it.

'So you know the Chief Engineer,' I said.

'My background is engineering, so when you meet another engineer, a proper engineer, you always have something to talk about.'

I didn't want to get into a discussion about what makes an engineer "proper".

'And Sweden is famous for the quality of its engineering.'

'Of course,' he said.

It was the most in depth conversation I'd had with him so far. I was keen to keep it going.

'I've always thought that Art and Engineering are close bedfellows.'

He gave me a strange look. I obviously didn't understand.

'I qualified in Göteborg and then moved to the States to join a large petrochemicals outfit,' he said.

That was a long way from what he was doing now.

'So what happened?'

He paused before answering.

'Oh what the hell,' he said, 'I killed two people that's what happened. Or at least I was the one that got the blame for it.'

I waited, took a sip of water.

'There are dangerous jobs that have to be done on a Chemicals Plant. After a year or two I had become qualified to carry out the Safety Assessments that must be done before the more difficult jobs can be started. I was young to be given such responsibility but it was an unpopular job and I was overconfident. At that time some of the attitudes to Health and Safety in the US would have reminded you of the wild west. I carried out my assessments more methodically than most.'

I began to see what must be coming.

'On the Plant I was working on we had perpetual problems with large powder silos that blocked and with the pneumatic conveying systems that needed regular maintenance. One of the more regular problem areas was the pick-up point at the base of the silo and to overcome this in normal operation the bottom sections used fluidising air mats to try and get the powder to flow more like a liquid.'

He paused, took a deep breath.

'I'd done all the usual checks, written up the safety procedures that needed to be followed, filled out and signed all the forms and had them signed off by a more senior Safety Officer. Three Maintenance Engineers then went underneath the silo and started to take off parts of the bottom section.'

His face hardened at the memory.

'Unfortunately the level gauges for this silo were defective and nobody, including me, had realised it. A powder bridge had formed at the base of the silo making it look like the silo was empty whereas in reality there was about 50 tons still in there. When the guys starting taking off the base section the vibration broke the bridge and brought the powder, like an unstoppable avalanche, down on top of them. One of the three was lucky enough to be thrown backwards and survived, but with serious injuries, the other two were buried alive and when they were dug out they were already dead.'

'But you said your assessment had been signed-off,' I said.

'For something as serious as workplace fatalities there has to be a fall-guy and that was me. The checking procedures were then changed so that such a catastrophe could not happen again, but that didn't help me. I tried to resign but the Company wanted to show strength in response to the adverse media. I was dismissed - it was the end of a promising career.'

'But there are other jobs for engineers in the US,' I said.

'My name was put in the press and in the inquiry report. I was effectively black listed. No one would touch me. I took it to heart. I guess looking back you would call it depression. Whatever it was I didn't sleep properly for months. I just kept hearing the sound of that powder crashing down. I was too ashamed to go home to Sweden. So when the money ran out I turned my hand to anything and everything that would make me a buck, that would help me to just survive. The deeper I got in, the more impossible it was to get back. I was lucky to be rescued by Dr Krai, I owe him a lot.'

Krai seemed to make a habit of rescuing people, although always for his own benefit. Picking up waifs and strays must have proven a fast and lasting route to loyalty and I knew how important loyalty was to Krai. Gunnar's openness was unexpected, the trip around the innards of the ship must have re-opened old wounds. He'd previously been so difficult to talk to but once he'd started to tell his story it had just flowed out of him, as unstoppable as the accident itself. I wanted to appear positive, to keep on his good side, he might prove useful.

'Would you ever go back to engineering?' I asked encouragingly.

'That is my dream,' he said.

'Maybe it's not impossible.'

He grinned.

'I have the qualifications to re-enter as maybe a 2nd Engineer. I have thought about it. A life at sea has its attractions. But I have bigger plans, Dr Anderson, much bigger. The only thing I don't have is enough money to make them a reality. If you have the money then anything is possible no matter what unlucky breaks you have had in the past. I'm young enough, I have time to live at least two more lives. I want to start my own company then I can be my own boss. That is the dream.'

'I wish you luck then,' I said.

'Oh, I don't need luck, Dr Anderson, just time, just a little bit more time.'

It didn't take a genius to see that there was something more bubbling up behind these words.

'And...?'

His phone was beeping. He looked at the message, put up his hand, and pushed back his seat.

'Time to go,' he said, 'Dr Krai would like to see you.'

Chapter 53

There were parts of my life on board that were beginning to show signs of becoming routine. We ate, we drank, we talked, we exercised, we got entertained, we ate, we drank, and Dr Krai called me into his suite after lunch to distract him from his pain with my scintillating conversational skills.

Even so Krai was becoming increasingly fractious. He was off-hand with Yana when all she was trying to do was to make him more comfortable and help him manage his pain. Marte would clench and unclench his fists when this happened, his mouth set tight. You could see how difficult he was finding it to control himself. He desperately wanted to intervene in Yana's defence but she would shoot him warning glances of restraint and reassurance, her big brown eyes pleading for him to keep calm.

Krai was on his balcony sitting in his wheelchair. He turned his head to welcome me and bade me take a seat. I declined his offer of a drink.

'So, David, I do so look forward to our little chats,' he said.

I could see the pain etched in his face. I thought I could hear the irony in his voice.

'I am myself a very amateur student of History, David, but am a sceptic. Just because something is written down doesn't make it true,' he said.

'Yes,' I said, wanting to get some kind of conversation going. It was easier to talk than to cope with an awkward silence. 'The Vikings for example have had a particularly raw deal.'

'What do you mean exactly?'

'It starts with the very word "viking",' I said, 'We've even named an era after it but none of those who lived in the 8th to 11th centuries would have recognised that as their epithet.'

Krai seemed interested so I carried on. I'd done some cramming on this and didn't mind sharing it.

'The word probably means "pirate" or "raider" and it's as appropriate as calling all Romans "invaders". At the very least it's a huge simplification. We know for example that at that time the Scandinavians were experienced seafarers, navigators, explorers, traders and settlers, acknowledged for their achievements in technology and the arts. It was 200 years later that the pejorative term "Viking Age" was coined by those who had no love for that chapter in England's history and, as there was no one left to argue, it gained a lasting historical foothold.'

'History being written by the victors?' asked Krai.

'Very much so. They were violent times and there is no evidence that the Scandinavians were any more violent than anybody else. But once a myth is repeated often enough ...'

Krai tried to laugh. It hurt him '…it becomes a fact.'

'Exactly,' I said, 'and a thousand years later their tainted historical legacy becomes fodder for the Hollywood studios. In fact it was Hollywood and works of fiction that invented the myth of the Viking burial, the Chieftain's body being placed onboard a longship, launched out into the sea and then set alight by a well-placed flaming arrow. Ridiculous.'

'A shame,' said Krai, 'it would seem such a suitable way to send someone on their journey into the afterlife.'

'Yes, a romantic idea but when you actually look at it, it makes no sense. The longships were the Scandinavian's technological advantage and took time and skill to build. They were far too valuable to be wasted. There were some ship burials but these were on land and not using longships. More gruesomely, if the deceased were not cremated before setting sail the heat generated by the burning ship would not be enough to fully destroy the body and there would be charred body parts floating ashore in the days that followed. Even on land the dead were cremated in pyres before being relocated and buried.'

'David,' said Krai, trying to smile, 'you have punctured my beliefs and I thought all Historians were romantics at heart.'

'Death is rarely romantic,' I said.

'I used to fear death,' said Krai, 'the idea of my consciousness re-dispersing into the ether from whence it came. But increasingly it just feels like another part of the order of things. As I learnt how to live, I now must learn how to die.'

His face contorted as another spasm wracked his body. Yana came forward and offered medication. This time Krai accepted it almost graciously.

'It is so easy to talk about other people's death or death in the abstract,' he said, 'but when your own death is becoming more real it is more difficult. It is difficult to part with life. But I know I've reached a point of no return. I must face the fact that my death is a near and present inevitability.'

He stopped, considering whether he should go on. I tried to look encouraging.

'Would you want to face it alone, David, if you knew you would not be forgotten?'

I froze. Go on Krai, I thought, go on, tell me.

His eyes shone, focussed on infinity, staring past and through me.

'David, we must all die. Is it better that it comes quickly, as a surprise, or that you can see the end, watch as it slowly approaches? Does such knowledge not allow a degree of forward planning? Should we feel sorry for those who are diagnosed with a terminal illness or for those with no inkling of their imminent end?'

I thought of my wife and fought hard to retain my self-control. My job was to let him speak, to find out what, if anything, he was planning to do.

'We've grown used to cures haven't we? You break a leg, you catch a bacterial infection and with a cast or a tablet you're fixed. But then, when the doctors say there's no hope, you don't believe it at first, it can't be true, you don't want to believe it. It's easy to forget how recent a thing it is to have so much hope on offer. But it is not an endless supply. Ultimately there is no hope for any of us.'

He was starting to ramble. I was wondering how strong a painkiller Yana had given him. Stick with it Krai, I thought, come on, tell me something.

'Death is just another part of life. I've seen enough of it, participated in enough of it, to know that. You can only join the dots of your own life when you start to look behind you. You can only begin to make sense of it all when you look back. It is only then that you can begin to post-rationalise it as the discernible track that you were always meant to be on,' he paused, 'I've had time to look back and you know something David, I've found that there are some dots missing,' he swallowed painfully, 'and I'm going to ink them in.'

His eyes closed.

'I've made my will, my affairs are in order. Remember Dr David Anderson, "Men are only as great as the monuments they leave behind" remember that David, it's a salutary lesson.'

Was this the logical voice of a reasonable man, the rational outcome of logical thought, or were these the beginnings of the ravings of a dying psychopath who was raging against the unfairness of the coming of his night?

I didn't need to know, all I had to do was to find out what he was planning and stop him hurting anybody except himself in the process.

Listening to him had made me more worried rather than less, but I was no further forward in my task.

Krai was continuing to speak but had begun slurring his words. I leant forward to try and hear what he was saying.

'Or carpe diem, "seize the day while trusting little on what tomorrow might bring"...'

By quoting first Napoleon and then Horace it was as if he were purposely taunting me, throwing my academic backstory into my face. I must be imagining it, I thought, I shouldn't be so sensitive.

'If you knew you were going to die tomorrow,' he whispered, 'what would you do today? With your help, David ...'

Krai drifted into unconsciousness. I wanted to grab him by the shoulders and shake him but Yana intervened.

'It's best that you go now,' she said, stepping around me to tend to Krai, 'Marte will take you back to your cabin.'

'What is going on?' I said, my frustration getting the better of me.

'He's dying, Dr Anderson.'

That's not what I'd meant.

Chapter 54

As Marte was depositing me in my room I told him that I needed some exercise to clear my head. He seemed to understand and told me he'd fix it.

I sat like a caged lion. All I wanted to do was to go to the gym and I'd had to ask permission and then sit on my hands waiting my turn.

The conversation, if that's what you'd call it, I'd just had with Krai had set me on edge. I felt anxious.

It was Atu that turned up to be my next babysitter. He looked about as happy as I felt.

'I've got news,' he said, 'Dr Krai will not be hosting dinner this evening. Instead he is going to the casino early.'

As he ate so little, I thought, it wouldn't make much difference.

Atu was tall, lean and sinewy. We signed in to the gym, changed, and took to adjacent running machines. As we ran we started to build up a sweat. At least I did. When I occasionally glanced across at Atu he was jogging at about double the speed I was and I could almost taste his disdain of my efforts.

Outside the gym's floor-to-ceiling toughened glass windows the sun was sinking down a cloudless sky towards a Pacific that was living up to its name.

After about 20 minutes I could feel the burn in my calf muscles, the tightness in my shoulders, and the sweat trickling down my temples. It was time to stop. I signalled to Atu and we slowed our machines and dismounted.

Atu's innate arrogance and lack of perspiration was annoying me.

'You're a good runner,' I said flippantly, 'I guess where you come from you have to be when nobody can afford a car.'

The next thing I knew I was pinned to the wall, Atu's hand around my throat and my feet barely touching the floor. I fought back my self-defence instinct, I had to maintain my cover.

'Never,' said Atu, 'never insinuate that my people are poor. They are married to their land, they are proud in their bearing.'

His piercing eyes seemed to have taken on a cat like intensity as they flared into mine, his face uncomfortably close.

'I apologise,' I said, 'it wasn't meant as an insult.' Although clearly it was.

He tutted and threw me bodily to one side.

'I don't like you, Dr Anderson, just remember that, tread lightly.'

And I'm not a big fan of yours either, I thought.

I recovered my towel and some of my dignity. Feeling unhygienically clammy I took the change of clothes I'd brought with me and headed for the showers and changing rooms.

Without really meaning to I had confirmed a couple of things about Atu. He had a short fuse if you touched the right spot and he could act impetuously, letting his emotions get the better of him. If I could find this out so easily then so could Krai. Atu had no shortage of weaknesses for him to manipulate.

When I emerged from my cubicle Atu was already washed and changed and waiting for me. He took my bag of soiled clothes and handed it over to the staff for laundering.

'Where would you like to eat?' he asked, his calmness restored 'remember this will have to do as dinner for you.'

It was early to be eating again but there was no point arguing. To make it simple I suggested one of the open air food stations where they were serving burgers and fries and had a bar alongside.

By the time we'd been served the sun had disappeared and the early evening air was beginning to cool and freshen, becoming much more comfortable for a body like mine that was designed for the Highlands of Scotland. The artificial lights bathed us in yellow, orange and blue, blacking out the night sky that hung above us like a blanket.

We munched our way through the burgers as we talked. After all the rich fare I'd consumed there was something slightly rebellious about enjoying such simple, fatty food washed down with bottled beer.

I took a large swig from one the two bottles of beer I'd acquired and tried to relax. Atu looked at me disapprovingly.

'I do not drink alcohol,' he said, sipping at a glass of fresh lemonade.

'Shame,' I said.

I sat trying to enjoy the ambience which was broken only by the occasional over exuberant splash in the nearby pool or an Australian accented shout for 'two more beers over here mate'.

'You're in good shape for an academic,' said Atu.

Taking into account our respective performance on the running machines and earlier around the jogging track I wasn't sure whether he was being sarcastic or not. It both took me by surprise and put me on my guard. Maintaining my cover as an academic was crucial, not to say essential, to the maintenance of my health.

'I just like to try and stay fit. A healthy body means a healthy mind. You, on the other hand, look like you're built for speed,' I said.

Atu laughed, white teeth shining against his dark skin.

'It is part of my life, part of my culture. We learn to run from the day that we're born. I can run all day, for me it's as natural as breathing.'

'You're sound proud of your heritage,' I said, 'How come you've left that behind to work for Dr Krai?'

The smile disappeared. Shit, I thought, I'm not very good at making friends.

'I've done what I had to do. I do what I have to do,' he said.

I decided to backpedal as quickly as I could from talking about his past and try instead to learn something about his present.

'And working for Dr Krai, it must be giving you what you need right now.'

His eyes were like black holes boring into me.

'Dr Krai can be both a generous and a demanding man. He has given me a chance. I do what I have to do. When you come from nothing anything is better,' I wondered whether this was a veiled jab at Marte, 'But for me who came from something and had it taken away there is always the ambition to regain what has been lost, and more.'

I'd obviously touched a nerve.

'I have within me the legacy of my ancestors, of trial, of achievement, of leadership. My roots give me the confidence to grow, to reach out my hands and seek out the sun. I can almost touch it.'

I wondered what he meant but could see from his face that I was on thin ice and I didn't want to push him too far. Before I backed away completely into inconsequential small talk however, I had one more question.

'What I can't understand,' I said, 'is why Dr Krai, who is clearly not a well man, would leave the support that is at his beck and call in the States and join a cruise ship where, with the best will in the world, he is more vulnerable?'

'I think you underestimate the abilities of Dr Yana Shavi. He could not have better care.'

I decided to have one more go.

'You know what I mean.'

He paused, looked thoughtful and then said, 'I have asked myself this question. Dr Krai has done nothing like this before. In fact, in my experience, he avoids travel unless it is absolutely necessary. So, I don't know Dr Anderson, I really don't know.'

This wasn't very informative and from the sparkle in his eye I was far from convinced that he was telling me the truth, but I could see that it was all I was going to get. I rubbed at my eye and noted that the swelling was almost gone. I was running out of time.

'It's not important,' I lied, 'it's just that if he'd stayed home I wouldn't be nursing these bruises and I wouldn't be compelled to enjoy his hospitality.'

The smile returned to Atu's face.

'Look on the bright side Dr Anderson, you've got to spend quality time with me and my friends.'

I tried to return his smile. Oh yea, I thought, I was so lucky.

'Tomorrow at 07:00 hours we dock at Suva, capital of Fiji, if you intend to go ashore you must tell us,' he said looking at his watch, 'Now I need to be in the casino.'

He took out a key-card and handed it to me.

'Do you remember our previous conversation?'

'The one about swimming,' I said.

'Exactly. Then here is a test. I find it a waste of my time escorting you every step of the way. It's just not important and it's boring.'

He wouldn't be getting any argument from me.

'This key-card will open your room door, everyone that matters is already in the casino, and so my little object lesson in trust will go unnoticed. Go straight to your room, Dr Anderson, and after you've let yourself in slip this key-card back under my door. We do understand each other don't we?'

'Yes,' I said, delighted at this small break in the wall of absolute control that I'd been tethered to.

Chapter 55

Later that evening Yana was sent back from the casino to be my theatre-buddy but before allowing me into public view she wanted to check me over and so walked me down the corridor, past the door marked "Medical Supplies", and into her surgery.

I took my customary seat in the examination chair.

'I haven't had a chance to thank you,' she said as she smoothed the makeup around my now pale yellow bruising, 'I enjoyed the hot stones massage a lot more than I thought I would and it was a nice surprise,' she paused, 'how much do I owe you?'

I laughed.

'Since Dr Krai's offer of hospitality I haven't had an opportunity to spend the dollars he generously poured into my onboard account,' I said, 'you don't owe me a thing, it was my pleasure.'

'Are you sure, I'm not used to taking something for nothing.'

From the serious look on her face I could see that she meant it.

'Take it as a thank you for looking after me,' I said, 'I saw the ship's medical facilities earlier today and it's made me realise the extent of the VIP treatment I've been getting.'

She blushed a little and continued to assiduously massage my bruises with the oils she was using to hasten their disappearance. When she'd completed the task she stood back and surveyed her handiwork. I could see in the mirror that the blue-black colouring had gone and had been replaced by a fading yellow-brown.

She took down the makeup and brushes from a nearby shelf and talked as she worked.

'The swelling in your hand is almost gone. It will still be a bit stiff but that will go, just keep opening and closing your hand to help it along. You had no immediate signs of concussion and that's been confirmed subsequently by your lack of nausea or bad headaches, dizziness and so forth. The cut on your head is healing nicely and since it's under your hairline it is not immediately visible. The bruising to your face is also almost gone, you've needed less and less makeup to keep it hidden and the bruising on your body is at the same stage. Another 48 hours, Dr Anderson and I will be recommending to Dr Krai that you return to your original room.'

'A shame,' I said, 'I was starting to like it here.'

She smiled.

'Sure you were.'

Part of me was going to miss it, the part of me that wondered how the hell I was going to stay close to Krai once I'd been dismissed back to my cabin on Deck 8. It seemed a long time ago that I was there, and a long way away from where the action was.

What it essentially meant was that I had 48 hours to find out what was really going on.

'Thanks,' I said.

I glanced at her face. She looked concerned.

'Is everything okay,' I asked.

'Oh yes, as I said, everything in your case is coming along nicely.'

So it wasn't me she was thinking about.

'Oh good, I was beginning to wonder if you were holding something back. Some tropical disease I've picked up that you didn't want to worry me about because it's deadly and incurable. I know how thorough you are in your examinations and professional in your care.'

'Hmm,' she said, ignoring my attempt at humour, 'that's just it.'

'What's just it?'

'I use many techniques to manage Dr Krai's pain and one of the most effective is hypnotherapy,' she paused, 'it's probably nothing.'

From the way she said it, it was obviously something.

'Go on,' I said, 'I can be a good listener.'

'For my own improvement I like to record some of the sessions, so I can watch them back later and see what I could have done better,' she said, taking her mobile phone out of her pocket, 'Sometimes I don't hear clearly what is said, people under hypnosis can mumble or whisper, especially if they are talking about a subject that they are sensitive about. Sex is the most usual of these.'

I shifted uneasily in my seat making a mental note to avoid hypnotherapy.

'I like to try to give positive and reassuring responses even if I don't really know what was said. I can always try to make it out, if I think it might be important, when I play it back.'

I was all ears.

'Listen,' she said, making her way through the icons

on her phone to the "Recorder" app and putting it on speaker, 'see what you think.'

A voice, unmistakably Krai's, could be heard whispering incoherently.

'Can you turn the volume up?' I asked.

'That's about as high as it will go, increasing the volume increases the distortion too.'

"…and when … hear … see … done … action … not words … remembered … yes …"

'What did he mean? He's never talked under hypnosis before other than to respond to my prompts. The way he looked when he talked worried me, I had to tell someone.'

And I was pleased that that someone had been me. It was a misplaced vote of confidence on Yana's behalf, but who else was there that she could talk to? The only other person I could think of was Marte but their relationship, Marte's own relationship to Krai and patient/doctor confidence were just three of the things that would complicate that conversation.

'I don't know,' I said, 'I can't hear anything that makes sense.'

'You're right,' she said switching off the phone and putting it back into her pocket, 'I'm just being silly.'

I had been in desperate need of some kind of lead and at least now I knew that Krai had something on his mind, and that it was enough to disconcert Yana.

'I don't think you're being silly,' I said, 'Dr Krai may be fragile but …'

I was going to say 'he is still dangerous' but stopped myself just in time. I had to be careful to maintain my cover of ignorance. I was not supposed to know what Dr Gabriel Krai was really capable of.

'…but if you need to talk to somebody…'

It was a good recovery. She smiled.

'Thanks,' she said, '

It was a slim lead, some mumbled words slipping out under the influence of hypnosis. I wondered if I was in danger of making too much out of it. It was a thin thread but I had no choice but to pull on it.

The theatre was well-filled and as the lights went down I nestled into my seat ready to be entertained. Yana sat alongside me fidgeting and biting her lip. I could tell that she felt that her place was with Krai rather than babysitting me.

The act was good; a female ventriloquist. Of course if you looked closely enough you could see that her lips were moving, but the solution to that was not to look too closely.

She was a slim attractively attired brunette and the first puppet out of the bag was an old man, with glasses, white hair, moustache and wearing a dishevelled suit.

'I think my wife is trying to get rid of me.'

'Why do you think that?'

'Every time I go out she paints the front gate a different colour.'

'Oh.'

'And changes the number on the door.'

'Oh dear.'

'And she waps my lunch in a woad map.'

'She wraps your lunch in a road map?'

'That's easy for you to say …'

Life goes on, I thought. The silliness of this act was a welcome relief to the seriousness of the world I was trying to fathom.

I'd just settled back for an hour of escapism when Yana's pager began to flash.

'I'm needed back in the casino, you'd better come with me,' she said.

I had not been following Krai's nightly visits to the casino but had understood he had been winning with monotonous regularity. But you can't go on winning forever, there's always going to be a time when the cards don't fall your way. Tonight looked like it was becoming one of those nights for Krai - and he didn't like it.

I could feel the tension in the air crackling like electricity. Atu had been revelling in Marte's previous enforced absences and was standing at Krai's right shoulder. Marte was on his left and looking unhappy. Gunnar was standing further off, surveying the room.

Krai's face was impassive but as soon as he saw Yana he beckoned her towards him. The casino was pretty full and Yana had to push her way through. I followed in her wake.

Krai dropped out of the next round, discarding his hand without even looking at it. He was so thin now that his body was hanging off the metal exoskeleton like washing on a line. Yana administered an injection into Krai's upper arm and leaned in close to whisper in his ear. He shook his head. Yana retreated a couple of paces looking concerned.

Whilst this was happening Marte had taken the opportunity to pull Atu to one side and have harsh words. Whatever it was he said, with a face as dark as a looming storm cloud, it was clear it wasn't meant as a joke. Atu just shrugged, grinned and returned to his original position.

I spotted Rosa, the Head Croupier, uniformed and smart, and moved across to talk with her. She pointed to a small, plump man in a Hawaiian shirt and khaki shorts. He had taken my seat at the table, she said, and for the last three nights had obligingly lost his stake early in the game and then left the casino grumbling about the unfairness of the cards he'd been dealt.

But "Lady Luck" is capricious and tonight the cards had fallen repeatedly and unassailably his way. He'd played no better than on previous occasions but time after time good fortune had smiled upon him.

As I watched the one remaining other player dropped out leaving only the small plump man and Krai to fight it out.

I could see from the difference in the piles of chips in front of them that the plump man had the advantage.

They played for a further 20 minutes with small numbers of chips passing from one player's pile to the other's and back again, without making much overall difference to the position. If Krai was going to win this one he would have to find a hand on which he could go "All in" and win himself back into the game. Such a move was eminently possible as Krai, even with his pain as an unwelcome distraction, was the better player by quite a long way.

Finally the decisive hand came, both players betting heavily on their chances. Before the last card could be dealt, the River, Krai pushed all his remaining chips forward.

'All in,' he said.

The plump man was sweating, hesitatingly he asked for the chip count to be confirmed and sat biting his lip, trying to decide whether to match the bet or throw in his hand and give the pot to Krai. As he was up in the game he had a lot to lose as even with average luck he should eventually win by attrition. But here was a chance to finish it now. He had a good hand. Was it worth taking the risk?

He counted out the necessary chips and piled them up ready to push into the centre. But then he froze. Time seemed to slow, the seconds ticking in time with the pulsing of his temples.

'Do you want to bet?' asked the Dealer.

The man looked across at Krai trying to read the answer in his face. But he couldn't – nobody could.

'Oh, sheeet,' he said, his American drawl pronounced 'ya naw man, yar only here the once.'

And he pushed his chips forward into the centre of the table significantly increasing the size of the pot.

The Dealer completed the flop, laying the fifth card on the table. In the middle lay the 4♣, 4♠, A♥, J♦ and J♠.

Krai slowly turned his cards exposing A♣ and A♦. Pocket aces, no wonder he was confident, with the cards on the table he had a Full House of Aces over Jacks. He didn't move. He read the reaction of his opponent.

With shaking hands the plump American turned over the cards in his hand. The J♣ and J♥ showed their smiling faces making a hand of four Jacks.

His whoop of joy could be heard from one end of the casino to the other. Krai's ashen face was fixed. When the little man offered his hand he did not take it but instead nodded towards Gunnar and then slowly, mechanically, raised himself from his seat at the table and made his way out of the casino, Yana at his side, Atu one step behind.

Marte came over and nudged my arm.

'Come,' he said.

We followed Gunnar who was only a few steps behind the little plump American who paused to talk to the Head Croupier.

'Ahm a winner,' he said beaming at her, 'you make sure all mah winnings get into mah account now won't ya. Ah don't want nothing to slip away if ya know what ah mean.'

'Certainly Mr Jackson,' said Rosa, a hospitality smile on her face. She was clearly used to dealing with all kinds of passengers be they winners, losers, happy or not, 'I'll see to it immediately.'

The American wobbled with pleasure and almost skipped out of the casino.

We followed him to the elevator, took the same one and got out at the same floor. He seemed oblivious to this close attention and made his way unswervingly to the pool deck, stepping out of the air conditioned interior and into the warmth and humidity of the night.

The Poolside Bar, still busy with late night revellers, was decorated with strings of coloured lights that danced on the surface of the adjacent swimming pool. The pool had only a couple of occupants and a bored lifeguard sat at a distance looking forward to the time he could close the pool for the night.

The victorious American ordered a drink and started asking if anyone had seen his wife, he had some good news for her.

Gunnar moved away and talked to one of the members of staff, a waiter. At first the waiter seemed to be saying 'No' but after a few minutes of sharp conversation he bowed his head and Gunnar returned to stand beside us.

'Watch,' he said.

I had nothing else to do, so I watched.

It wasn't long before the waiter approached Mr Jackson. We were close enough to hear what he said.

'Congratoolations sir, I unerstan' you winner tonigh'.'

'I certainly am,' said Mr Jackson.

'You hav free drink on us. I get you champagne.'

'That's great. Bring two glasses won't ya.'

The waiter returned promptly with a bottle draped in a white cloth. He walked slowly, near the edge of the pool.

Mr Jackson came gleefully towards him.

'Excellent, excellent.'

He didn't see the person who pushed him, just at the right moment, just when his balance could be easily lost.

For a second or two there were arms flailing, grasping for purchase on empty air, eyes wide in the artificial light, and then he hit the water.

It was the deepest part of the pool, he surfaced spluttering.

'I can't swim,' he shouted, 'help, help me.'

The lifeguard rose and moved as if he were swimming through treacle.

'For god's sake!' spluttered Mr Jackson.

All of the people at the bar heard him, they could hardly fail to, and they moved en masse to see what all the commotion was about.

The lifeguard signaled to the other bathers to leave the pool and jumped in the water.

Unfortunately for Mr Jackson the lifeguard landed on top of him pushing him well below the surface. In the frantic splashing that followed it at first appeared that the lifeguard was trying to finish the job of drowning Mr Jackson rather than saving him. The poolside audience looked on in a mixture of concern and amusement and when Mr Jackson was finally heaved unceremoniously out of the pool and lay like a beached whale all pretence at concern evaporated. As he continued to splutter and gasp for breath there was little communal sympathy. His fellow passengers were more inclined to mirth than to offering the kiss of life.

'Aah nearly died,' he groaned, tears running down his plump red cheeks.

At this point a large woman rushed out of the darkness and undulated to his side.

'Georgie, Georgie, are you okay darling?'

'Aah nearly drowned,' he coughed.

Marte glanced up. I followed his gaze. Standing on the mezzanine deck that overlooked the pool area was Krai, with Atu alongside him. His face was emotionless as he watched Mr Georgie Jackson's humiliation play out.

In all probability this episode would enter the pantheon of cruise ship folklore, being repeatedly retold and embellished behind the little man's back for the rest of the cruise, with suppressed laughter his constant companion.

I could hear the whisper of the servo motors as Krai turned away and disappeared from view.

'Dr Krai does not like losing and in particular he does not like losing to a weaker player,' said Marte.

I said nothing.

'He has been let off lightly,' said Marte, obviously feeling some further explanation was necessary, 'it is only a small public humiliation. I have known times when he would not have been allowed to resurface.'

I looked at my still slightly swollen hand. To be beaten by 4 Two's must be worse than 4 Jack's but I had been taken into Krai's keeping rather than being half drowned. For the first time in my life I felt a surge of gratefulness to a dead wasp.

Marte put his hand on my shoulder.

'Time to get you back to your cabin, Dr Anderson,' he said.

Chapter 56

Sitting outside on my balcony I wondered when it was that Krai had become more hands-off and elevated himself to the position of a "desk perpetrator", a man one step removed from the dirty realness of what he actually stood for, hidden behind the pen, the screen or the word; no longer witness to the consequences of the actions he sanctioned, the fist, the knife or the gun. For him the end results were the same and it must be so much easier to give the order when you do not have to clean up the mess. From my original briefing in London Krai must be a man who understood this separation because I had been told that he still chose to step in every now and again and do his own dirty work. To keep his hand in, just so he didn't completely forget how it felt.

It had been more than 4 days since I had last checked in to "The Store" and one of the reasons for that was that I knew my room was bugged. But I couldn't put it off forever.

I turned the TV on to a music channel and turned up the volume. I took a book, "The Viking Sagas", down from the shelf, sat at the desk and started to leaf through it taking notes, bending my body over my watch. The only way I could sensibly make the call was voice-to-text from my end and text from theirs. I manipulated the 'incoming' sequence and waited until I got the 'ready' response. I spoke in a low even voice, starting with my code name,

Agaricus
Ready...

In Dr G. Krai inner circle
Good...
Dr Krai dying
Are you sure?
Sure as can be
Pause.
Is that all?
Think something else
What?
Don't know...
I thought about the hints that I'd had of large amounts of money arriving shortly.
... but to do with large amount money
??
... Nothing else
OK, keep in touch
Choice?

When the call finished I looked at the scribbled notes I'd made so that if anyone checked later they'd find something.

The sayings of Har Havamal; Eddic poetry from the Icelandic Sagas of the "Viking age"

'Animals die and friends die
And we shall soon die
But fair fame will never fade,
for him who wins it'

It was dour enough to reflect my current state of mind, the guy could almost have been Scottish. I felt I was somehow surrounded by death but of legacy I had no idea, neither for myself nor, even less, for somebody like Krai.

I found it difficult to get off to sleep. To be so close to somebody else's pending death again, to be an observer of their decline brought back too many memories and my thoughts ran away with themselves.

As a rational human being I know there was a time before I existed and although I know this and accept it logically I cannot really comprehend it. At some finite, definite moment in time my consciousness sparked into existence. But I have no memory of that and my early years are patchy and hazy. My parents remembered my early life better than I do.

I know I exist in the moment and that tomorrow I will already have only a partial recall of what I did today. In a month I will not even be able to say with any real certainty what happened when.

Existence is such a strange beast, it slips like water between our fingers. We float by each other, each in a bubble of our own being.

As we grow older our capabilities first increase and then decline and in decline we are given no more consideration for what we used to be than we gave to others when we were flushed with our own youth.

The world changes, the sharp images we can hold in our mind of places, so clearly captured in memory that we could count the bricks in the walls, are artefacts of places that no longer exist.

There are people whose faces we can recall; although their voices are vague. People who we can see at different ages in their lives, allowing them a form of time travel, their timeline scrambled haphazardly by our act of recall.

I thought of my wife when we first met, then how she looked as the cancer spread beyond her ability to fight it, then to the day she brought our daughter home, smelling of warmth and milkiness, then .....

But the world carries on, time does not stop.

I drifted into an uneasy sleep, unsure of what tomorrow might bring.

Chapter 57

When tomorrow came we had already docked in Suva, on time at 07:00 hours.

With an extended urban population of 330,000 Suva is both the Capital of Fiji and the largest city in the South Pacific. Built around a hilly peninsula, it is a jigsaw of small passages, winding streets, shops, eateries, colonial buildings, and shopping plazas busy and bustling with business suits and students, tourists and locals.

I knew enough to know that "bula" meant "hello" and that Fiji worked on "Fiji time" a more laid back version of the space-time continuum.

Although I needed to get ashore, to taste a different kind of air and clear my head, I had decided to wait until the afternoon and had booked a tour. I was banking on Marte being my unhappy companion and hoping to talk more to Yana before we set out.

I was seeking a way to loosen Marte's tongue and my plans for our onshore expedition in Fiji had a fair chance of success. If it were not for this opportunity I would have stayed on board as I had been here before and there was a slim chance of my being recognised. Getting my cover blown was the last thing I needed right now, but with the risk being so small I thought it was well worth the taking.

In the meantime I was tucking into a cooked breakfast of bacon and fried eggs, over easy, white toast and black coffee.

From my balcony table I looked out over a harbour busy with vessels of all sizes, from massive container ships to local fishing vessels. Some of the smaller vessels had ventured close to the side of the ship, so close that I could see the whites of the fishermen's eyes.

After a perfunctory knock Atu entered my suite and strode through the room and out the open glass doors to greet me.

'Good morning, Dr Anderson. Did you sleep well?'

'Very well, thank you,' I lied, 'and you?'

'I always sleep well,' he said, 'it is the sleep of the pure in heart,' he laughed but I didn't get the joke.

'I have news for you, Dr Anderson. First it is Marte who will meet you in time for your trip ashore.' He didn't seem the least bit upset. I was pleased but tried not to show it. 'Second, and more important, Dr Krai would like to see you. I will take you to him.'

'But I'm not finished my breakfast,' I said, 'Have a seat, pour yourself a coffee.'

He looked down at my half-eaten plate of food.

'Ah-ha,' he said, and reached out, taking the plate from under my nose and throwing it Frisbee-like over the balcony rail. I watched it's trajectory as it flew out and down, tumbling towards the sea and some very surprised fishermen.

'You seem to have finished now,' he said, 'let's go.'

Chapter 58

Instead of Atu leading me to Krai's suite as I'd expected he marshalled me across the ship, took an elevator down a few decks and walked me along a familiar corridor.

Jacob was there, beside his trolley of cleaning materials and fresh laundry. It was good to see him again and I couldn't stop myself from slapping him on the back like a long lost friend and shaking his hand. He smiled and I found that strangely reassuring.

'How you do, Dr Anderson?' he said, 'I keep room clean for you.'

'I do … I mean I'm doing OK Jacob, it's really nice to see a friendly face.'

Atu opened the door and ushered me in. It was a strange feeling. Even though the room was now bereft of my personal belongings I still felt that it belonged to me.

Krai was wearing his exoskeleton and standing at my balcony rail. To see him taking ownership with such indifference was like a slap in the face. Yana was nearby, paying her habitually assiduous attention to his health. She stepped towards him but he waved away the proffered medication.

From what I could see his face had more colour than the night before and he seemed more energised.

'I find logistics fascinating,' he said as I walked over to stand beside him, Atu stepping aside and taking a seat at the balcony table, 'it lies at the heart of all human endeavour. Imagine the effort, David, that has gone into deciding what is required for the next leg of our cruise, placing the orders, transporting the items from all of their various starting points and gathering them here at the right time, in this one spot.'

'Quite remarkable,' I said, not quite so enthralled.

'And then all the checking, rechecking and careful stowage. It's all so complicated yet so easily overlooked,' he was warming to his theme, 'When we leave Suva we have 7 consecutive days at sea before we reach Hawaii. Imagine if essential supplies were missed here today, there would be no easy way to overcome the omission.'

I wondered what "essential supplies" might be, something that if omitted would be more than a mere inconvenience. After fuel I could only think of alcohol and the reaction to the point of rioting of those on pre-paid drinks packages.

'I'm expecting more medical supplies,' said Yana.

Ah yes, I thought, I'd forgotten about those. Krai was looking better and acting more alert and attentive but I'd forgotten that that was only due to the judicious administration of a complex mixture of chemicals.

The dockside was filled with movement. Forklift trucks cranked pallets up and down and moved them in and out of large warehouse spaces that lined the jetty. Pallet after labeled pallet was ordered in rows and checked.

Looking down on the activity from above I could see the multitude of different colours, sizes and shapes of the boxes, bottles and crates and in some instances I could make out their contents. There were crates of fresh pineapples, boxes of bottled beer, and sacks of flour, whilst many others were hidden from clear view under a covering of opaque polythene stretch-wrap.

'Look at all the effort,' said Krai, 'I wonder how many of the passengers spare even a thought for the logistics that is managed on their behalf, the amount of work that goes into placing the many different plates of food in front of each one of them every day. Or are they content just to complain if their steak is a little overdone or their fried egg is too runny.'

I could see each of the pallets being inspected by members of the crew and then marked off and countersigned on clipboards before disappearing beneath us into the bowels of the ship.

'It's certainly a major exercise,' I said.

'It is a useful coincidence, David, that your old cabin is in such a good position to view the loading. I hope you don't mind me using it.'

'Not at all,' I said.

Krai pulled a chair towards him and struggled to sit down waving away the helping hand that Yana offered him.

'Dr Shavi,' he said, 'I'm sure that you have plenty of other things you need to do, I think it's safe to leave us alone here for a little while.'

Yana looked uncertain, but she could see that Krai wasn't. She moved slowly out of the cabin and closed the door behind her. I thought briefly about hefting Krai out of his seat and over the balcony rail, the fall to the concrete dockside would most certainly kill him. But then I looked at Atu, he would probably be quick enough to stop me. Either way I didn't do it.

Krai looked at me, as if reading my thoughts.

'My mantra has always been to never go back on a decision,' he said, 'Once you have decided on a course of action then just do it, don't question it part way through, doing that is the path to disaster, do it and then take responsibility for the consequences.'

He stopped, I felt like he wanted me to ask him the obvious question so I did.

'Is that always the best policy? Surely there are times when you embark on something with conviction and determination only to come across new information along the way, information that effects your original decision, information that necessitates a change of course,' I decided to pad my question with some of my academic homework, 'History is full of such moments, and when the information is ignored, when conviction and determination turn to stubbornness and pigheadedness, look what happens. Look at Napoleon's ignominious retreat from Moscow for example, he overstretched his supply lines and ignored the most basic of things, the weather. Look at the slaughter in Europe when the Gallic tribes failed to adapt to the Roman approach to war, not realising that passion and numbers were no longer enough.'

'There is always something that will go wrong, or someone plotting your downfall,' said Krai, 'making a change is not a passive thing, David, it is done through action, action that creates change and leaves a legacy. It's the strong that decide and do, it's the weak who decide and don't.'

'Perhaps,' I said, 'perhaps.'

'My history is not lily white, David,' I knew that that was a huge understatement, 'but the world needs people who misbehave. Where would the FBI, the

CIA, the SIS, the FSB and all the other hundreds of Intelligence Agencies be without enough suspicion to go around? Think of the unemployment. How would we know what good looks like if there were no version of bad. If there were no vices in the world, no greed, then there would be no industry, no progress. If people did not personally gain by doing what they did they would not do it, or at least they would do it very badly. And then where would we be – living in a world of lethargy that's whining its way to the grave. A purely virtuous society has only one thing to look forward to - extinction.'

A bit harsh, I thought.

'Everybody has their price,' said Krai, shifting uncomfortably, painfully in his chair, 'Take yourself for instance. You, I suspect, would do something for me if the price was right.'

'What kind of "something"?' I asked.

Was he dangling a bait? Was I biting?

'Something that most people would find impossible but is within your power to do.'

'Something illegal?'

Krai made a strangulated noise, it obviously hurt him to laugh.

'That depends on whose laws you are playing by,' he said.

'Would I know precisely the job and the risks, the possible consequences?'

'You would know as much as could be known, and I'm sure would try to guess the rest.'

'But I'm only an academic,' I said, 'what could I possibly do for you?'

Krai avoided the question.

'$50,000, how would that sound?'

'That's quite a lot of money ...'

'But less than you could win in a single night of playing poker perhaps. Hmm, yes that wouldn't be temptation enough. How about $100,000?'

This was a very strange game he was playing. I didn't understand either the rules or where the game was headed, or why we were playing it.

'Generous,' I said, deciding to play along for the hell of it. If it kept him amused and made him relaxed then maybe he would let something slip about his reasons for being on this cruise. From his obvious discomfort it wasn't for the good of his health.

'Enough to make you curious? If someone was offering you $100,000 might it make you think? Or if say, you had a daughter and she was under threat, would that be your price?'

This hit me like a blow to the stomach. I tried to hide it. Did Krai know more about me, the Mark Wilson me, than was healthy?

'Dr. Krai there are things I would do for you for nothing. I would with pleasure discuss with you the ins and outs of any aspect of the Peloponnesian wars, I would buy you dinner, I would ...'

'But if it were something you didn't want to do but could. Could you be tempted?'

I was out of my depth here, floundering. Was Krai just teasing me for his own amusement or was I being tested, probed for weaknesses, manipulated? I decided this last question deserved a serious answer.

'I accept that we are all intrinsically curious,' I said, 'it's a portion of what sets us apart, and that we are open to propositions that may be to our advantage. Any decision would, in most cases, depend on the balance of risk versus reward, your interests versus mine.'

Krai nodded.

'Good Dr Anderson, very good.'

'I don't...' I started, but was interrupted as Yana walked back into the room.

'Is it OK?' she asked, 'if Dr Anderson wants to eat before he goes ashore ...'

'Yes, it's fine,' said Krai, 'we had just finished a very interesting conversation. He's all yours.'

She looked relieved.

As I was leaving he said, 'Enjoy your time ashore.'

'Thank you,' I said.

Before I was allowed to disembark Yana touched up my makeup. I was still confused about the conversation I'd just had.

In her white lab coat Yana looked the consummate professional. In more normal day wear her bearing and self-control might be confused with that of a teacher or a lawyer if it were not for the faint smell of disinfectant that would sneak through even the floral-citrus-clean complexity of the Chanel No. 5 she liked to wear and give her away as a member of the medical fraternity.

'I'm surprised Dr Krai can spare you to look after me. I hope you don't mind me saying but although he was livelier today overall he seems to be getting steadily worse.'

I saw tears spring into the corner of Yana's eyes and wished I'd kept my mouth shut.

'He refuses help, he is increasingly pushing me away,' she said, 'and there is less and less that I can do to help him. I'm just trying to make him more comfortable, I don't have the ability to make any significant improvements to his condition.'

'How long do you think he has?'

'I don't know, but it's not long.'

Chapter 59

Marte and I took off in a taxi. The driving was as crazy, the roads as suicidally bad as I remembered them when I was last here on honeymoon with my then new wife; a lifetime ago, in a parallel universe.

Marte and I had only had a light lunch because we were visiting a tribal centre and knew we were going to be invited to dine on the local food and drink. I was keen to introduce Marte to kava, which he'd told me he'd never tried.

Fiji is considered to be one of the happiest places on earth to live and certainly you are generally greeted with a friendly smile but there are some parts of their history that are best forgotten, their tendency to eat their enemies for example.

Historically there is no written language and their aural culture is maintained through ceremonies, rituals, songs, dance and stories.

There are some big, big men in Fiji; think rugby players that you might run into but wouldn't run past. They might wear blue skirts but there is nothing about that that you would want to snigger at.

It all brought back happy memories.

Suva harbour is a hub of commercial and military activity and as our taxi drove out of its confines I spotted a couple of midget submarines as well as the more regular Naval Patrol Boats known simply as NPB's. I pointed them out to Marte.

'Do you know the clever thing?' he said.

I said I didn't.

'There is now a military design of scuba gear that has built in carbon dioxide removal and oxygen pressure balancing.'

I looked suitably puzzled.

'So now divers can operate under water for a time without producing any tell-tale bubbles.'

'Oh,' I said, probably not sounding as impressed as I should have done.

We drove out of the city and up into the green. When we arrived at our village destination the first thing we noticed was that the houses were perched on stilts.

'Bula, bula, to survive the flooding,' our guide told us, 'when it rains it does not stop. Also it protects our houses from vermin and provides a good cool place to sit and talk when the sun is too hot.'

He pointed, 'Here is our coconut tree, the tree of life that gives us food, drink, wood to build, leaves to weave into mats and baskets, and fuel to burn.'

Marte asked about wages.

'Ho, average wage is $2 American per hour and if you haven't worked you don't get benefits,' he looked up to the skies, 'but graduates, ha, they can get $15,000 a year and maybe more. I try to get a son educated, it's better for the whole family.'

Before proceeding any further he gave us each a piece of kava root.

'This is the gift that you must bring to us,' he said, 'I give to you because you do not know our ways. I tell you when to give it back.'

He then took us to the main hall where we sat cross-legged on rush matting while several of the villagers prepared the Kava ceremony. From the number of brightly dressed people in the hall it felt like we'd been joined by the entire village, all of them smiling, friendly and repeatedly saying 'bula'.

The Kava ceremony was the main reason I'd hoped that it would be Marte that was forced to accompany me and our guide had already filled us in with the required etiquette. Although focused on my task of intoxicating Marte I also kept a watchful eye on those around us, hoping I didn't recognize anybody.

Before the ceremony started I managed to take our guide to one side and talk to him conspiratorially. I pointed to myself,

'Low tide,' I said, meaning that when it came to it I wanted a half cup of kava. Then I pointed at Marte.

'High, high tide,' I said.

The guide nodded and laughed.

When told to by our guide we presented the kava root as a gift to the village chief, which seemed a bit strange as they'd only just given it to us.

The chief was a big man dressed flamboyantly in reds and yellows.

We bowed, smiled, said 'Bula' to each other and clapped hands.

The kava was then ground up with a little water being added before it was strained through a cloth bag and into a large communal wooden bowl.

I was offered the first drink of the milky brownish liquid which was handed to me in a coconut shell bowl. I clapped once, my hands cupped to make a hollow sound then I shouted 'Bula!' and drank the contents down in one. Then I clapped three times and said 'Mathe'. From the smiles on our host's faces I'd either got it close enough or was the cause of wide amusement.

Then Marte had a go.

After this the village chief took a drink and then it was offered to everyone in the room, the men drinking before the women. I remembered my wife's less than enthusiastic reaction to this 'Don't expect it to be like this at home,' she'd said.

The kava looked like, and tasted like, a bitter version of muddy water. But it was not for its looks nor its taste that it was renowned. I could feel the tingling and numbness on my tongue. The drink is a mild narcotic and after two or three "half-tides" I began to feel relaxed.

Marte was drinking at least three times as much as I was and I watched as his body visibly softened.

Once the Kava ceremony was over, the real festivities began. There was dancing and singing and I'm a little ashamed to admit that when Marte and I were invited to join in; and we did.

There was also food of course, a banquet of stir fry, chicken, rice, bread plant, and tarrow root together with fresh pineapple and bananas. We filled our paper-plates and basically chilled.

By this time I was in a state of happy unconcern, full of well-being and contentment. Conversation came in a gentle, easy flow. Our guide recited for us a traditional Kava verse,

'The day of revealing shall see what it sees:
  A seeing of facts, a sifting of rumors,
  An insight won by the black sacred 'awa,
  A vision like that of a sacred god!'

My plan for loosening Marte's tongue was working well. There was only one slight flaw. Although I had drunk only a third of the amount of kava that Marte had I was not unaffected. In fact I was feeling relaxed to the point of near unconsciousness but tried hard to retain enough of a focus to squeeze information out of the newly friendly version of Marte that swam before me, his bald head slick with sweat.

Before I could ask him anything he started to speak.

'I have never met anyone like Yana Shavi,' he said, 'she is just...'

He tailed off and then he said, 'Do you think we have a chance?'

'We all have a chance,' I said, feeling at one with the universe.

'You're a nice man, Dr Anderson, a nice man and ... when the time comes ... I want you to know ... I'll protect you ... oh yes .. I won't let Atu have his way... no, you'll be alright Dr An-der-son ...'

'Protect me from what?'

'I won't let Atu throw you over the side ... You're a nice man ... but I can't tell you everything ... Dr Krai would kill me ... he's not so ill that he would forgive disloyalty.'

I was thinking about Atu, here was confirmation that his threats were not idle ones. He obviously didn't like me, even if I was a "nice man".

'Me and Yana, we need it to work,' Marte looked suddenly alarmed, 'she doesn't know, of course, but I'm doing it for her, for us, for ...'

His voice tailed off again and he staggered to his feet.

'We'd better go,' he said, taking our guide's arm and tottering towards the taxi.

I followed, thanking our hosts and wishing them well as I went. By the look of things the party wasn't going to stop just because their guests were leaving.

Marte reached the taxi and climbed into the back seat, closing the door behind him. I looked through the window. His head had lolled back and he had started to snore.

I thanked our guide and gave him some money as a sign of our appreciation.

'Bula!' he said.

It was at that moment that I was distracted by a loud voice, a little too loud for my heightened senses.

'Mr Wilson, Mr Wilson!'

The sound of my real name sent a shiver down my spine. I glanced at the prone Marte and turned quickly, distancing myself from the taxi.

A large man was rushing towards me, his familiar face all smiles. I remembered him. He had been one of our best guides when my wife and I had honeymooned on the island. This is what I had feared. I'd taken what I thought was a very small risk but now I was in danger of being given away. I put my arm around the man's broad brown shoulders and moved him away to a safer distance.

'Mr Wilson I remember. How Mrs?'

I didn't have the heart to tell him the truth.

'She's at home,' I said, 'I'm here on a business trip, just passing through.'

We talked for a few moments. He the more animated, his torrent of words full of happier memories. Filled with kava I rolled with the flow, he was reminding me of good times. I reached into my pocket and passed him I handful of dollars.

'No, no Mr Wilson, it not necessary.'

I pressed the notes into his hand and said my farewells. I may even have given him a hug. Then I strode unsteadily to the car and saw, with relief, that Marte had not stirred.

I had been lucky, my worst fears had been realised but I'd got away with it. I was walking a very thin line and trying not to fall off.

My head was swimming in a luxurious pool of lightness of being. I was incapable of taking greater advantage of Marte's condition because mine wasn't much better and he was unconscious.

I climbed into the front passenger seat alongside the driver and said, 'Can you take us back to the ship, please.' Or at least that's what I tried to say.

As we drove back the taxi driver would not stop talking.

'I have never travelled outside of Fiji,' he said, 'I see the rest of the world through other's eyes, what people like you tell me about the rest of the world is all I know.'

'If you're happy then stay here,' I said.

He continued to press me for information and I sought in my pleasantly fogged brain for a way of describing something of my world to someone from his. It felt as difficult as trying to explain the colour red to someone who couldn't see.

'We have lots of things we don't need,' I said, 'and some things we do, the trick is knowing which is which and trying to hold on to the right ones.'

The driver looked at me.

'Bula,' he said.

I must have satisfied his curiosity because we drove the rest of the way in silence.

Chapter 60

We rumbled past the Chinese donated cement works and back towards the Nereus that loomed like a floating apartment building above the waters of the harbour.

When we got to the quayside it was bouncing with the sounds of a brass band, uniformed in dark blue jackets and white sarongs, playing live and loud. The tubas, trumpets and trombones thumped out a joyful noise, the polished surfaces of their instruments flashed in the sunlight.

Marte was still groggy as he climbed out of the back of the taxi. He tried to smile and proceeded to empty his pockets into the open hands of the driver.

'Bula, Bula, Bula,' said the driver as the notes and coins continued to come. It must have been the equivalent of at least a month's wages. I just hoped he didn't waste it.

I glanced up towards my old room and saw Krai looking over the balcony, still watching.

He couldn't possibly have been there all the time we had been away, I thought, it must be a coincidence.

As we boarded I turned around one last time to the brightly clothed people playing music, dancing smiling, waving, cheering and shouting 'Happy cruising'. In an instinctive reaction I waved back before proceeding past the less joyful faces of the onboard security personnel and on, into the artificially lit bowels of the ship.

Marte looked rather sheepish as he hurried me towards my suite. Outside in the corridor we had to make way as a trolley load of new supplies was trundled past us and into Yana's medical storeroom.

As soon as I had been secured in my luxury cell I went for a long, cool shower. The water streamed over my head, neck and shoulders refreshing and re-awakening me. The effects of the kava were only temporary and I could feel myself de-levitating, remaking contact with ground zero.

As I towelled myself dry I thought about Krai on the other side of the ship and wondered whether he really had continued to watch the loading all day, his hands hard clasped to the ship's rail for balance, waiting until the last pallet had been brought onboard and the loading bay doors clanged closed behind them.

I wondered why he would be so concerned. We had taken on other provisions at Nouméa, albeit on a much smaller scale, without him showing the slightest interest. Maybe it was boredom on his behalf or maybe the prospect of the next 7 days at sea had given him a wish to savour the stability of operations on land for as long as possible before having to leave it behind in exchange for the rolling uncertainty of the ocean.

Feeling clean and wearing a fresh smelling change of clothes I retreated to the balcony with a glass of iced water to watch as the Nereus prepared to leave the harbour.

There was something significant about this moment of departure. The gangways had been taken up, the ropes freed and reeled in, the ship's horn, sounding like the bellow of a sea buffalo, had called out its deep, resonant farewell.

This was a point of no return. There was no going back. A moment, a time had passed, what had been had been and this was a new kind of beginning – a journey into an unknown future.

Now we would exchange the elemental solidity of the land for deep water and float away on a 200,000 tonne piece of sophisticated driftwood.

Slowly at first and then faster the big ship moved away. I raised my glass,

'Good on yer Fiji,' I said, 'all the best, and thanks for the memories.'

It was almost like leaving another part of my wife behind, here where our marriage had started. It seemed like it had all happened in a separate life, a lucky dream that was never meant to last.

Now the Nereus would become my whole world for the next 7 days.

As we left the sun was setting and darkness was already creeping in. As I watched a much smaller launch came alongside and the harbour Pilot stepped briskly onboard, the launch turned and spewing a white wake accelerated away.

We are better at arriving than departing, I thought, we arrive with smiles and laughter, we leave with tears and remorse.

I turned and slid back the glass balcony door, hesitated, and then stepped over the threshold and back into the cool interior.

Chapter 61

Yana came by and led me to her surgery. Before beginning her medical ministrations she told me that Krai would be having a private dinner with the Captain that evening and that therefore Atu would be looking after me. Knowing how much Atu disliked me this was not wholly welcome news.

As I sat myself back in the all-too-familiar examination chair I asked,

'How are you today?'

'I'm the doctor,' she said.

'I know.'

She smiled and continued with her handiwork until she seemed satisfied.

'There is one thing,' she said.

'What's that? As I've said I'm a good listener.'

She bit her bottom lip.

'Well, I shouldn't be talking to you about this ...'

'I'm harmless,' I lied, 'if there's more that's got you worried why not share it? A worry shared is a worry halved and all that.'

I was doing my damnedest not to sound over-eager when what I really wanted to shout was 'Come on Yana, spill the beans!'

She walked back and forwards to her shelves and cabinets, and then she made her decision.

'It's Dr Krai's pacemaker,' she said.

'His pacemaker?'

'That's right, I've known it was there of course, just under the skin, but today ...'

'Yes?'

'Well his skin is so translucent that today I couldn't help noticing that the pacemaker had started to flash, a pale blue pulse, once every 10 seconds or so.'

'Maybe it's a sign that there's a battery that needs replacing,' I said, 'or maybe it's always been flashing and it's just that the translucency of his skin has increased and you couldn't see it before, even though it was there all the time. Could it be something like that?'

She shook her head.

'The thing is that, although I don't know all of the medical interventions Dr Krai has had, and he has had many, I do monitor his current medical condition very closely,' You could say that again, I thought, 'I measure all his vital signs regularly in order to help him manage his pain,' she paused and looked me directly in the eyes, 'I do my best.'

'I know you do,' I said, not lying at all, 'So what's the problem?'

'The problem is,' she said, screwing up her face, 'that Dr Krai may have several severe medical conditions but if there is one thing that he has got it's a strong heart ... a heart that as far as I can see ... is not in need of a pacemaker.'

'But ...'

'Exactly.'

Atu, bless his cotton socks, came lumbering in at this precise moment making no attempt to hide his displeasure. I did my best to hide mine.

'Let's go,' he said, almost dragging me out of the examination chair.

My conversation with Yana would have to be continued another time and as soon as possible as far as I was concerned.

Marte's enforced absences had opened the way for ambitious Atu to wheedle himself closer to Krai, an opportunity that he was aiming to make the most of. Now that the shoe was on the other foot, however temporarily, he didn't like it, for him the sands had shifted in his favour and he had no intention of letting them drift back.

He marched me down to the all-day buffet.

'We'll eat here, and quickly,' he said.

He didn't eat. I filled my plate slowly and followed behind him to an empty table. He sat watching me. If he could have grabbed my knife and fork and force fed me he would have done it.

As I opened my mouth to speak he lost his patience, his black face showing his agitation as he leant far too close to me and growled,

'I know who you are!'

This was an unexpected turn. Had my cover been blown? I tried to remain calm.

'Yes?' I said, expecting the worst, hoping for the best.

'You're a pompous academic that talks too much, eats too slowly and asks too many questions. That's what you are!'

If there were points out of 10 for accuracy he wouldn't have scored past a 5. I almost smiled in relief.

'Sorry,' I said.

He glared at me, 'Are you finished?'

I wasn't.

'Yes.' I said.

He took the key card out of his pocket and threw it at me.

'See yourself back,' he said.

I didn't know where everybody else was but I knew they couldn't be in their rooms. Wherever they where Atu was desperate to join them.

As I entered the corridor I saw that the door to the medical storeroom was open and that more fresh deliveries were being taken inside.

I skipped past the metal trolley and locked myself obediently in my room.

Chapter 62

Not yet ready for sleep I sat nursing a not-very-good blended whisky from the mini-bar.

Although he had appeared more alive today it was clear that Krai was fast approaching the end of his life. As a boss he must have got used to living with a target on his back and maybe that was the reason he had taken this cruise, to distance himself from those at home that would otherwise be gathering around him like vultures. All he really had left was the opportunity to try and die in peace.

With such happy thoughts swirling around in my head I felt the need to talk to somebody, to make contact with another human being, one that I cared about. Despite the risks I decided to call my daughter.

In order to minimise the chances of the surveillance equipment picking something up that might cause concern I turned on the TV and hunched over my notebook. Hiding my watch from view I put through a voice activated call. Unusually for her, she answered straight away.

'Dad?'

'Hi,' I said, in as light a tone as I could muster.

'What's wrong?'

Could she instantly tell or was it just that I rang so seldom?

'Nothing's wrong,' I lied, 'I was just wondering how you were doing.'

'I'm doing just fine, where have you got to now?'

I told her.

'Sounds great.'

'Yeah great. And how is life with you?'

'Oh you know, busy with ...'

I basked in the sound of her voice, letting it wash over and through me as she related the minutiae of her life. Every now and again I contributed a 'really?', or a 'really!', or occasionally a 'really' of support and encouragement. It took me by surprise when she fired me a question,

'...so that's about it, my life in a nutshell. Now, why did you really call?'

I had to think fast. I could say 'I just wanted to hear your voice', or 'I'm a bit worried', or 'I love you'. I made the choice quickly, without thinking it through, and said,

'We'll eventually dock in Honolulu and I was just wondering if we could meet up for a day or so before I fly back to the UK?'

There was an uncustomary silence at the other end of the line, and then she said,

'Are you sure you're OK?'

As if it were unusual for a father to want to meet up with his daughter - kids!

'Well, if a father can't want to meet up with his only daughter without ...'

'OK, OK, don't get all het up about it. Of course I'd like to see you. When and where do you dock?'

I told her.

'OK, I'll look into my schedule and change it around if necessary. If you don't hear from me then assume I'm going to be waiting for you when you disembark,' she paused, 'with my arms open and tears in my eyes.'

Kids can be so lovably sarcastic.

'Let's not go too far,' I said, thinking she could probably hear the smile in my voice.

We finished the call soon after that with the usual platitudinous pleasantries.

It was only later, when I thought about it properly, that I realised what I'd actually managed to achieve. If Krai was planning something on arrival in Hawaii, which was logical, then I'd just invited my daughter into the danger area - and she'd accepted. The words "bloody idiot" sprang to mind and I made a note on my watch, for the day before we were due to arrive in Hawaii, to contact my daughter again and call off the meeting with some excuse that I'd manage to concoct in the meantime.

I also made a mental note to just answer a simple question truthfully, rather than trying an off-the-cuff answer designed to sidestep it. It would have made life so much easier. I now had a new self-created worry to add to my load.

To cheer myself up I decided to listen to some music on the mp3 player Yana had supplied me. But the fates conspired against me and the shuffle function delivered up Garth Brooks singing 'If tomorrow never comes'.

They say that music helps to calm the soul - this didn't.

Outside my window white lightning forked across a darkened sky, signalling a storm at sea. I counted... one.... two ... three - the air carried the low, deep, thunderous growl, more present, more immediate than the lightning. 15 minutes later the ship and the storm met and the rain was beating at the balcony windows.

Lying inside in the dark I was an observer to the scene, insulated from the storming elements that thrashed around me. I was an audience member, pampered and protected, safe and secure.

Maybe it was time to take away the protection.

I got up, slid open the glass door, stepped outside and let the wind pound me, the baptising rain soak me from head to foot.

Chapter 63

By the next morning the storm, a stark reminder of the power of the elements, had passed over and it was a clear blue day. I again took my breakfast out on the balcony. I was becoming boringly predictable.

I sat sipping coffee, gazing out across the rolling calm, looking out at nothing in particular, my eyes focused on the middle distance. I was in a mental no-man's-land of reverie when the first of the debris floated by.

It was a few moments before it registered. Corrugated metal sheets, wooden slats, palm fronds, plastic drums, mats of green and brown detritus brought together on the undulating swell. I wondered whose homes these had been a part of, what storm had broken them and carried them away.

The debris floated quietly past like a parade of destruction. It had taken me by surprise and I watched as it passed, mesmerised.

When Marte came to collect me he was notably silent on yesterday's shore excursion and seemed keen to drop me in front of Krai and then leave.

Krai sat in his wheelchair looking skeletal, but strangely energised, as if he was anticipating something important. I told him about the debris I'd seen floating by.

'People have a false sense of stability,' he said, not at all reassuringly, 'have you ever experienced an earthquake first hand?'

I said that I hadn't.

'All of a sudden the ground that you are standing on begins to tremble, the land on which you have built your home, the fields that you have tilled and harvested begin to shake, to move and slide beneath your feet. Fear is immediate and intense, there is nowhere to run, no safety in standing still. Homes that have always been a haven are now potential death traps as their structure shakes and crumble. Concrete slabs crash into the street, indiscriminate in their collapse onto living things. Bridges twist and fall, holes open randomly swallowing the unlucky.'

'It makes you aware of your mortality,' I said.

'Yes,' said Krai, 'our time is used up second by second, minute by minute, we don't get to go back and use it again or do it over differently. But of course in these days the rich can live longer than the poor, it's not the case that each human life has the same value. When it comes to it show me someone who would not value their own existence above that of the general populace, who would not use whatever they had or could find, steal or beg to live longer, and I'll show you either a liar or a fool!'

'I have amassed money and lots of it, enough for several lifetimes. It'll be no use to me when I'm dead. I have paid for the best care, medicines and technology to keep me awake for longer, before the last sleep.'

Krai was getting breathless and Yana wheeled over an oxygen cylinder. Krai put the mask to his face and breathed deeply, his face contorting with the effort. No matter how much he'd spent it looked like there wasn't much life left.

'What you see before you is the result of all of these endeavours,' he said, 'I have had at least 5 more years than was due me. My organisation still functions with me at the head, my key lieutenants still follow my orders.'

He was starting to talk more loosely although his self-control was holding, at least for now. I looked at the old, wizened man in the wheelchair, oxygen on tap, painkillers; somehow he still had the power to make me feel vulnerable.

'There is one last thing about my own time,' he said quietly, 'and that is that technology allows me to choose how and when it ends.'

I could feel the hairs on the back of my neck stand on end. I said nothing. I was content to let Krai continue to ramble.

He breathed deeply and waved away Yana's further offers of assistance.

'Do you know what it is like to feel no guilt, David? It feels free, it feels liberating. There are so few of us that can say that.'

'To feel no guilt is to stand out from the crowd, to feel nothing for others or for anything, to be alone by choice. If you do not have this virtue you cannot comprehend it, it is something beyond, outwith the human spirit. I feel no guilt David, none whatsoever.'

This was something completely contrary to my experience. For me the memory of past action, or chosen inaction, haunted my sleep. I could not escape my guilt, it bit deep and returned over and over again, a constant reminder of past transgressions - the reasons I was not heaven bound.

'You're right, Dr Krai,' I said, 'that is something I cannot comprehend.'

Krai gave a thin smile.

At this point Gunnar entered and asked if I was ready for lunch. I couldn't leave fast enough.

Chapter 64

Over lunch I was very quiet and Gunnar decided to fill the vacuum. He had already established his tarnished credentials as an engineer and now wanted to show me his wider intellect.

'It's interesting how tastes change,' he said, 'how someone's or something's reputation can transform over time.'

I wondered whether Gunnar was thinking about the recovery of his own reputation.

'Engineering is as much an art as a science,' he said, 'and I am an enthusiast for Swedish art.'

'Really,' I said, trying to sound interested.

I was happy for him to talk, it was a big change from our first meeting. The more I knew about Gunnar the less I understood him. He was young and impetuous enough to get himself into trouble. Being over confident and under prepared is a deadly combination.

'Great art is born out of adversity, Dr Anderson,' he continued, 'and in Sweden adversity produced one of our greatest artists.'

'His name is Carl Larsson and he was born in Gamla Stan, or what you would call the "old town" area of Stockholm. His parents were poor, his childhood unhappy, living in filth and disease, together in one room with his mother and brother and another three families. However at the age of 13 his talent for art was spotted during his time at the school for poor children and, almost miraculously, he was accepted into the Royal Swedish Academy of the Arts.'

Gunnar paused to see if I was still listening. I nodded encouragingly.

'He of course was completely out of place, he struggled, later moved to Paris, married and moved back to Sweden to start a family, and found to his own surprise that it was his paintings and prints of his own daily life that finally brought him to prominence and financial security.'

'Now he could think of his artistic legacy and it was his monumental works that he wanted to be remembered for, in particular a 6-by-14-metre oil painting that he was commissioned to prepare for a specific wall in the Swedish National Museum in Stockholm.'

'He completed the work in 1915 when he was already 62 years of age and suffering from declining health.'

'The painting, called "Midvinterblot" or "Midwinter sacrifice", depicts a scene from Norse mythology in which the swedish king Domalde consents to be sacrificed to the gods in an attempt to avert a famine that is endangering his people.'

'The painting was rejected by the museum even though it was they who had commissioned it.'

'Larsson was angry and predicted "that this painting will, one day, when I'm gone, be honoured".'

'And he was right. Tastes and decisions change over time and in 1997, 78 years after his death, Carl Larsson's painting was procured to hang in the space for which it was originally intended. It hangs there still and is now lauded as one of Sweden's most famous and accomplished works of art.'

'It's a dangerous thing to predict the future,' I said, 'having such confidence in his own work could be construed as simply arrogance. Although it's a shame he did not live to see that he was right after all.'

'And the subject,' said Gunnar, 'a leader who secures his own place in history by sacrificing his life for his people's. He knew he'd left a great legacy, it was time that had to catch up with his judgement.'

I'd often wondered what the benefit was of being lauded after you were dead. Works by Vincent Van Gogh that received at best a lukewarm reception when he was alive are now trophy pieces for billionaires commanding prices of hundreds of millions of dollars. What good has that done him - he committed suicide whilst living in a medical asylum. I'd rather be less ambitious and make a bob or two while I'm still around to enjoy it.

As we returned to my room I noticed that the door to Yana's medical storeroom was ajar and I glanced in. Something took me by surprise.

I waited until Gunnar had gone and then put my ear to the cabin door. When I was as sure as I could be that the corridor was clear I used the key card that Atu had given me the day before and let myself out.

There is always a chance your actions will be caught on camera these days. Surveillance cameras, CCTV, and every smartphone can potentially capture images that you would prefer they didn't. It's getting more difficult to get away with anything. I kept to the side and tried to tread carefully.

While I'd been waiting someone had closed the door to the storeroom. I tried Atu's key-card hoping it was a "Master".

The door clicked open and I went in.

The whole of the day before the crew had been loading and distributing fresh supplies, I knew Yana had been expecting additional medicines so there was no reason to be suspicious – but I was.

I switched on the light and started to look around.

The whole place was like an Aladdin's cave of bottles, boxes and medical equipment but it was directly in front of me that the wooden crates that had attracted my attention were stacked.

I went over to inspect them more closely.

There were six of them and their sides and tops were heat stamped with "Fijian Pineapple Rings" and "Bula Bula Brand". I remembered very clearly the chef's aversion to canned fruit and had never come across tinned pineapples being referred to as any form of medical treatment!

The lid of the first crate was loose, presumably removed for inspection. The wood was cheap and coarse so I wrapped a handkerchief around my hand for protection and removed the lid.

Inside the case were layers of greased packing material, unusual for tinned pineapples. I moved these layers carefully to one side and began to uncover stocks, barrels, and magazines. It was easy for me to piece the parts together in my mind and make out the weapons they would become when they were assembled.

I stood back and tried to take it in.

The parts belonged to the AKM, a development of the ubiquitous AK 47, a gun I was very familiar with.

Designed by Mikhail Kalashnikov it entered service in 1959 and has been in use ever since with over 10 million produced to date and rising. It is easy to assemble and disassemble and weighing in at only 3.4kg including a fully loaded 30 round magazine, is easy to handle. Capable of firing 39mm M43 cartridges at a semi-automatic rate of 40 rounds per minute and a velocity of over 700m/s it is a highly effective weapon. I knew my guns and this was a good one.

Even disassembled some of parts were too long for the crates and the barrels sat diagonally, poking an accusing eye in my direction. From the number of crates and the way they'd been packed I estimated there were enough parts to fully assemble 20-25 AKM's.

Shit, I thought, shit, shit, shit.

I replaced the parts, greased packing and the lid of the case as quickly and neatly as I could and then slipped out and returned to my room.

This discovery was far too important not to risk an immediate call to "The Store".

I went into the shower room, stripped off and turned on the water, setting the temperature to maximum. The small room was soon fogged as well as noisy.

I put in the call.

'Guns,' said Samantha, 'not unexpected I suppose. A man like Dr Gabriel Krai is unlikely to want to be without firepower. But why wait until Fiji? Why not just smuggle them on board right from the start?'

I had no answer to that.

'I'm going to talk to AB and get a decision on what we do from here,' she said, 'In the meantime stay vigilant and don't do anything stupid.'

I treasured her faith in me.

'Remember you have the authority to act. But only if there is imminent risk to life.'

Whose life, I thought, does it count if it's mine?

I told her that under these circumstances it was impossible to say when I could call in next. She said that she understood that, but not to leave it longer than 24 hours.

She had a way of making it clear that this was an order not a request. Her voice hardly changed in tone or level, but I got the message.

Chapter 65

I'd just got dressed when Marte entered my suite. He carried a large linen laundry bag which he laid over the back of a chair. Then he turned to me. He didn't look happy.

'Oh dear, Dr Anderson,' he said, 'Oh dear.'

I asked him what he meant and he held up my handkerchief. In my haste I'd obviously left it in the wooden packing case.

I could try to deny what I'd seen, but I could see from Marte's expression that it was already too late to try something like that.

'Why do you need so many guns?' I asked instead.

'You know you are always full of questions. It's not good for you. We all live by trust, Dr Anderson. When we buy a bottle of wine we drink it, we assume it's safe, we trust that all the people that have been involved in its manufacture and bottling have done so in a way that's not going to hurt us, we trust that not one of them has chosen to poison it, that all of them have carried out their tasks hygienically, competently. It makes you think doesn't it, how much we take for granted, how much trust we put in unseen, unknown others. But sometimes, Dr Anderson such trust is not justified. I am sorry to say that this is one of those times.'

I felt like I'd let him down. But what I'd actually done was uncover danger. I'd done my job, although unfortunately I'd got caught.

Marte reached inside his jacket and pulled a handgun from a holster couched under his arm. It was a Glock.

'For Dr Krai trust is the same as loyalty, and you know how he hates disloyalty.'

Marte calmly reached into a pocket took out a silencer and screwed it to the end of the barrel. He'd come well prepared.

'I know what I should do,' he said.

I'd been caught through my own stupidity. I deserved everything I got.

He raised the gun and fired twice.

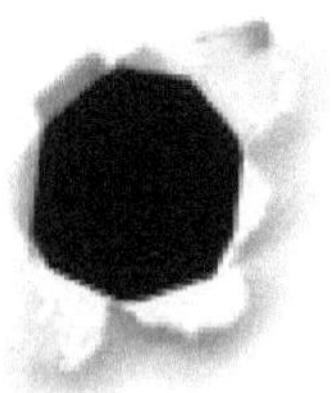

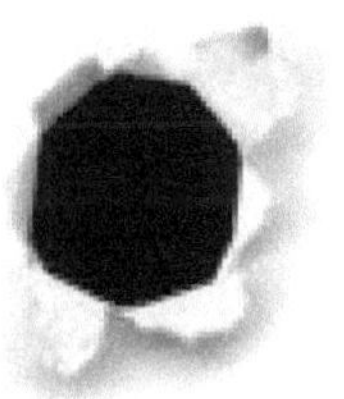

The two shots blasted into the pillow that lay on my bed.

Marte went over to inspect the damage and fired a third shot at closer range.

'You know you should be dead,' he said, 'so I expect you to be grateful and play along.'

I didn't know why I hadn't been shot. Marte read the question in my face.

'I've got enough on my conscience to last a lifetime and I would have to explain what I'd done to Yana. I'm not sure I could do that.'

He reached into the laundry bag he'd brought with him and withdrew a wine bottle full of a deep red liquid.

'Ox blood,' he said, 'there's plenty in the kitchens. Now stand aside.'

I obeyed.

He poured the blood over the bullet holes and surrounding area and then dripped a trail out onto the balcony and up onto the balcony rail. He then returned the empty bottle to the laundry bag and reached up to the top shelf of the wardrobe to pull down spare pillows which he stuffed into the bag.

'It needs more weight,' he said and moved to my bookshelf.

I watched as the Gallic Wars, Icelandic Sagas and even Marcus Aurelius disappeared into the sack. I felt like I should protest but realised this wasn't the time.

He hauled the bag onto the balcony, smearing the trail of blood as he went.

'Come and help,' he said.

Together we hefted the bag and flung it over the balcony rail. It's not many people who get the chance to help throw their own body into the sea.

The bag twisted and flapped as it fell, turning over and over. We watched as it hit the ocean surface many feet below. It sank quickly and I imagined it slowly descending through the blue then black depths finally settling more than 2 miles beneath us on the ocean floor.

Marte went to the door and checked the corridor.

'Let's go.'

I picked up my jacket and prepared to follow him.

'Surveillance?' I said.

'All that I have access to has suffered a temporary fault. Now move.'

He was nothing if not thorough.

Chapter 66

'You're a lucky man, Dr Anderson.'

We descended into the bowels of the ship. The lower we went the sorrier I felt for myself. There didn't seem to be anything I could do. I thought of running but the problem with a cruise ship is there's nowhere to run. At least I still had my watch and with that the chance to communicate to "The Store".

Exiting the service elevator at Deck 1 I could guess where I was being taken. Marte walked beside me holding my arm in a vice-like grip.

We walked past the medical room and then the door to the small morgue. I was relieved not to be going in there.

When we reached the jail the door was open, the key was in the lock.

'Please,' said Marte, motioning for me to enter.

The room was small and bathed in yellow artificial light, the atmosphere was claustrophobically close and the smell was of other people's urine.

There were the two sets of bunk beds and against the far wall the sink with a mirror above and the galvanised bucket below that I remembered from my earlier tour.

'What's going on,' I asked, 'why all the fire power?'

'Have you ever done anything you regret?' he said.

I could think of about a thousand things just off the top of my head.

'Yes.'

'Well, I've made a lot of mistakes, some I try very hard to forget.'

I knew what he meant.

'But now it's time I made a change. I don't know how much you know about Dr Krai but some of it is dirty work.'

I tried to look surprised.

'By a combination of bad luck but mainly through bad judgement I have nothing put away,' he said, 'no money, nothing to see me through a rainy day.'

I tried to look sorry for him.

'So this is my pension,' he said.

'What is?' I asked.

'Dr Krai is very ill, close to death, without him at the helm god knows what will happen to the rest of the organisation. I have protected him physically but he has protected me, without him ...'

'I still don't see...'

'At this late stage, when there's nothing you can do about it, I suppose there isn't much reason not to tell you.'

He paused.

I waited.

'The day after tomorrow we're going to take over the ship.'

I held my breath.

'By that time we will be 400 nautical miles from the nearest land and sitting on top of more than 3,500 metres of water. Dr Krai has worked everything out to the smallest detail, he always does, that's what he does best. I've worked for him long enough to know that. Everything is pre-planned. We're going to take over the ship. It's going to be the biggest hijack in history. And it's going to cost somebody $1bn.'

My mind was racing to try and catch up – and failing. It seemed an impossible idea and impossible to get away with.

'But why?'

'A challenge, doing something that's never been done before, the notoriety, who knows? All I know is that this is the biggest thing he'll ever do.'

Krai's legacy, I thought, the thing he wants to be remembered for. It made some kind of perverted sense.

'But he's dying.'

'Maybe that's why, it's now or never.'

'But it's impossible! You can't hijack a cruise ship, collect $1bn to release it, and then get away scot free. It's just crazy.'

I was letting my emotion show.

'How much is a life worth?'

'What?'

'How much is a life worth? The ship is worth half a billion dollars at least and there are 5,000 people onboard, how much are they worth? I think you'd value a life as being worth more than $100,000 wouldn't you? The mathematics seem very reasonable to me. And what about the value of avoiding the bad publicity, how much is that worth?'

'And if they don't pay up?'

He moved his arms in an upwards gesture.

'Boom,' he said.

'Boom?'

'There are also explosives on board.'

I just couldn't believe we were having this conversation.

'OK so you've got guns, let's say you gain control, let's say you negotiate a deal, let's even say it's paid into some offshore account that's immediately laundered, you're still on a cruise ship in the middle of the Pacific for Christ's sake, how do you get off?'

His calmness was winding me up.

'A helicopter would be tracked, a boat would be tracked ...'

I stopped, my own logic had given me the answer. I remembered a conversation from the Bridge. It had to be something that was difficult to follow. It was hardly credible.

Marte smiled as he saw my penny drop.

'A submarine!'

'I can't say,' said Marte.

'Where, how, when ...'

'I told you Dr Krai works everything out beforehand. He only tells me what I need to know.'

'So you don't know it's a submarine?'

'I have a brain Dr Anderson and I've had a long time to consider,' he shrugged, 'that's enough for me. The rest is trust in Dr Krai and doing my job. It's been a winning formula up until now.'

The shock of receiving this information dump after trying so hard to find out what was happening and getting nowhere was hard to cope with. Was there still time to do anything to stop it?

'Why are you telling me all this?'

'The first reason is because you're already dead, the second reason is that if anyone discovers you're not you soon will be, and the third reason, Dr Anderson is that I figure that if an intelligent person like you knows the seriousness of the situation he's in then he'll sit tight and not make a fuss.'

Self-preservation, it's a strong motivator.

'And if I behave.'

'Then when we've left the ship you can be found and released. In the meantime you'll be fed and the cell will be periodically cleaned,' he pointed to the bucket. I was in for an uncomfortable time surrounded by my own smells.

Marte left the cell pulling the heavy door closed and locking it. He looked back at me through the small grille.

'Just remember, Dr Anderson, you're a lucky man, a very lucky man.'

He drew the hatch closed and I could hear his footsteps receding as he walked away.

Chapter 67

I went to the washbasin and splashed my face in cold water. The mirror above it reflected back a worried face.

Taking my watch from my wrist I thought about how I was going to explain the situation succinctly and then attempted to make the call.

There was no signal.

I tried several times, with increasing frustration. This far down in the ship's hull and surrounded by metal walls, I couldn't pick up a signal. The cell was operating like a faraday cage rendering any communication device that depended on a radio signal useless, absolutely useless.

I returned the watch to my wrist, snapping the catch on the stainless steel strap back into place. I felt impotent.

Now all I had was time to kill.

Sitting on the lower bunk I tried to think.

Hijacking a cruise ship! It would get Krai the worldwide attention he was after, but how would he pull it off?

Why had nobody hijacked a cruise ship before?

Because it's almost impossible, I thought, that's why. I tried to compare the difficulty to that of an airplane hijack.

On an airplane, even a super-jumbo, there are 5-600 passengers and they're all strapped in. On this cruise ship there were 5,000 passengers and crew all largely uncontrolled and free to move around up to 14 Decks and tens of different locations.

The crew on an airplane, including the pilot and flight deck, number less than 30, on the Nereus it was more than 1,200.

The accessways on an airplane are narrow corridors that run between the seats, easy to monitor and control. On a cruise ship the movement areas are complex, spread out, making them difficult to monitor and almost impossible to control.

On an airplane a minority of passengers at any one time are out of their seats to go to the toilet or stretch their legs. On a cruise ship thousands of people are moving about between restaurants, bars, theatres, lounges, shops, spas, swimming pools or their separate rooms.

On an airplane a handful of determined armed hijackers could provide a realistic threat of freefall by threatening to shoot the pilots, destroy the flightdeck controls or blow holes in the fuselage, enough of a deterrent to keep most people behaving themselves. On a cruise ship you'd need an army to take over from Bridge to Engine Room and amongst the 5,000 passengers and crew it's inconceivable that there aren't at least a handful of "heroes" who would make life difficult for the hijackers. In addition, as the ship could be controlled from 4 different locations, two of them "restricted", it would be difficult for the hijackers to know if they'd really taken over absolute control of the ship or not.

It was also likely that there were a limited number of guns or other weapons onboard available to selected crew members trained in their use, weapons that could be issued quickly in an emergency.

And lastly, but not least in importance, on an airplane the availability of the means of communication to the outside world was limited and almost controllable. On a cruise ship the multitude of mobile phones, tablets, laptops, PC's and ship's communications made uncontrolled communication to the outside world almost a certainty. The presence of 42 different nationalities from American to Chinese, Malay to Russian made onboard communication control impossible. From uncontrolled communications followed the inevitability of attempted rescue missions.

I'd instinctively thought that hijacking a cruise ship was a crazy idea and now I was sure of it. Krai might be a psychopath, but he was not crazy. He would get his moment in the world's media spotlight but he couldn't possibly get away with it.

Or could he?

Whatever the truth the world was going to know in less than 48 hours.

Chapter 69

My night's sleep was a troubled one, a jumble of thoughts tumbling together.

Even if I could communicate with "The Store" I couldn't see a way that the attempted hijack could be prevented. There wasn't enough time.

Lying on my back on one of the hard mattressed bunk beds, using my rolled up jacket as a pillow, I tried to think through all that I thought I had learnt over the last few days. Krai must be doing this for the notoriety – a final fling ... his legacy ... doing something that had never been done before ... something he would be remembered for ... snapshots of conversation floated through my mind ... circling ...

...legacy...   ...death...   ...pain...

... pacemaker ... taking action ... decision ...

... all day watching the loading ....guns...

...explosives... ...instability at sea...

...Napoleon ... Caesar ... vikings ... history...
making your own legacy

... explosives

... death

making your own legacy ... explosives ... death

I stopped thinking and just tried to calmly put the pieces together.

It was an audacious plan for somebody with not a lot of life left in him, someone who wanted to be remembered, to leave some kind of lasting legacy, someone who was interested in history and in human nature. Someone who felt no guilt ...

Hijacking a cruise ship **was** a crazy idea.

I sat up with a start.

Krai wasn't going to hijack the ship. He was going to sink it!

Oh shit, oh shit, oh shit!

I knew I was right. Krai was a psychopath. Why else would he take on the discomfort of a voyage at sea unless he had a very good reason. He was dying and he knew it. He wanted to be remembered. It would have to be something big. Escaping with $1 billion to share around his entourage and then finding somewhere to curl up and die didn't fit. Blowing up a cruise ship and taking 5,000 people with him did!

I had to get out of this cell and bet my life, and I knew I would be betting my life, on proving it.

The only way I could possibly convince anybody was to confront Krai and hope that his arrogance got the better of him.

But I had to get out of here. If the ship went down and I was still sitting in here I put my chances of survival at zero, or less.

I took off my shoe and started hammering at the door with my heel. The sweat rolled down my face and back. Eventually the grille slid open.

'You must stop that.'

'I will if you just ask Jacob who was looking after me in cabin 8136 to come here immediately and talk to me.'

'I know who you mean, but why?'

'I've just remembered something I gave to him and I want to know what he did with it,' I lied, 'It's very important. I'll give you $100 if you do this for me.'

I returned to my jacket and took out a single $100 bill. I held it up for him to see and his brown eyes opened wide.

'Give,' he said.

'When you bring Jacob.'

The grille slid closed.

I waited.

Chapter 69

I could hear footsteps approaching. The grille slid open. I could see my new friend with the brown eyes and Jacob standing beside him.

'Here is Jacob.'

I rolled up the $100 bill and pushed it through the grille. Brown eyes inspected it, grinned and left.

'What you leave with me?' asked Jacob.

'It's OK Jacob, I didn't leave anything with you. I want you to do something for me, that's why I wanted to talk to you. I had to tell your friend something to get him to bring you here.'

Jacob scratched his nose, looking uncertain.

'Listen I trust you Jacob, I want you to go and bring somebody to talk to me.'

'Who?'

I described Marte, 'Do you know him?'

'We all know,' said Jacob, 'all crew know, we see, we talk about, he big strong man.'

'Go and tell him to come here,' I said, 'you can get near him easily, pretend you've come to clean the room. He'll be on Deck 14, Suite 1402. If he isn't there please find him, if you do this for me I'll give you $300.'

'Yaa, you want to talk bad.'

'Yes I do, it's very important, and here, give him this, to show I've sent you.'

I removed my watch and passed it through the grille.

Jacob turned and walked away, taking my future with him. I watched his retreating back until it disappeared from view.

I had to convince Marte that sinking the ship was Krai's real purpose and not just a mad ruse of mine to get out of jail and create trouble. I knew his weakness and I had to play on it.

20 minutes later Jacob had been paid his $300 and Marte was in the cell with me, sitting alongside me on the bottom bunk.

'I don't know why I came down here,' he said, 'you're starting to be a nuisance Dr Anderson; I wouldn't do that if I were you.'

He returned my watch and then glanced at his own.

'You have exactly 3 minutes then I'm due somewhere else. We've got things to do today.'

With so little room to manoeuvre I decided to go straight for the jugular.

'He's going to sink the ship,' I said.

For an instant Marte just sat, startled, and then he started to laugh.

'I mean it,' I said.

He stopped laughing.

'Do you have any proof at all for such a wild idea?'

'Yes,' I said.

'Let's hear it.'

'It will take longer than 3 minutes.'

Marte looked at me, studying my face.

'I think you're probably mad,' he said disdainfully, although I could hear a slight uncertainty in his voice.

He may me mad but he could see I was sincere.

'Can you take that chance?' I said.

He thought for a moment, took out his phone and saw there was no signal.

'Wait here,' he said.

He went out leaving the door open, which I thought was a good sign.

He returned a couple of minutes later.

'OK, I've reassigned some tasks, Atu is delighted. This better be good Dr Anderson. Go ahead, talk.'

I laid out my "evidence" before him piece by fragile piece. He listened, asking questions, passing comment along the way.

'I think you're being fanciful,' he said when I'd finished.

'Has Dr Krai ever lied to you?'

Marte thought for moment.

'No, I don't think he's lied. That's not his way.'

'Has he held back information, told you only part of the story?'

'Oh yes,' said Marte, 'many times. He does not overburden people with information they do not need.'

'And has he told you everything about his plans for the ship? You don't even know for sure how you're meant to escape.'

'But he'll tell me when the time is right, I trust him,' he shook his head, 'I trust him, Dr Anderson, a lot more than I trust you. I think I've wasted enough time listening to your nonsense.'

He got up to go.

'But can you take the risk?' I said.

He half-turned.

'My life is full of risks, Dr Anderson, I think I can manage a few more.'

'And Yana?' I asked.

He froze.

'What do you mean?'

'It's very simple, if I'm wrong then there is no immediate risk to you or to Yana, but if I'm right,' I paused, 'if I'm right Marte, then you, I, Yana and everybody else on this ship is heading to the bottom of the ocean. Are you willing to take that risk, not for you but for her?'

I'd played my last card, my Joker.

Now I could only hope.

Chapter 70

Marte hesitated and then turned and towered over me.

'What are you suggesting?'

'I'm suggesting that we test my theory.'

'And how do you propose to do that?'

I knew I would have only one chance at convincing him to help me.

'I want to interview Dr Krai under narcosynthesis.'

'What the ...'

'Narcosynthesis is a combination of hypnosis and barbiturates. Together the effect is to allow the unconscious to become predominant, to prevent the conscious mind from suppressing the truth.'

'A truth serum?'

'Something like that.'

'How do you know ...?'

'I said I was ex-military, but I didn't say which section.'

I hoped that would do.

'Yana routinely uses hypnotherapy to help Dr Krai manage his pain,' I continued, 'so we ask her to put him under hypnosis and intravenously administer the drug. For her own safety she would then leave and I would question Dr Krai on my own. You would make sure we were not disturbed.'

'And how do I know, how do I believe whatever proof you might say you get out of him.'

'Hand me back my watch and give me your phone,' I said.

I took my watch and made a Bluetooth connection to Marte's phone before giving it back to him.

'Now go outside.'

Once he'd left I switched on the microphone.

'That's how you know,' I said into the empty room, 'you'll hear every word spoken and then you can make up your own mind.'

Marte re-entered.

'These modern watches,' he said, 'it's amazing what they can do.'

'Have we got a deal?'

'I've listened to you this far,' said Marte, 'now I've got to know the truth.'

We left the cell together and walked towards the service elevator.

Chapter 71

Yana took some convincing though I knew she had her own concerns about what Krai had previously said under hypnosis and about the role of his "pacemaker".

Even though I was full of fanatical zeal for my theory I knew I could not have convinced her.

It was Marte who took her quietly out onto the balcony and left me to twiddle my thumbs in the examination chair.

They kept their voices low but I could see from their animated expressions and gesticulations that the flimsiness of my evidence and the utter madness of my plan was not lost on Yana. Finally Marte raised his voice enough for me to hear him say, 'Can we take that chance?'

Yana fell silent, turned to look out to sea, and stood cocooned in her own world of thought for what seemed like an age. Then, without a sideways look at Marte, she turned and re-entered the room, walking purposefully up to where I was sitting.

'I have something of Russian origin that might work,' she said, 'As his condition deteriorates I have more and more regular pain management sessions with Dr Krai. He is close to death and there is a possibility that this further medication may kill him. Because of that I will not leave him. I will bring a number of epipens with me and if needs be I will administer a shot of adrenaline. If we reach that point, Dr Anderson, at any time, then your interrogation will stop.'

'I understand,' I said.

'In that case I will collect together the necessary things and go and treat Dr Krai immediately. If we are going to test your theory, Dr Anderson then the sooner we do it the better.'

My thoughts exactly.

Yana took my watch so we could listen in to her conversation through Marte's phone. As she was preparing to leave she said, 'When I'm ready for you I will let you know.'

I nodded.

She had not looked at nor talked to Marte since returning from the balcony. He sat on the bed, a forlorn and dejected look on his face.

After Yana had left Marte approached me,

'If this is a wild goose chase ...'

He was too wound up to finish the sentence and stood clenching and unclenching his fists.

It didn't take a genius to work out what might happen if I was wrong. Part of me wanted to be, another part didn't.

Chapter 72

We waited without speaking, all the talking had been done between us, we were taking a dangerous step and we both knew it.

Then we heard Yana's voice and listened intently. She was talking quietly, soothingly,

'...and as you relax... more with every breath... imagine a dial... it's sitting in front of you... just imagine the dial... with five numbers around it...one to five... and now I want you to imagine... moving the dial from number one... to number two... and as you do that... imagine every muscle in your body... every nerve... every fibre... relaxing... simply relaxing..... now in your mind's eye... move the dial from number two... to number three...'

And so it went on, I had to snap my attention away to stop it from working on me!

'And as you turn the dial... you feel and you become... more... and more... calm... more... and more... relaxed... drifting... deeper... and deeper... becoming... calmer... and calmer...'

It was almost like listening to a religious chant. The focus then changed seamlessly from relaxation to therapy.

'...now I want you to notice where you're feeling discomfort... and put your attention onto that place... where you're suffering discomfort... and as your attention goes to that place... and in your mind's eye... you see another dial and you notice what number it is on... imagine doing that right now... focusing on the discomfort... looking at the dial... and noticing what number that dial is on... and now ... imagine reaching for the dial... and turning that dial down one number at a time... and as you do that... notice how your muscles relax... notice how the discomfort falls... it becomes less and less....'

And so on. Yana was taking Krai deeper into a hypnotic state, carrying out this session as if it were no different from any other, minimising the chance of Krai becoming suspicious. Eventually I heard from her voice that Yana was moving about and then there was a muted sound from Krai.

'…and this injection is to help you … to help you relax…you're feeling calm…deep…calm…relaxed.'

Yana's voice changed, it sounded more strained. She was betraying a trust, something she would never have done for me. If I was wrong there would be hell to pay, in a whisper she said, 'He's ready for you now, Dr Anderson.'

Chapter 73

With Marte alongside me I walked along the deserted connecting corridor and entered Krai's Suite.

After recovering my watch from Yana I switched on the recording function. Krai was in his wheelchair, Yana sat directly behind him. His eyes were open and he turned his head towards me as I moved one of the chairs so that I could sit directly facing him.

'This is a surprise,' he said.

'He's in an altered state of awareness,' said Yana, 'tread carefully.'

I decided to take it slow. I'd done this before, in a previous life, in a different world that wasn't so different.

Under the influence of a "truth serum" the hope is that the subject will be less resistant to suggestion, that the defences of the conscious mind can be bypassed and that the unconscious "truth-telling" mind can be accessed directly. In my experience it had rarely been easy, the mind is a resilient force; you had to approach cautiously.

'Dr Gabriel Krai.'

'Yes.'

'My name is Dr David Anderson.'

'I know who you say you are.'

Shit! There were some truths I did not want uncovered. Here was a suggestion that Krai knew more about me than I thought. I wanted to know if he did, but I also knew I must not ask.

'I understand that you had guns smuggled aboard while we were docked at Suva harbour.'

'Not smuggled, delivered.'

'You had guns delivered.'

'Yes.'

'And was anything else delivered?'

'Of course.'

'What else was delivered?'

'What I ordered.'

Not helpful, I tried a different tack.

'You know you are dying.'

'Of course, and soon, very soon.'

'And you want to be remembered.'

'Yes, everyone does.'

'What kind of legacy do you want to leave?'

'What is of value?' said Krai, 'To be remembered for good or for bad makes no difference the only thing that matters is to be remembered - for something,' he winced in pain, 'and here I am, prepared and ready to be remembered for doing something no one has ever done,' he tried to smile, 'something unique.'

Krai's breathing was uneven, but his voice was steady, his strength of purpose clear. I wanted Krai to take me to the answers, I was just a guide. I switched direction again.

'Do you care about the lives of the people on this ship, Dr Krai?'

He looked puzzled.

'Do they care about mine?'

I repeated the question, hoping that Krai's conscious mind would not keep blocking what his unconscious mind knew.

'Do you care about the lives of the people on this ship, Dr Krai?'

'No, but their lives are important to me.'

'Why?'

'As a sacrifice.'

I saw Yana tense, I hoped Marte was listening. It was time to stay silent and let Krai fill in the gaps.

'These people do not care about my life, a life that is ending. But you see I have laid my plans,' he pointed to his chest, 'when my heart stops beating, and it will stop beating soon, even if I must cause it myself, then ...'

He stopped talking, as if remembering some other question.

'Then?'

'Do you want to know what else I had delivered?'

'Yes, Dr Krai, I would.'

'Explosives, in the hold, amongst the pallets of supplies and ...' his face contorted, as if he were having an internal battle, 'and ...'

Yana looked worried. She took Krai's pulse.

'He's really very weak,' she said, 'you don't have much longer.'

'It is an audacious plan to hijack a cruise ship carrying five thousand people,' I said, 'are the explosives a negotiation ploy, a threat to damage the ship.'

'No.'

So here we were. The final question.

'Then what are they for?'

Krai's eyes shone.

'There will be no negotiation, only death. My death will trigger the explosives and the explosives will sink the ship, a proper modern Viking burial, Mark. I am just sorry that I will not see how fast the ship sinks, or get to count the survivors. No one has ever done this before... it is my legacy. I have left messages to be triggered, to inform the world's media, they will know my name, they will publish ... my legacy.'

He had used my real name! Tears were streaming down Yana's face, Krai could see them, he lifted a hand as if to try to wipe them away but Yana pulled back. Marte burst into the room, he had obviously heard enough.

'Do you really want to do this?' I said to Krai, whose face had turned ashen.

He was still looking towards Yana.

'His pulse is very weak,' she said.

Chapter 74

Marte moved forward threateningly, Yana held up a hand and he stopped in his tracks.

'And how are you to detonate the explosives, Dr Krai? You started to tell us before, please carry on.'

Krai's lips pulled back tight, froze for a moment and then relaxed, the hypno-truth therapy was having an effect but he was fighting it.

'My life is the switch,' he said, 'or rather, my death. When my heart stops beating,' he shrugged his shoulders.

It was not difficult to guess. Whatever it was he had in his chest was not a pacemaker but a monitor, detecting his heartbeat, switched on only when the explosives were safely on board. If he died, if his heart stopped beating then the detonation would be triggered.

If we killed him we'd all die, or as many as could not get into lifeboats before the ship went down. Judging from the lack of attention to the evacuation drills when we first boarded and the inevitable panic that would ensue. I could just imagine the mayhem. A seat in a lifeboat would become one of the few things that the onboard $ could not buy. The idea of an orderly disembarkation was farcical.

But what if we let him live, if we kept him alive?

Krai seemed to get the joke, his mouth formed a thin smile.

'Control is so important,' he said, 'you must remain the one in control, Mark.'

He'd used my real name again. There was no mistaking it this time. His voice was weak and hardly audible, I just hoped that neither Yana nor Marte would register the slip; after all there were more important things to worry about right now.

'What do you mean?' I asked, dreading the answer.

'My life is ending, what does it matter if it is now, or in a few days or in a month,' he paused, swallowed, his mouth dry, 'I have control over when.'

I looked at Yana, she shook her head.

We didn't get it.

And then we did.

Krai bit down. He must have had a false tooth that abruptly released its poison because foam appeared on his lips.

'Oh my god,' screamed Yana, darting forward and forcing Krai's mouth open, 'it looks like cyanide to me. I must get an antidote quickly.'

She ran from the room, Marte close behind.

With Yana and Marte out of the room, Krai beckoned me closer. His voice was weak and sputum dribbled from his mouth. I leaned in to hear what he was trying to say.

'Weakness ... do not be weak, Mark ... you learn to survive ...sometimes you need others to stop ...'

His eyes closed and his head tilted backwards into unconsciousness.

I didn't have time to worry about what I thought I'd heard, he was probably delirious.

Much more important were the actions we must now decide to take and the speed we took them.

Things started to happen quickly.

Yana returned and injected Krai.

'Dicobalt edentate,' she said, 'it can help with cyanide poisoning but Dr Krai is very weak. I can't guarantee to keep him alive for long.'

Marte returned with the Captain who looked very flushed.

'Is this true?' he said, looking at Krai's recumbent figure.

'Yes, I'm afraid it is,' I said, 'did you have any idea what was going on?'

The Captain shifted uneasily on his feet.

'After travelling the world a captain's pension is not much to be looking forward to,' he said, 'Dr Krai promised me no one would get hurt, that it would be over quickly and that if I co-operated there would be a large amount of money sitting in an off-shore bank account with my name on it.'

He was sweating.

'I believed him,' he paused, lowering his eyes, 'because I wanted to believe him. Giving him the access he wanted, allowing unexamined goods onboard...'

He looked up, his steeliness returning.

'I haven't lost a ship yet,' he said, 'and I don't intend to start now. I'll turn around.'

'How long will it take us to get back to Fiji?' I asked.

'At full speed approximately 24 hours.'

'I'm not sure we have that much time,' said Yana.

'Then what do you suggest?' he said, 'I'll do whatever is necessary to safeguard the ship and all the people on board.'

'Stop the ship,' I said, 'and I'll take him off.'

Chapter 75

'Are you crazy?' said Marte.

Very probably, I thought, very probably.

There were explosives somewhere in the hold, we didn't know how much and we didn't know whether they were booby-trapped or not. We had a half-dead psychopath who had linked the beat of his own heart to the detonation.

It wasn't just me that was crazy - it was the world.

'We can't keep him unconscious, if he dies the explosives detonate, if he regains consciousness and sees he's out of choices he'll find a way to detonate the explosives, he may even have another, simpler, method of detonation. He's a dying, desperate man. So if we don't take him off the ship what do we do? All other paths seem to lead to the same outcome - disaster.'

'How long can you keep him alive?' asked Marte gently, turning to Yana.

'I'm already out of my depth,' she said, 'he's so frail that there's a risk I'll overdo the medication. I think we've got hours but if he starts to falter ...'

'What good will it do to take him off the ship?' asked the Captain, 'He's not going to be any more reasonable out there than on board. I don't think it's a wise strategy to count on the mercy of the devil, Dr. Anderson.'

'That's not my idea,' I said, 'the first reason to get him off the ship is that if his pacemaker is the detonation transmitter then the farther away he is the weaker the detonation signal will be if he dies.'

'But we don't know the range,' said Marte.

'I know. I said that was the first reason. The second reason is that once I am far enough out not to be seen I'm going to dump Dr Krai into the sea.'

There was silence.

'Because,' I said turning to Captain Hayadal, 'as Gunnar so clearly told me on the Bridge radio waves do not travel through salt water.'

'So that when he drowns the detonation signal will not reach the ship,' said the Captain.

'Exactly,' I said

There was more silence.

'I will have to go with you,' said Yana, 'he will need monitoring to the very last. I'll bring more adrenalin to inject if we need to.'

Marte looked at Yana, 'We'll take the FRB. I'll take the wheel.'

The Captain looked anxious.

'Alright,' he said, 'I'll issue the necessary instructions but I'm going to have to evacuate the ship, the risks to life are too high, and slowing the ship to a stop will take us 20 minutes.'

'I'll use that time to disable Atu and Gunnar,' said Marte, 'I don't want them running loose at a time like this,' he looked across at me, 'Dr Anderson, you're going to have to help me. You're the bait.'

Chapter 76

'Trust me,' said Marte, although I didn't think I had much choice, 'come.'

He led me back to the cell but this time he left the door unlocked. 'Wait there,' he said.

I wasn't in the mood for waiting, so after a few minutes of mounting impatience I arranged one of the bunks to make it look as though I was lying asleep in it. Then I went outside and found a corner I could hide behind.

Soon Marte returned with Atu and Gunnar in tow, they were arguing.

'I thought he was dead already,' said Atu.

'Why do you need both of us?' asked Gunnar.

I watched them enter the cell. There were a few seconds of silence followed by shouting and the sounds of a scuffle.

Then Atu emerged looking flushed.

I stepped out from my corner.

Atu saw me and smiled, 'Oh, Dr Anderson, I am going to enjoy this.'

'Come on Atu,' I said, 'show me you mean it.'

His eyes glared and he rushed towards me. I was counting on his impetuous anger to give me an opening.

It did.

I waited, balanced on the soles of my feet. At the last second I struck out with my right hand and hit him in the neck, right on the vegus nerve. I was impressed by my own accuracy.

Atu's momentum carried him forward and he slumped against my chest before sliding down to the floor, unconscious.

'I told you I'd been in the military,' I said to his still form, 'sometimes you can be too ambitious for your own good.'

At that moment Marte emerged from the cell. He took in the scene and looked surprised. He pointed at Atu.

'What happened?' he asked.

'Atu tried to get past me.'

'And how ...'

'I just got lucky,' I said.

'Hmm,' said Marte, reaching down to grab Atu's legs, 'Give me a hand.'

I took Atu's shoulders and together we carried him back into the cell and laid him out on a lower bunk. Gunnar was already stretched out on the other one. The two thin silver lines still attached to his chest told me how he'd been subdued and I followed them back to the discharged taser gun that lay on the floor. A second discharged taser lay alongside it, but its silver lines lay forlornly awry.

'I took on too much,' said Marte, 'I told them that you'd miraculously survived and that we'd better make sure this time otherwise Dr Krai would be displeased. They were surprised but not overly suspicious. Atu was particularly pleased.'

I was a bit put out that "making sure" of me had been accepted as such a popular activity. I'd done my best to make friends.

'I tasered Gunnar first, but I underestimated Atu. He was too quick and too strong for me and he got out.'

'I know,' I said.

'I wanted to secure Gunnar before going after Atu and I was surprised you weren't in the cell. I didn't know how many problems I still had to tidy up. So I injected Gunnar with a sedative Yana gave me to immobilise him for 24 hours or so. As it happens it was a blessing in disguise that you were outside. Atu could not possibly have passed up the opportunity of saying "hello".'

'Pleased to help,' I said.

Marte took a second syringe from his pocket and injected Atu's thigh.

'Two down,' he said.

We walked out of the cell, slid the communication hatch closed, and locked the door behind us.

'Next stop Deck 4,' said Marte.

Chapter 77

By the time we got there the Captain had slowed the ship and completed the clearing and closure of the starboard section of Deck 4 from which one of the Fast Rescue Boats (FRB) could be launched.

Yana was also there with Krai who was wearing his metal exoskeleton and sitting in his wheelchair unconscious. Yana was assiduously monitoring his condition.

Two crew members stood by the davit ready to lower the FRB. The crates of "tinned pineapples" I had seen in the medical storeroom had already been loaded and the FRB shone a deep orange in the afternoon sun. At nearly 7 metres long it had a top speed of 30 knots and with a hull filled with polyurethane foam it was virtually unsinkable, which was reassuring.

One of the crew stepped forward and gave us each a lifejacket, which seemed somehow incongruous, and I helped Yana with the securing of the straps on hers. She then slipped one over Krai's head.

Lowering an FRB from a slow moving cruise ship is no easy task. Operating the davit from a local consul one of the crew swung the FRB outwards so that it was at deck level for boarding. A second crew member then unlocked and opened the gate in the guardrail before standing to one side and letting us step aboard.

As we would be relying on Marte's proven ex-navy experience to drive the FRB, he stepped aboard first, taking his place by the steering column and hooking the engine emergency cut off switch cable or "kill switch" onto his shoe. At least if he were pitched overboard for any reason the engine would stop.

I lifted Krai onto my shoulder, a task made a little more cumbersome by the presence of the lifejacket, and boarded.

Yana followed.

Krai was remarkably light even accounting for the exoskeleton and in my mind's eye I saw a different kind of kill switch flashing blue through the skin on his chest.

I dumped him onto one of the moulded plastic seats. Yana gave me a severe look and sat beside him continuing to monitor his health.

'I can't keep him going for much longer,' she said, 'if I give him more adrenaline it might finish him off, if I don't…'

Krai stopped breathing, his mouth fell open, his eyes closed.

'Give him the adrenaline,' I said, 'We've got to get him away from the ship while he still has a pulse.'

The FRB was lowered into the water.

Above me I could hear the captain's announcement begin over the Public Address system,

'Bing, bong'

'Ladies and gentlemen this is an important public announcement. In accordance with the rules of the Company we are today going to carry out an at sea evacuation exercise. There is nothing to be alarmed about, it is purely a statutory exercise undertaken to ensure that all of our safety procedures are tested routinely. I now ask that you please proceed calmly but quickly to your proscribed muster stations where crew members will be waiting …'

I could imagine the communal groaning. All we were trying to do was save their lives.

Marte started the engine, held the FRB steady, nose pointing slightly away from Nereus's hull and disengaged the main hook securing it to the davit. On his instruction I loosed the secondary cable and we powered away into the undulating blue.

Chapter 78

With Marte at the throttle and Yana hovering over a recumbent Krai we sped away from the sheltering shadow of the cruise ship's bulk and out into the indifferent sea.

The sharp 'V' of the FRB's reinforced fibreglass hull knifed through the water, the two hundred horsepower engine churning a turbulence that foamed behind us.

Marte steered us expertly out and across the swell, cranking the speed past 20 knots, our course perpendicular to that of the Nereus.

We didn't speak, the air was full of the noise of the engine and the rising, rushing water.

After only a few minutes I looked behind to see that the cruise ship had significantly diminished in size and now looked like a toy floating a world away.

Marte slowed and then stopped the engine. Unhooking the kill switch he stepped from behind the steering column.

The sea was calm, the sky was clear.

'You know what we have to do,' said Marte.

I looked across at Yana.

'He's very weak,' she said.

I reached forward, loosened and removed Krai's lifejacket. He wouldn't be needing it anymore.

'Let me do it,' said Marte.

I took hold of Krai and carried him to the side of the boat, the shift in weight causing unsteadiness.

'Are you sure that the detonation signal can't travel through the water?' said Yana.

'I'm sure of the science,' I said, 'and I'm very sure that the risk of the signal travelling through air is much greater.'

"The signal travelling through air", I thought. What I meant was if Krai died here on the boat instead of drowning underwater. How easily we sanitise the unsavoury.

'Are we far enough away to let him die naturally?' I said.

'Maybe,' said Marte, 'are you willing to take the risk? And even if you're right what do we do then, do we stay out here waiting to be rescued? We can't go back, we don't know how long the detonation signal will be active, we could simply be taking it back within range, and then...' he moved his arms to mimic an explosion.

Yana looked at me pleadingly, 'I cannot do anything more,' she said.

With the lifejacket off, the blue light could be seen, the pulsing seemed to be slower.

'Let me do it,' said Marte again.

'No,' I said, 'it's OK.'

I swung Krai's body over the side, holding on to his arms. His legs entered the water.

The shock of the cold must have done something because his eyes opened and he looked at me, a look of bewilderment. Marte and Yana were behind me, only I could see Krai's face.

I froze but held his gaze. His lips moved. I think he said, 'It's OK, Mark.'

With a convulsive shudder that took me by surprise he shook himself free and I watched him go. The weight of the exoskeleton took him down, his mouth opened but it was no good, you can't scream under water.

I continued to watch as he sank, his shape dissolving into a ghostly outline and then almost nothing, nothing, gone.

I straightened up and turned to face Marte and Yana.

'Now we'll see whether the science is right or not,' I said.

Chapter 79

The FRB bobbed up and down on the surface of the Pacific like a cork, lifeless and at the mercy of the waves.

Marte heaved the wooden crates containing the AKM's over the side.

'Better to be beyond temptation,' he said.

Then we waited, Turning our heads to look back at the dark profile of the Nereus we could see small yellow dots bobbing around it. The evacuation was in progress.

We floated gently, the water slapping lethargically against the side of the boat.

We waited in silence, avoiding eye contact, looking into our own different distances. We just kept watching the Nereus and waiting for some kind of sign.

We waited for 10 minutes. I looked at my watch as each second crawled sluggishly past, each minute lasting an hour. Slowly the pointers moved, slowly the immediate danger passed, slowly our belief turned to hope, turned to fact.

There was no explosion.

Marte was the first to speak, 'That's long enough,' he said, moving back to the steering column, 'let's call the ship.'

He picked up the handset of the radio communicator.

'FRB 1 to Bridge, over.'

We heard Captain Hayadal's voice in reply. There was a hiss of static but it was a strong signal and we heard him clearly.

'Bridge here, go ahead FRB 1, over.'

'Items successfully disposed of, any messages at your end, over.'

'Evacuation proceeded as anticipated, no unwelcome messages received, over.'

'Understood, Bridge. We're going to start heading back now, over.'

'Okay FRB 1, we'll ready starboard davit for you and will complete evacuation drill and start re-boarding procedures, over.'

'That's fine Bridge, thank you, over and out.'

'No … thank you, out.'

There was no feeling of celebration.

Marte gunned the engine. I was grateful for the voice-shrouding noise as he turned the FRB and we headed back towards the Nereus.

There was nothing honourable about what we, or more correctly I, had done. It was sordid and nasty. There had been no viking funeral for Dr Gabriel Krai, no sacrifice of innocents to accompany him to his watery grave. If I had anything to do with it the news of his demise would be suppressed, it was not newsworthy and there was no reason to give it air time.

It must have been clear to Marte and Yana that I had not acted as an academic would be expected to act in these circumstances. My cover was blown even though the detail of who I really was happily remained hidden.

Is it alright to do a bad thing in order to prevent a worse one?

Krai was dying when we took him on board but he was not dead. We'd kept him alive so that we would have control over his moment of death. We took that away from him.

I didn't feel like a murderer although technically I probably was. If you gave me the time over again I would do the same thing.

From the perspective of Krai's organisation I could only imagine the turmoil that would follow his departure. The head of the snake had died and the now the rest of the body was left to writhe. I felt like someone who's shout had started off an avalanche but was neither underneath it nor likely to have to stick around to clear up the mess.

Chapter 80

Back on board the Captain was waiting to greet us. He had something to get off his chest.

'I have been the victim of my own fear and greed,' he said, 'fear that I could not cope with a life beyond the sea and greed for an amount of money that would take away that fear.'

He hung his head.

'I'd convinced myself that if someone like Dr Krai was set on violence then people on board, people under my protection as their captain, would get hurt, maybe even killed, and that my decision to collude was neither selfish nor brave but sensible, a way of reducing those risks. And the pay off,' he shrugged, 'I pretended that that was secondary, something that I would almost deserve. Wouldn't you pay to keep your family safe?'

I didn't answer, I didn't have to. All I said was,

'My role was specific to Dr Krai and his organisation. Any report that I give will remain within those boundaries.'

The Captain raised his eyes and held out his hand. I shook it, he still had a strong grip.

Then I turned to Marte and Yana who had been helping to secure the FRB.

'I trust you to keep things under control,' I had no idea how many of the crew were contracted to Krai, nor what they would do now, but I thought Marte would know.

'Yes,' he said glancing at Yana who took something black out of her medical bag and pointed it at me.

'I think this belongs to you,' she said.

It was my phone! I took it. It was like welcoming back a long lost friend.

'I'm going to return to my original room,' I said, 'I have some overdue calls to make.' I looked back at the captain, 'I think we all do.'

Tears were trickling down Yana's cheeks. I shook hands with Marte and promised to seek him out later.

I made my way to my room dodging through a seething mass of disgruntled passengers.

'Bloody stupid drill.'

'Never had anything like this before, bureaucracy gone mad.'

'I was halfway through lunch …'

'It was a complete waste of time.'

I looked around at the jostling people, they were just ordinary people, going about their normal business, flowing to and fro. Somebody bumped into me. They didn't apologise. I didn't care. They were oblivious to their narrow escape.

Just for a moment it hit me, what I'd done and how close we'd been to disaster. I stood there, at the edge of one of the stairwells, holding onto the cold chromed banister, silvered like a mirror.

'Are you OK?'

It was an older lady; white hair, neatly dressed, small and quietly spoken. I recognised a Scottish burr in her voice. I just looked at her.

'I need to get past you,' she said, 'I need to hold onto the rail I'm afraid. Don't want to fall you see.'

I smiled. I was in the way. Rather than being interested in my condition she needed me out of her way. I shuffled aside, releasing my hold.

'Thank you, young man,' she said, grabbing the banister as if it were a lifeline.

'You don't look too good you know,' she said, a stick in one hand, stair-rail in the other, the movement in her hips wooden and slow as she creaked past me, 'You young men, you really need to watch you're drinking,' she said, her back to me now, 'keep it under control lad, before it controls you. You look awful. But I daresay you deserve it.'

I wasn't sure what I deserved. A drink was what I needed, not what I'd had.

It wasn't long before I was sitting nursing the single malt that I'd asked Jacob to bring me, feeling better after a quick shower and a change of clothes. I felt the time for rushing was over.

I picked up my phone and called in to "The Store".

Samantha remained quiet as I summarised what had happened as succinctly as I could.

'Are you sure he's dead?' she asked.

'I didn't see him swimming away.'

'No need to be flippant,' she paused, 'so as far as you are aware there is still an unknown quantity of armed explosives on board?'

She made it sound worrisome.

'But no detonator.'

'Just because you've removed one trigger doesn't mean there aren't more,' she said.

Fair point. Maybe I had assumed Krai's removal from the scene meant the crisis was over. Maybe I was wrong.

'Don't you think it likely that Dr Krai would have a back-up plan?'

Now I thought about it, it did seem very likely.

'Following your last call we made dispositions to the military base on American Samoa,' there was a short pause, 'I requested their immediate dispatch 10 minutes ago, while you were speaking. Please alert the captain that there will be incoming visitors.'

I wondered who "we" were, what "dispositions" meant and what or who had just been "dispatched".

'Can I give him any more detail than that?'

A short pause.

'10 to 12 American Navy SEALs, members of the UDT section, are flying towards you in a Chinook helicopter equipped with larger fuel tanks to give them the range. Current eta is 1 hour 57 minutes.'

I wondered why she couldn't have been more precise the first time.

'Anything else?' she asked.

'When do you want me to leave?'

Another pause, as if she were consulting with somebody on another line.

'It is not in our interests to have you on board once the situation is under control. There are too many people who might ask too many awkward questions.'

I thought of the times recently that I had been accused of just that.

'We take pride in being inconspicuous as you know. You could even say it's one of our USP's.'

'I'll let you know when I've left the ship.'

I called the Captain and passed on the glad tidings. He didn't seem to universally welcome the intrusion.

'How do you know?'

Good question, I thought, how would an academic know that a helicopter load of US military were on their way.

'I'll have to pass on that one,' I said and ended the call.

Impolite I know, but effective.

Chapter 81

Near death experiences tend to put things into a new perspective, sort the important from the immaterial.

It's the people that annoy you that you miss the most. My wife annoyed me. From the very first moment we met I knew she was different, the way she tantalisingly half-ignored me, throwing me off balance - and keeping me there.

She got under my skin and soon I could not imagine a time without her. When we broke up (my fault) I felt more naked and alone than I had ever felt. It took me four months to win her back and in the winning knowing "the deal" we were both making. Trust. Belief. Faith. A friendship that was also a love-ship.

And when the cancer that had somehow got into her body, the cancer that I wished had been in my body instead, creased her face in pain, I held her hand and told her white lies about what the future would be like. And she smiled and pretended to believe me.

And when she was gone I...

You can't learn grief from a book, you can't choose when or how you learn to cope, but if you live long enough it will surely be something that creeps up and grabs you by the heart. You have to learn to live with it, because it never leaves, it just matures into a gentler hurt, less sharp and less raw. But it can still flare up, sparked into life by some insubstantial thing, an association or a memory.

I wondered what my daughter found most annoying about me. Was it my ability to ignore her messages?

Was it my oblique half-sentence talk when I finally called, leaving her to work out the riddle of what lurked between the lines? Or was it one of the several thousand other reasons I had given her to be annoyed with me over the years?

There was only one thing that annoyed me about her. She was always late. Her mother used to say, mainly with affection, 'That girl will be late to her own funeral'.

It was as if her biochemistry was constructed with an in-built delay, her circuitry designed with an additional capacitor. The good thing was that the delay was predictable; 5 minutes late for a call, 30 minutes late for a meeting.

I called her. I was conscious that I owed Teresa a decision, that I hadn't called her in days. I wanted more of my daughter's opinion before I jumped one way or the other, but I knew it was time to jump.

She must have thought it was somebody else because she picked up immediately.

After the usual small talk I said,

'I've got something on my mind,' thinking I was letting go of a secret.

'I know.'

'You know?'

There was the sound of exasperation. The kind of sound a mother makes when her young child does the same daft thing over again.

'Dad, of course I know. Don't you think I know you at all?'

Hmmm, OK then, maybe I wasn't the tightly closed book I thought myself to be.

'I need some advice and I've got nobody else to ask.'

'Nice to know I'm top of a league table of one,' she said.

I had to smile, it lifted the tension a little, my tension.

'Do you think...,' I started, but then stopped.

'Yes, most every day,' she said, and then, 'come on Dad, spit it out, how bad can it be.'

We were about to find out.

'You know the woman we talked about? Did I tell you she'd asked me to make my mind up?'

'You told me you treated her like a whore.'

I wasn't sure this was helping.

'Your Mum... would I be disgracing her memory ... you know ... if ... maybe ... you know.'

I stopped, relieved. I don't think I could have put it any more plainly than that.

There was a pause, a long pause. I was wondering if we'd lost connection if not technologically, then emotionally. Had this been the stupidest thing I had ever done? Fancy dragging my daughter of all people, with a life and worries of her own, into my own turmoil, it wasn't fair. I was about to say 'sorry' and crawl my way out of the conversation with as much self respect as I could when she broke the silence.

'She's asked you to make a decision?'

'Yes, a decision, you know, whether I'm serious or not.'

'Smart woman, she obviously knows you pretty well.'

I wasn't sure what that meant but it didn't sound as if it was meant as a compliment.

'And?' she said.

'And I don't know if I'm,' I stumbled, trying to find the right word, '... allowed, sort of, to even think ...'

I trailed off. I was wishing I'd never started this.

'You loved Mum.'

True.

'She loved you.'

I hoped she did. We had our ups and downs but overall I think she did; most of the time at least.

'And she didn't mean to die.'

True. She didn't want to die. That bastard cancer had been impossible to beat even though she did her best. She did her best.

'And you'll always remember her.'

'And love her,' I said.

'And love her,' repeated my daughter, 'And what do you think she would want now?'

That was just it. I didn't know.

'I think that Mum always wanted the best, wished for the best, for us all.'

True.

'I think she would give you her permission to be happy.'

This sunk in slowly, 'permission to be happy', is that what was bothering me? Did I feel like somebody needed to give me their permission to be happy; somebody that it was now impossible to get permission from?

'So you wouldn't mind?'

'Dad, you're ridiculous.'

Thanks, I thought.

'Can I meet her?'

'No.'

'Why not?'

'Too early,' I said.

'Does she actually know?' she asked.

'Know what?'

'How you feel.'

'Well maybe, maybe not, it's complicated, I've been quite busy recently,' I answered indecisively.

'You're an idiot,' she said, the words softened by the tone.

'Thanks,' I said

'Listen, good luck Dad, I hope it works out.'

I hoped so too and realised it was the first time that I'd actually hoped that.

We prattled on for another 10 minutes and then after promising, with my fingers crossed, that I would keep her informed of progress the call ended with a reminder,

'See you in Hawaii,' she said.

I reflected on what she'd said. I had her permission, I had my daughter's permission to be happy. How ridiculous. I was beginning to wonder who was the parent and who was the child in this relationship.

I could not understand why but I wanted to jump into the air and click my heels. In the privacy of my room I tried it - it wasn't a great success.

Chapter 82

There was as yet no sign of the helicopter. It was time to take my life, or my future life at least, by the scuff of the neck and give it a shake.

I decided to take the chance. I decided to call Teresa.

'Hello?'

'Hello,' her voice sounded hesitant, suspicious. It wasn't a great start but at least she hadn't cut me off.

'It's me.'

I just wanted to ensure identification was unequivocal.

'I know. Your number came up on my phone.'

OK then, that seemed clear enough. Now what?

'So?' she said.

She was clearly thinking the same thing.

'I was just wondering how you were.'

There was a slight pause.

'My temperature is within the range called "normal", I do not show any symptoms of serious disease and all my limbs and organs seem to be in reasonable working order.'

She was still pissed off with me then.

'I'm very pleased to hear it...'

'Are you,' she snapped, 'why would you care one way or the other? What does it mean to you? You're so "independent"!'

Ah, there was a word I wouldn't be using much in the future.

'Well,' I said helplessly, 'I didn't like the way things turned out in Sydney and I just wanted to see if you were OK.'

'Why?'

Good question, this was getting less and less comfortable. Why had I called her?

'Because…' I trailed off, buying more time.

'Well?'

She wasn't going to give me any.

'Because I care about you dammit, because I care.'

The words just rushed out, beating my brain to the acceptance of the fact. But after I'd said it I knew it was true. There was no-one more surprised than me.

'Say it again.'

So more calmly this time,

'I called you because I care. I care about you.'

The sweat was streaming down my face. I felt like I'd spent an hour in the gym, and the gym had won.

There was another pause. I could hear her thinking.

'Well it's a start I suppose,' she said.

A start, a start! I'd poured out my heart more effusively than I'd done to any other human being since…

I stopped myself thinking. I wanted to stay in the present. Things were complicated enough.

'How much?'

The question surprised me. Was she asking for a quote? Did she need a loan?

'How much?' I said.

'Yes, how much do you care?'

The best I could come up with was,

'Enough to call you from a cruise ship at $10 a minute.'

She laughed. It was good to hear her laugh.

'You've got to make up your mind,' she said.

'Err right.'

'You know how I feel.'

Did I? I had no idea how she felt, but this didn't seem the right time to ask.

'So you'll think about it?'

'Sure... er ..... I mean yes, of course, yes.'

'Good, well don't take too long.'

'No, no I'll try not to.'

'Try?'

'I mean, no, no, definitely, I won't.'

'Good, then we'll talk again soon.'

It wasn't a question.

'Yes, yes, soon.'

'Then goodbye till then.'

Click.

It has always been my conviction that the male and the female of the species homo sapien are in fact two different species. And of the two it is the female that is blessed with vastly superior emotional intelligence. I had a vague idea that Teresa and I had reached a mutual crossroads and that I'd promised to do something to point the way. What I had agreed to I wasn't too sure, how long I had was even more vague.

The unmistakable sound of the twin rotors of a Chinook helicopter brought me back to the present and I left my room and made my way to the helipad at the Nereus' bow.

Chapter 83

We stood at a safe distance and watched the Chinook descend slowly and thunderously onto the helipad.

I love this helicopter. One of its kind had snatched me safely out of tricky situations more than once. If I ever bought myself a helicopter it would be a Chinook.

This version was painted the US military shade of battleship grey. As it descended I could see the open side doors and as soon as the wheels touched the deck people were jumping out. There were seven of them; four with Colt M16A3 semi-automatics slung over their shoulders, bulletproof vests, and helmets with visors, two with dogs.

The seventh looked like he was in charge and he made a beeline for the Captain who I was standing next to. The bars on his collar told me he was a Lieutenant, the trident on his badge gave confidence of safe hands and the holstered Beretta M9 hanging from his belt signalled he was not to be messed with.

The Captain stepped forward and held out his hand.

'Captain Sven Hayadal,' he said, 'welcome aboard the cruise ship Nereus.'

The Captain was clearly nervous. The Lieutenant took his hand and shook it, hard.

'Lieutenant Carter, I'm pleased to meet you sir, I understand you have a situation here.'

'I'd like to explain it to you,' said the Captain, 'would you follow me to my cabin.'

'Yes, sir,' said Lt. Carter, 'my men can wait for me here. One thing though, this Chinook has been fitted with extra fuel tanks to give us the range to get as far as you guys out here. Could we start the refuelling while we talk?'

'Yes, of course,' said the Captain, 'I'll give the instruction.'

Marte and I were invited along and introduced to Lt. Carter. Sitting around the table in the Captain's suite we tried to bring him up to speed as quickly as possible.

'So if I've got this right,' said the Lieutenant, 'you've got live explosives in the hold. You don't know where, you don't know how much and you don't know how dangerous.'

That was indeed our immediate concern. The Captain agreed.

'We were warned this could be the situation,' good old Samantha, I thought, 'so we've brought a couple of sniffer dogs along and, if you don't mind Captain, I'd like you to explain the layout of the ship to me and my men so we can get started.'

'I've talked to the Company Head Office,' said the Captain, 'and of course I'll help you in any way. As you would expect their main concern is for the safety of the passengers and crew.'

'Are you asking if we need to evacuate the ship?'

'I suppose I am.'

'First things first Captain, baby steps. Let's see what the dogs sniff out and then we can make a plan.'

With time on our hands I arranged to meet Marte and Yana and grab something to eat from the Buffet Restaurant. In the meantime I returned to my room and called "The Store".

I gave Samantha an update.

'You were lucky you were still within the extended range of the Chinook and that we could use some resources already based in American Samoa and fly in others quickly from Hawaii,' she said, 'another day or two out into the Pacific and things would have been a lot more tricky.'

I didn't feel lucky. I was floating on an ocean over 2 miles deep in a steel bucket which was only afloat because it currently had no holes in it.

There were a few more matters to cover, things to double-check, but we rattled through these quickly.

'I'll write a report and give AB a full briefing within the next hour,' she said, presumably checking something on one of her other screens, 'let's hope the explosives are not booby trapped.'

Yes, let's hope so, I thought.

Chapter 84

Knowing I would have to hand back all of the outstanding credit in my onboard account at the end of the assignment and also knowing that there was a lot more in there than I started with, I did some shopping on my way to meet up with Marte and Yana. I thought it only fair.

'Are our two friends in the prison cell still OK?' I asked as I bit into a hamburger. Once I'd smelt the food I'd realised I was more hungry than I'd thought.

'I've checked on them,' said Yana, 'they're still unconscious and I've made them as comfortable as possible.'

We ate in silence for a while.

'What are you going to do?' said Marte.

'About what?'

'About me and Yana.'

I was battling to see what he was on about.

'What are you going to tell the Lieutenant?'

I thought about this.

'I'm going to tell him, although why he should listen to me I don't know, that I think that you and Yana could be a big help in getting this ship safely to Hawaii. After all Marte, you know who on board is linked into Dr Krai's plans and who isn't. That's valuable information right now.'

'And me?' asked Yana.

'I'll tell him you're a first class doctor.'

The silence returned and I munched my way through my remaining french fries.

'And then it's up to you,' I said, 'maybe you should go and look up Lieutenant Carter.'

After they'd gone I ordered a speciality coffee and sat gazing out over a calm ocean that undulated like a silk sheet ruffled in a summer breeze, the smooth tops smeared in sunlight, the troughs hiding in shadow.

About an hour later I sought out the Captain and found him together with Lieutenant Carter and Marte on the bridge.

He was just finishing a public announcement telling everybody that the evacuation and re-boarding had been a great success and the landing of a helicopter and the presence of the military was all part of the exercise, and there was nothing to worry about. All the bars and restaurants were open and to show their appreciation of everyone's patience and cooperation the Company had authorised free drinks for the next hour for all passengers.

You could almost hear the stampeding feet.

He finished by saying that the ship would soon be back underway and that he was confident that by increasing the ship's cruising speed for the next 24 to 48 hours he could make up the lost time.

'We've done a first sweep of the storage areas with the dogs,' said the Lieutenant, 'and have found 9 explosive devices hidden within pallets, in crates, sacks and so on,' he paused, 'They appear to be quite rudimentary in design and we have already deactivated 3 of them.'

'Isn't that a dangerous thing to do with everyone still on board?' I asked.

The Captain was smiling, an expression he had not worn for some time.

'The Chief Engineer has been involved,' he said, 'he's looked at one of the defused bombs and is absolutely positive that, even if they had all gone off, they are not powerful enough, nor in the right places, to sink the ship. Don't get me wrong they would have caused damage and made quite a mess but it would not have been terminal.'

'The only way to sink a ship this big is to blow up the engines and ignite their fuel,' said the Lieutenant, 'or do it from the outside. All these explosives were going to do was make a very messy salad.'

I wasn't so pleased to hear this. Did this mean Krai had underestimated what it took to sink the ship? Did it mean we did not have as much to fear from his death as we had thought? Did it mean I did not have to kill him?

I tried to smile, but it was forced. Lieutenant Carter turned and put his hand on Marte's shoulder.

'This man has been very helpful and I suggest he stays on board with me.'

'It's up to him,' I said.

Marte nodded his assent.

'Once we've completed deactivating the explosives,' said the Lieutenant, 'they'll be put aboard the helicopter and removed from the ship. In addition the two men in the prison cell, first names Atu and Gunnar I understand, will be stretchered off together with another 10 members of the crew Marte has identified as potentially dangerous.'

They really had been busy, I thought.

'I and 4 of my team will remain onboard the ship until we reach Hawaii so there will be plenty of space for you on the helicopter, Dr Anderson, if you wish to leave.'

Samantha's words were ringing in my ears.

'Yes please,' I said.

'Then go pack, Dr Anderson, the refuelling should be complete in 30 minutes and there's no reason to dawdle.'

'I'll make sure that your passport and other papers are returned to you,' said the Captain.

As I was packing Yana entered my cabin.

'Thank you,' I said, opening and closing my hand, 'for your medical attention.'

'That's OK,' she said.

I knew there were lots of questions hanging between us the loudest of which was probably 'What happens now?' I also knew that she was smart enough to know I didn't have any answers, so she didn't ask.

'Do you think it's safe?' she said, 'the explosives I mean.'

'If they mess up I think we'll hear about it pretty quickly,' I said, 'but they're the experts so we have to trust them.'

I'd changed into my travelling gear and was wearing black trousers, blue shirt, casual jacket, and was busy pushing the rest of my things into suitcases. Without being asked Yana started to fold my clothes and help me to pack.

'There is just one thing,' she said, taking something out of her pocket, 'I'd completely forgotten about this, what do you think I should do with it?'

'What is it?'

'When Dr Krai was very weak he told me he was concerned about the consequences his death would have,' she said, 'he told me that if he should die onboard then I should use this phone, that it has a pre-programmed number in it and that the person I called would know what to do. He was very anxious that I understood how important it was.'

'May I?'

She handed it to me, it looked like a phone.

'Can I take it?' I asked.

'I wish you would.'

I slipped it into a jacket pocket. I'd look at it later as it might well contain information useful to "The Store".

I was ready to go and it wasn't long before I had said my goodbyes and "Thanks" to Jacob and was shaking the Captain's hand, nodding to the Lieutenant and taking the offered ear defenders as I stepped on board the Chinook and started to strap myself in.

Although there were two stretchers already on board, one for Atu, the other for Gunnar, and the 10 other people that Marte had identified as dangerous were also strapped in, there was still plenty of room. Off to one side I noticed a large elongated container marked ROV.

'What's that?' I asked of one of the flight crew.

'It's a Remotely Operated underwater Vehicle, sir,' he said, 'we use it for laying underwater mines,' he paused, 'or for removing them.'

'You mean like a midget submarine,' I said.

'Not really, this is unmanned and operated from above water.'

I gave him a thumbs up and went back to getting myself settled for departure.

Krai was a paradox. A man who could be ruthless, who prided himself on detail, but who put explosives on board that could not have delivered his desired result. It was a strange mistake to make.

I thought back to Suva harbour and to Krai's attention to the loading, on his keenness to talk to me about logistics when I could have been sitting on my balcony on the other side of the ship, drinking whisky, watching the other boats and ships, some in close proximity, and looking forward to going ashore.

Hold on a minute!

What if Krai called me over not to watch the loading but because he didn't want me to be on the other side of the ship. My mind was racing. Why, why would that make any sense? Then I remembered. When our taxi was leaving the harbour area I'd noticed – two midget submarines!

And what had the Lieutenant said, 'The only way to sink a ship this big is to … do it from the outside.'

The doors of the Chinook were closed. The pilot had started the take-off routine. The rotors were powering up. The noise was increasing.

I jerked upright, punched open the clasp on my seatbelt and pushed my way through to the flight deck. The explosives in the hold were only a distraction!

'Stop!' I shouted, 'Stop! The bastard has mined the ship!'

Chapter 85

Leaping from the helicopter I ran to the Lieutenant.

'He's mined the ship,' I said, 'I'm almost sure of it.'

To say the Lieutenant was startled would be an understatement.

'Give me 5 minutes to explain,' I said.

'It had better be good, I don't want anybody making a fool out of me.'

Despite his misgivings he gave instructions for the helicopter to stand down and await further instructions. No one looked happy.

When we were in private I told the Lieutenant who I worked for. I wanted him to take me seriously rather than consider my ravings as those of an amateur.

'I hate vigilante groups,' he said.

I wanted to argue that we were not a "vigilante group", we were an organisation that filled in the gaps. I wanted to argue my case, but I didn't. There wasn't time, we had more important things to do.

'Now lookee here, I thought we'd been briefed pretty good but how's about you start by telling me just what has really been going on?'

I gave him an outline sketch which was mainly factual.

'And Dr Krai was dead when he fell overboard?'

But not totally factual.

'His hand was on the trigger,' I said, 'he was a clever guy, he wasn't going to do all this and get the explosive charges wrong.'

I told him what I thought had really gone on while we were docked in Suva harbour.

'I see.'

'Listen,' I said, 'maybe I'm wrong, maybe Dr Krai underestimated what it took to blow a hole in a cruise ship, maybe his orders got lost in translation along the way. But what if I'm right? Can we take the risk?'

He thought about it, all the time never taking his eyes off my face. It was disconcerting, but I refused to look away.

'We've got the equipment and this is what we're trained to do. Let's take a look.'

We sought out the Captain as quickly as possible and filled him in on the intended underwater inspection. He was both incredulous and freshly anxious for the safety of the ship and all on board.

'Whatever you need, just tell me,' he said, he was getting repetitive.

The Chinook was emptied of its passengers; Gunnar and Atu carried back to the cell, the others held in the nearby medical room under armed guard.

I was with Lieutenant Carter and Captain Hayadal sitting in the helicopter cockpit gazing at a screen. Off the port side of the Nereus a lifeboat had been lowered into the sea. Two divers had donned their gear and rolled backwards off the side and down into the water. They were wearing headphones and headcams and the screen we were watching was split in two so that we could see what both of them were seeing.

Like all large cruise ships the Nereus had a draft of about 9m and the divers separated and followed the hulking metal sides down through clear water.

'Search the stern of the ship first,' said the Lieutenant into a stick microphone that protruded from the console and communicated directly with the divers.

'Yes, sir', 'Yes, sir', crackled back.

The images moved slowly as the divers followed the hull towards the stern. The metal surface looked clear. I was beginning to wonder if I was wrong. Maybe I was just paranoid. If I was wrong, at least we'd made sure. That was a good thing wasn't it? As soon as the inspection was finished I'd just apologise to the Captain and the Lieutenant for being overzealous and then get off the ship as quickly as possible.

We peered at the split screen in silence. There was nothing to see, we just kept watching. It seemed like an eternity. I was losing faith in my judgement.

'There!' shouted the Captain pointing.

Suddenly the hull was no longer smooth. On the left hand screen we could see what looked like a black pimple. The diver went closer, the anomaly grew bigger and clearer. A voice crackled into the cockpit.

'Limpet mine found, sir, my immediate judgement is that it is a Piovra type. I'll look for distinguishing features.'

On the right hand screen another pimple appeared.

'Limpet mine found in place on the hull, sir, will investigate.'

'Very good, continue searching the entire hull and then report back to me.'

Lieutenant Carter turned to me.

'Well, it appears you were right.'

'Is it safe?' asked the Captain, 'do I need to evacuate the ship again?'

'You've been hauling these things through the Pacific Ocean at 16 to 20 knots,' said Lieutenant Carter, 'I think a visual inspection can be considered safe. Once the inspection is complete we'll need to consider what to do next, that's when it'll get interesting.'

'How many do think there will be?' asked the Captain.

Lieutenant Carter shrugged.

'9,' I said.

'9?'

'It's the number of Judgement,' I said.

I didn't say any more, they could look it up if they wanted to.

Chapter 86

The inspection took some time. I went up to Deck 12 and walked around the jogging track. When I came to the front of the ship I stood by the rail and looked out and down over the groups of passengers, the landed helicopter, the sharp 'V' of the bow and into the rolling blue of the sea. I felt very small in this desert of water, with a surface that covered so many things, an ocean that treat good, bad or indifferent with the same disinterest. I thought how quickly the wake of our ship would disappear, how memory would swallow events.

The sun was hot on my face. I turned, went inside and sought out a malt whisky with ice.

The Lieutenant had thought I was crazy. I'd thought I was crazy.

I opened and closed my hand in memory of a sharp pain. Krai was behaving like the wasp; even though he was dead he still had a sting.

At least we'd found out before it was too late, although the knowledge was uncomfortable. As Samantha had said, there must be a second detonator; Krai wouldn't go to all this trouble without a back-up plan. Not long ago I thought the ship had been made safe but now it felt like we were all sitting on a time bomb.

As luck would have it 9 limpet mines were found stuck to various precisely vulnerable places on the ship's hull. The explosives in the pallets may have been made by amateurs, but according to Lieutenant

Carter, the limpet mines had been placed by professionals. We were on the Bridge and he was speaking to the Captain and me.

'These are nasty little bugs,' he said, 'they're magnetically attached and sometimes this type of limpet mine is fitted with a small internal turbine which detonates the mine after the ship has sailed a certain distance.'

I thought about the Pacific crossing, the day that we would have been 400 nautical miles from the nearest land and atop a sea of 4000m depth. Maybe I'd just found Krai's back-up plan.

'What do we do now?' I asked.

'We've got the right gear. We'll use the ROV that it was suggested we bring along.'

Good old Samantha, I thought, always more than one step ahead.

'Do I need to evacuate the ship,' asked the Captain, 'again?'

'The problem is that at the moment we have a free sea, if you put lots of bobbing lifeboats full of people out there, they could seriously get in the way.'

'But what happens if it doesn't work?'

'Then we'll hear the explosion.'

This wasn't the reassurance the Captain was looking for.

'I don't know,' he said, 'I can't put passenger's lives at risk.'

'Do you want us to leave and you can take the risk of turning back to Fiji or travelling on to Hawaii?'

'When there might be other triggers or detonators on board,' I added helpfully.

'Exactly,' said the Lieutenant.

'Do what you have to do,' said Captain Hayadal, 'I'll move the passengers to their muster stations but won't start an evacuation until I believe I have no choice.'

'Very good. Now let me explain the procedure. First we'll need the use of your 2 FRB's.'

'That's no problem.'

'Then when they're in the water with my men onboard we'll take the Chinook airborne and lower the ROV into the water, passing the control cables to an FRB and then setting it loose from the helicopter.'

'The Chinook will then re-land and the ROV will proceed to the first limpet mine, located in the least damaging area and carry out a deactivation and removal procedure. We can relay the ROV camera to the Bridge if you'd like to watch what happens.'

It sounded very complicated to me, but you have to do what you have to do. We were lucky to have members of the UDT (Underwater Demolition Team) and trained US Navy SEALs (Sea, Air and Land special operations forces) on board. Samantha had done a great back-up job of choosing them and getting them here. I for one was very grateful.

The initial steps went very well although I'd underestimated the down draught from the Chinook and watched as the FRB's were battered around, fighting to retain position as the ROV was lowered.

Once the ROV was made operational and the camera relayed to the Bridge we sat around the screen watching. Marte had joined us. Lieutenant Carter gave us a running commentary on what we were watching.

'The first important thing is that we have identified the type of limpet mine we're dealing with. From our Design Manuals we think we know exactly where the detonation mechanism is located within its shell but, because it wouldn't be pretty if we got this wrong, we're first going to use the ROV's sonar to check this out.'

'Could the sonar trigger it?' I asked.

'Possibly.'

I decided not to ask any more questions.

We watched as the ROV manoeuvred close to the first limpet mine.

'They'll now be looking at the sonar image onboard the FRB.'

His phone rang, 'I see, roger that, you may proceed,' he said.

'They've confirmed the sonar images against the Design Drawings, I've authorised them to proceed and try and neutralise the detonation mechanism.'

I didn't like his use of the word 'try'.

The ROV changed position so that it was directly over the mine. A robotic arm with a cowling on the end then moved out and covered the mine.

'OK,' said Lieutenant Carter, 'we won't be able to properly see this next step but what's happening is that the alignment tool built into the ROV arm is locating the firing mechanism precisely.'

'Firing mechanism?' asked the Captain.

'Yes, we are going to fire a projectile into the mine. The aim is to take out the internal detonation control system.'

I wanted to ask how dangerous that was, but I'd learnt from my previous question.

Captain Carter took another call, 'OK, go ahead,' he said.

'I've just authorised the shot.'

We held our breath.

The image on the screen juddered. Expelled gas and water at high pressure and energy disrupted the view but there was no great explosion.

'Good,' said the Lieutenant, 'that's always the most dangerous part.'

Thanks for telling us now, I thought.

'Now we use a different mechanism to demagnetise the limpet mine by using electrical alternating current that randomises the orientation of the magnetic dipoles.'

'Ah, right,' I said, 'of course.'

I didn't really care that the technique was as clear to me as mud, as long as it worked.

We turned back to the monitor. A different contraption now straddled the mine. Lieutenant Carter again gave the go ahead and I watched in fascination as the elongated limpet mine detached first at one end and then the other and started to fall backwards, rotating slowly end over end as it sank downwards and out of sight.

'Just eight more to go,' said the Lieutenant.

Chapter 87

I stopped watching after number 4, it was starting to become routine.

When the entire hull was clear the Lieutenant insisted on a repeat diver inspection of the entire underwater surface to ensure that nothing had been missed. During this last procedure disgruntled passengers were allowed to leave their muster stations and had their displeasure salved by the application of $200 to each onboard account.

The helicopter was reloaded with the 2 stretchers, Gunnar and Atu would never believe the excitement they'd slept through, and the crew members identified by Marte as potentially dangerous. We also had a crate of the defused explosives from the hold. They seemed very puny now compared to the danger of the limpet mines.

As I prepared to board the helicopter Marte approached me,

'Go well,' he said.

'Thanks,' I said, 'and good luck.'

He gazed back to where Yana was standing.

'I have my luck,' he said, 'I don't need any more.'

I could have disagreed. Who knew where life was going to lead him next. But I just nodded and stepped aboard the Chinook. Just inside the entranceway I turned back one last time.

'Anything else?' shouted the Captain, 'Are you sure you're really going to go this time?'

I gave him a thumbs up and shouted back,

'Enjoy your retirement, you've earned it.'

He smiled. The five stripes on his sleeve glinted in the sunlight.

I was definitely ready to leave.

About half an hour into the flight to American Samoa two of the soldiers unstrapped themselves and opened the back drop-down door of the Chinook. It was disconcerting to see the white-topped waves passing beneath us at such speed.

One of the soldiers pushed the crate of defused explosives towards the edge.

The other shouted in my ear, 'Although they're completely safe we don't need 'em back at base.'

Forensic evidence, I thought, DNA sampling? It was too late to argue anyway as the crate had reached the edge and toppled over and into space, hitting the water behind and beneath us.

About 3 seconds later a huge plume of water shot into the air, the sound of an explosion following closely on its heels. I watched as the eruption fell back on itself, crashing back into the sea and sending out circular waves of its own that dissipated and then disappeared.

The soldier shouted in my ear again, 'That's the other good reason,' he said, 'just in case we were wrong.'

As we sped towards American Samoa I thought about all the remnants we were leaving behind, littering the ocean bottom; crates of automatic weapons, explosive debris, Dr Krai, and, buried in a sack smeared with ox blood and stuffed with pillows, the Meditations of Marcus Aurelius. I wondered what the fish would make of it all.

Chapter 88

American Samoa is a group of five volcanic islands and two coral atolls located some 2,600 miles south of Hawaii. It is an unincorporated territory of the U.S.A. and is a well respected source of US army recruits.

We landed on Pago Pago, at the US Military Base. A number of Samoan recruits were waiting for us in their XXL sized camouflage pattered uniforms. Sporting Colt M4 carbines they seemed like men it would be foolish to argue with, or meet on the other side of a rugby tackle.

Gunnar and Atu were carried off still dead to the world. I partly lamented that there would not be the opportunity of saying a proper goodbye. I wished Gunnar well; he was still young enough to attempt another new start. Atu would have to make do without my best wishes.

The other crew members, none of whom I knew, were escorted away in handcuffs, their heads bowed, they looked very sorry for themselves. The last I saw of them they were being helped into a series of black limousines with impenetrably dark windows.

'Amazing there were so few people involved' said one the soldiers.

I didn't really care. My job had been to find out what Krai was up to (Tick) and if necessary intervene to save life (Tick). That was it and that was enough for me.

My flight onwards to Hawaii was a few hours away and I was invited into the military mess by my new Samoan friends.

The food was very basic but no less wholesome for that. I got on very well with my hosts and a large quantity of beer was drunk. The experience reminded me that when you're military or ex-military you remain a part of an extended family that stretches around the world. Our different experiences brought us together. I enjoyed the banter, the swearing, the drinking and the back slapping when it was time for me to leave.

At about 11pm I was poured on to a Hawaiian Airlines flight HA 466 bound for Honolulu. It was an Airbus A330-200 and my Premium cabin seat was at the front.

I declined all further offers of refreshment or entertainment and as soon after take-off as possible I put the seat into its horizontal position, curled myself up and went to sleep. I tried not to think of the $1500's the ticket had cost me.

It was a 5hr 30 min non-stop flight and I had to be shaken awake in time for landing.

Conscious that somewhere between leaving the ship and American Samoa I'd crossed the International Dateline I had been given the unique opportunity of living the same day over again.

Once through Customs I got a taxi to the Hilton Hawaiian Village Waikiki Beach Resort and thought about the question 'If you had your time over again what would you do differently?'

So much had happened recently it wasn't an easy question to answer. Would I change any of the things that I'd done? One thing did occur to me and I decided that as soon as I got into the hotel I'd try and call Teresa.

The place I was staying was like a beached cruise ship with all of the amenities I'd been used to but none of the ocean swell. I was in a suite on the 16th Floor with a balcony and a sea view, just for old time's sake.

I called Teresa. She answered.

'I've got something on my mind,' I said.

'Really?'

There was the sound of exasperation.

'Do you think...,' I started, but then stopped.

'Come on Mark, say what you want to say, how bad can it be?'

People kept asking me that … and once again we were about to find out.

'Do you think that we could give this a go?'

'What do you mean by "this"?'

'Well us.'

'Is there still an "us"?'

She wasn't making this very easy.

'Well you answered the phone.'

'I've been brought up to be polite,' she said.

I felt a little relieved. I could feel the smile in her voice.

'I'd like to give it a try,' I said, 'Would you?'

There was a pause, a long pause. Had this been the stupidest thing I had ever done?

She finally broke the silence.

'Yes,' she said.

That was a welcome surprise.

'Are you sure, I mean I'm not the best catch in the world …'

'Are you trying to talk me out of it?'

'No, no, it's just that, you know…'

She interrupted.

'Where are you?'

I told her.

'I'll see you tomorrow,' she said.

Chapter 89

I was settling into the room, unpacking, putting my clothes away. I was about to hang up my jacket in the wardrobe when I felt a hard outline in one of the pockets. I took the object out and examined it.

It was the phone that I'd taken from Yana. It was slim and light and in all the excitement I'd forgotten all about it. I held it in my hand and turned it over. It looked just like an ordinary mobile phone, albeit a small sized one.

I switched it on.

The screen lit up and an icon appeared that looked like the back of a white envelope inside a blue rectangle. A "1" in white within a small red circle hovered over the upper right hand corner.

I paused.

Why would Krai have given this so particularly to Yana? And why the strange instruction to only activate it after his death? He must have known Yana very well, her trustworthiness and her honourability. I would have been playing with the thing about half an hour after I'd got it.

I put my finger to the icon and a message flashed up asking if I wanted to "Proceed" or "Cancel". I touched "Proceed" and the phone went immediately to voicemail. I recognised Krai's voice,

'Yana, if you are listening to this message then something has gone wrong and I am afraid you are my back-up.'

This wasn't what I was expecting. I started to feel a chill.

'I have tried to help you over the years. I have tried to protect you from suffering the kind of life, the kind of hardships that I have had to endure.'

'Your mother was a gentle soul that I could not save and I am sorry for that, she was caught in the crossfire, an innocent caught inside my problems.'

'You are now also caught in my problems. I will no longer be able to protect you, but I do not want you to be alone,' there was a pause in the message, you could hear Krai's breathing, 'As I've been talking a detonation signal has been sent from this phone, you may have heard the noise of explosions. I think it's for the best …'

I stopped the message.

Had I got this right? Krai was telling Yana he was her father? And as a caring father his final act was to kill her - as an act of mercy!

I thought about the Vietnamese-Australian family I'd briefly met. Ken and Thanh and their daughter Linh had been through so much, survived, and come out on the other side as such a close unit. I thought about my own daughter. Who the hell did Krai think he was!

I took the phone and smashed it under my heel and put the pieces back in my pocket.

I wasn't god but I wasn't going to burden Yana with this information. I didn't even want to think about Krai's warped logic and whether he had any possible justification for using his own daughter as his back-up detonator.

I called "The Store".

'I'm safely arrived in Hawaii,' I said.

'I trust the help that we sent you was useful,' said Samantha. I knew that she would already know that it was and I also knew that she would know that I knew that she knew. She liked to play.

I gave her my own summary of just how useful.

'I have already received a briefing from a separate source,' she said, 'you've been too long getting back to us. We needed to know more and faster.'

I took the admonishment on the chin. She was probably right. I wasn't even interested in who the "separate source" might be. Good luck to him or her.

'What I still find strange,' she said, 'is that having gone to all that trouble Dr Krai failed to have a back-up detonator, something simpler than a pacemaker linked to the beating of his own heart.'

I thought about the pieces I had in my pocket.

'Yes, that is strange, although Lieutenant Carter did say that the mines may also have been set to detonate once the ship had travelled a certain distance.'

'That must be it,' she said unconvinced, 'We'll need to tidy a few things up. I've talked to AB and he'll contact you in a couple of days, in the meantime enjoy Hawaii.'

I will do my level best in that regard, I thought.

While I was waiting for Teresa I took myself off to Pearl Harbor. I needed to slough off the skin of Dr David Anderson, I was beginning to wear it too comfortably, and return to being plain old Mark Wilson. Pearl Harbor seemed as good a place as any to do just that.

The first thing you notice about Pearl Harbor today is the enormous number of tourists pushing and shoving their chaotic way from area to area whilst pools of US Military personnel try to keep some semblance of order.

It's extraordinary that coming up to 80 years after the event so many people remain so fascinated in what happened.

At 7:48 a.m. on 7th December 1941 the American fleet based at Pearl Harbor was attacked from the air by 353 Imperial Japanese aircraft that had been launched from six aircraft carriers and attacked in two waves. It was all over in 90 minutes and left 2,403 Americans dead and 1,178 wounded, 18 ships sunk or run aground and 188 U.S. aircraft destroyed.

Of the battleships all but the USS Arizona were later recovered, repaired and lived to fight another day.

The USS Arizona sank with the loss of 1,177 officers and crewmen after a bomb hit its powder magazine and it violently exploded. The wreck still lies at the bottom of the harbour and is today straddled by a memorial built above, but not touching it and can be visited by US Navy shuttle boat.

Was this a version of what Krai was trying to achieve for himself? A disaster so memorable that it could not be forgotten. If the 5,000 people on board the Nereus had been lost it would have been more than double the death toll of Pearl Harbor. Their family and friends would surely have remembered their loss, perhaps annually for decades, for generations even.

But I was here to shake these thoughts off.

I took the US Navy shuttle boat out to the remains of the U.S.S. Arizona. On the way back I leant close to the rail and dropped the pieces of the phone Krai had given Yana into the water. I was doing this on Yana's behalf but without her knowledge. I was purposely withholding this information from her.

As I departed the memorial grounds to return to the hotel I said my goodbyes to Dr David Anderson, academic, lecturer in Ancient History at St Andrews University, Fife, Scotland and resumed the life of Mark Wilson some of whose trials I would never be able to shed irrespective of whatever cloak of identity I might like to assume.

You always carry with you who you are.

Chapter 90

Maybe it's me being in touch with my feminine side but I do like a mojito and I'm pedantic enough to demand, if at all possible, that the sugar be supplied from sugar cane juice and the mint from spearmint.

I'd just been down to one of the hotel bars to supervise the preparation. The rather put-out bartender needed a couple of $20 notes in order to be persuaded to add the lime slowly over the sugar cane juice and spearmint leaves before using a wooden muddler to gently mash the ingredients together, taking care to only bruise the leaves and release their essential oils.

I had chosen a 3 year-old white rum from Barbados, The Real McCoy, that was then added reverently to the mix and briefly stirred.

The performance had gathered a small appreciative audience and they watched with me as my now flushed but friendly barman added two whole ice cubes and an invigorating squirt of soda water.

Finally each work of consumable art was garnished with two lime wedges and a final fresh spearmint leaf.

I carried them carefully back to my room and looked forward to savouring the combination of sweetness with the refreshing smack of the lime and spearmint flavours against the smooth kick of the rum.

It was at this moment that the phone rang. I couldn't ignore it as it was "The Store". In fact it was AB himself. I felt honoured.

'Well done,' he said.

Under normal circumstances such lavish praise would have been very welcome, something to store away and tell the grandchildren, should I ever have any. But right now I wasn't completely reconciled to the trade I'd made; one life for 5,000. It seemed like a good deal but somebody had still died by my hand. Having had it circle around my head a couple of thousand times I had convinced myself I hadn't had much choice. But that didn't completely clear my conscience.

As we spoke I looked out through the window towards the harbour. I could see the Nereus berthed dockside. She had arrived in Honolulu in the early hours. People I knew and people I didn't know would have already ventured ashore.

Responding to a request from AB I repeated a brief resume of the summary report I'd already sent to Samantha. I spoke carefully because I knew that the call would be being taped for the record. AB interrupted me a couple of times, asking astute questions, and I added the required details unhesitatingly. I could hear his tone become less clipped and more relaxed as the official niceties came to an end.

'This was a damn near run thing,' he said.

'Yes it was,' I replied, 'we got lucky.'

'You did a good job. There are a lot of families who will never know how much they owe to you.'

He was making me blush.

'And that's the way we would like to keep it, isn't it sir,' I said.

'Quite right, quite right,' said AB, he paused for a

moment and then he said, 'Why do you think he didn't just blow the damn ship up the first day out?'

'I'm glad he didn't,' I said, 'it would have been very messy and I'm not that great a swimmer. It seems to me he'd made his plan and was determined to stick to it. He'd decided before he ever set foot on board the way he wanted to go, the when, the how, and the where.'

'And the why?' asked AB.

'I guess he had his reasons,' I wasn't used to having such an adult-to-adult conversation with AB. We weren't equals and never would be.

'Yes, I guess he did,' he said, 'I guess he did. By the way we noticed there was quite a lot of money in your onboard account.'

'Ah, yes.'

'So much so that I've felt it right to deposit £10,000 of it into your personal bank account. Think of it as a bonus.'

A bit mean, I thought, considering how much was in there.

'Thanks,' I said, 'very generous.'

He paused, I was aware of the sound of running water behind me.

'Where are you?' he asked.

I've always believed in keeping a safe distance between my private and professional lives, this was getting close to the line. However I was wise enough not to lie.

'I'm still in Honolulu, sir,' I said.

'Sounds more like Niagara Falls,' he said. I hoped this attempt at wit would be sufficient to curtail the conversation.

'I hope you're enjoying it,' he said.

'Thanks,' I said, 'I am.'

'Well, I can't keep chatting all day. I've got people waiting to see me. Is there anything else I need to know?'

'No, sir. I'll submit a full written report to go with the summary as soon as I can.'

'Don't dawdle.'

'No, sir.'

Click.

I switched off the phone. Behind me I heard a soft rustling and turned around.

Teresa was naked. Silhouetted against the backlight from the bathroom she was drying herself with a pure white cotton towel.

Outside our hotel room window the sun shone and somewhere there were beaches that stretched pale yellow and dipped their toes into the azure blue of the Pacific. But much more importantly Teresa was out of the shower and we had 45 minutes before we were due in the lobby to meet my daughter. Assuming she arrived on time!

I had the matching pair of Rolex watches I'd bought on the Ship already gift wrapped as a surprise.

Now we only had to think about what we could do for the next 45 minutes …

1 Week later - Press Cutting

Gangland Billionaire Lost at Sea

Dollar billionaire Dr. Gabriel Krai has been reported missing presumed drowned. He disappeared from the cruise ship Nereus about ten days ago.

Dr G. Krai was known to be in increasingly poor health and it is believed that he may have fallen overboard when out at night on one of the public decks.

The cruise company and the police authorities have each issued statements to the affect that although this "is a most sad and tragic accident" there are no suspicious circumstances. We understand that a search at sea yielded no signs of Dr Krai and that no further investigations are planned.

Dr G. Krai made his fortune over a period of 30-40 years in what have euphemistically been called "entrepreneurial gangland activities". He never married and there are no surviving children.

We await news of his will and the disbursement of his substantial assets.

9 Months later...

Beep, beep, beep...

I could see it was my daughter calling.

'Hello'

'Dad, hello, wow, I mean ... thanks ...'

This was an unusual way for my daughter to start a conversation. I thought of her now as a mature, thoughtful young woman, someone who could be relied upon. This was out of character.

'Has something happened?'

Call me perceptive.

'Dad, Dad, don't tease, you know.'

I didn't, I really didn't.

'We're so grateful, and it's come at such a good time.'

My daughter was living in with her boyfriend. I'd met him, he was OK. They'd known each other for a while, about 6 months longer than I knew she even had a boyfriend! She didn't ask for any advice from me.

But I still didn't know what she was talking about.

'And $100,000 ... out of the blue, where did you get it? Are you sure you can spare it?'

$100,000! It took a second or two to sink in.

'When did it arrive?' I asked, fishing for more information.

'Just today, straight into my account, the bank rang, just like you asked them to, to let us know - wow, what a surprise!'

Surprise indeed. Who could have...?

A shiver, sharp like an electric spasm ran down my back. I stiffened. Into my mind came the memory of a conversation, a conversation that meant little to me at the time, a conversation with Dr. Gabriel Krai. His words came back to me,

'If you were offered $100,000 to do something you didn't want to do but could, would you be tempted, might it make you think?'

I'd done something I didn't want to do, but I hadn't done it for Krai, definitely not, and I certainly didn't want to be rewarded for it.

I'd had evidence that Krai had blown my cover when he used my real name but here was the confirmation. Maybe he knew all along, maybe my phone was easier to hack into than I thought, but for whatever reason he had decided to keep me around. Maybe he knew all the time how things were going to work out, maybe I was just an extra option, another pawn in his game. Maybe he wanted to be stopped but knew he couldn't stop himself.

People are crazy.

I just hoped my daughter would not expect any more surprise donations of this nature in the future.

'Dad?'

Her voice pulled me back into the real world. My daughter may as well keep the money. I'd earned it.

'Great,' I said, trying to summon up some enthusiasm, 'I've had a windfall and wanted to surprise you.'

'Well you certainly did that. We're moving house you know,'

I'd forgotten.

'So it's come at a really good time. It'll make things a lot easier.'

'I'm glad,' I said.

'And Dad ...'

'Yes'

'I've been meaning to tell you, but I wanted to be sure, you know?'

I stayed silent.

'But this seems like a good time,' she paused, 'Dad...'

I stayed silent.

'I'm pregnant Dad, I'm going to have a baby, and you're going to be a grandfather.'

I'd better start getting to know this boyfriend a whole lot better, I thought.

There must have been a gust of wind from somewhere because for some reason my eyes started to water.

'Wow,' I said.

3 Years Later …

AS THE CROW FLIES

The Mobility Research Institute which is funded entirely from bequests opened its doors today for the first time.

Professor Wren the President of the Institute told us, 'The purpose of our work here is to find practical ways in which the most modern technologies can be brought to the aid of those in need, primarily by either increasing physical or virtual mobility.'

When asked about the financing of the Institute Professor Wren said, 'Without the foresight and generous bequest of our most prominent though anonymous donor this building and the work we hope to do here simply would not be possible'.

Professor Wren refused to be drawn on the name of the donor but said that they had decided to use the brand name "Crow" for commercialisation of their inventions. He and his team had felt that these birds, like new technology, had something of a mixed reputation and that the image of a bird in flight would symbolise the freedom of movement that it was their ambition to improve.

With some ceremony the accompanying logo was released to the press and this reporter hopes that it signals the start of a positive and productive period of both invention and practical application that will deliver benefit to many in the years ahead.

[Kraai is Dutch or Afrikaans for Crow – it is both a Noun and a Verb]

Agaricus

Agaricus is a type of mushroom whose genus contains some of the most commonly cultivated and consumed mushrooms in the Western world. It also includes a stinky variety that can cause stomach cramps, nausea, vomiting, sweating and diarrhoea (although for unknown reasons a minority of people can devour these particular fungi with no ill effects whatsoever) and at least one that is deadly poisonous.

They are distinguished by their chocolate-brown spores and a stem that elevates them above the substrate on which they grow and from which they take their nourishment.

Agaricus Homo: A sub-species generally kept in the dark and frequently fed with lots of well-rotted manure.

ACKNOWLEDGEMENTS

Thanks again to all those who have given me support and constructive criticism on my journey to completing this book. Especially to those who have edited various 'rough' versions of the manuscript over its long and painful gestation and those who have given me insightful remarks on plot, pace and character development. All your help has been both essential and greatly appreciated!

To Crime & Publishment (C&P), Graham Smith, Michael J. Malone, Matt Hilton, Les Morris and the tens of others who have given me the benefit of their knowledge, their moral support and the encouragement I needed to persevere until I got to finally write 'The End' – which brought both a relief and sense of 'so what now?'. Also to C&P my thanks for teaching me the method, structure and process of how to put a book together and when and how to ask for help..

Thanks to Fiverr for the artistic and creative contributions to the cover artwork. It was a collaborative process and I enjoyed it – Thank you.

My respects to Moffat Crime Writers and the 'Twisted Sisters', especially Linda, Ann, Irene, Jackie, Beth, Rose, Fiona, Christine, Andrew and Derek. It is fun talking Crime with you all and learning from each other's experiences on this journey of writing and publishing.

To Janet Williamson for previous useful editorial support that I've learnt from and carried forward with me, and to the mighty M. W. Craven for his time and undiluted feedback (especially on the Use OF Capitals; and semi-colons!).

Thanks also to Ian Rankin for a brief and chance conversation in Kendal about cruise ships, death and deep freezers.

And finally my thanks to Janet Langley for putting up with the seemingly 1000's of hours it took me to write this book, for reading the manuscript and for making constructive suggestions for improvement – most of which I listened to.

Praise for the "Agaricus" books:

"The narrative is excellent. This is a really well written book… Krai is a superb creation."
M. W. Craven, *Author of 'The Puppet Show'*

"Mark Wilson is like Bond with a conscience"

"Page turner, unexpected twists and turns… a recommended read"

"…a new approach to a traditional genre. Liked it."

"the main characters are flawed and complex, just like us all…"

"Enjoyed it, look forward to the next instalment"

"…a really good read. Recommended…"
H. Citeau, USA